Walking the Crimson Road
Perrie Patterson

ISBN: 9781708478148

This book is written as a work of fiction. The story has been created by the author's imagination. Places, buildings, restaurants and hotel names are accurate. Location for the National Championship game was per the author. The weather in Cape Cod in late March early April was made more appealing for story purposes. Cover photo was taken November 2019 in front of the University Club, Tuscaloosa, AL just prior to the Alabama VS LSU game.

Printed by Kindle Direct Publishing in the United States
First printing edition 2019
www.perriepatterson.com

For my mother...

Nell Patterson Hixon, who loved the Crimson Tide. She signed Bear Bryant's checks when she worked at the university in the late 50's. She taught me to "stick with it," because hard work pays off. She passed before I finished this book, but I told her about it two days before she died. Love you, Mom!

And to my all-time favorite professor...

Wilma Green, who was an inspiration to everyone who took her course, and anyone who knew her. I loved when she would share stories in class about having taught Joe Namath and Kenny Stabler. Her tragic death broke my heart.

With this being my first book, it's an honor to dedicate it to these two important ladies in my life. I did it, Mom!
#rolltideforever

1
#Bigflex

"Rebecca, I know how busy rush week will be, but I expect a daily text." My mother's loud voice jolts me to attention in the cramped backseat. Quickly, I pop one of my AirPods out.

"Mmm, hmmm," I mutter, half-ignoring, half-listening.

Dad's driving the family SUV. It's stacked to the hilt with storage containers and my Vera Bradley luggage heading straight into my sophomore year at Bama. My roommate, Bella, and I have been texting and chatting all summer about our room design. Although she spent most of her summer with another Phi Mu sis, Lexi, working at summer camp, we found time to plan our decor.

"That reminds me." Mom looks over her seat at me. "I need to call your sister and make sure she's up and studying."

Lauren didn't make the drive this year. She's retaking the ACT tomorrow for like her third time.

Get ur butt up, act like ur studying, mom's calling.

I whip off a quick text to my sis, hoping she gets it in time. She seems to have answered, because I hear Mom ask what time she's meeting with her tutor.

Dad tilts his head toward the backseat as he drives. I can barely see him over all my stuff piled to the roof. "Mom and I are proud of you, honey." There's a bit of early morning gruffness to the sound of his voice. "You had a successful freshman year. We know you'll accomplish a lot this year, too."

"Thanks, Dad," I reply, not knowing what else to say, but a warmth spreads inside me. He's usually not one to dole out compliments, so when he says something, he means it.

In high school I had great grades, forever the straight-A student, and earned a scholarship because of them and my ACT score. I've never given my parents any trouble or reason to worry, unlike my sister. I grimace at the memories of Lauren sneaking out of the house her first two years of high school to meet up with her friends who undoubtedly were up to no good. I was way too scared to dare do anything like that and much too focused on my grades. This time last year I had just turned eighteen, and I was feeling nervous and anxious about starting college with 40,000 other students. A smile creeps over my lips. But now I'm starting sophomore year with a bang. I made the *Crimson Cabaret* dance team last spring. I've been dancing since I was three. But, you know, I've always thought the *Crimsonettes* were cool with their baton twirling skills, maybe I'm a little jelly. I'll stick with dancing, it's what I know. Besides making the dance team, I'm *super* excited to be moving into my sorority house. Bella and I decided to room in the house together after becoming fast friends during rush last year. We bonded instantly over our love of the Jonas brothers, AJR, and other favorite bands.

B, I'm so excited. R u almost there?

About 45 minutes. HBU?

"Dad, how much further?"

"Can't wait to get rid of us, huh? About twenty miles, sugar," Dad replies. He can be a goof, sometimes, but that's dad for you.

I think 40 minutes, see u soon.

I put my phone aside and glance out the window in a daze, thinking about the year and what it'll be like. My dream of becoming a journalist is on the verge of becoming reality. The classes I'll be taking will allow me to write for the campus newspaper and school magazine this semester. My YouTube channel that I've been uploading my vlogs to has over a hundred followers, so far. That's cool, but I'd love to gain a lot more. I suck in a deep breath, and a tingle of inspiration washes over me. I breathe out slowly, closing my eyes, thinking how much fun Bella and I are going to have this year.

The car makes a sharp right turn, pulling me out of my dazed thoughts. Craning my neck, I see the red brick paths come into view. Tons of cars and students with rolling carts are scattered about. Piles of trash bags, stuffed and overflowing, sit next to empty TV and mini fridge boxes lining the sidewalk. I'm glad to be here a week early to help with sorority recruitment. *Will this year's freshman be as nervous as I was last year?* Recruitment week is crazy, fun and exhausting—so glad pledging is behind me. This year I'll be working behind the scenes on decorations and helping organize the girls for their interviews. It'll be work but fun.

In the distance the stark, whitewashed stone of the Phi Mu house looms in grandeur. I feel a catch in my throat, and a surge of adrenaline charges through my veins. *This is going to be amazing.* I dreamily stare at the massive, white columns flanking the house entrance. No, this year will be more than that. S*tellar.* It's going to be a *stellar* year. I can feel it.

2

#Besties

Finally here, I step out of the air- conditioned car. The late August heat feels damp and thick on my skin. I hear Mom complaining about the affect humidity has on her hair. I roll my eyes and throw my duffle bag over my shoulder.

"The heat index is 95 according to the car," Dad says, popping the trunk open.

"Bex!"

Turning around, I see Bella running toward me. Colliding, we squeal in excitement and bubble over laughing as we talk over one another. Mom and Mrs. Campbell share a hug. And Dad and Mr. Campbell exchange a hardy handshake while Bella and I move into the line forming for room assignments. From our place in the line, I watch as my parents begin unloading my things out of the car. Once we have our room keys, Dad helps with the heavy boxes, then he and Mr. Campbell head out to find something more interesting to do besides room design. Our moms, on the other hand, are all about it. And I, of course, am convinced the status and success of our year will be based on how well we achieve decorating perfection.

Bella and I chat a mile a minute while unpacking. After making our beds and putting out cute pillows, I think it's time for our moms to leave. I'm grateful for the help, but Bella and I plan to hang pictures, put up curtains and get the room looking like the top photo on the Dormify blog. A little later, when Mom finishes hanging my clothes in the closet, I casually ask, "Do you think

Dad's back? I know you guys talked about wanting to get on the road before it got dark."

Bella winks at me and turns to speak to her mom. "Not trying to rush you, but I think we've got it from here," she says.

"We get it." Mrs. Campbell gives Bella her raised eyebrows look.

"Remember, it will be homecoming before we're back." Mom looks at me sternly. *Must I remind her this is my second year? Geez! But to be fair, last year, me, Lauren and Mom were bawling our eyes out when they got ready to leave.*

"We expect phone calls, and texts regularly," Mrs. Campbell adds. "We trust you both to make good decisions. I know you'll keep each other in check." Her eyes dart between me and Bella.

Mom smiles, puts her hand on Mrs. Campbell's shoulder, and gives it a squeeze. She tears up a little walking over to hug me.

"I'm so proud of you, Bex. I know not to worry about you. You've always proven yourself to be reliable, honest, and hardworking. It's just hard leaving, knowing it will be a few months before I can see you again."

I love my mom and dad. They've always been so supportive. But she needs to let go. I'm feeling more confident this year and ready to find my way. Believe me, this year I feel more than ready. I hope she sees that.

Bella and I walk with our moms downstairs to the living room, where we find our dads in a sea of more dads talking Alabama football. After tear-filled hugs, Bella and I stand together outside the front door waving as they walk to their cars. With our parents out of sight, we run inside to continue our decorating frenzy.

"Look, Bella." I enthusiastically pull out a collection of large cast iron hooks. "I'm hoping we can use these to hang clothes, and other stuff."

Bella picks up the largest one. "These are funky and artistic even without anything hanging on them."

Bella and I are prattling on about which picture layout looks best when our friend Lexi walks in. Meeting in the doorway, the three of us embrace in a group hug, giggling.

"I'm so excited to see you guys. How's unpacking going?" Lexi asks.

"Not too bad." I sigh. "Much faster after everyone left," I say, looking at Bella sheepishly.

"I know, my parents just left, too," Lexi says. "Mom was trying to do everything. I finally sat down and just watched until she got the hint that I didn't want her help anymore It seems she would already know I wasn't interested in her help after last year." Lexi laughs. "I've got to go back to my room." Lexi says glancing at us. "I have one more box to unpack." She walks toward the door. Her black hair pulled into a high ponytail looks slick and shiny. It swishes back and forth as she walks into the hallway. "I'll catch up with you guys later during dinner," she says looking over her shoulder.

Poking my head into the hall, I snag her attention. "Lexi, I can't wait to hear more about the Young Life camp where you and Bella worked this summer."

Twirling around, she yells back, "We met a really nice guy that worked as our lifeguard and boat driver. He goes to school here, too. He's perfect for you, Bex," she purrs.

Shaking my head, I laugh at that comment before walking back into the room. Bella's staring at the wall with a dazed look on her face. Pointing, she says, "Let's try to hang the decorative hooks first then the large memo board."

We complete the room with framed art above our beds and a mirror between the closets. Kate, one of our big sisters, pops her head in, scanning our room curiously.

"There's our Blake Lively look-a-like. Y'all's room is looking very sophisticated," she says, grinning a me.

I give her a half smile as she hands me the rush week schedule of events.

"We have a meeting tonight after dinner," she trills excitedly.

I tack the schedule on our new memo board with a hot pink push pin.

"We'll be there. Thank you." I glance at Bella then watch as Kate pops back into the hallway. I animatedly mouth the words, "Why does everyone think I look like Blake Lively?"

"Cause, you do." Bella giggles.

"I don't see it beyond the long, blonde hair and blue eyes——but whatever."

Bella laughs. "How about the mile-long legs? Or the fact that you're a drop-dead, gorgeous bombshell who just happens to be as laid back and easy going as the girl next door. Face it, Bex, you're the "it girl" package without the sass and drama that most girls who look like you always seem to have."

I give her a soft smile. Bella is super cute. She has long, wavy brown hair down the middle of her back, a dark tan from working at summer camp, and amber eyes. One reason we get along so well is that neither of us likes drama. Bella's always up for something fun. And she's super chill.

Changing the subject, I ask, "What dresses did you bring for preference and open house days?"

"Hang on, I'll show you."

We hang our dresses and set our shoes on either side, stepping back to admire them.

"Perfect," Bella ponders. "I'm loving these decorative hooks already."

I open another container, pull out my Kate Spade agenda, notebooks and pens, and spread them on top of the desk. I set a cute lamp next to the agenda and plug it in.

"I bought a lamp for the room, too." She gets hers and puts it on the nightstand.

Standing side by side, we carefully study the room to see if we need to add or move anything.

With hands on her hips and her head slightly tilted, Bella announces, "It's perfect."

"Yes, it looks very stylish and swank. We did a great job." I give Bella a high five. "Best roomie eva!"

Bella smacks my hand. "Back at ya."

"Let's take some pictures and send them to our moms." I pull my phone from my back pocket. Bella photobombs the last picture, cracking me up.

"Sophomore year, we're here," she says, laughing along with me.

"The best year yet. It's almost time for dinner. Let's go downstairs," I say, as I hit send on the text to my mom.

In the hall we hear cheering, then applause breaks out. Reaching the bottom stair, we see our sisters gathered around Tonya, a Phi Mu alum who has just arrived.

3

#Savvysisters

The excitement is tangible as all of us settle into a spot at the long banquet table for our first meal of the semester. Tonya sits at the head of the table, as our Alumni guest of honor. We're hanging on her every word while she tells us about winning the Miss Alabama pageant a few weeks ago. She plans to help us with our chapter philanthropy project later this year. Everyone takes a turn sharing an exciting summer vacation story. Through the stories and laughter, our sisterhood bond deepens. After dinner, Bella, Lexi and I take seats next to each other for our first chapter meeting of the year to discuss rush week and the T-shirt design for our first date-night social event of the season. Our chapter co- presidents, Amanda and Caroline, have a hard time calling the meeting to order, because it's so loud with everyone talking at once. Lexi's roommate, Jessica, puts two fingers in her mouth and launches an ear-piercing whistle, shocking us into silence.

Lexi passes me a clipboard with the voting sheet attached. "I like this design." She points to the page. I nod in agreement.

After the votes are taken on the shirt design, we've decided on pale pink with a mason jar image on the back featuring a black and white checkered print bow tie tied around it. The theme and date will be printed in a circle around the image, and our Phi Mu symbol will grace the front pocket. The design choice is practically unanimous.

"The T-shirts will be shipped here in a week, and we'll order extras for the guys you invite, if they want one," Amanda announces.

Our meeting carries on with reminders of assignments for tomorrow as recruitment gets underway. This whirlwind week will go fast as we meet and greet hundreds of new pledges. After reviewing our rush week assignments, Bella and I go back to our room to call it a night. Sitting on my bed, leaning against the pillows, I watch Bella plug in the Keurig.

"This is going to be such a fun year," she bubbles. "It felt like the glistening, white, marble floors in the foyer grinned at me when I walked through the doors this morning," Bella says in a mock theatrical tone that makes me laugh.

"I know what you mean. I had butterflies when we pulled up in front of the house earlier. You're lucky your parents let you bring your car this year. My sister's been driving mine back and forth to school. I can basically say it's hers now. I'm hoping I'll be able to have a car on campus soon."

"Yeah, but you can always ride with me whenever you need something. A lot of girls in the house have cars, too, so it shouldn't be a problem. Last year we walked everywhere we needed to go anyway."

"Last year we hardly left campus. We're sophomores now time to spread our wings," I say, waving my hands above my head.

Bella laughs, giving me a silly grin. "How far are you going to fly?" she asks.

"Limitless possibilities are in store, I'm sure of it," I announce with an air of confidence. "I think it's time for me to soar into new adventures and leave a bit of the old boring me behind."

"You know you're not boring right? Maybe a bit strait-laced but you are never a bore," Bella says, giving me a serious look.

"I just want something exciting to happen this year since last year I had just turned eighteen and was quite the cautious

13

freshman. So, I'm claiming this year as the year of the "yes." My Instagram made be fire, but it's time to kick it up."

"Year of the yes? Uhm, okay." Bella looks skeptical but gives me an air high five. "To living our best lives," she says, as she sits back on her bed, holding her laptop.

The glow of the lamplight causes a coziness vibe to settle in as I snuggle down under my duvet. "Just a reminder," I say, glancing at Bella. "I'm not a morning person, so I'm setting an alarm."

"Neither of us is an early bird, so definitely set an alarm, girl. I'm going to crash soon too."

Suddenly I get the giggles, remembering rush week last year. "Bella, remember when we were waiting to go into Zeta and we had our shoes off sitting on Lexi's blanket and we all had those battery- operated mini fans, trying to hold those and eat at the same time then it started to rain and we were trying to grab all our stuff, running away as if we were being chased by an ax murderer?" Bella laughs and pulls her mini fan out of her drawer and turns it on, holding it out toward me. After the giggle fit, I drift off to sleep dreaming of rush week and Bid Day.

*****

Bid Day starts out at the crack of dawn at the stadium. Lexi, Bella and I had to get up an hour before everyone else to place the cards in our section. I feel like I'm sleep-walking as I put bid cards on the seats. Once we're done, we sit down in the front and watch the pledges file in. The roar of the thousands gathered comes to stark silence as they wait with bated breath for the signal. As the countdown begins, the sounds of ripping envelopes turns to cheers for the houses that selected them. Squealing, crying, yelling, and the pound of thousands of feet running behind giant Greek letters back to their sorority houses kicks off retreat weekend. I'm excited about this trip. We're

14

going to Stone Mountain in Georgia. It makes for a long weekend, since we won't be back until Monday night, and first day of classes begins on Tuesday. I love a short week, too.

With three days of sisterhood bonding underway, we load the buses with overnight bags in tow. After everyone is seated, the luggage compartments look like a Vera Bradley store exploded. Lexi, Bella and I sit next to each other and settle in for a full-on gossip session.

"I was in charge of arts and crafts, and Bella was in charge of the zip lining station. Carolina Landing Young Life Camp is the best and a really fun place to work. Bex, we would totally love for you to sign up to work with us next summer." Lexi sounds enthusiastic and hopeful.

Bella adds, "Don't forget we were going to tell her about the hot guy we met."

Lexi nods. "Oh right, his name is Grant, and he's on the swim team here at Alabama. He was our go-to lifeguard, and he ran the boating station. He's actually from South Carolina and will be starting his junior year. He told us he worked with Wyldlife the summer before, and the summers before that he worked as a lifeguard."

Bella chirps, "He's a Chi Phi, and I can't believe we've never met him on campus before."

I say, "Yeah, I know. I'm sure we've passed him sometimes. Maybe we were even at some of the same parties. But I mostly talked to other freshman guys last year."

"I remember seeing him last year at one of the Young Life events," Lexi says. "But I agree with you, I was always more comfortable talking with other freshmen."

I give Lexi a coy smile because I'm about to ask her a personal question.

"Do you still have a thing for that band guy, what was his name, Patrick?" I ask. Lexi gives a shy grin.

I know Bella was crushing on a guy from the band last spring, too. I turn my attention to Bella, who blushes and nods her head.

15

"Spill the tea girls, we've got almost an hour before we arrive."

4
#Allthefeels

*Strong women know they have enough strength
for the journey, but praying women know it's in the
journey, where
they'll gain strength.------- Luke Easter*

The quote shared during last night's house Bible study is on repeat in my head this morning. The glorious first day of class has arrived, and I'm feeling ready for the world. I even got some sun the past few days during our sisterhood retreat from kayaking on the lake and hanging by the pool, so I'm looking tan again. I down my last bite of bagel and snap the lid closed on my mug.

"Bye girls." I stand, pushing my chair under the table. Bella leans toward me, giving me an air kiss while still chewing her bacon. "Go get it girl," Lexi says, giving me a thumbs up. With a wave, I'm out the door and into the warm sun this beautiful late August morning. I pop my earbuds in and listen to some Sam Hunt as I step onto the sidewalk and make my way over to Reese Phifer Hall.

Scurrying up the steps, I bounce into the grand foyer, then pause and stare up at the huge chandelier in all its glory. I think about snapping a photo for my Instagram but quickly change my mind, not wanting to look like a total dork.

I'm extremely nervous about taking a class from a Pulitzer-Prize winning author. Feeling both thrilled and scared as

I walk into Rob Brigg's writing class I know it'll be a great experience and a check off my college bucket list.

The enormous lecture hall is already crowded. It only took me five minutes to walk here from Phi Mu house, but these people must be serious about getting to class on time. I see an open seat, but unfortunately it requires scooting past some guy to get to it. As I step over his feet, I trip slightly but catch myself before falling flat on my face.

I give him a meek, *I'm sorry* smile. Embarrassed, I sit down. The guy looks familiar, but I've never met him. Trying to peek at him without being noticed is hard. When I look back, his eyes catch mine, and his smile is brilliant. He introduces himself as Lane.

"Hey, Lane. I'm Rebecca, but my friends just call me Bex."

"Cool. Nice to meet you, Bex. Are you a journalism major?"

Before I can answer, Professor Brigg walks to the podium, clears his throat, and gathers everyone's attention. As the lecture starts, I can't get my mind off this guy sitting next to me. He smells amazing; his fragrance is intoxicating and sexy and makes me feel like I'm breathing in nitrous at the dentist office. How a man's cologne can make me feel lightheaded, I have no idea. I need to focus on taking notes but, *holy cow*, not only is he gorgeous, he smells unbelievable and appears to have just stepped out of a Ralph Lauren ad. He has the intense good looks that makes me think lustfully of what in the world I might do if left alone with this much hotness.

After forty-five minutes of listening and note taking, I've just finished my first lecture in creative writing.

As I'm gathering my things, Lane says, "You never finished answering my question."

I look at him, taking in his handsomeness and realizing I forgot the question. "Oh, yeah, sorry about that. I forgot what you asked me." A nervous blush warms my face.

"If you were a journalism major?"

As we walk up the lecture hall steps toward the door, I notice he's not wearing socks with his very expensive-looking leather loafers.

"I'm actually a creative media major, but I'm working toward a minor in journalism. How about you?"

His smile is beautiful, and his hazel eyes are electric. Facing him directly, I realize why I thought he seemed familiar. My mom coaxed my sister and me into watching some of her favorite movies from the eighties. My parents are always talking about how the best music, movies and fashion came out of the eighties. He looks a lot like the rich, flashy blonde guy from one of those John Hughes films, but I can't remember the actor's name.

"I'm actually an English major and planning to double major with art history. I really wanted to take one of Rob Brigg's writing classes. I read a lot. Usually a lot of history. I've read several of his books, since they're about his past, his family members, and the South."

"Same. I've read three of his books. But I mostly read chick lit."

"Chick what? he asks, with a short laugh that doesn't feel intimidating. "Listen, Bex, I've gotta truck it across campus now, but it was nice to meet you."

Just like that he's gone, and suddenly my head is clear.

"Bex! Hey, Bex!"

I turn and see Bella waving at me frantically. I wave back and walk toward her.

"Hey, Bella, what's up?"

"Nothing. I'm heading over to Bidgood for my marketing class. You wanna walk with me?"

"Sure. I'm going in that direction anyway."

Bella and I are both from the South and are used to the late August heat. It's easy to spot kids who aren't southerners by what they wear those first few weeks of school. We point out a few as we're walking and laugh about their probably being from Michigan or Washington State or somewhere. I love our game of *where's that look from.* We made it up last year when we spent so much time together during recruitment week.

Bella's from Louisiana, near New Orleans, a city called Covington. I remember she said it was the same town where that hot actor from *The Vampire Diaries* is from.

I look over at Bella. "I'm going to Palmer, for math, but I've got almost twenty minutes before it starts."

"I have two more classes near Bidgood after my marketing class ends. Maybe I'll see you before I go to band practice," she says as she turns to dart up the stairs into Bidgood Hall.

"Don't forget we're going dress shopping after class tomorrow with Lexi, and Cat. So carve out some time to go," she shouts back at me before disappearing into the building.

"Okay, bye!" I yell back and continue on my way to the other side of campus. Even though the late August sun is beating down, it's a beautiful day that shows off the ancient oak trees, thick green grass of the quad, and ivy growing up the sides of the stately brick architecture. As I make my way near Ferguson Plaza, I can see people walking in and out of the center fountains that spray up from the pavement. On a hot day like this it, would be nice to walk through them, but I don't want to be late, so I make a right turn and head for the math building.

Math is as dull as can be, and unfortunately no one smells remotely amazing. Afterward I go back to Phi Mu to gather my things for dance team practice and maybe squeeze in a nap. The room is empty and quiet when I walk in, perfect for a catnap. As I start to snuggle down, my phone dings a text. I look to see who it is—just Mom checking on my first day. I quickly text back, *Great, but gotta go to practice.* I set a thirty-minute alarm for my nap and drift off to sleep. When my alarm buzzes me awake, I shake off the grogginess. Opening our room fridge, I grab an energy drink, throw my bag over my shoulder, and open the door as Bella barrels in.

"Hey, Bex, how was your first day?"

"Cool. I think pretty close to perfect. How about you?"

"Same. Can't complain. Anything new?" she asks, opening the closet to get out her trumpet for band practice.

"Yeah, I *have* to tell you about this guy I met in my creative writing class, but I'm going to be late for dance if I don't hurry."

"Sure. See ya, Bex. Have a great one. We'll catch up on all the details tonight."

"Definitely," I say scooting out the door. Thinking about *new guy* from my journalism class, makes me smile and creates a lightness to my step. I bounce onto the sidewalk and decide to vlog about my day as I make my way over to dance team practice. I'll title this vlog *"What to do when you trip over a hot guy in class."*

5

#Shoptillyoudrop

My phone starts ringing as my first morning class ends. I slide it open and shove it to my ear.

"Ready to go shopping? Can you meet us for lunch at Rama Jama's at one?" Bella asks breathlessly, like she's in a hurry.

"Yep, but I'll be a few minutes late. My last class ends at one, so order me a grilled cheese and a diet coke. I'll Venmo you."

It's twenty after by the time I hurry into Rama Jama's. Everyone's chatting, eating and laughing. Cat tells me to sit next to her. She introduces me to her friend Ryan. I think she says he plays baseball. Cat plays softball for Alabama and knows lots of guys on campus. She's a Tri Delta who met Bella through Lexi, and they met me through Bella. We generally hang out together, including some of Cat's friends every now and then. Lexi plays the flute in the *Million Dollar Band*, and Bella plays the trumpet. They're good friends with several band guys and even the dude who plays the part of *Big Al*, our school's elephant mascot. I kinda know Alex too, a.k.a. *Big Al*, because the mascot is at the basketball games and hangs out with the dance team and the cheerleaders. However, at Alabama, football is the *King of all sports*. I'm thinking this when I notice how cool a couple of the football players look walking into Rama Jama's for lunch.

"Hot," Cat whispers to me as she casually points to one of the football players who just strolled in. I smile at her in agreement as I take a bite out of my grilled cheese.

Seconds later our star QB saunters in, mingling with the crowd, giving fist bumps, and back slaps as he makes his way to the counter to place his order. Ryan has stopped shoving food into his mouth, and we're all sitting there awestruck as if the president just arrived.

Cat leans into the table and whispers, "Guys, one of my sorority sisters, Sara, was bragging about hooking up with him last weekend."

Lexie arches an eyebrow. I roll my eyes. Cat looks at me then in a mocking tone says, "Sorry Bex. Too much for those virgin ears of yours?"

I stare at the French fries on my plate.

Bella spurts, "Watch it." and points a finger at Cat like she's about to give a lecture. Cat taps out a loud drumroll on the edge of the table with her fingers. "Anyway," she says, standing. "time to blow this pop stand. See ya, Ryan, the girls and I gotta get our shopping on."

Ten minutes later, we arrive at the store and make our way to the dress department since we're trying to find something for our first social of the season. Last year we had to wear black because we were freshmen. This year we get to wear any color we want. Cat's got a social of her own for Tri Delta. I'm not totally sure of the theme, but since she and Lexi know each other from high school, she hangs with us, almost as much as with her own sorority sisters.

Surrounded by tall racks, Cat and Lexi start pulling things and chatting about how they love the colors. Bella squeals when she finds a dress in teal crepe with quarter-length bell sleeves. We ooh and ahh over it. I pick out a red sleeveless number with a simple lace trim around the bottom.

We're searching for a fitting room, when out of the corner of my eye I see the men's cologne counter. Without any self-control, I shove my dresses onto Cat's arm.

"I'll be back in a minute," I say to the girls. "I'm going to look at the men's cologne for just a second." I call, over my shoulder, already in a sprint.

At the cologne counter, I grab the first fragrance I see and spray it on a card and sniff. The sales lady comes over to offer assistance and hands me a container with coffee in it.

"Here," she says holding the container for me to take. "This will clear your palate. Take a sniff before trying the next one."

She gives me another bottle. After smelling the coffee, I spritz another scent. I continue my way down the counter as she continues talking to me about how this is new or that one lasts longer.

"What are you looking for?" she asks.

"I'd like to smell everything, if that's okay."

"Of course. Be my guest. Let me know if I can help you with anything." She walks over to the women's cologne, leaving me to my own devices.

I continue my smelling journey down one side and around the other. I've pulled aside four fragrances but keep going because there are so many.

I'm in the middle of smelling one, thinking I may be getting close to the final few when I hear, "Bex! What are you doing?"

It's Bella, and it looks like she's already made her purchase. I stare at her, frozen and feeling sheepish.

"Bex, we've tried on our dresses." She sounds flustered. "Lexi tried on yours, too, and bought both of them. Cat and Lexi went to look at earrings. What are you doing over here? It looks like you spilled a bag of rice, there are so many white spray cards on the counter." She looks at the counter then at me.

"You know how I told you about the guy I sat next to in my creative-writing/ journalism class?"

Bella nods.

"I thought maybe I could figure out what type of cologne he was wearing."

24

Bella cracks up and tries to speak between bursts of laughter. "Bex, how many have you tried so far? And what's that on your face?" She steps closer to me, examining me further. "You have brown flecks all over your chin."

I'm starting to feel a little embarrassed and maybe slightly crazy. "I've been sniffing coffee beans in between each tester. At some point, I decided to take the lid off, and I've been shaking it before each sniff. I guess maybe some of the residue got on my face."

Bella rolls her eyes. "Of all the crazy things, this has to top them. Well, did you find it?"

I point to the bottles I've set aside. "I've narrowed it down to these four, and I think I've tried almost everything."

Bella looks slightly annoyed. "We should probably get going," she says.

"Wait. I have an idea. I want you to spray a card with one of these." I slide the bottles closer to her. "I'll try and choose with my eyes closed."

I quickly smell the final three fragrances just in case those need to be added to my collection. I open the coffee container's lid and take a deep sniff, careful not to get any more stuff on my face.

"Okay, I'm ready. I'll keep my eyes closed. Don't say anything. Just spray the card and hand it to me."

Bella tells me to turn around. "Close your eyes, and hold out one hand," she says while spraying something. She sticks a card in my hand. After trying all four, I seem to keep coming back to the same one.

The sales associate walks over and asks, "Have you ladies found what you're looking for?"

"Yes, I think I'd like a few samples of this one," I say, handing her the card, forgetting I don't know which one it is yet.

"She means this," Bella says, handing her the bottle.

With a patronizing smile, she hands me a bag with three samples inside. We thank her and turn around to see Lexi and Cat walking toward us.

"Hey, guys." Lexi says, as she walks up with her shopping bags. "I bought two dresses since you never tried yours on. You can borrow one, of course."

"Great. Thanks, Lexi."

Cat butts in, "What were you guys doing?"

"Bex has smelled every men's cologne in the store trying to find the one that some guy she sits next to wears," Bella complains, with irritation in her voice.

"Is it someone I know?" Cat questions.

"I don't think he's a baseball player, but he looks like a model, dresses really nice and smells even better."

Lexi perks up. "Do tell. Can't wait to check this guy out."

"He reminds me of an actor I saw in an eighties movie called *Pretty in Pink*.

"Oooooh, I've seen that," Lexi cries. "Is it Andrew McCarthy?"

"I don't know the actor's name, so I'm not sure. He's got blonde hair, hazel eyes and he's kinda tall."

Lexi nods. "Right, you mean he looks like James Spader. Or, more specifically, a very young James Spader."

Rolling my eyes, I answer. "Sure, maybe."

Back on campus, Lexi, Bella and I head to Phi Mu house to hang in our room until dinner. I grab my computer and look up James Spader movies and sure enough, that's who Lane looks like. I pull up images and show the screen to Lexi and Bella, who are busy going over notes and homework, which I should totally be doing, too.

Lexi confirms. "Yep. That's him."

Bella looks at the screen. "OMG, Bex! I totally get why you're so ga ga over meeting this guy. He looks like hot-Ivy-League-prep-schooler-meets-Hollywood-heartthrob. Good luck with that." She turns her attention to Lexi. "Lexi, you know Bex got a sample of the cologne she thinks he wears."

Lexi sticks out her hand. "Gimmie." Snapping the lid open on the bottle, she sniffs and grins. "You're right, this smells

26

like heaven. It's a Tom Ford fragrance. Does he smell like Harry Styles?"

I look at Lexi with confusion then realize she may be right. Harry Styles has been said to wear a Tom Ford fragrance with notes of vanilla and cashmere.

Now, I give Lexi a more confidant glance. "Mhm, maybe he does."

Bella inhales deeply. "Speaking of delicious smells, I think it's *Waffle Wednesday*. I'm ready to eat. She sets her notebook down and stands up, stretching.

"Oh, good. I hope they have fresh fruit toppings and whipped cream like last time," I say, standing, tossing the cologne onto my bed. I follow the girls out the door then turn and look back at the samples. *Yep, I'm definitely squirting that all over my pillow later tonight.*

6
#Friyay

It's Friday, and I'm glad the first week of school is over. All my classes have gone well, and I'm looking forward to tomorrow night's social. Bella and Lexi invited dates and decided I needed one, too. Now I have a blind date. *Yay!* I've never dated anyone seriously. Back in high school, I dated and had a few crushes, but no one I felt strongly about. Mostly, I kept my grades up, danced, went to practice, and hit repeat. I've never been one to stay out partying or drinking a lot. I've always tried to stay on track. A lot of it has to do with my upbringing, my church, and my family. I've always had a *good-girl* reputation. That's probably why I stopped getting invites to some of the parties that my friends were going to in high school. I guess I'm too much of a rule follower. I feel the need to change that starting soon.

Here on campus there's never an end to the number of parties or social events, most of which seem pretty casual. Bella and Lexi have a lot of guy friends they've met from being in the band, and they volunteer with Young Life, a non-denominational outreach, allowing them to meet even more people. I've gone with them to Young Life a few times. It's fun and involves a worship band and dressing up for theme nights. I think whoever they've chosen for my blind date will be someone they met there. At least that's the impression I've gotten from the hints I've picked up on.

After my last class, I head toward Starbucks. I want to catch up on homework before the weekend starts. At the counter, I order my favorite chai drink, find an empty table near the window, and pull out my work with an air of confidence and a goal of getting things accomplished. While getting settled my phone dings with a text. It's Bella wondering what I'm up to.

I'm at star$.

Do you want to go to Gallette's to hang with some ppl 2night?

Sure. What time?

Cat's friend will let us in. We should get there early, around 8:30 or a little b4.

When we know someone at the door who can let us in, that's usually when we decide to go out. Until we're of age we don't have much of a choice. The plan is to each buy one drink but don't stay too long, hoping not to get caught. I won't turn twenty-one until August, right before my senior semester starts. Last year a group of us ordered fake ID's from China, but I feel weird using mine. Again, I'm feeling that I'm too much of a rule follower, but I'm determined to do something daring this year, I'm just not sure what that is yet.

Hours later and dressed to impress, Bella and I meet Cat on the sidewalk outside of Gallette's.

"Hey, girl," Bella says when we walk up.

"It's early and not hopping yet," Cat says. "We should be able to get a table while waiting for the rest of the gang." Cat motions toward the bouncer manning the door. He sees us and lets us through. A few minutes later, Lexi and Patrick arrive with Ryan and Jack and a really cute guy I've never met.

"Bex, this is Grant," Bella introduces us when the guys sit down.

"Hi, Bex, nice to meet you." He reaches to shake my hand.

"So how do you know Lexi and Bella?" I ask, kinda already thinking I know the answer.

29

I remember this is the guy Bella and Lexi met while working at summer camp. A week ago, they told me all about him during our long bus ride to our sisterhood retreat. Grant has a killer tan, dark brown hair and soft brown eyes. He has a really handsome face and striking cheekbones. Let me just say it like it is, *he's hot!* We chat each other up with a lot of small talk. He's easy to talk to, and he definitely passes the vibe check. Cat's friend, Reese, shows up and joins our group, and we struggle to find another chair. It's starting to get crowded as more people pack in to kick off the weekend. I see some girls from dance team and wave to them as they move through the club.

Our group grows into eight then ten after Cat invites a few more friends to join us. We leave to walk down the strip and grab something to eat. By sticking close to Grant, I'm finding out more about him and his hobbies. He's talking about a fishing trip in Destin last spring break when he caught a thirty-pound marlin.

Our group heads into our fav restaurant hang out, Buffalo Phil's. A band is setting up while we're ordering and starts tuning and testing the microphones. The first song they play is "Livin' on a Prayer" by Bon Jovi, and by the third song, we're up dancing and singing to "Don't Stop Believing" by Journey. The band switches from 80's to our decade and does a good job with "Mr. Brightside" by The Killers. This is why I love college so much. I'm caught up in the music, have a slight buzz and am dancing and singing like there's no tomorrow. Everything in the world is right now. This moment is all that matters. I'm feeling totally free. I have my friends by my side, good music is blaring, and my world pauses into a perfect sliver in time. As I drink in the mood, the band slows down and plays "Sweet Caroline," and we sing it at the top of our lungs. After the song ends, we notice it's way after midnight and decide to walk back to the house.

As we're walking toward Phi Mu, I'm smiling, thinking what a great night. People are still milling about, and I see a group of guys, laughing and singing, coming up the other side of the road. I do a double take and realize it's him. *It's Lane. The gorgeous and delicious smelling guy from class.* Our eyes meet for a brief second, and I turn and look back again. I feel a draw, a slight pull like an invisible force, and then I hear, "Look out, Bex!" "Watch out!"

Bella is yelling my name, bringing me back to reality.

"Bex, you stepped off the curb and almost got hit by a car." Bella's voice has a concerned tone.

Grant starts asking if I'm okay. I'm totally startled and dazed but manage to say, "Yes. Sorry guys, I'm fine."

I make it the rest of the way home in one piece. Stopping before I go inside the sorority house, I smile at Grant.

"I'm looking forward to tomorrow night," I say, giving him a hug. His jaw brushes against my hair as we pull apart.

"I am, too. It was nice to meet you, Bex. See you tomorrow night."

He turns toward the sidewalk and gives a slight wave before he walks away with the guys.

Back in the room, Bella's talking about how much fun tonight was and starts asking me questions.

"So, Bex, did you have fun? What do you think about Grant?"

"Bella, I saw him." I ignore her question because my mind is on Lane.

"What? Who?" She looks at me, confused.

"Lane, the guy in my creative-writing journalism class. I saw him walking on the other side of the street, going the opposite way, and he saw me, too."

"Are you sure it was him?"

"Yes. We looked right at each other, then I turned around to make sure. That's when I stepped off the curb. I swear, Bella, it was like a force was pulling me toward him."

Bella smirks at me. "Girl, you need to watch it and be careful not to get too carried away. You're already acting like a fool in love."

We have a good laugh. "You're right," I say. "I need to stop before I become some crazy stalker. I appreciate you introducing me to Grant. He seems like a really great guy."

31

Changing into my PJ's, I inform Bella, "I don't have anything until practice at one, so I'm sleeping in."

"Me, too." I hear as I turn off the lamp.

"Goodnight." I snuggle down under the covers. Closing my eyes, I think, *Oh, dear God, am I acting like a middle school girl with a crush on a famous YouTuber?"*

7

#Phisandbowties

Bella and I are in our room with the music up loud, jamming out to Judah & the Lion while getting ready for our Phi date social. I check my hair and makeup in the mirror to make sure it's on point. As I'm standing there, I hear a knock on our door. I open it to find Amanda waiting to give instructions.

"I need you guys to come down and help with set up," she says, before hastily closing the door.

Downstairs, Amanda assigns us a variety of jobs, and we join our sisters working on last minute tasks. After blowing up forty balloons and putting out plates and napkins, we have the house looking festive. We take pics with our Phi big sisters, and our housemother gets a group shot of all of us on the staircase. Glancing at my phone, I see it's time for our dates to start arriving.

I greet Grant out on the front patio and introduce him to each girl as we walk past. After wandering around the house giving Grant the tour, we grab some drinks and head over to the photo booth. We search through the cute props. There are all sorts of hats, sunglasses, long gloves and even a gold tuxedo jacket. I pick up a giant bow tie on a stick and Grant picks up a giant pink bow. Grant holds the bow over his head, and I hold the bow tie under my chin, laughing and making faces at each other during the photo session. Taking his hand, I pull him over to snag a spot to sit and get cozy. I scroll through the photos we just took on my phone.

"These are really cute," I say and show Grant the pictures on the screen.

"You probably wouldn't be able to take a bad picture if you tried," He says looking into my eyes.

"Awwww, you are sweet to say that."

I smile at him. I think he's nice and has a great sense of humor, and, of course, he's hot. I'm not drawn to him by some invisible force like the one, last night that made me walk off the curb while starring back at Lane. But I do want to get to know Grant better.

We make our way outside to hang out near the band. Since last night's dancing was so fun, we pick up where we left off. As we get closer to the DJ, we can see Jack and Patrick doing the "floss" with Bella and Lexi laughing hysterically. Grant joins the guys and the three of them show off, entertaining us with their dance moves. The evening is turning out to be pretty cool. I'm feeling very relaxed around Grant. Dancing with him is a lot of fun allowing his fun-loving side to shine. When it's time to say goodnight, I walk Grant out the front door. We stop near the sidewalk, and he reaches for my hand and holds it gently.

"I had a really good time with you tonight and last night," he says looking at my hand he's holding then he looks up and holds my gaze. "I'd like to get your number and maybe get together and do something tomorrow." The look in his eyes is hopeful and adorable.

"Sure, I usually go to church on Sundays with some of the other Phi Mu's. Would you like to meet me there?" I ask, thinking he'd probably be interested.

He agrees, so we exchange numbers. "I'll text you in the morning before I leave the house," I say, looking into his eyes for a brief moment before he leans in for a kiss. His kiss is soft and gentle, almost polite with a sweetness that makes me blush as we whisper goodnight.

34

I think he's certainly a gentleman and everything a girl would want in a boyfriend, but he's just not Lane. I'm determined to put forth the effort to get to know Grant better, and tomorrow we'll have an opportunity to be alone to talk. It'll be great, I tell myself as I walk up the stairs. I see Bella and Jack saying goodnight near the foyer and wave to them. Wandering into our room, I kick off my shoes and flop onto the bed, almost forgetting about washing my face. I drag myself back up and into the bathroom to start a facial routine. After putting on the new Burt's Bees mask, I walk back to the room and decide to vlog about this hydration treatment mask as I wait for it to dry. When Bella walks in, I shut off my vlog and head back to the bathroom to wash the mask off. Slipping back into the room with glowing skin, I say goodnight to Bella, and snuggle down under the soft sheets. I fall asleep quickly, dreaming about rock bands and boys with bow ties.

8
#Mondaymood

Monday, ugh. Why does Monday have to rhyme with fun day because who thinks Mondays are fun? I am totally not a morning person, and neither is Bella so waking up in order to get to an eight thirty class is like a zombie scene from *The Walking Dead*. We grumble and grunt and stumble around, trying to wake up. After a shower and a Diet Coke, I feel a little more alive. I gather my bag, slide my feet into a pair of flip flops, pull my hair into a bun, and say good-bye to Bella. As I'm shuffling to the sidewalk, I see Amanda, my Phi big sister. She's one of our chapter co-presidents, a senior, and she's on dance team with me. She's someone I admire with strong leadership skills. She's a talented dancer, *and* she's stunningly beautiful, as tall as I am with glossy auburn hair. I'm glad she chose me to be her Phi little sister this year.

"Hey, Bex," she says stopping in front of me. "Don't forget we changed practice time today. It's at four, instead of six. We're meeting on the gym floor at Coleman."

"Thanks, Amanda, see you then," I say with a smile, turning the corner to head to my first class. Although I didn't forget the time change, I still appreciate the thoughtful reminder.

Classes go by quickly for a dreaded Monday. It's sunny and warm without a cloud in the sky, a perfect September day. I decide to grab some rays and sit out on the quad, which is buzzing with people sitting on blankets, playing frisbee and eating lunch. Plopping down in the grass, I use my backpack as a headrest, pull out my Ray-Bans and put them on while I hang and chill, watching some hot guys throw a Frisbee. I'm zoned out when I get a text, and at the same time someone pops up next to me. I look up to see Lexi standing above me.

"Hey, whatcha doin'?" Lexi asks, sitting next to me in the grass.

"Nothing much, just watching those cuties," I say, pointing subtly.

"I know, right? It's a beautiful day." My phone dings again. This time I look at it.

Lexi smirks and asks in a singsong way, "Who is it?"

"It's Grant. He wants to know if I can hang out with him at the cliffs today."

"Oooo, sounds romantic."

"Yeah, I know, but it's one thirty now, and my practice time changed, so I can't go."

I quickly text Grant back to let him know my schedule and ask for a rain check.

"So, you've been on a few dates with Grant now, how's it going?" Lexi asks with a silly schoolgirl grin on her face.

"After church on Sunday, we ate lunch at that busy brunch place on the riverfront. He's really funny and started telling me these corny bicycle jokes after some bikers passed us on the boardwalk while we were waiting for our table to be ready. He had me laughing so hard I was snorting."

"Cute. I knew you guys would hit it off," Lexi says smiling. "By the way, the chapter meeting tonight is about homecoming. Bella signed us up for decorating."

"Wait, for what?"

"The homecoming lawn decoration committee. We're supposed to meet after *Love Island* is over."

"Great," I say, not very enthused. "Fortunately for you and everyone, I'll be there, since my practice time for today got moved up."

Before I left this morning, I'd packed a change of clothes in my backpack for practice, so I wouldn't have to walk all the way back to the house then all the way to Coleman. I'm loving just sitting in the sun on the quad for a few hours and getting a little homework finished. After Lexi and I shoot the breeze, she says she has another class to get to and tells me she'll see me tonight. It's almost time for me to go to practice, so I put my homework away, put in my AirPods, choose a song by The Killers and begin my walk toward Coleman Coliseum.

Everyone seems to have the first routine down, so after we've gone full out for the fourth time we're dismissed. I catch a ride back to the house with Amanda, and we arrive just as everyone is sitting for dinner.

Afterwards, Bella, Lexi and I grab a few chairs, carry them into the living room, and settle in for the traditional Monday TV drama either *Love Island* or *The Bachelor*. During the commercial breaks, we chat about who's cute and who seems fake. The show ends and our homecoming meeting is called to order. We vote on the theme and afterward count the tallies. Caroline, the senior in charge of the homecoming float and lawn decorations, announces the winning theme, *Disney Dreams Come to Life Along the Crimson Path*. We move on to discuss the homecoming choreography dance and pass around signups for those who want to participate in the homecoming sorority basketball games.

Only the fourteen girls who have committed to competing in this year's dance stick around for the rest of the meeting. Phi Mu is serious about the choreography competition. We usually win every year or come in second. This year I made sure Lexi and Bella were up for the challenge, and they promised to give it a hundred percent. As the meeting wraps up, we finalize the day, time, and location for dance practice and the days and times that will be set aside for working on the lawn decoration and the parade float. When the meeting ends, everyone seems pleased with what we accomplished.

After my busy Monday, I'm glad to change into PJ's and lie down. My mind wanders to thinking about tomorrow's creative writing class and if I'll see Lane. Maybe I should avoid him?

The next morning, I'm purposefully early for my creative writing class. I think I'll try to avoid *you know who*. I don't want to become a stalker, and I am really interested in Grant, so it's probably best to avoid further contact with hottie. I find a seat on the end of a row near the front on the far left. I'm rummaging around in my backpack getting out my notebook, pen and phone when I hear...

"Hello." I turn to my left and see Lane standing next to me. My breathing hitches with his presence.

"Can I squeeze by and sit next to you?" he asks, smiling down at me.

He looks a little casual today in chambray shorts with red elephants on them and a white Southern Tide T-shirt with leather loafers and no socks. He smells amazing, of course, and I feel like I've got my mouth hanging open, hoping I'm not drooling all over my shirt.

"Of course." I stand so he can pass.

He sits down, turns to me, and asks, "So how was your weekend?"

"Great, and yours?" *Oh, and by-the-way, I moved to a different seat trying to avoid you. But OMG you are beyond beautiful. Bex, get a grip.*

"The usual," he says and clears his throat. "Did I see you out with your friends on the strip Friday night?"

Blinking nervously, I answer, "Oh, yeah, you're right. I guess that was you I saw walking with a group of guys across the street."

"Yeah, that was me," he says with a gorgeous smile.

Professor Brigg glides in and starts writing on the board, so we grab our pens and start taking notes. After class Lane stands and turns toward me.

"See ya, Bex. I've gotta scoot." He shoots me a million-dollar smile that could give toothpaste commercials a run for their money.

"Bye," I murmur and feel dreamy and loopy until he's out of sight. I thought by getting to class early today I might avoid him altogether with my low-key determination to forget him and move on. But it looks like I can't, and, honestly, I don't really want to. I'm drawn to him. Maybe it's only physical attraction, which is obvious, I mean, he's gorgeous and smells like Harry Styles, but it feels like more than just good looks and sexy cologne. I scurry across campus to get to math, then later choreography practice, and after that dance team practice, so I shake off the *what ifs* and go on my way.

9

#Fallfever

Grant asked if he could redeem his "rain check" date from a few weeks ago when I was too busy. He and I are having a picnic at Lake Tuscaloosa before the weather starts turning cold. Fall is in high gear, and the leaves on the trees in and around the tops of the cliffs are a gorgeous array of oranges, reds, and yellows. We spread out our blanket and picnic basket on a flat rock over-looking the lake. Grant surprised me by bringing a bottle of sparkling cider and some plastic cups. I just threw a couple of bottles of water and two granola bars into a bag.

I chuckle. "Wow. Aren't you the Boy Scout ready for duty?"

He laughs and leans in for a kiss. We quickly fall into easy conversation, talking about everything from how homecoming festivities are going to classes, tests, and what we're wearing for the Halloween party. This year we're doing a swap with the Chi Phi's for Halloween, so Grant and I get to decide on matching couple's costumes. Grant opens the picnic basket, pulls out plates, and sets them down next to the blanket. He has cheese, grapes, strawberries, apple slices, crackers and prosciutto.

"I wasn't sure what you'd like, so I got a little of everything," he says with an adorable grin.

"Grant, I'm so surprised," I say smiling back at him. "If I didn't know you were an accounting major, I'd have guessed you to be in hospitality and restaurant management. This is an impressive spread."

Laughing, I lean back into his chest as he wraps an arm around my waist. Together sipping on our drinks, we enjoy the view looking out onto the lake. There are only a few people out here today, so we have the perfect spot at the top of a huge rock overlooking the main part of the lake. Usually, in the spring this place is hopping with swimsuit clad college co-eds jumping off the cliffs into the lake, lying out and partying with their friends.

"So," Grant says, "let's talk Halloween costumes. How about Dr. Who and the Tardis?"

I shake my head. "I'm not a Dr. Who fan. How about a skeleton bride and groom?" I suggest.

He doesn't seem too taken with that one.

"A magician and his rabbit?"

"Nah." He smiles then says, "But that is kinda funny. How about a zombie couple? Or maybe a pizza slice and a delivery guy?"

"I don't want to wear a pizza costume. How about Danny and Sandy from Grease?"

He tips his head from side to side and says, "Maybe. Okay, how about Gatsby and Daisy?"

"That would be totally cool. I really like that one, and I think dressing like a Twenties' flapper girl would be pretty easy."

"Awesome! *The Great Gatsby* theme it is."

An hour later and before we pack up, we take a selfie with the lake and fall colors in the background. We fold the blanket, gather our basket, and head back to campus. Back at the house, I help the rest of girls with our homecoming lawn display. It still amazes me that simple chicken wire and tissue can create amazingly realistic designs.

After dinner I find a quiet spot downstairs in the library near the window that overlooks the front lawn and study for a while. Taking a break, I respond to an email from Mom letting her know how everything is going. She loves details. After a few more study hours, I stand, stretch my arms over my head, and yawn. I look up and notice Amanda looking in at me from the hallway. She quickly looks down and starts typing on her phone. I guess she doesn't need me, so I continue working. After a while I notice it's gotten dark, so I glance at my phone for the time. I had turned the ringer off so I wouldn't be tempted by it while I was finishing my homework. I have two missed texts messages, six SnapChats and several likes on my latest Instagram post.

With my laptop under my arm, I head back to my room. Bella's working on something that looks serious, but she stops and looks at me when I walk in.

"Hey." I say, throwing my bag down. I plop onto the bed to answer a text from Grant.

"Hi, were you at the library all night?" Bella asks.

"No. I was downstairs in the library here in the house."

"Man, I've been studying for like three hours, and I'm so over it right now."

"I feel."

"So how was your picnic with Grant today? You guys are getting along great. I'm so happy for you." She looks at me, giddy, waiting for me to spill the tea.

"It was really cool. He brought a whole picnic. I was impressed at the thoughtfulness that went into everything he packed, including two kinds of cheese, fruit, and a bottle of sparkling cider. I know he said let's get together at the cliffs for a picnic, but I just thought, you know, he meant hang out with snacks and chill for a while."

"Wow, oh my gosh, Bex, that sounds like something off *The Bachelor*."

I shrug, "Eh, I guess. The views were amazing with all the fall colors. And we chose our Halloween couple's costumes," I say, in a slightly excited tone.

"That's awesome. What did you choose?"

"*The Great Gatsby,* I'll be Daisy and Grant Gatsby."

"Aw, how sweet. You guys will look so cute. I'm glad things are working out between you two."

43

"Yeah, I think they are. I moved to a different seat in my journalism class trying to avoid interacting with Lane," I say meekly.

Bella perks up and sits up straighter on her bed, waiting for me to expand my thoughts. "And ..." she says.

"He found me," I grin. "and mentioned the other night walking home from the strip when I saw him with that group of guys across the street, then almost got hit by a car when I looked back."

Bella laughs. "He found you, huh? Like you were trying to hide from him?"

"Well, yeah, I moved way down toward the front row on the far left- side, completely the opposite of where I was sitting before, trying to avoid talking to him. But it didn't work. He asked to sit next to me."

"Okay, like he sought you out and found you? Maybe he's a vampire?" Bella laughs at her own joke. I roll my eyes and change the subject.

"Speaking of vampires have you thought about a costume?"

"Lexi and I are talking about wearing something matching."

"I'm sure you'll come up with something original." One hand covers a yawn, and my other gives her a thumb's up. I lie down on my bed as a question rolls around in my head. *Why did Lane want to find me?*

10
#TrickorTreat

On Halloween, the Phi Mu house, along with the other sororities on the row, participates in Sorority Row Trick or Treat for the families in the community. Our house has rented a snow cone machine, and we have eight freshmen running that. The rest of us are ready to hand out candy. The house is decorated to the hilt with orange and purple lights, giant cobwebs and oversized spiders in the bushes.

I put on my flapper costume and feather headband. Using my favorite Morphe eyeshadow pallet, I spend a lot of time doing my eye makeup for tonight. Bella and Lexi are dressed as sock monkeys, and they look totally hilarious. On our way downstairs, we stop and take pictures with our Phi sisters. I take a selfie and text it to Grant, so he can see my costume, since he's my other half tonight. He texts back *Hot* with a fire emoji next to it.

After we pass out all the candy, Bella says, "Lexi and I are planning to meet up with Patrick and Jack at the Delta Kappa Epsilon house later. I only want to stay at Chi Phi about an hour."

"Grant is coming here in a few minutes, so if you guys want, you can ride over with us to the Chi Phi house."

Bella nods. "Sure. Later Jack can come get us. I want to go to DKE because I hear their parties are not to be missed."

I shrug at Bella with indifference. I know they want to go there to hang with Patrick and Jack.

Lexi says, "You and Grant will look so cute together tonight."

45

"Thanks, Lexi. I'm going to the bathroom." I announce, heading upstairs. Bella and Lexi follow me.

"We better go now while we can. It will be hard trying to get in and out of these sock monkey costumes in the frat house bathrooms," Bella says, jogging up the stairs.

As I'm touching up my makeup my phone dings with a text.

"Guys, Grant is downstairs," I say in an excited rush.

We walk out to meet him. Grant lets out a loud whistle when he sees me. Bella snaps a picture of us. She and Lexi look adorable as sock monkeys, and I take a few of them for Instagram.

Lexi leans near my ear. "Let us know if you guys get bored later. You should come by the DKE house at some point and find us."

I smile. "I'll see if Grant wants to do that, I'll text you guys later."

We hop into Grant's jeep. He's removed the top, and Bella and Lexi stand in the back, singing at the top of their lungs to 24K by Bruno Mars as we drive off.

Inside the Chi Phi house, the smoke machine has made the air as thick as pea soup, and the music is so loud we scream to hear each other. Bella and Lexi move toward the DJ and start dancing. Grant goes about introducing me to his Chi brothers as we wander through the house. A couple comes over to talk with us and tells us how cool our Gatsby costumes look. They're dressed like zombie's with blood and chunks of flesh oozing out of their faces. *I'm glad we didn't choose to go with that costume.* I notice Amanda and Caroline are dressed as skeleton zombies.

"Hey, Amanda," I say, getting her attention. "Y'all's costumes look great, and your face paint is impressive."

"We watched lots of makeup tutorials on YouTube to achieve this level of awesome," she says, posing with her hands under her chin.

We all laugh as Caroline compliments Grant and me. "I love your costume choice. It's very original."

46

"I watched makeup tutorials to get my make up just right for tonight, too."

Grant adds, "Yeah, me, too."

We crack up laughing. I think Grant's sense of humor is endearing. We continue to make our way through the crowds. I see a guy dressed like Chuck Bass from *Gossip Girl*, and his date is dressed like Blair Waldorf. I ask Grant if he's ever watched the show, and he shakes his head.

"What do you like to watch on Netflix?" I ask.

He rattles off *Supernatural*, *Stranger Things* and *Always Sunny*.

"I've heard of *Stranger Things,* but not the others. So, I'm guessing we're not into the same TV shows. I'm sure I'm typical for a girl my age, most of my friends watch the same shows I do. I'm a huge *Gilmore Girls* fan. It's my all-time favorite Netflix binge."

"You should watch *Stranger Things*. I think you'd like it."

"I always pick a series during the summer and try to watch as many episodes as I can." I name a few more to give him an idea of my taste.

My phone buzzes, it's Bella saying she and Lexi are leaving in a few minutes. Grant and I move toward the DJ. He's playing "Swish Swish" by Katy Perry, and it's impossible not to dance. After an hour, I start to get hot and sweaty. We move outside to get some air and escape the pea soup fog. I notice someone throwing up in the bushes, so we walk to the other side of the lawn. I ask Grant if he feels like going down to the DKE house to hang with Lexi and Bella. I text them to see if I can get one of them to answer. Five minutes later I get a text from Bella, *Come on down.*

Delta Kappa Epsilon is the oldest fraternity on campus and known to be exclusive to southerners, politicians, and blue bloods. It was introduced to campus by someone from Yale University in 1847 and is part of *the Machine,* a secret society made up of elite chosen members from the original Greek houses

47

on campus. You must be selected by someone who's already a member. They've been known to control campus politics. I haven't paid much attention to them myself, and their identities are a mystery, so no one knows who's in the secret society anyway.

The Delta Kappa Epsilon house we're going to tonight is not the original house that was built. That house was torn down years ago to increase the size of Bryant-Denny Stadium so it could hold over a hundred thousand fans during home football games.

Even though the newer house is beautifully designed and decorated, I sense an old feel as we walk in. It feels like walking into history. There's a distinct smell of cigar smoke, leather and bourbon. As we walk through the front door, I notice the large room on the right. It's as big as a ballroom, with dark carved wood embellishments on the walls and ceiling and floor-length heavy brocade curtains with thick tassel tiebacks. A huge oil painting hangs above a massive wood burning fireplace, which has a roaring fire crackling and popping inside. I guess the huge painting must be of their founder. The fireplace itself is also large and impressive.

Bella's friend, Jack, and Lexi's friend, Patrick, are both third generation DKE legacies, according to Bella when she gave me the scoop on her crush. They became good friends with them after many hours of band practice. I assume Patrick or Jack have bragged about being in DKE. It must be the reason the girls are so determined to hit this party tonight, and a little crush doesn't hurt.

We continue through the house. I almost bump into what looks like a bear statue covered in blood with half its head torn off. *Gross.* They also have guys dressed like undertakers walking around with trays in hand. I suppose their pledges have the job of being waiters tonight. I also notice a giant Grim Reaper statue with glowing red eyes. And, last but not least, they have a coffin full of Jell-O shots. I think it's all completely creepy, but at least we're not choking to death on a fog of smoke at Chi Phi house anymore.

Grant and I make it to the back of the house to a large room that has French doors open to the patio. The DJ is set up outside. Lexi and Patrick are dancing. Grant and I walk up to them and yell, "Hey Guys." Lexi stops dancing, throws her arms around my neck, and hugs me, spilling her drink on me.

Patrick high-fives Grant, and Lexi says, "Bella's here somewhere."

I scan the crowd, looking for another sock monkey. I spot Cathryn, a senior on my dance team. She's with a date, and they're dressed as Vampires. I continue peering through the crowd for Bella, and then I spot Lane. He's dressed like a Roman soldier. He's with a couple of guys and a girl. He doesn't notice me. Good. Now all I need to do is find an excuse to leave quickly. *Think Bex, think.* Suddenly, I feel someone behind me covering my eyes.

Bella yells, "Guess who? I'm so glad you guys came down here to hang with us."   She's chatting nonstop about how this is the best party ever, and it's the hottest house on campus and *blah, blah, blah.* I'm not listening, because I'm still trying to figure out how to leave fast, when Grant walks up with two beers and hands me one. I'm not a huge beer fan, but it's a Bud Light, so it's practically water anyway. Bella grabs me and Grant by the arm, dragging us toward the DJ. All six of us move out on the dance floor and really get into the music. Immersed in the crowd, I start having a lot of fun dancing with everyone. For the moment, I forget about seeing Lane.

When it's time for a dance break, we go inside to find somewhere to sit and chill. We walk to the front room and sit on the leather couches near the door. I ask Jack and Patrick if they'll get us some bottled water. While they're gone, Lexi and Bella start to look sleepy and lay their heads back on the sofa and close their eyes. Grant comes over to sit by me and reaches out to hold my hand.

He leans his head into my neck and whispers quietly in my ear, "You look beautiful tonight, if I haven't already told you."

I glance down at our hands folded together on his knee. When I look up, I notice Lane walking down the hallway, and he's looking *right* at me. He smiles and looks like he's about to walk over when some guy stops to talk to him then turns to leave. I look at Grant, who's laid his head on my shoulder. I reach out and touch his cheek. He raises his head and leans in to kiss me. I kiss him back a little more passionately than normal, and he seems to get the message quickly. He moves closer to me and puts one hand on my leg, while his other hand slowly caresses my neck. Even though I'm totally caught up in kissing him, he's not who I was just thinking about. I feel weird kissing him, knowing I'm thinking about Lane, so I stop. I smile shyly and say, "It's getting late. Let's see if Bella and Lexi are ready to ride back to the house."

When we arrive in front of Phi Mu, Lexi and Bella say, "Goodnight, see you later Grant" as they hop out of the back of the jeep.

"Tonight, was fun," Grant says, leaning in kissing me.

I stare into his dark brown eyes, thinking he looks hot in his 1920's costume.

"Yes, it was a total blast; a Halloween not to forget." I pull away, reaching for the door. "I'm tired and can't wait to get all this makeup off. Thank you for everything. Goodnight, Grant." I say, sliding out of his jeep.

Bella's in the room in an awkward position, trying to unzip her sock monkey costume. I help her with her zipper, and she un-zips me as I slip out of my costume.

"Let's sleep really late tomorrow. It's Sunday," I say, tossing my dress onto the bed.

Bella looks at the clock on the desk and says, "Yeah, totally. It's two a.m., and I don't want to think about anything for the next twelve hours."

In the bathroom, it takes me a while to get all the eye make-up off. As I'm walking back to our room, three girls stumble down the hall, giggling. One says, "Hey, Bex, what's up?" Her voice is slurred.

"Hey. A fun Halloween?" I ask.

"Got a date with a Chi Phi next weekend," she says, holding the door open to her room so her friends can go inside. Sounds like a successful Halloween. Mine on the other hand has been interesting for sure.

11
#Goals

Neither Bella nor I stir until mid-afternoon. It's Sunday, and the house is still and silent. November has gently arrived and presented itself in soft solitude. Tiptoeing down to the kitchen we pour ourselves some juice and pop some bread into the toaster. We know we need to work on the lawn decoration today, and I think Caroline said today's plan is to begin at four o'clock. Bella and I gather some bottled juice, toast, and granola bars, and take them back to our room. I'm not planning on getting in the shower for at least another thirty minutes, so I pull out my computer and my day planner and look at all my assignments and commitments for the upcoming week. I see a note in the margin for today that says, "5:30 filming."

"Crap!"

Bella screams. "Oh My God! You scared me to death."

I laugh and say, "I'm sorry. It's just that I remembered I am supposed to film a commercial ad for one of my classes today, and I may have mentioned to my group that I had a few friends that would be helping with it."

Bella looks at me, points to herself and asks, "You mean me?"

"Yes. Did you forget I asked?"

"Uhm no. Now that you mention it, I do remember you asking me and Lexi and Grant about helping you with a project."

"Whew." I snatch my phone quickly and text Grant a reminder. I'm hoping he's up and around. He answers, *Hey babe.*

Hope u r having a great first day of November.

Absolutely, now that I've heard from u, my day just got a 100%.

I'm hoping u can still help me with my project today.

I remind him of the plan to meet up with my group to film the soda ad for my class project at the river walk. He shoots me back a text.

See u at 5:30.

I send a text to the three guys in my group to remind them and one to Lexi. I gather my hair into a messy bun and take a quick shower. When I get back to the room, two of the guys have texted back that they'll meet me at the river walk, and Lexi has answered me with a question.

Is Bella going?

Yes.

Great. Sounds cool.

I remind Lexi about working on the lawn decoration before we leave. She texts me back a "thumbs up" emoji.

After working on the lawn decoration for over an hour, we hop into Bella's car and head to the riverfront and park near the paddle board rental. When we get out of the car, I see my classmates setting up cameras and other equipment. We walk down to the dock where I introduce them to Bella, Lexi, and Grant. After filming the ad, the guys say they're going to hang around and take some still shots of the bottles with the river in the background. They've created impressive looking labels, making them look like a real soda brand.

"Send me the final clip to look at before we have to turn it in," I say, waving bye as I turn around and walk toward my friends. When Grant asks if he can take me to dinner at Steamers on the strip, I accept. It feels like a good way to wind down the day.

We wave bye to Bella and Lexi and hop into Grant's jeep. At Steamers, Grant and I grab a booth and order Cokes.

H smiles and reaches for my hand over the table. "I'm glad to spend more time with you today."

"Yeah, me, too," I smile back.

I order a shrimp Po-boy, and Grant orders wings. While we're eating, we chat about homecoming.

"How's y'alls lawn decoration coming?" he asks.

"It's looking good. It's almost finished."

"Do you have special plans for game day? Will your parents be coming in for homecoming?"

"Yes. They have a spot on the quad with a tent. They tailgate with good friends who are alums, complete with TV and a catered meal."

He nods and says, "My parents have come the past two years but decided not to come to the game this year. Can I pick you up at the house sometime after the parade ends? Maybe we could walk to the quad together and meet up with your parents."

"That sounds perfect. I'm not riding on the float. I'm marching behind the band with the dance team. After the parade I'll quickly run over and say hi to Mom and Dad, then I'll go back to the house, change clothes and hang for a while."

"I'll be riding on the Chi Phi float. I'll text you sometime after the parade ends, and we'll meet up."

We continue eating, and Grant asks me about dance team. I explain that we'll be performing at a home game on November 14th.

"I can't wait to watch you perform," he says, with a huge grin.

I smile back, biting my lower lip. "Yeah, I'll probably be a little nervous if I know you're in the crowd."

I text him the rest of the basketball schedule for the season and explain that we usually perform prior to the game starting and at halftime. "The next home basketball game will be the Friday before homecoming. It'll be a busy week for me. My parents will be there. You can meet up with me and meet them right after the game is over."

"Yes, that'll be cool."

"We'll still plan to go by their tent on Saturday. We can get a quick bite before the game."

He gives me a sweet smile, brushing his fingers across mine. "I'm looking forward to homecoming with you. Before you know it, it'll be Thanksgiving, and we'll be stuffing ourselves with the big bird."

This makes me laugh, and I'd just taken a bite of food. Trying to cover my mouth while laughing only makes Grant laugh harder. He has a great sense of humor and an easy- going nature that puts me at ease.

Grant asks, "Will you be going home to Atlanta for Thanksgiving?"

"Yes, we have plans for my mom's birthday, which falls on Thanksgiving this year, but those aren't final. She said something about wanting to go to an island off the coast of Georgia."

"I'm planning to leave after the Iron bowl. Are you going to stick around for that game?"

I nod. "I wouldn't miss that game for the world." We laugh knowing no one would want to miss the biggest college rivalry game in the state."

"I can't leave until after the basketball game that week. My parents will be at that game, too, and I'll catch a ride with them. I usually get a ride back to school with a Phi Mu sister who's also from Atlanta. We plan to come back the first Sunday in December. I have to dance at the basketball game that night, too."

Grant looks serious and says, "Do you realize it's the first of November, and we've planned the entire month out over dinner?"

I smile, feeling nostalgic. "Yeah, November will go by fast, then it's Christmas break, and by the time we come back from that, we'll have more than half the year completed."

On the short ride back to Phi Mu, I ask Grant when his first swim meet will be. I know he swims at six thirty every morning before school, but I haven't asked him about coming to a meet.

He smiles and says, "I had a lot of home meets in September and only one home meet in October. Since we'd just met, I didn't want to push a swim meet on you. They tend to be long and sometimes a little boring for most people."

He pulls up to the curb in front of the house, reaches for my hand, and says, "But there's a home meet this week against Auburn."

"I'm there. What about the rest of the month?"

"There are several away meets in November." He squeezes my hand.

We're still holding hands and making plans for where I need to go for the swim meet when he takes his other hand and plays lightly with my hair. Then he puts his hand on the back of my head, pulls me closer, and kisses me gently. When I finally pull away, we say goodnight. He lifts the hand that he's holding up to his lips and kisses it while looking into my eyes and murmurs, "Sweet dreams."

He slowly releases my hand. I smile back and think he's the perfect guy-next-door-take-home-to-mom-type. I like him a lot, but do I like him, *like him*?

Walking into our room, I see Bella at her desk. She turns around when she hears me.

"Hey, aren't you glad to have that commercial assignment over with?" she asks.

"Totally. Because I have a lot more stuff coming up right before homecoming, plus we have choreography practice twice next week. And Grant has a home swim meet on Thursday. Would you want to go with me?"

"Not really, I've heard they can be boring. But if you really want me to I will."

"Nah, that's okay, I'll text Cat. She'll probably go just to look at the hot guys with their dripping wet bods and tight speedos on."

Bella doubles over in laughter. "Girl, you know it," she, says.

12

#Canyoukeepasecret

I get to my usual seat for creative writing and realize Lane hasn't come in yet. At the end of class, we receive our end of term assignment that will technically be our grade in the class for the semester. The paper states our assignment is writing up to a 2,000-word story that can be fiction or nonfiction. The good news is this is our final grade and takes the place of our exam. It's one exam I don't need to study for. I also notice it's due sometime around Christmas break.

After class is over, I hurry down to catch Professor Brigg before he leaves the room.

"Excuse me, Professor Brigg, could I get an extra assignment sheet for a friend?" He smiles and says, "Yes." He hands me the extra paper and, as I turn to leave, I scan the room. Outside along the sidewalk I watch to make sure I haven't missed seeing Lane. I realize I haven't seen him since the party Halloween night. It was a little surprising finding out he's a DKE. I stuff the extra paper inside my notebook and head across campus for my next class.

Later, I have to pick up my dance team uniform and pom poms for the homecoming parade then go to practice for the choreography competition. We have practice three times this week in order to get ready for the big event. It's only Tuesday, and I'm already hoping for weekend vibes to come soon.

******

Another week, a new Monday, and more homecoming preparations to keep me crazy busy. Glancing through my agenda, I double, and triple check my schedule for practice times and things I need to turn in for classes. I have a math test to study for, and I've been asked to submit an article on homecoming to the *Crimson White* school newspaper. I'm flipping through my notebook when I see the paper I picked up for Lane. I hope to see him in class tomorrow since he missed last Tuesday. If not, maybe I'll check with Cathryn and see if she knows him, since I saw her at the DKE house Halloween. What was I thinking getting this paper for him? Like what is he going to say? And why I am so worried about giving it to him. Gawd, I still have a total crush on the guy. *Geez, Bex, get over yourself already. You have lots to work on, including the lawn decoration.* We plan to put the final details on it after dinner. After that, I'm looking forward to a little chill time in my room.

Later that evening after dinner, I get up from the table to throw my trash away. I feel a tap on my shoulder. Turning around, I see it's Amanda, and she's signaling me to come downstairs, which is a very odd thing for her to do. No one ever goes down to the basement, and why is she being so secretive? I leave my tray and follow her down the stairs when she signals me over to the side away from the lights.

"You've been chosen," she whispers. "You need to come with me tonight."

"Chosen for what?" I ask a little too loud because Amanda places a finger to her lips, signaling me to be quiet.

"You'll see," she whispers. "Meet me at my car at eleven thirty. You're riding with me, and you'll find out everything once we get there. Be careful not to tell a soul."

"Okay," I squeak.

She turns to head up the stairs. That was weird. *There goes my quiet evening.*

Everything seems totally normal while we're working on the lawn decoration, but in the back of my mind I'm desperately curious as to why so much secrecy with this *chosen thing*. I'm a little spooked and a bit confused, but I decide to go with Amanda.

At eleven twenty, I casually walk out of the room. Bella's busy working on something and doesn't seem to notice. In the parking lot I see Amanda standing next to her car. She sees me and unlocks the doors. Getting in I question where we're going but Amanda just answers me with, "You'll see."

We drive for a while and end up on a dirt road in the woods. I see a few parked cars. We pull up next to one. I start to feel nervous.

"Come on, let's go," Amanda urges, getting out of the car.

"Why are we here?" I ask, but Amanda just keeps walking. I send up a quick prayer. *Dear God, please don't let me die in the woods tonight.*

Amanda turns on her phone light, and we continue along the path which ends at a clearing. That's when I see more people. As we get closer, I recognize a few faces, then I spot Lane. I gasp aloud as if I've stumbled on something, thrown by his presence. Amanda asks, "Are you okay?"

I pull myself together and answer, "I'm fine, just stepped on something."

She leads me over to a table with a bowl, candles, and a flag of Theta Nu Epsilon. A guy asks me to raise my right hand and take the pledge of complete secrecy of everything I will see, say and do while here. I follow through with the pledge, and he hands me a candle. Amanda takes my hand and leads me to our place within the circle.

The only light is from a few lit candles. One of the leaders begins by lighting a candle within the circle. Each person touches a candle to light their own.

We're asked to recite a pledge in Latin. I don't know it, so I'm standing quietly. When the pledge ends, someone walks around with a bowl and presents it in front of each person.

59

He concludes, saying, "As you dip your left hand into the bowl, any violation of the oath, or of the secrecy of our society will cause the blood to appear on your left hand, never to be removed."

Okay, by this time, I'm freaking out, and wishing I hadn't come. But when he steps in front of me, I dip my left hand. When he steps back, I notice someone wearing a black hooded robe with a skull and crosskeys embroidery on the top left standing in the center of the circle. I can't see who it is. The person in the cape calls the meeting to order. It's a guy's voice. Do I recognize that voice? The order of business seems completely normal, all about supporting our Greek candidates and remembering to vote for our supported SGA president and something about commercial media focus, promotions, and influence. I'm only half-listening, since I've been thinking about wanting to leave ever since I got here. Suddenly, there's a loud chant in Latin and everything goes dark. I quickly blow my candle out. I notice light from a flashlight, and everyone quickly disperses. Things are packed up and gone in a matter of minutes.

Amanda turns on her phone light and hands me a piece of paper with words written in Latin and says to memorize the pledge and the chant.

"Next time we meet you'll be voted in, and you'll recite the chant by yourself at the official ceremony."

I'm not sure how to respond, but as I start to say something, I hear my name.

"Rebecca." I turn around and see Lane. "Can I drive you home?" he asks.

"Yes," I say breathless, staring at him like I've been turned to stone.

Amanda says, "Bex, I'll see you back at the house later." She gives Lane an annoyed look and walks away. Interesting, she gave him a watch-it-bro look, very protective of her sorority little sis, sweet.

We're left standing in complete darkness. Lane turns on his phone flashlight and points it at his car just a few feet from

60

us. When he opens the passenger door for me, I slide into the delicious smelling leather seat. He gets in on the other side, his golden wavy hair glowing from the dim interior light. He starts to push the ignition button but instead, he turns and looks at me. His hand moves to my knee. We're looking right into each other's eyes, and time seems to have completely stopped. I've forgotten the weird, spooky ceremony since all my focus is on the beautiful creature, no make that god, sitting right in front of me. I drink in the intoxicating scent of his cologne, and I'm transported to another dimension. Thoughts of Grant's hot swimmer's bod, slick with water, rising from the pool during the swim meet last week are nothing compared to this.

He whispers, "I'm glad you came tonight."

I gulp, and all I can eek out is, "Me, too."

He looks like he wants to kiss me, and I really want him to. Instead, he squeezes my knee, which sends a wave of butterflies swarming into my stomach.

As he starts the car, he says, "I better get you home."

Oh, but I don't want this to end. I quickly say, "I missed seeing you in class last Tuesday morning."

He glances over at me with the most dazzling smile and says, "Yeah, I was out of town. I had to fly to New York for a family thing."

He slowly backs the car onto the gravel road, and we begin driving down the dark path out of the woods and back into civilization.

"I picked up the assignment for you. I can give it to you in class in the morning."

He glances at me and says, "Thank you, Bex, that was very thoughtful."

I smile. "Sure, no problem. I actually got to speak to Professor Brigg when I asked him for an extra paper for a classmate." I giggle when I say that, because we talked about how intimidated I was to take a famous author's class.

He reaches over and turns on the radio. A song by the Eagles called "Hotel California" is playing softly. *How fitting?* A weird song about stabbing some beast with steely knives seems very appropriate after experiencing some secret Greek society introduction. When the song ends, he looks over at me.

"I saw you on Halloween at my fraternity house. It looked like you were with some of your friends and maybe a date?"

Oh my gosh, is he poking around to see if I have a boyfriend? Trying to keep calm, I answer him coolly. "Yes, my roommate and my other Phi sister Lexi are good friends with Jack and Patrick. I was with a guy named Grant, he's a Chi Phi." I leave it at that, because of yet Grant and I have only been on four or five dates.

We pull up to the curb along the front lawn of the Phi Mu house. He turns the radio way down. Then he picks up my left hand, pulls it towards his mouth, and touches the back of my hand gently with his lips. Butterflies are doing somersaults in my stomach while actual drops of water are running down my under arms. I think my heart is going to pound out of my chest. He whispers, his breath warm on my hand, "You looked beautiful as Daisy." He kisses my hand and says, "Goodnight Rebecca."

As he releases my hand, I say, "Goodnight, I'll see you tomorrow."

I run into the house, up the stairs into the bathroom, where I sit on the marble floor. It's one a.m., and I hope no one is up wandering around. I need to re-coup alone in the bathroom before going to bed. I'm breathing heavily, not from running up the stairs but just from the feeling I had when he was holding my hand and looking at me. It's like nothing I've ever experienced in my life. *I must be in love. This must be what love is like.* The butterflies doing flips, the heart palpitations, the heavy breathing, all incredible things just from being around Lane. It's like being transported into another world. I realize I don't even know his last name or where he's from. But he said something about New York tonight. I get off the floor and splash water on my face a few times to come back into reality. I brush my teeth, sneak back into my room, crawl under the covers and breathe deeply as I calm down, drifting into sleep.

The alarm is going off, and I hear Bella from a distance as I slowly wake up.

"Bex, Bex! Wake up, Bex!" I open my eyes and look at the time. It's already seven forty-five. I usually get up at seven thirty for a hot shower.

I sit up in bed and say, "Sorry, Bella. I'm totally wiped out."

"Where the heck were you last night? I didn't notice you were gone until it was after midnight. I just thought you were in the bathroom."

"Yeah, I had a stomach thing and stayed in the bathroom a while last night."

"I hope you are feeling better this morning."

"I think I'll be okay," I say slowly getting out of bed and feeling really weird that I just lied to my best friend.

I grab my stuff, take a super-fast shower, brush my teeth, and come back into the room to dry my hair. I want to wear it down today and put on a little more makeup than usual—— maybe due to my encounter with Lane last night. I get ready at break-neck speed. I don't want to be late for class, so I run down the sidewalk all the way to Phifer.

Slowing down as I enter the lecture hall; I quickly scan the room for Lane. I see him sitting in the seat next to where I usually sit, down front on the left. Hustling down the steps to the seat next to him, I notice there's a book and a pen sitting on top of the desk. Lane sits with his long legs stretched out and his feet crossed at the ankles. His shirt is unbuttoned a little lower than normal for a classroom setting, and I get a peek of his chest. I see a tiny bit of blonde hair, but he doesn't have too much, which I think is just right. He's looking at something on his phone.

I interrupt him, "Hello." He looks up at me, smiles a huge, perfectly white smile, and picks up the book and pen off the desk next to him.

"Good morning, you're just in time," he says.

I sit down, open my backpack, get my notebook, and pull out the assignment. I hand him his copy.

"Ah, yes, the dreaded assignment. Thank you, Rebecca."
When his eyes meet mine, I blush and turn a burning shade of red.

When the lecture begins, we're fascinated by Professor Brigg as he shares his experience writing for the *New York Times*. He reported from war-torn countries, often in life-or-death situations, to capture stories that earned him the honored Pulitzer prize. When the lecture ends, Lane stands and looks at me. "Bex, I'd really like to get your phone number."

I tell him my cell number and watch as he puts it into his phone.

"Well, you know I've got to get to my next class across campus, so I've gotta scoot." He winks at me.

I say, "Okay." But he's already walking up the stairs to the hallway.

I wonder if he has any idea how crazy I am over him? He's always so calm, collected, perfectly polite and interested in everything I say. I just can't get a read on his feelings. I think the closest I came was last night when I really felt something from him. Not only the way he was looking at me, but the way he was talking to me, making me feel like I may be the only girl in the world.

I have twenty minutes to get to math, but I hurry, because I want to go over some notes before the test. In class, I quickly open my notes, while in deep concentration, I get a text. Glancing at my phone, I don't recognize the number, so I drop it into my bag. When I finish the test, I gather my things then I remember the text, so I get my phone and look at it.

Hey gorgeous, from an unknown number that has a (212) area code.

Who's this? I text back. Within a few seconds I get a response.

Your secret admirer. I laugh at that and text *Lane?* I quickly get another text.

Do you want to meet me for a bite to eat?

I do, but I have two dance practices today and just can't squeeze another thing into my day. I text back, *Not today, maybe another time.*

Hard to get drives me crazy.

Reading that last text makes me drop my phone on the floor. I say, "Crap" a little too loudly. People turn around to look at me picking up my phone off the ground. I just can't respond to that last text. I add Lane to my contacts smiling to myself.

*****

Later, during choreography practice, Bella notices I'm back to my old self. She was probably worried that I was coming down with a bug after I told her I'd been in the bathroom most of last night. She walks over to me during a break.

"You look more chipper than ever," she says. "I guess you're feeling better?"

"Oh, yeah, lots better." I beam. She has no idea. I lean down to pick up my water bottle and notice a text from Grant. I open and read the text quickly. *Thx again for coming 2 the swim meet. It was good 2 see u, I know u r busy. Can't wait 2 see u dance at the game.*

I quickly text back a smile emoji, but my smile has faded. What am I doing?

13
#Thetidewillturn

On Sunday afternoon, we set up the homecoming lawn decoration in front of the house and work on adding the final touches. My hands are full of tissue paper when I get a text from Mom asking about the game Friday night and if I can get their tickets to them when they arrive. *Come to the house around noon, I'll have your tickets and the calendars. Luv u.* Slipping my phone back into my back pocket, I wander over to Bella and Lexi who are carefully creating flowers at the bottom section, using three colors of tissue.

"Do you guys want to walk with me while I get pictures of lawn decorations and painted windows? I've got to get some cool looking stuff for a project in my digital media class, and I need some for the article on homecoming I'm writing for the newspaper."

"I would, Bex, but need to study tonight," Lexi says with a sad face.

"I'll go with you," Bella says, packing the extra tissue away. "In fact, I'll judge the other sorority lawn displays with a British accent as we go," she says, in a fake British accent. I laugh so hard I'm wiping tears away.

"Have you been watching 'The Great British Baking Show,' again? Are you going to do your accent tomorrow afternoon when we're working on the canned food sculptures?" I ask, stopping in front of the KD house. Instead of answering me, she begins describing their lawn decoration, beginning with the elephant standing on one foot, crushing a bear, all in a very loud theatrical British accent. Two girls giggle at us when they pass us on the sidewalk. Both Bella and I double over laughing.

"I do think our canned food display for the food bank will be interesting this year, since our theme is the Disney castle," I say.

"I agree. Caroline bought special Disney stickers for the food drive sculpture because she wanted to make sure it tied in with our lawn decoration theme, too."

"You know she's all about getting the points and winning," I add, "and she's participating in the blood drive to gain points, since she's not doing choreography this year. This week is *so* busy, but in a good way."

"My favorite will be the basketball games." Bella sounds certain. "I can't wait to go up against Cat and her Tri Delta team."

By the time we get to the restaurants and shops on the strip to take pics of the homecoming themed painted windows, I get a text from Grant. *Want to get together tonight?*

Bella and I are out on the strip getting pictures for my digital media class. He asks if he can help, and I text back, *Sure.* Within a few minutes, Grant pulls up in his black jeep. Bella and I hop in and continue down University Blvd. When I'm done, we decide to grab drinks at Innisfree Irish Pub.

We get a table near the outdoor patio and order Cokes and nachos. We chat about the canned food sculptures that we'll be working on tomorrow, and I ask Grant if he signed up to play basketball Tuesday.

"I did, but I'm not that great at basketball, so please don't judge."

Bella and I laugh and say, "Same."

Bella adds, "But Cat is playing on the Tri Delta team, and she's good. They'll probably be the team to beat. Oh, and let's not forget our girl Bex here is performing at the first home basketball game Tuesday night."

Grant grins. "I've been planning on that for weeks."

We laugh, and I take a sip of my drink. When I set it down, out of the corner of my eye I spot Lane walking in with a girl hanging on his arm and her head on his shoulder. He's with another DKE that I know I've seen before. I think I might have seen this same girl on Halloween at their fraternity party. I feel a stab of jealousy just seeing another girl with her hands on him. I'm shocked that I would be so jealous, since I barely know him. She could be his girlfriend, for all I know. They walk past us into the next room, and as they do, Lane looks over and sees me staring daggers at him. He suddenly looks sad and moves away from the girl, but he keeps his eyes on me. He gives me a wink and a half smile, and they move to their table out of view. Bella and Grant are talking about something and haven't noticed my distraction. I feel a bit embarrassed because Lane noticed I was staring.

"Hey, guys," I begin. "Let's see if we can get our check. I want to get back to the house and work on editing the pictures I took tonight and write a little for the article on homecoming I have to submit in a few days."

Grant signals our server for the check. We chip in and pay in cash, so we don't have to wait on change or sign anything, then we quickly leave. I'm more quiet than usual on the ride back to the house, I think Grant notices. He takes my hand, kisses it and asks, "You okay?"

I smile sweetly at this adorable guy. "Yes, I'm glad you were able to join us. Thank you so much for the ride back to the house. I think I'm just overwhelmed with the work I need to finish tonight."

"Thanks, Grant. This was a much- needed study break," Bella chimes from the backseat.

When we pull up to the house, I lean over, kiss Grant, and say, "See you later."

"Bye, babe." He pulls me back over for another sweet kiss.

Bella and I hop out of the jeep and head up to our room to begin studying and homework. I work on my article for the

Crimson White until I notice it's getting late. I set my alarm and turn out the light in hopes of getting some rest before the most fun week of our lives begins. As soon as my eyes close, I hear my phone ding. I grab it and look at the screen. It's a text from Lane.

It's not what you think. I'm not dating anyone. But I see you might be????????

He has eight question marks behind the text.

Rather than answer, I text back, *I'm asleep already. I'll see you Tuesday.* I use a smiley face emoji and add one last text, *Thx for clearing that up.*

I roll over, trying to go to sleep, but now I'm curious. He wants me to know he's not dating anyone ...

******

I make it through Monday, and our canned food display turns out to look a little like the Disney Castle. We add some cute Disney stickers so that everyone gets the main idea of the design. After we finish the sculpture, Lexi, Bella and I head over to choreography practice. After that, I have dance team rehearsal at Coleman. I catch a ride back to the house with Amanda after practice.

When we get into the car Amanda says, "You know Lane was the one who chose you for the secret society."

"Oh really?" I look at her, surprised. "Do you know if he has a girlfriend?"

She gives me a serious look, like she may not want to answer. "No, as far as I can tell he's never dated anyone seriously. But I do know Lane is from a very wealthy family in New York, and he's a total playboy."

I respond, bemused, "But I thought that DKE's only allow southern guys or legacies in?"

"He is a legacy, and he's from a wealthy family. He got in with a southern connection, I'm just not sure who. Look, Bex, just be careful with him. He's a heart breaker."

69

"Thanks, Amanda. I appreciate the advice and the information. I'll be sure to keep that in mind." Amanda's a senior and obviously has known Lane a while now, so she probably knows best. I should take her advice and ignore my feelings for Lane. *I should* ... and after all, Grant's a great guy and uncomplicated.

When we get back to the house, everyone is eating so I grab my plate and join Bella and Lexi at the table.

Bella says, "You need to ask Caroline for your basketball jersey for tomorrow afternoon's competition. The uniforms were passed out before dinner."

"Okay," I say. "I'll make sure to get it after I finish eating. I've also got to get some work done on the homecoming article I'm writing, since it's due Thursday."

Lexi says, "By then you'll have info on which sorority won the lawn decoration competition and which house won choreography."

Bella butts in, "And who wins the basketball tournament."

I raise my glass in a mock toast to that statement. "I'll put in a blurb about the bonfire and the parade, too. Since this is my first featured article for the *Crimson White,* I want it to be great."

The next morning, I wake up feeling more refreshed than usual. I throw on some ripped jeans, a Phi Mu sweatshirt, thick socks with fur lined boots and my knit beanie, since it's a chilly 48 degrees this cold November morning. I grab a Diet Coke out of the fridge, say bye to Bella, and head out the door to Phifer Hall. I walk in, find my seat, pull out my phone, and start checking my messages.

As I sit reading notes, sipping on Diet Coke, Lane's voice startles me.

"Good morning, beautiful."

Lane is standing next to me with a huge smile, perfectly coiffed hair, and a gorgeous Burberry scarf around his neck. *Gawd, he's a vision.* His shirt is unbuttoned a little further than it should be, and I am for sure drooling on myself. I let him past to get to his seat.

70

"Good morning," I say smiling up at him. "You look very nice today."

"But never as beautiful as you." He leans in very close to me.

A whiff of his cologne transports me into Neverland. I can't help but blush. All the advice Amanda gave me last night flies out the window. He leans closer and whispers into my ear. His breath is warm and gives me tingles as it touches my skin. "You are the most beautiful girl on the entire campus."

"Look, Lane, you don't have to flatter me," I begin. "We aren't dating, and I shouldn't be mad at you for being with another girl. I'm dating Grant, anyway."

He's still very close to me, but his smile has disappeared. His look is intense and questioning. "But do you want to be dating Grant?"

Before I can answer, Professor Brigg walks to the podium and begins talking. He talks a lot about our project that's due over Christmas break and wants us to begin working on it over Thanksgiving and not waste time. He lets us out thirty-five minutes early since its homecoming week. I'm thankful for the extra time, but now I have an hour to kill before math. Afterward, I'm meeting the Phi Mus over at the rec center for the basketball tournament. I packed my shorts, jersey and an extra water bottle in my bag last night so I wouldn't forget them.

As we stand and gather our things Lane asks, "Will you walk over to Ferguson with me? I have a few minutes to kill since we got out early."

"Sure, but aren't you on your bike?"

"I am, but you can ride on the front handlebars if you don't mind holding your backpack."

When we get outside, I watch Lane unlock his bike and decide I can do this. "Let's try it," I say.

It's hard to get up on the handlebars, but Lane picks me up under my arms and lifts me. I get situated and off we go, riding across the quad over to Ferguson, laughing the entire time.

Outside Ferguson, I hop off and Lane locks up his bike and says his class is not far from here. We walk inside, buy some drinks, and find a seat on an empty sofa in the common area. When I go to sit, he grabs me and pulls me onto his lap with a huge smile on his face.

"Remember I asked you if you really wanted to be dating Grant?"

Oh God. I slide off his lap and onto the couch next to him. I don't know how to answer that. I stumble with my words. Nothing is really making any sense and a lot of uhm sounds are coming out of my mouth.

I finally look right at him and say, "Lane, I like you a lot. There's a lot about you that intrigues me. Tell me something that I don't know. Well, I guess there's a lot I don't know about you. Our chats in class every week have been nice but . . ." Lane interrupts me before I finish.

"What would you like to know?"

He smiles and puts his arm around my shoulder and pulls me closer to him. With his other hand he lifts my chin, focusing my attention on his beautiful hazel eyes. "Rebecca, I'm more than crazy about you."

Wow, my mouth goes dry. That sends butterflies on roller coasters into my stomach, and my heart starts beating fast. I can't process clear thoughts anymore. He's still staring at me.

"I'm going to take that response to mean I may have a chance with you." He kisses the tip of my nose and says he doesn't want me to be late for math and he'll see me later. I never ever want to move from being this close to him, but he stands, offers me his hand and helps me up. He turns around, giving me a wink as he looks back over his shoulder, knowing I'm still watching.

I pick up my backpack and head to math. I walk in, right on time. Hopefully my teacher will have the same pity on us that Professor Brigg had and let us out a few minutes early. He does, so I text Bella and Lexi that I'll meet them at the rec center basketball courts.

72

At the rec center, I go into the bathroom to change into my jersey then stretch out with a few other Phi Mus on the court who are ready to play. When the rest of our team arrives, we play two thirty-minute sets of five-on-five. We win both, so we have to play the Tri Delta's, that means we play against Cat and her team. This time we get beat by three points and are out of the tournament. Cat's team keeps winning, so they play until they're one of the top four teams. Bella and I watch Cat's second game before we leave. By this time, it is almost four thirty. Walking past the other courts, I see the Chi Phis playing the Pikes. I tell Lexi and Bella to wait while I get Grant's attention. He sees me and waves back. A feeling of guilt like hot liquid burns through me. *He's such a nice guy, why am I not totally into him?*

I rush into the house then into the shower trying to shake off the negative feelings. Pictures at Coleman with the dance team and Big Al are in less than an hour. I need to focus on getting ready, no time for weird feelings.

After getting into my Crimson Cabaret uniform, I meet Amanda downstairs and we walk to her car, get in and make our way to Coleman. We scurry up the stairs and hop into place, ready to greet fans. We do fan meet-and-greets for forty-five minutes prior to game time, even signing our calendars for those who ask for autographs. Once the picture taking sessions are done, we walk to the dressing room to freshen up and get ready to be announced before the start of the basketball game.

Five minutes before the start of the game, both teams are warming up on the court. The *Crimson Cabaret* are all lined up, ready to run out and perform our first dance. I've been telling myself all night, *Don't think about Grant watching, it's just a normal night and a normal game.*

The fight song starts, and we take our place at center court. They introduce us individually. I'm up and do a kick and a wave, when I hear, "We love you, Bex!" from somewhere in the crowd. We hit our routine and run off the court high fiving each other back in the dressing room. It feels good to hit. Now we just need to nail our halftime routine.

It is a great feeling to have the first game jitters behind me. The Cabaret cheers along the sideline for the rest of the game. During time outs, the cheerleaders, and Big Al rush to the center court to do their thing.

Bama wins the first basketball game of the season. As I'm running into the locker room to change, I hear my name, and I look up to see Grant waving at me from the bleachers. I wave back and tell him I'll be right out. After changing, I walk out with Amanda and a few teammates to find Grant waiting for me.

Grant takes my hand and says, "Your halftime dance was great. You look amazing tonight, Bex. I love your hair." He points to the stack of calendars I'm carrying, asking, "Can I have one?"

"I have to give some to my parents along with their tickets on Friday, so I was bringing them back to the house with me, but, yeah, I have an extra."

I hand him a calendar. He flips through it to find I'm the month of July.

"Your picture is gorgeous." He bends to kiss me as we walk out to the parking lot. He opens his jeep door, and I hop inside. When he pulls in front of the house, I give him a quick kiss. But he pulls me in closer and *really* kisses me.

I break the kiss then tell him, "I have to go, it's late. I'll see you Friday."

"I hate to leave you, but I know it's late." He looks crestfallen, so I give him a soft smile as I slide out of the jeep.

In the shower, I begin to wash off the sweat and makeup from the performance. I close my eyes and let the hot water run down my face. I start thinking about Lane and feel a little weird about my relationship with Grant. I'm really interested in Lane. Although he hasn't actually kissed me yet, he's kissed my nose and my hand. He hasn't officially asked me out, either. I'm trying to make sense of it and figure out if I am cheating on Grant. I'm sure cheating would only happen if Lane had already asked me out and we'd gone on a date. So, I'm probably not a cheater? I'm still feeling confused when I get out of the shower. I dry off and

74

put on some Nike pros and an old T-shirt. I sit on my bed and pull out my agenda and start going over everything I need to do for tomorrow when my phone dings with a text. Thinking it's Grant saying good night again, I casually look at it. It's from Lane.

Your performance was incredible.
I didn't see u tonight.
I saw both of your performances before I had to leave. I'm sry I wasn't able to stick around to see u afterwards, but I wanted to.

Whew, good thing he didn't stick around. Another text from Lane comes in.

Let's meet at the bonfire on Thursday night. Meet me at the top of the Gorgas library stairs behind the first column.

Mmm, I think a secret rendezvous sounds fun. I text back giddy with excitement. *Okay, I'll find u.*

I'll text u when I get there.

OK, I reply. Now I'm really starting to feel like a cheater, but I ignore the feeling and focus on my assignments and read through my plans for tomorrow. I have two classes I believe will be cut short due to homecoming. I also have choreography competition tomorrow night. I have a note written out to the side to submit the homecoming article to the *Crimson White* before three on Thursday. Looks like it'll be a busy day.

Bella arrives back after hanging out with Jack after the game. I decide to put away the lustful feelings I have for two different guys and ask her about her date. When I start to nod off, I tell Bella goodnight and fall asleep dreaming of dancing in a ballroom with a mystery man who makes me feel like I'm floating on air.

75

14

#Yasqueen

The computer screen has gone blurry, I've been staring at it too long, thinking about my next paragraph. When my phone rings, I almost jump out of my skin. I look at the screen. It's Mom calling.

"Hey, Mom," I answer.

"Hi, sweet girl, how's your busy week going? What are you doing at the moment?" she asks.

"I'm working on the article for the newspaper I have to turn in this week, and tonight we have our choreography competition, so I don't have time to talk. Can I call you back later?"

"Yes, of course, hon. Do your best tonight. We love you. Bye, darling, we'll see you in a few days."

"Bye, Mom." I set my phone down and turn back to the assignment on my computer screen just as Lexi and Bella burst into the room.

"What time do we need to leave for the competition?" Lexi asks.

"We should be ready to leave before six. We'll take a few pictures first. The first act is supposed to start around six thirty." I glance at the time then turn back to my computer and continue working.

Bella and Lexi are trying to be quiet, but I hear them talking anxiously about styling their hair in tight buns. Bella rummages around her dresser, looking for white glitter to sprinkle in our hair. She pulls out our costumes for tonight and hangs them up. I give into their excitement, close my computer, and start working on my hair.

Sparkling with glitter in our hair, our competition team bunches together on the staircase for a group picture then another one outside in front of the lawn decoration. We carpool over to the theater, where we kill our routine. While watching the rest of the sororities, I notice Cat sitting in the back with Reese. I wave them over to come and sit with us.

They sit behind me. Cat leans over the seat and whispers, "You guys had an amazing performance, totally loved it."

Coming from Cat, that's a huge compliment. I whisper back, "Thanks for sticking around waiting on the results with us. We have our fingers crossed for first place."
Amanda turns around in her seat and says, "I think we've got this, girls." She was right, Phi Mu wins first place in Choreography.

We chant and sing all the way home. Back at the house, we center the trophy on the fireplace mantle after we've all taken kissy pictures with it. I post one of me, Bella, Lexi, and Amanda holding the trophy with our lips on it.

Grant sees my post and comments, "Congrats to my favorite house and favorite girl." His comment makes me smile. I can't believe homecoming week is more than half over. As I lie in bed trying to fall asleep, I think of the night, the cheering crowds, and my best friends. And someone who won't stay out of my dreams.

******

Classes are cut short on Thursday, so I get to walk back to the house to work on my article for the *Crimson White*.

Bella looks up when I walk in. "Hey, Bex, I was just about to walk to the kitchen to grab some lunch. Do you want anything? Or do you have more classes?"

"No, I'm done, just need to get this article submitted. Can you bring me a PB&J?"

I grab a bottle of water from our fridge in the room and sit down to work. Situating everything on my desk, I see a text from my mom that I didn't notice, since my phone stays on silent during class. Glancing through the message, I see she's just excited about seeing me this weekend. I whip off a quick text back to her.

Bella returns with a tray of food, hands me my sandwich then sits back on her bed to work on something.

"I'm going to the bathroom," I say, standing. "Will you read over this and see if you can find anything wrong?" I hand Bella my laptop.

When I return, she hands it back and says, "Love it, time to submit."

Always the perfectionist, I re-read it one last time just to make sure.

A while later Lexi pops in. As she sits on our fuzzy rug and gets comfy, I offer her some grapes we just pulled from the fridge.

"You guys going to the bonfire?" Lexi asks.

"Yes, I'm meeting Lane there." Bella and Lexi stop what they're doing and stare at me, their eyes wide, their mouths agape. "What guys?" I ask. "Someone say something."

Bella stutters, "Bex, wha, whatcha'ya mean, you're meeting Lane there? Aren't you dating Grant?"

Lexi adds, "Yeah, Bex, you've been dating Grant for two months now. He's such a catch. Don't screw it up."

"I know. I really like Grant. But you guys just don't understand how I feel when I'm with Lane."

Lexi says, "Spill the tea girl."

I describe how I get a thousand butterflies when he looks at me and how I feel like I'm transported into another dimension when I smell his cologne or get close to him. I tell them he's so confident and shows so much genuine interest in what I say. It makes me feel like time stops when we're together.

78

They're still staring at me, so I say again, "It really feels like when I'm with him time is frozen."

Bella says, "I don't know, Bex. Grant is such a nice guy, and we don't really know Lane. We only know that you've described a good-looking hottie that totally knocks your socks off. I guess I thought you were basically over him and really into Grant."

"Yeah, I know we talked about how I needed to forget Lane because I was sounding like a crazed stalker smelling all the colognes at the mall. Which I know was definitely stalker-like. But I've seen him in class every Tuesday for months and I haven't been able to get over him."

Lexi's eyes are big, "So you've been cheating on Grant this whole time?"

I shake my head. "No. I don't think I've really cheated on Grant yet. Lane hasn't actually kissed me, he's kissed the top of my hand and my nose, and he's asked if I really want to date Grant. He's fished around that he's interested in me. I got a text from him on Tuesday night. He saw my performance but left right after half time. Then he sent another text asking me to meet him at the bonfire."

Bella interrupts, "So what you're saying is you're about to cheat on Grant?"

"I don't know, guys. Is it cheating on Grant if Grant and I aren't really that serious yet? I mean, he hasn't given me his pin and he hasn't asked me to be exclusive."

Bella looks sympathetic. "Bex, I think you know Grant is totally into you. He may not have asked you to be his girlfriend yet, but it's coming."

"I agree with Bella," Lexi says. "I think if you end up actually kissing Lane at the bonfire tonight, then you'll have cheated on Grant."

"Okay. I'm going to be committed to only talking to Lane at the bonfire tonight. Nothing else, I repeat, just talking."

79

Bella smirks. "After all you've just told us about how you feel when you're around Lane, you think you'll be able to just talk to him?"

I put my hands over my face and scream in frustration, "Guys I really don't know."

Lexi puts her arm around my shoulders. "Look, Bex, we're here for you. Text us if you need us. Do you know if Grant will be at the bonfire tonight?"

"I don't think so. He'll be coming back from an out-of-state swim meet. The bonfire starts at seven thirty. Let's plan to walk over there together. He told me to meet him at the top of the steps of Gorgas behind the first column."

Lexi makes a face. "That's weird. He doesn't want to meet you out in the open?"

"I get the feeling there's a girl that likes him, and he doesn't want to see her. He may think I need to hide from Grant because I did tell him that I was dating him."

Bella closes her homework. "What did he say when you told him that?"

"He asked me do I *really* want to be dating Grant."

"What did you say?"

"I said, 'I'm not sure, but I really like you.' So, I really didn't answer his question directly. I think he got the impression I like both him and Grant. Look guys, my brain is total mush when I'm around him."

Bella rolls her eyes toward the ceiling. "Oh, good grief."

"Well girlfriend, hottie or not, text us when you feel comfortable with him. If you don't text us, we're bringing in reinforcements and coming to look for you," Lexi says with a fierce mama-bear face.

"My girls," I say, smiling. "all for one, one for all. Love you guys," I reach over to Lexi and Bella. We collide into a group hug before I fling the closet doors open to decide what to wear to the bonfire.

I work on my makeup and curl my hair similar to the way I wore it on Tuesday night during the *Crimson Cabaret* performance. I choose a solid V-neck long-sleeve T and pair it with a soft flannel, add my favorite ripped jeans, monogramed leather boots and knee- high boot socks. I grab my Denim jacket, spray my favorite perfume, then turn around, and ask Bella what she thinks.

"I think you're going to be in trouble. And you better keep in touch by texting us like Lexi said, or we may have the campus police come looking for you."

"I promise," I say. "And I'll keep the volume on my phone turned all the way up."

We meet Lexi in the living room then walk outside and down the sidewalk toward the quad and the bonfire, which will be lit by the time we arrive.

As we're walking near the bonfire, I feel my phone buzz in my pocket. I pull it out and look at the screen. It's a text from Lane saying he's at the top of the steps of Gorgas. I text him back. *"I'm walking past the bonfire now."*

"Hey, guys, Lane is here."

They both reach out to squeeze my hands, and say, "Be careful."

"I'll text you guys if I need you," I say as I turn and walk away.

I walk up the steps of Gorgas, and when I get to the top step, someone grabs my arm and pulls me. I gasp in fear and let out a small yip sound. Then I realize it's Lane. He pulls me to him, wraps both his arms around my waist, and is looking down into my eyes with a big grin on his face.

"Hey, you."

My skin is all tingly. I stand frozen staring at him. He moves his hands from my waist up to my face, cups my face in his hands, and says, "I want to kiss you so bad."

Tears pool in my eyes because God knows I really want to kiss him, too.

He pulls me tight to his chest and says, "Shh, it's okay. Tell me what's wrong."

81

He strokes my hair with one hand and continues to console me softly with his voice.

"Please, baby, tell me what's wrong."

Looking into his beautiful eyes, I say, "I want to kiss you, too, but I can't." The tears begin to fall.

He pulls me toward him and holds me for a long time, stroking my hair.

He kisses the top of my head and says, "Rebecca I would never do anything to hurt you. I want you to know that."

I look at him, "I know, it's just that I'm dating Grant, and he doesn't know how I feel about you. And I don't know what to do. I really want to be with you. I also don't want to hurt Grant. He's a really great guy."

Lane pulls me in tighter then looks down at me with sympathy in his face.

"I know that's a hard decision," he says. "I know you have a pure heart and that's why you are so upset over how this is making you feel. It's one of the reasons I care about you and one of the reasons I'm so crazy for you, Rebecca. You are pure in heart and soul. Everything about you is wholesome."

He wipes the tears off my cheeks and pulls out a pocket square from his jacket and hands it to me. I dab it under my eyes, then he takes my hand and leads me to the steps.

"Let's go sit down."

We walk down the steps of Gorgas Library and go inside the little rotunda located on the side of the Library. Inside, we sit on the floor with our backs against the wall. Lane puts one arm around my shoulders and pulls me close. I lay my head on his shoulder, and he takes my hand in his, slowly bringing it up to his lips, gently kissing it. Then he brushes his lips across my hand and over my fingers. His lips are so soft, and I notice he has his eyes closed. I close my eyes, too, and we sit there for a few minutes just being quiet and still.

He turns toward me, looking a little sad, and says, "I will wait for you as long as you need me to."

When he says that I kiss him. My apprehension is gone, and I only want what I want in this moment. He pulls me in tight, holds my face with one hand, and pulls me in tighter with his other hand. I feel like I can't breathe, and my heart is beating wildly in my chest and I am breathing heavy as my arms wrap around his shoulders. With our hands clasped around each other and our lips locked, I think how much I never want this to end. I want him so much. As we slow our kisses down and try to catch our breath, he whispers my name, then grips the back of my head, pulls me toward him, and he kisses me passionately until my phone starts ringing and interrupts us. I pull my phone from my pocket and lay my head on Lane's chest to look at the screen. Lane is stroking my hair and kissing the top of my head. I notice the caller ID say's Bella. I answer it.

"Just checking on you," she says when I answer. "Are you okay?"

"Yes. I'm good. Everything is going well."

"The bonfire is about over. Lexi and I are walking back to the house. Do you want to go with us?"

"I'll get a ride back with Lane, and I promise I'm fine."

"Okay, if you're sure, we'll head back."

"Thanks, Bella. I'll see you back in the room later. Thanks for checking on me roomie."

I set the phone down next to me. Lane is smiling at me, and I smile back. I curl up into his lap, and he tilts my head back and strokes the side of my face with his hand then runs his fingers down my neck to my shoulder and follows it with a trail of kisses. I close my eyes, pull his face to mine, and kiss him passionately. His tongue moves slowly, entangling with mine. It's soft, and sexy and feels amazing. I stop for a second and look into his eyes and whisper, "I wasn't expecting this to happen, but now I may never want to let you go."

"I never want you to let me go."

Leaning into my neck, he places sweet kisses just above my collar bone then kisses the tip of my nose. "But I know I better get you back before you turn into a pumpkin, and we can't have that."

I giggle. "Yeah, it's getting late, and tomorrow is a big day. I only have one class, but I'm meeting my parents around lunchtime, and the dance team is performing at the basketball game tomorrow night."

"I know I'm planning on being there, and I'm staying the whole time."

"Grant will be there."

"I'll give you as much time as you need with that situation. I want you to deal with it on your own time. I don't want to interfere. When you're ready, I'll be waiting."

We stand, and I notice all the windows in the rotunda are fogged up. We walk toward his car, which is parked near the library. He opens the passenger door. I get in and smell the familiar leather. He gets in on the other side, reaches out, pulls me toward him then whispers in my ear, "You're perfect, sexy, and beautiful." The way he says it, gives my stomach a flutter.

When we pull up in front of Phi Mu. He gets out and opens the passenger door for me. It makes me feel so special. He takes my hand in his, and we walk hand-in-hand to the door. He stops, leans in, and kisses me on the cheek.

"Goodnight, Rebecca, sweet dreams." He turns and walks back to his car.

I open the door and step inside but watch him from the window. My eyes follow the car as he drives away. I float up the staircase into the bathroom. I go about brushing my teeth and washing my face, but the whole time I'm floating on a cloud and can't stop smiling. I quietly sneak into our room and look to see if Bella's awake. She's asleep. I look at my phone to see what time it is, and I can't believe it is almost midnight. I set my alarm for my Friday morning class then drift off to sleep dreaming about being somewhere with a roaring fireplace, a very special someone, and *happily ever after*.

15
#Goodvibesonly

The alarm wakes me from a beautiful dream. I hit snooze.
Ten minutes later it wakes me again, this time I turn it off and
look at my phone to see that it's almost nine thirty and I have a
text from Lane.

Good morning beautiful.
It's a good morning now that I've heard from u.
Good luck tonight. You'll be awesome.

I shower, throw on a hoodie, jeans, and my Converse. I
braid my hair quickly down the right side and secure it with a
hair tie, grab my backpack and walk out the door to my Friday
Spanish class. As I'm walking across the quad I check to see if
our professor canceled class for today. I mean—it is the day
before homecoming. It's not canceled, but he graciously cuts it
short by fifteen minutes. After class on the way back to Phi Mu I
text my parents to see if they've arrived on campus yet. Bella's at
band practice, so I do a quick room clean and look for the tickets
for tonight's basketball game and tomorrow's homecoming
football game, and the calendars that my parents want.

Mom texts back. *About 5 min. away.* I pick up the tickets
and calendars and head down to the main living room to sit and
wait. Mom and Dad walk into the house, and we greet each other
with hugs and kisses. They chat with some of my Phi sisters
while I pop into the kitchen and grab a couple of glasses of tea.

When I hand Mom her glass, she says, "We need to check into the hotel at three. Before we do, we want to take you to lunch."

After a short walk to the strip, we're seated at a table at Buffalo Phil's. Mom smiles at me and says, "It's been almost three months, and even though you're good about texting and emailing, I know there's more going on. We want to hear all about it." Mom pats Dad on the arm to get him to set the menu down and pay attention, as if I'm going to tell her something she doesn't already know.

I start with my busy homecoming week. "We came in second on our lawn decoration, we lost the basketball game to the Tri Delts but won the choreography dance competition."

Dad asks about classes and assignments. I tell him about some of the filming, and writing I've had to do for some of my classes. Mom wants to hear about Bella, dates and parties. I explain how I was set up for a date back in September.

"His name is Grant. He's a Chi Phi and is on the swim team, and he's really nice. You guys will get to meet him tonight after the basketball game, and he'll be my date at the homecoming game."

"I know you've shared a lot with us over the phone, but we love hearing it all again in person," Mom says. "I remember you telling us about meeting Grant and that Bella and Lexi set you guys up. And you guys seem to be still getting on?" Mom gives my arm a squeeze.

I smile and nod without saying anything, because I know I'm not being a hundred percent honest about my feelings for Grant. I don't say anything about Lane, and I don't *dare* mention that I've been chosen for a secret society.

On the walk back to the house after lunch, I text Amanda about getting a ride and head up to my room to change into my uniform.

Before the game Mom and Dad stop by the *Crimson Cabaret* fan table. I give them a big smile as they approach.

"Remember to meet by the entrance after the game," I say, leaning in for hugs.

"We'd like to take you and Grant to dinner afterward," Dad says, pecking me on the cheek.

"Can we talk about this after the game?" I ask, thinking I don't want to make this into a parents-meet-the-boyfriend thing. I have a feeling after this weekend I'll to need to have a serious talk with Grant, and I am dreading it like the plague.

After our fan meet-and-greet, our team heads to the locker room to change into a different uniform for tonight's performance.

Amanda nudges me. "I saw Lane and a group of DKE's in the stands."

"That's cool," I say nonchalantly, trying to act like it's no big deal.

After she gave me advice to stay away from him, I don't want her to think I like him or anything. I shake it off and wrap my mind around the performance and pretend like I won't know anyone in the crowd. That's about the only way I'm going to get through this night. I say a quick prayer and take a deep breath. We line up, hit the floor, and blow our routine away. We're pumped up, excited, and high fiving each other as we walk off the court.

After the game, I text Grant to meet me upstairs near the entrance. I change quickly and walk out to see Grant with one of his friends. My parents are on the opposite side, talking to some of the other dance team parents. I walk over to Grant first, give him a hug, and tell him thank you for coming. He introduces me to his friend Parker. Dad waves at us from across the way and we walk over. When I introduce Grant to my parents, he reaches out to shake hands with Dad.

Mom says, "How about we get dinner close by? Is Cypress Inn okay?"

Mom and Dad follow us in their car, and I call ahead for a table for four. We're seated along the window overlooking the Black Warrior River. Mom and Dad ask Grant about school, his

87

major, and about the swim team. The conversation is easy and relaxing, but I start feeling a little weird. I had pushed thoughts of who was at the game out of my mind and tried not to think about Lane, even though I knew he was there. Now that everything is calm and the night is winding down, I'm feeling uncomfortable that I'm with Grant *and my parents*.

Tossing my napkin onto the table, I glance at Mom, "It's getting late, I should get back since I'll be up early for the parade. I'll stop by the tent after the parade ends. Grant and I plan to stop by again before the Elephant Stomp marches into the stadium."

Dad turns to Grant and says, "It was nice to meet you. We'll plan to see you both, tomorrow."

I leave with Grant. He pulls the jeep up in front of the Phi Mu house and leans over to kiss me. I know he wants to kiss longer than I really want to sit out in the jeep, so I invite him inside for a while. There are a lot of people going in and out of the house tonight. Because of homecoming, all the families and alumni are wandering in and out all weekend. I know once inside we won't be alone. I ask Grant to sit in the living room while I go to the kitchen. Lemonade and tea pitchers are sitting out, so I fill two glasses and carry them with me to the living room. I hand Grant his glass and sit next to him.

"I really like your parents," he says taking the glass of lemonade from me. "They're very nice and easy to talk with. Why didn't your sister come this weekend?"

"She's on a weekend church retreat," I say, as I lean back on the couch sipping my drink. After talking about our homecoming plans tomorrow, I glance at my phone for the time.

"Look, it's close to midnight." I start to get off the couch. "I need to get to bed." I fake a yawn.

He agrees it's late. I take his hand and together we walk to his jeep. He stops before opening the door, leans in and kisses me goodnight, and just so this doesn't turn into a long make-out session, I give him a quick kiss then back away and turn to walk back to the house.

When I walk into my room, Lexi and Bella are sitting on the floor talking to someone on FaceTime.

Bella looks up. "How did meeting the parents go?"

"It went really well. We had dinner together."

Lexi tells the FaceTime person she has to go and sets the phone down. "I haven't gotten to talk to you since last night at the bonfire when you walked away to find Lane. I'm sure you already told Bella all about your secret rendezvous with him, but I want the scoop, too."

Bella shakes her head. "Not really, Lexi, she just told me they went and sat in the rotunda and talked for an hour then he brought her home."

"You're kidding? You were able to just talk to him for that long?" Lexi asks.

"Yes," I say. "We talked, and he was so sweet. I told him how confused I am about my feelings for Grant, but pretty sure of my feelings for him. I told him I need to confess to Grant that I may want to just be friends."

"How did he take that?" Bella questions.

"He was kind and gentle and very sincere in telling me that I should take as long as I need to decide. He told me he would wait for me as long as I needed him to."

Lexi bursts, "Good Freaking Grief! He sounds too perfect. There's got to be a catch somewhere."

Bella barks, "I agree. He looks like a model, dresses like he just walked out of a magazine, appears to be super wealthy, and he's taking your feelings into consideration and putting you ahead of himself?"

Lexi adds, "You forgot to mention he smells amazing, and it is intoxicating." We burst into uncontrollable laughter at that comment.

I finally say, "From what I can tell, he's Mr. Perfect."

Bella mumbles, "Well, we could actually say that about Grant."

Lexi goes on, "Right, I agree with that. You seem to have two amazing guys falling all over themselves for you. I'm impressed you were able to just talk to him and nothing else happened between you two."

Bella asks, "So nothing else, no kissing?"

"No comment."

Bella and Lexi throw pillows at me. "You are so in trouble," Bella says, as she pounds me with another pillow.

"Well, how does he kiss? Bella, asks.

"It was me who caved. I kissed him first, but he most definitely kissed back, and he's an amazing kisser, like the kind of kiss you get lost in."

Lexi insists, "This is *way* better than *The Bachelor.*

Bella looks at the clock on the desk and says, "Guys, it's almost one a.m. We have to be at the parade in line ready to march at nine."

Lexi walks to the door and says, "Goodnight girls." With a wink she's out the door.

I throw on an old T-shirt and climb into bed, making sure my alarm is set. Bella clicks off the lamp and rolls over, mumbling something that sounds like, "Get some sleep, girl." She's right, I need to sleep, but after our conversation about kissing Lane and with the excitement of homecoming tomorrow, I'm suddenly not sleepy. I think about texting Lane, but don't. I fall asleep while contemplating how to break the news to Grant.

16
#Gameday

Homecoming morning is a buzzing. Everyone's rushing around in and out of the bathrooms. The house is overflowing with parents and alumni downstairs taking pictures and reconnecting with old friends. Since Bella, Lexi and I will be near each other in the parade, we can leave at the same time. I fix my hair, add some red glitter to my eyes, and look at myself in the mirror checking to make sure my uniform is straight. I grab my silver pom poms and walk outside with Bella to wait for Lexi.

My phone dings with a text. I look at the screen. Its Lane. *U looked beautiful last night.*

Thx, ur not so bad either. I add the wink emoji.

Bella notices I'm smiling at my phone and not watching where I'm walking and yells at me.

"Bex! you're going to walk off the curb into traffic again."

I reply in a sing song voice, "Just got a sweet text from Lane."

She rolls her eyes, and Lexi just shakes her head.

The parade marches down University Blvd. For miles there are thousands of students, families, children, and alumni lined up along the road to watch. The cheerleaders, band, Big Al, the Crimsonettes, Crimson Cabaret, the fifty sorority and fraternity floats, the law school float, and local dance teams come cheering their way past the fans. The rush of excitement and

91

elaborate pomp and circumstance from the parade feels like a spiritual high.

Once we get to the end of the parade route, I quickly make my way to the quad to say hello to my parents and our friends who share their tent during home games. The tent is festive with balloons and Bama flags. Their catered meal smells delicious. I fix a plate and sit with Mom and Dad to eat a quick bite. After taking a few pictures with my parents and their friends, I remind them I'll be back a little later with Grant. I meander my way through the thousands that have gathered today, finally making my way back to my sorority house.

When I get back the house is packed, and people are spilling out onto the front lawn. Since Amanda was voted homecoming queen this year, the local Tuscaloosa News is here filming and interviewing her. I walk past the camera crew and a large group of people. I say, "Hi" as I pass them on the way to my room. Walking inside, I close the door to the noise, then change into something more comfortable. After changing, I get a text from Grant asking what time he should come by. *Is 3:30 okay?* He answers with a 'thumbs-up.'

Bella walks in with half her band uniform off, looking hot and sweaty. She plops down onto her bed and looks at me sadly. "I need a nap before we have to play for the Elephant Stomp.

Laughing, I say, "You don't have time for a nap."

She slips off her shoes and her band uniform. She gives me a pleading look. "Will you fix me a plate for lunch and bring it up?"

"Sure thing, since you're my favorite roommate."

When I get back to the room with Bella's lunch, I pull out what I am going to wear tonight, hang it on one of our hooks on the wall, and select a pair of boots to go with my dress. I've chosen a solid crimson, soft knit with long sleeves that has flow and movement around the bottom. I re-curl my hair, touch up my makeup, add a strand of pearls, and matching earrings. I work my feet into killer, knee-high, black, suede boots.

Bella slips her band uniform back on and looks at me before she walks out the door. "You look amazing," she says.

"Don't forget to stop by my parent's tent on the way over."

A few minutes later, Grant texts me he's outside, so I meet him on the sidewalk.

He greets me with a kiss. "You look incredible."

"You look nice, too."

In reality, all the fraternity guys look the same, navy blazer, khaki pants, white shirt and red tie. We walk to the quad and over to my parent's tent, arriving as they're putting some food away. We sit and talk with them for a few minutes before Mom asks Grant if he'd like something to eat.

"We have barbecue sandwiches, beans, salad and apple cobbler," she says picking up a plate. "Bella stopped by about ten minutes ago and said hello," Mom adds while scooping up apple cobbler for Grant.

We watch the Elephant Stomp pep band make its way past us toward the stadium. After helping Mom pack up the rest of the food, I give my parents hugs and tell them I'll see them in the morning. Grant takes my hand in his as we walk over to the stadium to watch the game.

We beat the Mercer Bears 42-0. Since the Phi Mu house is close to the stadium, we go there after the game, grab water bottles, and hang for a few minutes. Bella and Lexi walk by, wave and run upstairs. I know they're going to be a while, since they need to shower and change for the parties tonight. I text Bella and Lexi that Grant and I will probably just hang at the Chi Phi house most of the night and to be careful.

Bella texts back. *U b careful.* I know she is being a little sarcastic. Careful *was* my middle name. But throwing caution to the wind feels way more interesting this year, maybe just a bit anyway.

Lexi texts back. *Have fun and stay out of trouble.*
Wow, what do they think I'm going to be doing?

Grant and I walk to Chi Phi through the quad. On home game days there's no way to drive around campus with literally a hundred thousand or more people walking around. We stop at Denny Chimes, the statuesque monument located in the center of the quad that chimes on the hour. He takes my hand and pulls me down to sit next to him on the steps.

With a big smile, he says, "Bex, I'm so glad we met. You are such a great girl. I want you to know I'm starting to have serious feelings toward you, and I hope you feel the same." He lets go of my hand, opens his coat pocket, and pulls out a small box.

He takes the lid off and says, "This is my Chi Phi pin, and I'd like you to wear it. I'd like for us to only date each other. Will you be my girlfriend?"

I stare at him without saying anything, then I clear my throat.

"Grant, I'm very flattered, and I don't know how to answer that just yet. I certainly wasn't expecting this.

"It's okay. Please take your time thinking about it. I just want you to know how I feel." He kisses me on the cheek.

"I need to think it over for a few days." *Ugh, how am I ever going to tell him how I really feel now?* I silently yell to myself.

He puts the pin away and seems a tiny bit disappointed but not totally put off by my non-acceptance. When we stand, he takes my hand. We walk down to the Chi Phi house ready to enjoy the homecoming party.

After midnight, I ask Grant if he can take me back. By this time the families and alumni have mostly cleared out, so the roads are drivable again. Grant opens my door, takes my hand, and helps me out of the jeep. He walks me to the front door, and because I don't want to stand outside and kiss him, since there are still people milling around, I ask, "Do you want to come up to my room for a few minutes?"

When we get to my room, no one is there. I offer him something to drink from our fridge. He looks around at

94

everything. I tell him which bed's mine and show him a few framed pictures on my desk. Bella walks in and looks surprised to see us. She says "Hi", creating the perfect moment for me to say goodnight to Grant.

I take his hand, "Grant, I'll walk you downstairs. It's been an awesome day." I give him a quick hug and kiss when we get to the foyer.

He whispers, "Goodnight, Bex," as he walks through the front door.

Back in the room I say, "Bella, you're not going to believe this."

She looks at me, her eyes big, "What?"

I walk over and sit on her bed.

"Grant sat me down on the steps of Denny Chimes and offered me his pin and told me he was developing very strong feelings for me. He asked me to wear it and for us to date exclusively."

Bella's eyes are bulging out of their sockets and her mouth is hanging open.

"What did you say?"

"I said I wasn't expecting this, and I need a few days to think it over."

"That's an understatement." Her words drip in sarcasm. "You need to tell him how you really feel."

"I know I do. But I just don't know when the right time will be yet. Since my parents are in town, I think I'm going to skip church and have breakfast with them before they leave in the morning. Do you want to come with me?"

"Sure, what time?"

"Mom said to come to their hotel in the morning, and when I get to the lobby to text them. There's a breakfast buffet at their hotel until noon. I'm going to set an alarm for nine, if that's okay with you."

"Sounds good. Goodnight," she says rolling over to go to sleep.

"Goodnight," I say, crawling into bed. But sleep is hard to come by, so I pull out my journal and write down my thoughts on what I should tell Grant.

The next morning while Bella and I are eating breakfast with my parents, I get a text from Lane and from Grant back-to-back. I turn the volume off on my phone and put it into my purse. My parents start talking about Grant and ask Bella if she knows him.

Bella explains, "I've known Grant about a year. We were camp counselors together at Young Life summer camp. Lexi, Cat, and I are involved in Young Life and do some volunteer stuff with them. Sometimes Bex goes with us when she doesn't have dance practice."

Mom asks, "Will your parents be in town for the Auburn game?"

"Yes," Bella answers. "They're coming in a few days prior to the game. I'll drive back to Louisiana when they leave and be home with the family for Thanksgiving."

"We should get together with Bella's family for dinner after the Auburn game," I suggest.

With hugs all around, Bella and I say goodbye and walk over to her car. I pull out my phone and read and reply to the text messages from Grant and Lane. Thoughts of Grant are clouded with stress, so my mind quickly switches to daydreaming about Lane. *I've got it bad.*

17
#Relationshiporflirtationship

Now that basketball season has intersected with football season, the *Crimson Cabaret* has another home game performance on Tuesday night. Our practice times have changed from every afternoon to just Sundays and Mondays. The huge rivalry football game called the "Iron Bowl" against Auburn University is coming up this Saturday.

"Bella, don't forget we need to make plans with your parents for dinner together after the game," I say, picking up a notebook off the floor.

Stretching out on her bed, Bella says, "My family will love getting together with everyone, and Saturday night should work. I'll text mom now and make that happen."

I move over to Bella's bed and tell her to scrunch over so we can scroll through Netflix to find a show to binge on.

"I'll probably only get one episode in before practice," I say, opening my laptop.

Amanda pokes her head in our room and signals for me to follow her.

I walk into the hall and say, "I know that practice has moved to Sunday afternoons."

"That's not why I'm here."

I close the door to our room so we're alone in the hallway.

Amanda whispers, "We have a meeting tomorrow night. If you need help memorizing your Latin, I can help."

"I forgot about that. What if I'm not interested?"

"Look, accept it as an honor to be chosen. Most of the Greeks involved in the secret society have high powered connections and go on to successful careers because of those high-ranking contacts. Most of them have families that have a great deal of political power as well, and . . .," she pauses then says, "There's a certain someone who would be terribly disappointed if you didn't except the offer." She looks into my eyes and holds my gaze for a beat.

Then, reluctantly I tell her, "Okay, I'll ride with you to practice, and we can work on it then."

I walk back into the room and sit next to Bella.

"What did Amanda want?" Bella questions.

"Nothing much, just dance team issues, nothing major," I lie, knowing that I can't tell her secret society stuff, anyway. "How about this one?" I say, changing the subject and pausing the screen on *Stranger Things*. "Grant told me it was really good."

"Speaking of Grant, have you decided what you're going to do about his pin proposal?"

"Not exactly. I know I need to talk with him honestly and one-on-one but, I'm not sure how to go about getting together with him and bringing it up."

"You could see him on Wednesday night at our Young Life event."

"Yeah, talking to him then might be easier."

After the first episode, we're totally hooked, and I am wishing I could watch more. Bella says she'll wait for me to get back from practice to watch the next episode. She promises to do homework and study while I'm gone.

I say, "You're the best," as I run out the door.

When I get back from practice, I promise Bella we can watch another episode of *Stranger Things*, as soon as I glance through my agenda for homework assignments first. I see I need to write an article for *Alice* magazine, the trendy magazine featuring University of Alabama students as models, photographers, and a student writing staff.

"Bella, I need to come up with an interesting article for *Alice,* and I have to do the layout and photos, too."

"Why don't you write about binge-watching or just something like ... Is binge watching good or bad? And do a poll on campus."

"Yeah, sounds like a topic to think about."

After the second episode, I really want to keep going, but I'm beat and so is Bella from our big homecoming weekend. We can't keep our eyes open. I turn out the light and drift off to sleep dreaming about strange aliens speaking in Latin.

******

Mondays seem to be my busiest day. I have three classes, all in Phifer Hall, which makes life easy, and afternoon practice for the dance team. We also have our chapter meetings on Monday nights. And now, I have a *secret society* meeting tonight, too.

Amanda had me practice the Latin chant to and from dance practice today and again on our trip to who-knows-where into the dark of the night. I've taken five years of Spanish but never Latin. I asked her to translate it for me. The words *Credimus sumus et honorem illuminati determinatae instructus ad consequi* translated from Latin to English mean *We believe, we are, with honor, enlightened, determined, equipped to achieve.* It sounds so normal in English but being chanted in Latin, *super sinister.*

We arrive on the dark, creepy path in the woods. When we get out of the car I'm blindfolded and led to a spot. After I've felt three taps, I am to recite the chant. I can feel someone behind me. There is hesitation. I wait, then I feel three soft taps on my shoulder. I begin.

99

"Credimus sumus et honorem illuminati determinatae instructs ad consequi." More voices join in and begin chanting softly at first, then louder until there's a sound like a small explosion. The blindfold is removed. There's now a fire on top of a stone table in the center circle, maybe that was the explosion. Someone hands me a mask and a black hooded robe. I notice everyone has them on. They look like they're wearing masquerade masks. I quickly slip the cape and mask on, then take my place in the circle, and the blood bowl is passed. I notice tonight the entire circle is lit with candles along the outside. After we dip our left hands into the bowl and clean them with the ceremonial hand towel, the names of the student government candidates are revealed. Each one is read from a piece of paper then lit on fire and engulfed in flames on the stone table. We're instructed whom we'll support for the election with promotions and campaigning. We're to control all the Greek votes. A leader asks if there's any news or grievances that need to be addressed. Nothing else is said, and suddenly all the candles go out. Just like that we're in complete darkness.

Amanda turns on her flashlight. "We're going to the after party now."

"What? An after party for what?"

"Because we inducted a new member, there's a celebration in a secret location."

"I hope you've noticed I'm getting a lot better with going with the flow, but I'd love a heads up about an after party before-hand. I have an early class on Tuesdays," I say, with an eye roll. Amanda snickers at that comment. We shed our masks and robes and toss them into a large trunk as we walk quickly to the car.

When we get into her car, Amanda hands me a black dress. "Put this on."

I noticed she was wearing a black dress, but I didn't think anything of it. I quickly change clothes in the car, thankful it's late and dark. We end up on campus at a building farther away from where I normally go. Somehow, we get into the building

100

and down to the basement. I am dumfounded the alarm hasn't gone off. How we're able to just walk in is a mystery.

Only candles light the dark room, casting large shadows on the walls. Black tablecloths cover the tables. The room is set for a party. There's a sound system and red rose bouquets sit on all the tables. A buffet is set up with a spectacular display of fruits, cheeses and a mini bar. I'm standing in stunned silence, just staring at everything, when someone walks up behind me and whispers in my ear.

"Looking for someone to sweep you off your feet?"

I turn around to find Lane smiling at me. He looks so good he takes my breath away. He's wearing what almost looks like a tuxedo, black jacket with a red rose on the lapel. His white shirt unbuttoned just far enough to be super sexy, a black silk scarf, black pants and expensive-looking shoes fit his image. He hands me a long stem rose and asks me to dance. The music playing is a slow song, so we slow dance. Everyone at the party is having a good time drinking, eating, laughing, and dancing.

"This is quite the impressive secret party," I say. "How in the world are we able to be inside a basement on campus without the alarm going off?"

"A perk of being in a secret society," Lane says with a smirk.

Mhm, this does feel nice——private parties, a secret society, and a mysterious, gorgeous guy who's interested in me. Yeah, I can get used to this. Lane pulls me close, and we dance for a while. The entire time I'm wondering how all the stuff got set up so fast. Minions, I'm sure. I feel like I'm dating Chuck Bass without having to be the snotty Blair Waldorf. I laugh aloud at this thought, and Lane looks at me, smiling.

"What's so funny?" he asks.

"I was just thinking this reminds me of a movie scene or something from a TV show where everything is perfect. From a viewer's standpoint you watch it and wish it was real and wish that was you on the screen. Now I feel like that's me, I'm in a movie or a TV show where life is perfection, and I get the hot main character."

He laughs. "Oh, this is very real."

When the song ends, we move to sit on a fancy, antique looking sofa that's also a part of the party decor. I pull out my phone to see what time it is.

"I should get back." I look into Lane's eyes. "You and I have an early class in the morning."

His grin turns almost to a frown when he answers. "Yes, you're right, it's late. I'll take you home."

Lane takes my hand, and the butterflies do loop-de-loops in my stomach. I'll never get tired of feeling so giddy when he's near, even thinking about him makes me giddy. An idea pops into my head.

"Hey, let's get a selfie," I say. "I don't have any pictures of you. I'll send it to you, so you'll have a picture of me too."

"I have the *Crimson Cabaret* calendar in my room at the fraternity house."

With a look of surprise, I say, "Oh, I could have autographed one for you and given it to you personally."

He lifts an eyebrow. "I asked Amanda for one a while back. I'm not really using it as a calendar. I have it set to the month of July, and it's sitting next to my bed. It's my favorite picture."

"I was having a good hair day."

He pulls me close and whispers in my ear, "You have a good hair day every day."

He lightly kisses my neck. We walk to his car then drive to Phi Mu. He opens the door for me and takes me by the hand, helping me out of the car, then he kisses the hand he's holding.

"Goodnight, Rebecca." He lets go of my hand, and I turn to walk toward the house. I float up to my room to find Bella sound asleep, thank God, because I have no idea what I'd say about coming home at this hour on a random Monday night. I slip out of the dress, then I crawl under the covers and set an alarm for later than I should and drift off to sleep dreaming about scenes from *Gossip Girl.*

18
#Dreamingisfree

Tuesday morning the alarm goes off, and I open one eye and look over at Bella. She's sound asleep. I turn on the Keurig and give her a nudge. She makes an un-comprehendible noise and rolls over.

"Bella, I turned on the Keurig," I say, poking her.

When I come back from my shower, Bella's sipping her coffee. I pour myself a chi tea latte into a to-go cup and open my closet to pick something to wear.

"A lot of people are coming to the basketball game tonight," Bella says, setting her cup down.

"Cool." I give her a thumbs up. "I gotta go. I'm running late," I say, rushing out the door to class."

As I'm walking up the steps to Phifer, I remember the last week of August when school started—how nervous I was to be taking a Pulitzer Prize-winning author's class. Now I get excited every Tuesday, but not about hearing a lecture from Rob Brigg on creative writing and journalism. But because I know I'll see Lane. I get there before he does this morning and settle in while sipping my tea.

Lane walks in and winks at me. "Good morning," he says, sitting down. "What day do you plan to leave for Thanksgiving break?"

"I'm planning to leave on Wednesday afternoon after dancing at the basketball game. I'll ride back to Atlanta with my parents. We leave for Cumberland Island the next day."

"That sounds like a fun trip."

"It's my Mom's birthday, which rarely falls on Thanksgiving, but this year it does, so we're celebrating at The Greyfield Inn."

"I've heard of it. I'm not sure yet if I'm leaving on Monday or Tuesday."

I nod, sipping my tea. "I'm hoping Tuesday's classes will be cut. I don't have anything on Monday that I need to attend, but I do need to work on my article for *Alice* magazine. I have to write it and do the layouts. I'll be busy with that on Monday."

"What are you writing your article on?" Lane asks, setting his bag down.

"I think I'm going to take a poll on Netflix binge watching. Is it good or bad? Once I have all the interviews, it's a matter of writing the article and laying out pages and photos. I can do that while on break if I don't finish before I leave."

Professor Brigg walks in, and class begins. He lets us know to be on the lookout for an email next Monday as to whether class next Tuesday will be cut. After class, Lane and I walk up the stairs together.

Standing outside the lecture hall, he takes my hand, kisses it, and says, "I'll be at the game tonight thinking about you."

Grinning back at him, I say, "Thank you, I appreciate that."

He gives me a wide smile as he leaves for the opposite side of campus. I walk on to my boring math class, but math doesn't get me down. Tuesday has become my favorite day of the week.

I finish classes for the day and arrive back at Phi Mu in time for lunch. I set my bag near the stairs and walk into the kitchen to grab a bite to eat. I see Lexi eating lunch, so I sit next to her.

"Hey, Lexi," I say, setting my tray down.

"Hey, how's it going? Ready for the game tonight? I hear a lot of people are coming. Bella and I, of course, I think Cat and some of the softball team are coming. Ryan and some of the other baseball players will be there, too."

"Fun," I say, biting into a chip.

"Yeah, we're going to have a big cheering section for you during your halftime performance tonight." She laughs, and in a playful voice says, "I bet Grant and some of his Chi Phi brothers or swim team friends will be there."

"Yeah. I think Lane will be there, too. He told me this morning in class."

"Oh, wow, big cheering section, for sure," Lexi says.

"It's a big game against Duke. It's not really me they're coming to see."

"Ha," Lexi huffs. "Oh, it's definitely *you* some of them will be there to see."

Finishing the last bite of my soup, I turn to Lexi. "See ya tonight. I've gotta get ready for pre-game fan-fare."

Bella, Lexi and Cat are waiting for me after the game. Since we played Duke it was a loss but fun to watch, especially when our forward dunked on Duke's point guard.

Bella says, "Cat and Ryan left for Heat Pizza to save tables. We're going to meet everyone there."

As we're walking to the car, we see Jack and Patrick, and notice a few more DKE's in the parking lot. And I see Lane. He's walking with that same girl I saw him with several weeks ago at Innisfree. They don't really look together, and they're with a larger group of people, so I guess I shouldn't think anything of it. Bella and Lexi wave to Jack and Patrick, which causes Lane to notice, and he waves back at us.

"Oh, my gosh guys, did you see that?" I ask.

"Yes, we finally got to see Lane in person. He is very attractive," Lexi says.

Bella smirks. "Yeah, but it's also dark out here."

"Really, Bella? Always the sceptic?" I say, giving her a shove.

Heat Pizza is hopping. Grant has saved me a seat next to him. We order five pizzas to share and enjoy a very casual, fun

106

evening together. Everyone is having a great time, and I'm enjoying being with my friends and Grant.

Grant asks, "Do you want to go to the Young Life event tomorrow night?"

I nod since I have pizza in my mouth when I finish chewing I say, "Yes, I've made plans to go with Bella and Lexi."

"Great, I'll see you there." He smiles and brushes his hand across my knee under the table.

Later, after dinner, I give Grant a hug and kiss on the cheek as we say goodnight in the parking lot. I'm hoping he doesn't think anything about me just giving him a hug and a peck on the cheek. After all, we're in a parking lot with a lot of people around, so maybe he thinks that I'm being shy, polite, or very lady-like. In the back of my mind, I know I have to talk to him tomorrow. On the way home, I explain my plans to Bella and Lexi.

"I'm planning on talking with Grant alone at some point tomorrow during Young Life."

Lexi says, "I'm praying for the best for you in that situation."

Bella chimes in, "I understand that's what you need to do, and after talking to Grant you'll feel a lot better."

"I'm sure I will," I say, although I don't feel certain about anything just yet.

19
#TBH

Bella, Lexi and I walk into Young Life as a worship band is playing a familiar song from North Point ministries. We sang this a lot on Sunday evenings during my high school worship services. It has beautiful lyrics. Everyone is worshiping and singing along, so I join in singing softly and feel emotional at the touching truthfulness of the words from the song.

Oh, your grace so free, washes over me, you have made me
new, now life begins with you. It's your endless love pouring
down on us, you have made us new, now life begins with you.

By the second verse I have tears running down my cheeks, but I continue singing, worshiping, and praising.

Ash was redeemed only beauty remains, my orphan heart was given a name. My mourning grew quiet, my feet rose to
dance when death was arrested, and my life began.

Free, Free forever we're free. When death was arrested and my life
began.

I needed this uplifting tonight. I know being honest with Grant about my true feelings is the right thing to do, but I feel sick. After the worship band finishes, the leader for Young Life speaks for a few minutes. The talk is about loving God, living differently, and leading the way for others to follow. Reminding us to keep up a strong streak with God, with a SnapChat reference, that brings a crowd of laughter. The ending statement he leaves us with is that God is our strength and our foundation.

We break into small groups for discussion questions and prayer requests. The high school students each have a college group leader they're paired with. I follow Cat and Lexi, who volunteer together. They lead a group of high school girls from Tuscaloosa Academy. We gather in a circle, and Lexi opens with a short prayer. I pray a silent prayer for myself to make good choices. It's hard to know if you're on the right path. Sometimes knowing which road to take or which road will lead you to happiness or a positive future is almost like a guessing game. I suppose that's why we need to be reminded to keep a strong streak going with God and know he's our rock and foundation when we have an unsure path or a hard decision to make. I'm feeling this struggle tonight with my decision about Grant.

After our groups break, we have a few minutes of social time. Some people wander into the game room to play pool or ping-pong. The high school students cluster together with animated conversations and selfie taking. I tell Lexi and Bella that I'm going to find Grant and ask them to wait for me. Bella squeezes my hand. I see Grant with his group. They're just breaking up from their small group session, so I walk over. He notices me and smiles. I ask if we can go somewhere to talk. We walk into the next room and find a quiet corner and sit facing each other.

I'm nervous as I begin, "I've been thinking about what to say for weeks. I really like you a lot. I feel I need to be totally honest with you. This is hard for me to say, but I have strong feelings for a guy in my creative writing class. His name is Lane, and I met him on the first day of class, and we've recently told each other we like each other."

Grant's expression changes and he reaches for my hand and puts his hand on top of mine.

I'm starting to sniffle but continue, "I feel like I haven't been fair to you the past few weeks. I have confused feelings for you, but I care about you. I like you a lot. Recently, I've come to the decision that I have stronger feelings for this guy in my class, and these strong feelings grew when I found out he had feelings for me, too. I felt I needed to say something to you about it."

I'm crying now, and Grant wipes a tear from my cheek, but I keep talking.

"I'm so sorry, I don't want to hurt you in anyway. I feel so bad, but I know I need to tell you the truth."

Grant looks mournful and says, "I am glad you told me. I have strong feelings for you, Bex. I was hoping you felt the same way about me."

"I've been confused and unsure of what to do," I say glancing up at him. "But I know I have to be upfront about what's happening, and I've been thinking about what to say and when to say it for several days. I wanted to be able to talk to you about it in person. I am still confused about my feelings, but because I have stronger feelings for someone else, I just don't think we should continue to see each other. I want to be fair to you."

I'm still a blubbering mess, and Grant looks teary, too. I reach over and give him a hug.

"I'm so sorry," I whisper.

"I care about you, Bex, I'll always think you're a great girl. I'm glad you were honest with me."

I stand, tell him bye and to have a good Thanksgiving. I walk into the game room, find Lexi and Bella, and ask if we can leave.

On the way back to the house, through my tears I tell them everything I said to Grant.

"How did he take it?" Lexi asks.

"He was sad. We both were. He was understanding. It was one of the hardest things I've ever had to do, but I feel a weight has lifted off my shoulders knowing I was honest with him about my feelings."

"Bex, you did the right thing by being honest," Bella begins. "I hope you made the right choice and things work out for you and Lane," Bella says, glancing in my direction as she drives.

When we get back to the house, I pass out a few of my Netflix poll questionnaires for the magazine article. Then I text Cat about the piece I'm working on and ask if I can get a few Tri Delts to take the poll. I tell her I'll meet up with her in the next few days. I also need to pass a few out in class tomorrow. I think I have about twenty done, so far, and I want to get at least forty more.

Bella and I head up to our room. She changes into her Pj's and sets the alarm on her phone then puts it on her side table and turns off the lamp and says, "You doin' okay?"

"I'm feeling better," I say, as I crawl under the covers.

"I know you did the right thing being honest with Grant. I want you to know I support your choice, because you're my friend and I want you to be happy."

I look over at Bella in the dark. I can barely make out her face, but I know she's looking at me. "I'm going with my gut, and I don't want to hold back. Lane makes me feel alive, and beautiful, and he's very attentive to me. Not that other guys weren't in the past. There's just a feeling that I get when I'm around him like an electric charge. I'm drawn to him. I don't know why, but I think he's the sexiest, the hottest, and the coolest guy I've ever met in my life."

"Bex, girl, I know you've got it bad."

20
#Zaddy

ESPN is set up on campus this morning for the Iron Bowl. Lexi and Bella leave early to play for the pep rally on the quad. The game is at two, and the campus is electric with reporters and camera crews filming "Game Day" live from our campus. I'm feeling lazy this morning and glad I didn't have to wake up as early as Bella and Lexi did for the festivities.

We have plans with my parents and Bella's family for dinner after the game. I texted Mom yesterday and told her I was planning on sleeping in this morning but would come to their tent to have lunch with them. I'm thinking about getting out of bed when my phone dings with a text. Thinking it's probably Mom, I casually glance at it. The caller ID says Lane, my stomach does a flip.

I'd love it if u could sit with me at the game today.

I can. I talked with Grant a few nights ago about how I was really feeling, and I told him the truth. My fingers shake nervously as I type out the text.

How did that go?

As good as can be expected.

It makes me happy u told him, I'm hopeful u feel better.

I feel less confused for sure. I'm thrilled u texted me.

Can I pick u up?

I'm meeting my parents at their tent for lunch. I don't think it would be a good idea for me to bring u to meet them just yet. They just met Grant a few weeks ago.

112

I understand. I'll meet u in the stadium. See u soon.

After lunch with my parents, I remind them to come to the house after the game so we can drive to dinner together.

Mom asks, "Where should we go tonight?"

"One of the restaurants near the river close to the Amphitheater would be nice," I answer. "I'll see you guys after the game." I lean in and hug Mom then Dad.

I put on my black pea coat and button the top button. I stick my Ray-Bans in my coat pocket and hurry across the street into the stadium to the loud roar of a hundred thousand fans as I make my way to the student section.

I pick up a shaker and stuff it down the side of one of my black boots and walk up the ramp. As I walk into the bright sunlight, I scan the student section for the DKE's and pick Lane out in the crowd easy. As I make my way over, he notices me, smiles, and reaches for my hand. He pulls me into his arms, kissing me softly then whispers into my neck, "You take my breath away."

I breathe in his scent and feel as if I'm high in the clouds suspended in time. My stomach has monster butterflies. He takes my hand and kisses it. The stadium explodes into Sweet Home Alabama by Lynyrd Skynyrd. The student section erupts in singing along and shaking our red and white pom shakers to the beat. All you can see is red and white moving in unison, all but the section of orange and blue Auburn fans.

Lane has a monogramed flask of whisky in his coat pocket and pours a little into a cup of Coke. He offers me a sip. I'm not fond of whiskey or scotch or whatever it is, but I take a sip and it warms me up. A feeling of calmness washes over me. I'm glad the game is in the middle of the afternoon. It's a beautiful late November day with the sun bright and warm on our shoulders.

At halftime we're beating Auburn by seven points, so it is anyone's game, and the stands are full of cheering fans. As the band performs their impressive halftime show, I point Bella out in the trumpet section. I tell Lane that my other sorority sister

113

Lexi plays the flute. I remind him that they're friends with his fraternity brothers Jack and Patrick. As the band makes their way back to their section to the right of where we're sitting, I stand and wave to Bella. She sees me and waves back. The sun is low in the sky and will be setting a crimson sunset soon. As the sun gets lower, it's in our eyes for a moment so Lane pulls his Wayfarer sunglasses out of his coat pocket and puts them on. I search my coat for my Ray-Bans. When I put them on, I glance at Lane. He looks like he just walked off a movie set, and it makes my heart skip a beat. He turns and kisses me on the cheek and nuzzles my neck.

With a sly grin he says, "Can I take you to dinner after the game?"

I frown, disappointed. "My parents and Bella's parents have plans to get together. Maybe we can see each other a little later this evening?"

He gives me a big smile and kisses my hand he's holding.

The third quarter begins, and Auburn has the ball. They score a touchdown, and we hope to block their extra point. We don't, now we have a tied game. We get the ball back, and our QB sets up for a pass. He throws downfield and lands it right into the receivers' hands, a perfect catch. He breaks a tackle and keeps running. He runs all the way and scores. *Whoo Hooo! Roll Tide!* We make the extra point, and we're up 21-14. The fourth quarter approaches and we kick off to Auburn with a roaring *Roll Tide.* Auburn moves the ball down the field on the next play, they get to 4th down at the 30 and decide to kick a 47- yard field goal. They miss, and we get the ball back. The stadium erupts in singing Dixieland Delight——the student version, of course. We score again and beat Auburn 28-14.

In Alabama, this rivalry against Auburn is huge. We don't feel we need to tear down goal posts, rush the field or roll toilet paper in trees. We win, and we win big. We're grateful for our traditions and our fans. We believe in playing with grace, class, blood, sweat and tears, things passed down from Bear Bryant about winners never quitting and quitters never winning. Hard work and determination win games. Attitude, passion and teamwork prevail. We believe in our team, our commitments, and our goals. Winning is a fact of life at Alabama; it's just what we do. As the final seconds tick off the clock, the student section leads the stadium in our final chant and cheer of the night … "Hey, Tigers! We just beat the hell outta you! Rama Jamma Yella Hammer, Give'em hell, Alabama!"

The sun setting behind the stadium washes the sky in a gorgeous shade of crimson. Lane and I follow the brick paths over to Phi Mu. He kisses me and tells me bye, but we're still holding hands, not letting go, so we kiss a little more. Short, sweet kisses that long for more. In between those kisses he whispers, "I miss you already."

"I miss you more."

One more kiss and we stretch our arms out, fingers barely touching, finally letting go. I watch as he walks away.

Making my way into the living room, I see Mom, Dad, Bella's parents and her younger brother Cade enjoying each other's company. I ask if Bella is back, but just as I say that, she and Lexi walk through the front door. They walk over to us, still in their band uniforms, and we talk about where we'd like to go for dinner. I ask if Lexi wants to go, too, but she says she has plans with her parents and grandparents tonight. Bella and Lexi run up to the room to change into something more comfortable. I hang back with the parents and introduce everyone to Lexi's family while we wait.

During dinner it's hard for me to keep from smiling. I'm thinking about Lane and how happy I am that I got to spend the day with him. My parents ask me about Grant, and if he's already left for Thanksgiving.

"I believe he's leaving in the morning to go home to South Carolina for the rest of the week." Fortunately, they don't ask anything more.

Bella's parents are funny. We spend a lot of the evening laughing at their stories. They invite us to come to their home in Louisiana and enjoy the French Quarter and maybe even come during Mardi Gras. Alabama may end up in the National Championship game in the Super Dome New Year's Day. It would be perfect for us to go then. Bella's parents offer to make plans for us to stay at their home.

Our parents drop us off at the house after dinner, and mine go back to their hotel so they can drive back to Atlanta first thing in the morning. Before we say good night, we make plans to go to church with Bella's family.

When we get back to the room Bella asks, "So, was this a first date with Lane today?"

"I guess we could call it the first official one. Being with Lane is easy. I don't feel guilty like I did before. I'm glad I had the talk with Grant about my feelings, but my heart hurts a little to think about it. When I'm with Lane, it's like I'm in a bubble with just him, each moment is perfect. It's hard to explain."

Bella looks at me funny, like *whatever* and doesn't say anything. I look at the clock. It's only eight thirty, but Bella looks like she is done for the night, putting on her pajamas and making hot chocolate.

"Do you want some hot chocolate? We can chill and watch Netflix," she asks while stirring her cup.

"I kinda wanna watch, but I kinda wanna see Lane."

I send Lane a text and let him know I'm back from dinner. His texts back immediately. *I'll walk over and get you if u feel like hanging out for a while tonight.*

Since I'm still dressed, I text him back. *I'd love to.* I look over at Bella sipping her hot chocolate.

"I'm going to hang out with Lane, but you go ahead and watch the next episode of *Stranger Things.*"

A few minutes later Lane texts me saying he's outside. I grab my coat and practically hop downstairs and out the door. When he sees me, his face lights up with that perfect smile of his. He's wearing a long black wool coat, with a plaid Burberry scarf. I walk up to him all smiles. He leans down and touches my nose with his and takes my hand. We walk along the sidewalk over to the DKE house, laughing and talking as we go.

At the back of the house, we slip in through the back door. Outside, leaning against the house, are pieces of their homecoming float. The sign on it says, *"The Road to Success Is Paved in Crimson,"* but it's been rained on. Now it looks like it's written in blood. We walk inside. Loud music greets us, and the party's in full swing.

We walk down a hallway that leads to another, opening into a larger room where most of the party people are hanging out. In most frat houses, this room is known as the 'band room,' with high ceilings and rafters. I glance up at the ceiling and notice all the pairs of shoes hanging above us. Once pledging is over, the former pledges often toss their shoes up——the certain pair they've had to wear all year. Lane greets everyone as we walk past, and in the distance, I see the girl that I've seen Lane with several times. She's talking with several other girls and doesn't see us. We walk into a smaller room that looks like either an office or a small study. It has a fireplace on one wall. A bay window on the far wall overlooks a corner of the lawn. Lane walks over to light the fireplace and then goes to a mini bar and asks if I'd like a drink. He returns to me with the drinks in his hands, and we sit on a couch near the fire.

He hands me my water and says, "I'll be flying to New York on Monday afternoon and will fly back here on Sunday."

He takes a sip of his drink and sets it down.

"I plan to get back late on December second, too. But I won't be able to leave until Wednesday, due to the afternoon basketball game."

"Tell me again about your family's Thanksgiving plans."

"We're going to Cumberland Island, off the coast of Georgia, to a resort called the Greyfield Inn. My mother's birthday falls on Thanksgiving this year, and she wanted us to spend the holiday there."

"I remember now. I've heard of Cumberland Island and The Greyfield Inn."

117

I think it seems strange that someone from New York would know about Cumberland Island, which is an uninhabited island that one can only get to by ferry off the coast of South Georgia, but whatever.

"This will be my first visit there. How do you know about it? It's pretty exclusive and remote, just a small island. You have to take a ferry to get there."

"A family member of mine had a book or an album where they'd taken a trip there a long time ago. It's a very beautiful and special place. I think you and your family will really enjoy it."

"Will your family be going anywhere on Thanksgiving?"

"We always have a family reunion during the week of Thanksgiving. There'll be lots of extended family gatherings that I'll have to attend."

"Tell me a little about your family," I ask, getting comfortable and kicking off my boots.

"I have three sisters, all older. The youngest of the three is Megan. She's working on her law degree and just started her second year of law school at Yale. My oldest sister is married and has two small children. She has twins that are six years old, and her name is Renee, her husband is Matt. My middle sister graduated from Brown, and now she works as a publicist for a publishing company in New York. Her name is Macy. She recently got engaged, and they'll have their wedding in June."

"Wow, you were surrounded by girls growing up."

"Yes, but I have lots of uncles and male cousins, and I spent a lot of time with them sailing, skiing and camping over the years." He gets up to poke the fire.

"Does your family live in Manhattan?"

"Yes, but we moved there from the Washington, DC area when I was about eleven."

He sets the fire poker down, and we stretch out on the couch and get comfortable. I put my legs across his lap, and he notices my socks with puppies on them.

"I have a thing for cute socks." I laugh.

After a few minutes of chilling and chatting, he begins to massage my calf muscles, and I'm finding it sexy and relaxing. He pulls me in close and kisses me, and I'm lost in the feeling. Time stops, and all I'm able to think, do or feel is all wrapped up in kissing Lane. It's like a drug. He's an amazing kisser, either naturally or just very experienced, whichever doesn't matter, because it's so perfect. *He's so perfect.* It becomes very passionate, and I have to stop to catch my breath. Both of us are caught up in the moment. I sit up and lean into his chest and hold him, kissing him along his neck.

"It may be time for me to get back to the house," I say, because I realize this could have easily gone beyond my comfort zone.

He looks at me, smiles and kisses the top of my head.

"Yes, it's probably time to get you back."

He picks up my coat and helps me put it on. We walk out the front door, and I glance at my phone to see how late it is. The party at the house is still going, and I wonder how anyone sleeps on nights like these at a frat house. It's after midnight and cold as we're walking back, and I'm kinda wishing we'd taken his car. The Phi Mu house is a welcome sight. We walk to the door, and he kisses me on the cheek. I close my eyes and drink it in. I open my eyes, knowing I'm grinning so hard my face hurts. I kiss him again and pull him in tight. He kisses me back with heated passion then pulls away and whispers, "Sweet dreams, sweet Rebecca" and turns to leave. I stand there starring at him dreamily until he's out of sight. Then I run into the house and up to my floor.

Back in the room, I set an alarm in order to get Bella and me up and ready when her parents pick us up for church in the morning. She must have fallen asleep watching *Stranger Things* since her laptop is sitting next to her. I close the computer and set it on her desk. Then I get ready for bed and fall asleep dreaming of a certain New Yorker.

After a great morning at church and brunch with Bella's family, I call Cat to see if I can come over to the Tri Delta house and pass out surveys for my article in *Alice* magazine. I know she's getting packed up to leave for Thanksgiving either today or tomorrow. She doesn't have too far to drive to get home like Bella does. But I don't want to keep her from getting things done.

I run over to Tri Delta with my folder of surveys and pass out fourteen of them. Cat and the other girls gather for a staged photo in front of the TV with a Netflix show of their choice on the screen. After snapping photos and collecting the surveys, I thank Cat and give her a big hug wishing her a Happy Thanksgiving. I finish my surveys at a dorm across campus, where I find another ten people to fill out my poll. I stage a few photos of them in the living room of their dorm in front of the TV set to the show of their choice. I jot down a few names before stuffing the papers into my folder and head home. Back at Phi Mu, I see Amanda just as I walk in.

"Hey, Bex," She says when she sees me. "If you want a ride to practice, you need to hurry."

"OMG, I zoned out and forgot about practice. Let me grab my bag," I tell her as I shoot up the stairs.

I burst into the room to find Bella getting ready to leave for band practice. I grab my stuff, say, bye and run out the door.

As we're driving over to Coleman, Amanda says, "I know you're dating Lane."

I don't look at her, but I mumble, "Yeah. I really like him, Amanda, and so far, he's been the perfect gentleman."

She doesn't say anything else about it though the mood in the car is off. I don't think she liked my answer.

After practice we talk about our plans for Thanksgiving. She's super excited, to be able to get away for a few days to see family in Dallas.

When I get back to the room, Bella has her suitcase out and has started packing. I sit on my bed to organize and count my surveys. I get a text. Thinking it's from Lane, I excitedly pick up my phone, but it's from Mom saying they've gotten a flight out of Birmingham for Wednesday evening to Fernandina Beach, which is where we'll catch the ferry on Thursday morning taking us to the Greyfield Inn.

Sounds good. I'll c u guys on Wednesday.

I go back to work organizing information for my article, crop the pictures I took and upload some things to my computer. Bella finishes packing, zips her bag and groans. "I need to set an early alarm to get up and leave when my parents arrive," she says, while changing into her Pj's.

"I'll definitely get up and walk you downstairs in the morning," I say cheerily.

Tired from working on my article, I flip off the light and fall asleep while planning an idea for a new vlog post.

21
#Slay

My master plan today is to go to Phifer Hall to work on my magazine article in the lab. Most classes have been canceled for today and tomorrow, but I'm still waiting for an email from Professor Brigg about our creative writing class. Since I don't have to be anywhere early this morning, I'm still chillin' in my Pj's. Bella's packed and ready to leave for Louisiana. Lexi and her parents left yesterday afternoon. The rest of the week will be quiet around here since most people have already left for Thanksgiving.

When Bella's family arrives, I walk with her downstairs and help by carrying one of her bags. When I get back upstairs, I think about crawling into bed for a few more minutes and almost do until my phone dings a text. My heart skips a beat as I read it. *Hey gorgeous, I'm missing u this morning. How about we grab a coffee before I fly out?*

Yes, I want to see u too.

Cool, I'll pick u up in 30.

I run to the shower and get in and out in five minutes. I look around the room for my books and files on my article and stuff them into my bag with my computer. Just as I'm putting those into my backpack, my phone dings. It's Lane letting me know he's outside.

Brisk cold air grips me when I walk out the door. I'm glad it's not raining, but the cold air tells me winter is approaching as I walk toward the car. Lane sees me, jumps out, greets me with a kiss and opens the door. The car is warm, and the smell of beautiful leather is familiar. Lane smells amazing. I put my hand on his knee as we drive to the coffee shop. When we stop at a red light, he picks up my hand and kisses it softly.

"The one by the outdoor plaza has good coffee and breakfast," Lane says, glancing at me and still holding my hand.

"Yes, I know the one," I respond. "I usually try to avoid that area because of all the cute shops. I know if I go inside one, I'll probably end up buying something," I say giving him a grin.

The coffee shop is quiet, peaceful, and almost deserted when we walk in. I order a chi tea latte and banana bread. Lane orders an Espresso and a bagel. We grab a table by the window.

"My flight leaves at two thirty, so I have a few hours."

"Not if you have to drive to Birmingham. Unless you're taking me with you, and I don't know it yet?" I say, tilting my head toward him and batting my eyelashes.

"I wish I could take you with me. I'm flying out of Tuscaloosa on a private plane straight into JFK, and I'll have a car waiting."

I stare at him, dumbfounded, and say, "Wow, that must be nice."

Lane gives me a bit of a cocky smile, reaches across the table and takes my hand and caresses my fingers with his thumb.

"It looks like you have your computer with you. I need to show you something on it, and I want to ask you to do something for me."

"Sure." I pull my computer out of my bag and link to the store's Wi-Fi.

He pulls his chair around next to mine. I breathe in his cologne, and for a brief moment I think I've slipped into heaven. He asks if he can type on it. I smile at him dreamily and slide the computer in front of him. He says he is typing on a secure secret site and pulls up a Twitter account. He says this is a special account no one can trace and can only be pulled up from a computer.

"This is the anonymous account that will be used for promoting the SGA candidate, and it's the Twitter that all the Greek houses follow. I want to show you how to log in and tell you the password. The password will need to be changed every few weeks. You can only share it with me."

He explains he wants me to run promotional tweets on our SGA candidate from now until the election. Then he says there's also a private log-in for an Instagram account which is anonymous, as well.

I remember this being mentioned during the secret society meeting. I'm a bit surprised he's trusting me with this important task but thrilled he does.

"The Instagram account will also need to be logged in from a computer, and the password will need to be changed every few weeks. This will keep the posts from location traces."

He explains the accounts need to remain anonymous, and all Instagram photos, posts, sayings, and images need to reflect positive Greek life as well as positive promotion of our Student Government candidate.

"We need to tag all fifty-seven sororities and fraternities in the post. Is this something you think you'll be able to handle?"

"Of course, not a problem," I say, trying to sound assured of my abilities on social media and secret accounts. Creative media is my major. I don't say I would do anything for him, but at this point I'm so ga- ga over him he could ask me to do anything.

"I can certainly run a Twitter and an Instagram for the SGA candidate we're promoting for election. I don't mind at all, I'm glad to help," I say, beaming.

"The most important thing is that these accounts remain secret and completely anonymous."

"I understand. I'll keep everything under wraps."

"Besides the promotional information that will be posted to the accounts, we'll also post party announcements. Those parties will include a free open bar and chance to meet the candidate. Once we're back from Thanksgiving, I'll give you the date and location for that event so it can be promoted."

He shows me how to keep passwords on an app in my phone and reminds me again to change the password for both accounts every two weeks. I tell him it won't be a problem for me to keep it secret. When I log out, I notice an email from Professor Brigg, so I open that before I close the computer.

"Hey, there's an email from Professor Brigg," I say, and I read it aloud.

"Tuesday classes this week have been cancelled. I hope everyone has a happy and safe Thanksgiving holiday. Please work on your final assignment. These are to be submitted online to my class link no later than December 30th. This is not only your final grade for my class for this semester, but I will be selecting one story to be submitted to *The New Yorker.*" I stop reading and gasp. I look at Lane, he looks as surprised as me. I go back to reading the email. "I've worked something out with the editors at *The New Yorker* as well as the opportunity to be published in our very own campus magazine *Alice*. I can assure you there will be much publicity that will go with having your story selected." It's signed RB. After reading the email, I close my laptop and look at Lane.

"Wow," I say. "Having a famous author as a creative writing teacher has all the perks. It would be awesome to have a story published in *The New Yorker.* Someone's career would be on fire after that."

Lane laughs and says, "Bex, you need to write a good story."

"I haven't even thought about what I'll write about yet, have you?"

Lane shakes his head. "I've thought of a few ideas, but that's about it."

While I'm packing up my computer I mention, "I still have to finish my assignment for *Alice* and get it turned in over Thanksgiving. In fact, I'm going to the writing lab over in Phifer, and I'll be there most of the day working on that."

125

Lane looks at his watch. "I hate to leave, but I need to get you back so I can catch my plane." We walk to his car, hand-in-hand. He opens the passenger door for me, and I set my bag down. He pulls me close, and I turn to face him. He kisses me gently on the lips, pulls the Burberry scarf from around his neck, and wraps it around mine.

"Something to remember me by."

"I've admired you wearing this scarf, and I love it."

"Keep it safe for me until I see you again."

I'm smiling from ear to ear as I get in the car. We drive back toward campus with "Too Damn Young" by Luke Bryan playing on the radio, and I sing along. It's a sexy song about two teenagers in love. Lane picks up my hand and kisses it and says, "You can dance, sing, and you're beautiful, a true triple threat."

I giggle. "I'm really going to miss you. Who's going to flatter me and make me feel like a movie star over the holiday?"

This comment makes him laugh, and he reaches over and squeezes my knee.

When he pulls the car up to the front steps of Phifer Hall, he leans toward me and we kiss sweetly for a few minutes. He pulls away, smiling a perfectly beautiful smile.

"Be good. I'll text you later," he says, still smiling at me.

"Be safe." I blow him an air kiss as I get out.

I grab my bag, walk up the steps, turn, and look back as his car drives away. I take the elevator up and walk into the writing lab. At a large table I spread out my papers, books, pens and my computer. Sitting down, I adjust Lane's scarf around my neck. *I'm never taking this off.*

I get to work compiling the names of each show by most popular and place them into a graph on my computer. After compiling the shows by vote and designing the graph, I decide to break it down further and do a top five guy favorites and a top five girls favorites. Then I add the top ten all around Netflix favorites. Once I have the graphs entered and lists created, I decide to walk down the hall and grab a cup of tea or a Coke, whatever I can find. Two girls I recognize as editors for *The*

Crimson White, campus newspaper are standing near the counter talking when I walk in. I turn on the Keurig and look around for some cups. They're talking about SGA elections. Eavesdropping on their conversation is too tempting.

"It's such a scam," I hear the one with the long cornrow braids say. "They think they can do anything on campus they want. I want to call them out and expose them. They shouldn't be allowed to be so secretive."

The other one responds, "I know it should be run as a fair election, not some bought and paid for candidate that wins just because all the Greeks voted and dominate the entire thing."

I slowly place my cup under the machine and hit the start button wanting to stick around longer and hear more of this. The taller one notices me and says, "Hey, aren't you in my creative writing class with Professor Brigg?"

I look over at them and answer her. "Yes. I'm in that class. My name is Rebecca Brant."

"Right," she says. "I read your article on homecoming in *The Crimson White*. I'm the current editor in chief. You did a good job on that. What are you working on now?"

"An assignment for my creative media class. I have to submit an article to *Alice*."

"What's it about?" she asks.

"I took a poll on campus to gauge the top Netflix binge watching shows. It asks the question is binge watching good or bad?"

Her eyes light up, and she turns to her friend and says, "I have the perfect idea. We should have Rebecca write an article for *The Crimson White* on fair SGA elections and call out *the Machine* on not allowing the student body to vote their choice. They've dominated elections since the beginning of time. Even run business owners in town out of business and funded and controlled state elections. What do you think Rebecca?"

I stumble around with my words, not knowing how to answer her. She walks over to me and sticks out her hand for me to shake.

127

"I'm Olivia." She points to her friend. "This is Beth."

"It's nice to meet you both," I say, looking from one to the other. "Olivia, I recognize you from class."

Olivia nods, "Yes, Professor Brigg's class," she says, "And Beth is one of the assistant editors at the paper. So, what do you say? Do you want the job?"

I quickly say, "I don't think I should be the one to write on that topic I'm only a sophomore. I think a serious article like that should probably come from a senior or junior writer, at least."

I add a smile to let her think I like her idea, and I'm hoping she takes my advice and thinks of someone better suited.

"You know you're right," she nods. "A senior would be good. It is a serious article and needs to be taken that way. I also think it needs to come from someone who's Greek."

I smile at them and say, "I just came to get a snack. I've left my computer and my things spread out on the table. I need to get back to work."

I wave bye and dash down the hall. I'm breathing heavily and feel a little light- headed after that shocking revelation of information. I'm part of *the Machine* now. I know that's what the secret society's been called by Independents. I try to put it out of my mind and get back to work on my Netflix article, but I make a mental note to tell Lane about it sometime later when I talk to him. I put the graphs into the layout program on my computer, add a title and a few photos. I make room for my copy and click save. I need to work on this again tomorrow and get it finished and submitted. I also need to squeeze in time on Wednesday to pack and be at Coleman for the fan meet-and-greet.

I pack up my papers and computer, put them into my bag and walk out of Phifer, down the sidewalk toward Phi Mu. I walk in the front door and see Amanda talking with someone in the living room. As I pass through the hall, I wave. Now I can see who she's talking to. It's *that* girl, the one I've seen with Lane. I bump into a table, looking at them and not watching where I'm going. I yell "OW!" Amanda and the girl laugh.

128

"Be careful, Bex," Amanda says. "We have to dance the day after tomorrow. I don't want you tripping and injuring yourself."

I smile and say, "I'm good. See you later."

With a slight wave I run up the stairs into my room, close the door, toss my bag onto the bed and slide onto the floor. I sit there with my knees up and my back against the bed, trying to think what to do. I'm freaking out because Amanda seems to be friends with this girl, and Amanda warned me about Lane. This is the girl I've seen him with on more than one occasion and once with her hands wrapped around his arm. My mind is racing a mile a minute. I want to call Bella. I look at the clock to see what time it is to determine if she's still driving or if she's home yet. I get out my phone and call.

She answers with a hardy, "Hey, roomie."

"Hey, are you home?"

"Yes, I got home a couple of minutes ago, so perfect timing."

"I'm freaking out here, and I need to tell you something."

"Oh no! Bex, are you okay?"

"I'm fine. But Amanda is downstairs talking with a girl I know I've seen Lane with, and I've seen her several times at the DKE house during parties. The first time I saw her with him she had her arms wrapped around him, and they were walking into Innisfree the night we were there with Grant. That same night Lane texted me he wasn't dating anyone. I never mentioned seeing the girl that night because I was with Grant, and I wasn't dating Lane, anyway. When I saw him walk in with her, I gave him a dirty look, and I know that's why he texted me he wasn't dating her. He wanted to assure me I had nothing to worry about. After that text we started talking about our feelings toward each other, and the truth came out about how he felt about me and how I felt about him. You know the rest of the story."

I remind her of the last home basketball game when we were walking through the parking lot to meet everyone at Heat Pizza.

129

"Remember we saw a big group of DKE's together, and you guys waved to Jack and Patrick and that caused Lane to look over and wave at us?"

"I remember that."

"I saw her with their group then. But the only time I saw her with him when it really looked like they were together or at least thought they were together was the night they walked into Innisfree."

"If you're worried that Lane is dating this girl or maybe has dated this girl, you should be upfront and come out and ask him."

"I don't want to do that. I don't want him to think I'm suspicious of something he has already cleared up weeks ago. I don't want to bring it up with him again. I was a little freaked out seeing this girl downstairs when I got home, and she seems to be friends with Amanda. She warned me to be careful with Lane and told me she thought he was a total playboy. My imagination is running wild. Maybe this girl dated Lane, and they broke up?"

"You may want to do some snooping."

"Okay, I could try to fish something out of Amanda and get details from her."

"It's probably nothing to worry about. Your imagination is just running crazy. It probably has to do with everyone leaving campus for the break, and everything will be back to normal once school starts back."

"You're probably right. I may be overthinking this." But in the back of my mind, I'm scheming a plot to interrogate Amanda. "I'll call you later, Bella."

I set my phone down and as soon as I do, I get a text. I look at my phone and see that it's from Lane. His text is so sweet. *Hey beautiful, I'm in the Big Apple surrounded by millions of ppl, but I'm lonely without u.* My heart pounds and skips a beat at reading his text. *I'm lonely too, but I'm really alone. There's hardly anyone in the house tonight. I wish I could be with u.* I add a heart emoji. He sends a kissy face emoji.

My mind has forgotten all about the stress I was feeling from the encounter with the unknown girl downstairs, and I decide to go in search of dinner.

When I get down the stairs, I hear the TV on in the living room, so I walk in to see who's watching it. It's Amanda, *that girl*, and two other senior Phi Mu sisters, Kate, and Caroline. They're watching *The Office* on Netflix.

Amanda looks at me and says, "Hey, Bex, we just ordered two pizzas if you want to join us, they'll be here any minute."

"Sure, Thanks." I plop down onto the couch like everything's cool, but I'm back to freaking out about who the heck *is* this girl. As soon as I think that, it's almost as if Amanda read my mind.

"Bex, this is Ashley, my old roommate from my freshman and sophomore years. We roomed together at Tutwiler."

"Hello, nice to meet you." I smile a friendly smile at her.

Ashley says, "Hey." And turns back around to finish her conversation.

She totally ignored me. I guess this can be a positive thing at the moment. When Ashley's done with her dramatic story, she turns and looks right at me.

"You look familiar, have I met you before?" she asks.

"No," I say curtly.

As soon as I say that, Amanda blurts out, "You know you've seen her before, she's on the dance team with me."

"Oh right." Ashley shrugs.

I breathe a deep sigh of relief and feel safe again. The doorbell rings and Amanda jumps up to get the pizza.

"I'll get us some bottled water," I say, as I spring off the couch.

I give everyone a water and sit back down. Amanda hands me a plate and says to grab a slice. I take two slices, and we continue chilling out, laughing and eating pizza. We watch three more episodes of *The Office*. After the third episode ends, I tell everyone goodnight and walk upstairs to bed.

131

I take a shower and throw on a sweatshirt and flannel pajama pants then crawl under the covers and text Bella the info on Ashley.

Hey, I went downstairs earlier, and the girl was still here watching TV. I met her. Amanda introduced me. She's Amanda's old roommate, her name is Ashley. She's a Kappa Delta. I pull out a notebook and start working on the copy for my article. A few minutes later, my phone dings with a text from Bella.

So, they're friends? How does she seem?

"*She's a little snobbish the way she talks and acts.*"

Bella sends a laughing face emoji and adds, *She's a KD.* I text back *IKR.* Then I tell her that I hung out with her, Amanda, Caroline, and Kate, and we ate pizza and watched several episodes of *The Office.*

Did u find out anything else about her? Do u think she and Lane dated? Is she pretty?

She's gorgeous and a total diva, but IDK if they dated or not. Maybe I'll find out more 2morrow.

After writing copy for my article, I close my computer and think about texting Lane again. I send a quick *Goodnight* text with a pink heart emoji. I don't need to set an alarm, so I set my phone down and snuggle up with Lane's scarf and close my eyes. I fall asleep and dream that I'm at work on an episode of *The Office* in a cubical next to Ashley, who's being a total bitch diva to everyone.

22

#Fam

My eyes pop open, and I glance at the clock, feeling happy to have slept late. I sit up, unplug my phone, and scroll through Instagram. Lexi has a cute post. It looks like she's having fun at her grandparent's house baking cookies and pies. I keep scrolling and liking a few more pics when a text from Lane pops up.

Good morning, I hope u have a great day. I'm thinking about u.

Just woke up, ur the perfect person to talk to first thing. I just woke up, too. U were the first thing on my mind.

I am beaming with a smile from ear to ear, giddy and happy.

Miss u 2, I send a kiss emoji.

I meander downstairs to get breakfast. Caroline is in the kitchen eating a bagel.

"Hi, what's for breakfast?" I ask.

"There's cereal, bagels, donuts, and some fruit in the fridge." She points to a tray on the counter.

I poke a bagel into the toaster and put some strawberries into a container and take it back to my room. I open the article I'm working on and add the copy I wrote last night. After working on it for an hour, I click save and close my computer. I turn on the Keurig and make myself a chi tea. After a long hot shower, I throw on comfortable leggings and a hoodie. Trying to decide what I should take on the trip, I hang up a few dresses and blouses on our decorative hooks and leave them there until I can gather the motivation to get out my suitcase and pack. A text dings from my phone, glancing at it I can see it's Mom.

We'll see you tomorrow morning, and we plan to take you to lunch.

Okay, as long as I'm back at the house by 1.

Tossing the phone down, I make my bed, fluff the pillows, and pick Lane's scarf up from where I slept on it. Wrapping it around my neck puts a smile on my face and in my heart. I pack up my notebook, papers, and computer and walk over to Phifer. It's almost deserted in the copy room. *Awesome, no interruptions.*

I finish the copy, double check it and re-read everything six times. Then I hit submit. I email the link to my professor and include a note saying it's been submitted to the editor for *Alice*. I know if there are any changes needed that the editor will email them to me, and I'll be fixing those while I'm gone for Thanksgiving. I close my computer and tuck it into my bag. When I get back to the house, I don't see anyone around.

Poking my head into the kitchen, I look around for some microwave popcorn. The microwave dings, and I pour the popcorn into a bowl and carry it up to my room. I want to stay in, and binge watch *Stranger Things*. Before I start watching, I quickly text Bella.

"Hey, what episode of ST r u on?"

five.

Oh good. I'm about to start three.

I'll wait until ur caught up to watch more.

I grab some nail polish and start up episode three. I touch up the polish on my fingers and toes while I veg out watching my new fav show. When I'm done, I look at my phone. It's late, but I text Bella that I'm on Episode five. We watch it together while on Facetime. When the show ends, I tell Bella I've got to go so I can pack.

I go through my closet again, and I stare at the clothes I've hung on our wall hooks and choose two dresses that don't wrinkle. I hang them next to my selections from yesterday, then

134

gather my makeup and pack everything into a duffle bag. I get out my uniform for tomorrow's game and hang that on a hook, feeling confident that I have everything I need. My phone dings with a text from Lane.

I want to b the last person u talk to tonight and wish u sweet dreams.

I've just finished packing and was just about to go to sleep. It's good to hear from u. I miss u.

I sleep with his scarf again and make a mental note to remember to pack it in my bag before I leave tomorrow.

In the morning, my alarm jars me awake. I sit up and check my phone. I see a text from Amanda, telling me what time she wants us to leave for the game today. I text her back, shower, and clean up the room. I take my bags downstairs and set them next to the table in the entrance foyer then I go into the kitchen and snag a Diet Coke. As I'm walking into the living room, I see Mom, Dad and Lauren walk through the front door.

Lauren and I run toward each other. Excited to see her, I throw my arms around her and squeeze. We haven't seen each other since I left for school late August. Lauren's a senior in high school and a cheerleader so she's been just as busy as I've been with Friday night football games and busy weekends. We have a lot of catching up to do. She starts telling me about school, her friends and a guy she likes. Dad picks up my bags and takes them to the car. The four of us walk to Buffalo Phil's for lunch on the strip. Lauren and I are monopolizing the entire conversation while Mom and Dad try to throw a word in every now and then. After lunch they walk me back to the house to get their car. Lauren says, "Mom and Dad are taking me shopping. I'll see you at the game."

"Have fun, I'll see you guys there." I wave bye, then walk into the house and up to my room.

I work on my hair and makeup, put on my uniform, and pick up my bag with my change of clothes for later. I look around the room and make sure I have everything. As I'm walking over to Amanda's car, I get a text from Lane.

Break a leg. I hope that's the right thing to say to someone who's about to perform.

I laugh out loud and text back. *That's in the theater, silly but thank u.*

Amanda asks, "What's so funny?"

"A sweet text from Lane."

"It seems to be going well with you guys."

"Yes, he's wonderful," I say cheerfully.

"I'm glad of that, but I would still keep one ear to the ground. My old roommate Ashley dated him for a while on and off. She was crazy head-over-heels for him. He didn't really treat her that well, or at least he didn't like her the same way she liked him. She doesn't realize Lane is dating you yet. I've tried to keep her from getting wind of it. She's still trying to win him back."

I stare at her in disbelief, the smile gone from my face. I'm shocked.

"Amanda, I had no idea. I saw her with him earlier this month at Innisfree. He was very clear with me that he wasn't dating her, but I know I've seen her around him a lot."

"Yes, she wants him back. Just be careful. Ashley's family is wealthy and politically powerful, just like Lane's. They're cut from the same cloth."

Amanda turns up the radio and starts singing along to "Your Song" by Rita Ora, and I try to let the music drown out what she just told me and get my head in the game for our performance. But this song makes me think about Lane. At the colosseum, we meet up with the rest of the team and Big Al for photo ops and autographs with fans.

We're finishing our last photo when I see Lauren and Mom waving at me as they're walking in. I wave back and motion for them to come over. I hand the photographer my phone and Lauren's and ask him to take a picture of me and my family with Big Al.

We perform the very first dance we did at the first home game. It's so familiar to us we do it perfectly. After the dance, the team lines up along the sideline, and we continue to cheer on the basketball team for the remainder of the game. We win! Big Al, the cheerleaders and my team, pose for a picture for the newspaper with the game's top scorer and the head basketball coach.

I wave to Mom and Dad as I walk into the locker room to change. I pack my uniform away and change quickly, adding Lane's scarf to my outfit.

Amanda walks toward the doorway. "Have a great holiday." She waves as she walks through the door. I turn to face her and see Ashley standing in the hall. Scrambling, I take Lane's scarf off and stuff it into my bag. I don't want Ashely to see me wearing it.

"I hope you have a great Thanksgiving, too. I'll see you when I get back." I pick up my bag and head out to meet up with my family.

I get in the backseat with Lauren, and she shows me a bunch of pictures on her phone from her busy weekends, her friends, cheerleading and football games. I follow my sister on Instagram, but I love that she's willing to share each picture and the stories behind them so we can get caught up. She asks me to show her some pictures from this semester. I pull up all the pictures I've taken since the end of August. There are a lot of pictures of Grant, so I explain about getting set up on a date with him by Bella and how I've actually met someone else I like more. I keep scrolling and pull up the only picture I have on my phone of Lane and me.

Lauren's eyes get big. "Hey, he totally looks like that guy from that eighties movie."

"That's what I thought on the first day of class when I had to step over him to get to an open seat. Ever since then we've sat next to each other. I've had a thing for him since day one."

I explain a little about our secret meeting at the bonfire and how I broke the news to Grant. And how nice Lane was to wait for me to be ready to really date him. Lauren's eyes are glued to me.

"Wow," she says, looking a bit star struck.

137

At the airport, we get in line for boarding passes. While I'm standing there, I pull out Lane's scarf and put it around my neck. While walking through security, I see Ashley and Amanda together. I watch them walk from security to their gate. We pass them, but they don't notice me. I see that they're both flying to Dallas on Delta.

I text Lane before I get on the plane. He texts back, *Let me know as soon as u land.*

"Do you follow Lane on Instagram?" Lauren asks, once we're in our seats.

"I haven't asked him about his Instagram yet, but I should probably start following him."

My Instagram's not private so he could be following me, and I might not know it yet. I still follow Grant, and he follows me.

Lauren taps my phone screen. "Pull up Grant's Instagram so I can see his posts."

She sees several posts with me and Grant together and makes the comment that we're a cute couple.

"Yes, I know he's a great guy."

"He's really hot and looks athletic."

"He's on the swim team, and he also wake boards and skis on the Alabama water ski team."

"This must be your year Bex, dating two really hot guys that are crazy about you. I'm going to search for Lane on Instagram. What's his last name?"

"It's Lane Townsend. His middle initial is K. Let me know if you find him."

"His Instagram is private," Lauren says showing me her phone screen. "You're going to need to send him a request. He has over 3,000 followers, wow, impressive."

I click request on his Instagram. My Instagram name is not my real name, so people that follow me really have to know who I am. I decide to post the photo of me and the family with Big Al that the photographer took of us right before the game today. I caption it "BAMA family meets REAL family." "Happy

Thanksgiving." The flight attendant walks by and tells us to turn off our phones and to make sure they're in airplane mode. I won't be able to check to see if Lane notices I sent him a friend request for almost an hour.

Lauren and I chat about what we want to do once we get on the island. We discuss riding bikes and going to the beach. I tell her I didn't bring a suit, because I figured it would be too cold. I lean over the seat and ask Mom what the weather will be like while we're there. She tells us it'll be between 50 and 60 degrees. So, Lauren's idea of going to the beach won't involve a swimsuit. It's not long until we land in Jacksonville and rent a car to drive to Fernandina Beach. It's almost an hour drive, so I text Lane on the way to the hotel.

Hey, we r n the rental car.

I see u are following me on Instagram now, @dancergrl.

Yep, that's me. Thx for accepting my friend request.

Ur more than a friend to me. That stuns me, and I smile and gush. Lauren notices my extreme gushing.

"Who are you texting?" she asks, looking at me with a gleam.

"Lane, he's following me on Instagram now." I continue texting with Lane.

What time will u arrive at the hotel?

In about 40 minutes.

Can I call u in an hour?

Yes, I'd love that.

*****

After we get to our rooms, Dad sets his bags down and asks us about dinner.

"We're going downstairs to the restaurant, do you two want to come with us?" he asks.

"I'll meet you guys there in a few minutes," I say, walking into my room. Lauren wanders down the hall following Mom and Dad.

I slide the door open to the balcony and walk out to look at the boats in the marina. I feel the wind in my hair and smell the salt air. I love being at the beach and near the water. My phone rings and I look at the caller ID, its Lane. My heart skips a beat.

"Hello." I answer quickly.

"It's so good to hear your voice." His voice sounds smooth and comforting.

"Me too, I've missed you a lot."

"Are you about to go to bed?"

"No. My parents just went to the restaurant to eat a late dinner. I told them I'd be down in a few minutes."

"I won't keep you long. I just wanted to hear your voice and talk to you."

"I'll call you tomorrow after I arrive on the island."

"It would be better if you called me later tomorrow night, maybe after ten thirty. I'll be at a family residence most of the day tomorrow and there'll be a lot of people around and I want to be able to talk to you without distractions."

"You're right. Tomorrow's Thanksgiving and a busy family day. I'll call you tomorrow night."

"I'm looking forward to it. Goodnight, Rebecca."

23
#Blessed

Cold wind whips through my hair as we board the ferry to the island. I wrap Lane's scarf around my neck and over my mouth then button up my wool pea coat with a gloved hand. Lauren is bundled up with her hood up and ear buds in. The scenery along the water is incredible. We even see dolphins following along next to our boat. The sun is shining, and there are only a few clouds in the sky. The forty-five-minute ferry ride is rich in wildlife sightings and gorgeous marsh scenery. As we disembark at the dock, the beach shows the tide is low, and the muddy bank is exposed with thousands of fiddler crabs. Lauren and I are like little girls excited to see live creatures on the beach. Mom comments she loves the bareness of the aged driftwood sitting along the shore.

A Greyfield Inn representative greets us and the other ferry passengers at the end of the dock with trays of sparkling water and homemade honey scones topped with cream and strawberries. Another man in uniform comes along and takes our luggage and loads it onto a trailer pulled by a golf cart. He leads the way from the dock to the Inn.

We stroll down a sandy path covered in a canopy of ancient oak trees dripping in Spanish moss. I take a few pictures with my phone as we walk. I'm in awe of the spectacular untouched beauty of this wild landscape I see stretched out before me. There's a peacefulness and calmness here that I've yet to experience, a solitude that encompasses grace, beauty, and the freedom of each living animal untouched by human hands. There are very few cars. In fact, the only cars allowed on the island are those driven by the National Park crews or the workers at the Greyfield. There are no roads, just a single sandy path that stretches from one end of the thirty-mile island to the other. The rest of the island is thick in trees, covered in moss and dense low growing palm fronds native to the island. We pass large amounts of what appears to be horse poop along the way, causing us to watch where we step.

Dad turns to Lauren and me. "There are hundreds of wild horses living on the island as well as deer, bobcats, and other wild animals."

I glance at Lauren, "I can't wait to go out and explore."

She nods, and says, "Same."

Our walk from the dock ends in front of the grand and glorious Greyfield Inn. It's large and stately. A staff member greets us at the bottom of the massive staircase and tells us a little about the Inn. "Thomas and Lucy Carnegie built it in 1900 for their daughter. In 1962 it was converted into an Inn by the granddaughter of the Carnegie's named Lucy Ferguson." He mentions we'll see paintings of Lucy in the main living room. He goes on to explain that this is the only mansion still in use on the island today, but two other mansions were built around the same period for other wealthy New Yorkers who vacationed here during the 19th century. To the south, we can explore the Dungeness castle ruins and to the north we can explore Plum Orchard. When he hands everyone their keys, we learn our bags have been placed on our rooms. Lunch will be in the main dining room just after a cocktail reception in the living room. Following other guests, we make our way upstairs to our rooms to relax and change into something more formal.

Later, walking into the cocktail reception, I notice a lot of young couples without children. I also see some older couples and then one large family including a guy who looks to be Lauren's age with a younger brother and sister of middle school age. They look like they're with their parents and grandparents.

142

Mom and Dad head over to get some wine while Lauren and I wander over to the fruit and cheese table. I notice the oldest boy from the extended family looking at us.

I nudge Lauren. "You might have a secret admirer at two o'clock on the right. Don't look now, but I think he's walking over here."

"Hi, I'm Brian," he says, looking right at me.

"I'm Rebecca, and this is my sister Lauren, I say, turning toward Lauren who's eating a piece of cheese off her plate, acting uninterested.

"I'm a sophomore at Alabama, and Lauren is a senior in high school. We arrived an hour ago." I want to make sure he knows which one of us he needs to concentrate on.

"Cool, my family got here yesterday. I'm also a senior in high school. I'm from Atlanta," he says, smiling at Lauren.

I elbow Lauren to answer him. "We're from Milton, just north of Atlanta," She answers then gives me the side eye.

Taking my plate, I wander off to talk with Mom and Dad, who seem to be involved in a conversation with another couple. I can tell I'm no longer needed to help Lauren along in her chat with Brian.

After cocktails and social time, we're escorted into the dining room for a wonderful Thanksgiving meal. We enjoy a five-course lunch that takes a lingering hour and a half to finish. We have a great time talking, laughing, and catching up on family time. One of the Inn employees comes around table to table to capture photos of each family group. By the time lunch is finished, it's three o'clock. Lauren and I tell Mom and Dad we're going to our room to change clothes, then take some bikes out and explore the island.

Back in the room, I charge my phone and change out of my dress and heels. I pull on a sweatshirt, leggings and a baseball cap. Lauren changes into something similar. Grabbing some bottled water from the room, I ask Lauren if she has some sort of small drawstring bag we can use. She has her Kavu, so I stick our water bottles inside, zip it closed and hand it back to her. We walk outside into the breezy late afternoon air and get two bicycles out of the rack.

Unfolding the map, I say, "If we turn right, we'll go south to the Dungeness castle."

"Sure, let's go that way." Lauren hops onto a bike.

We set off down the sandy path shaded with massive oak trees and Spanish moss. Deer poke their heads out of the dense foliage along the way. It's a struggle to film with my phone and peddle the bike at the same time, but because the island is so incredible, I'm okay with risking a crash. We arrive at the Dungeness castle, park our bikes, and walk toward the ruins in order to get up close and look around. The castle was burned by arson years ago. What's left of it is hauntingly beautiful. Rich brick and stone structures covered in ivy and moss stand stately and impressive. Lauren and I take turns taking pictures of each other along the brick walls and iron gates. We walk around the back of the castle remains and see wild horses grazing lazily in the grass. They are beautiful. They allow us to come fairly close, but when we try to touch them, they scuffle away.

We spot a guy with a camera and tripod set up inside what's left of a large fountain. I walk over and ask him to take a photo of us with the ruins in the background. I hand him my phone and Lauren's. He snaps of couple of photos of us then hands our phones back.This island is truly a photographer's haven.

Suddenly, we hear something strange coming from the woods beyond the fountain.

Lauren points in the direction of the weird sound. "Let's see if we can find out what's making that noise."

We walk to the edge of the wood and see another lonesome path near what used to be an old green house and standing to one side of the path is a deer and its fawn. The doe is pounding her front left hoof on the ground and making a screeching sound with each pound. It almost sounds like a bird's screech. She's staring at something straight in front of her, but we can't see what it is. Lauren and I video them for a few minutes

144

until they gallop off like gazelles. I motion for Lauren to follow me.

"Let's see if we can figure out what she was so concerned about."

We stop where the mama deer was but don't notice anything unusual, so we continue along the path, thinking it may lead to the ocean.

A deserted beach is at the end of the path, where we find thousands of fiddler crabs. It's like attack of the crabs, although as we walk toward them, they scurry away. After finding a spot in the sand to sit, Lauren and I stare up at the sky washed in a beautiful orange sunset hovering low above the ocean.

"This has been a wonderful day," I say as I tilt my head back, drinking in a full breath of salt air. I love the beauty and wilderness of this island."

Lauren agrees. "I'm glad I get to share this with you."

I pull out my phone to take a photo just as a text from Mom shows up.

What are you and Lauren doing?

We r sitting on the beach just south of the Dungeness ruins watching the sunset.

Dinner is being served near the fire pits picnic style. You should make your way back to the Inn.

Standing, we jog our way back down the path to our bikes and race back toward the inn. Parking our bikes, the smell of barbeque cooking fills our senses. Walking around to the side of the Inn, we see several fire pits blazing as well as tables lit with candles. A large buffet is set with picnic style foods and salads. Lauren and I fix a plate and walk over to join Mom and Dad.

Dad asks, "How were the ruins?"

"Really cool. We saw deer, wild horses, and a beautiful sunset on the beach just below the castle. We talked to a photographer and asked him to take a photo of us with the castle in the background." Lauren pulls up the photos she took and shows them to Mom and Dad.

"What did you guys do while we were gone?" I ask.

145

"We did a little kayaking and took a nap." Mom looks relaxed. "What do you think you guys will want to do tomorrow?" she asks.

"Let's ride bikes again and maybe go north this time. What do you think, Lauren?"

"I'm up for it," Lauren says between bites.

"Do you guys have any specific plans?" I look over at Mom.

"We're planning to ride bikes and probably go to the Dungeness ruins." Mom gives Dad a nudge. If you do go riding again tomorrow be sure to take a picnic lunch with you and keep in touch with us throughout the day." Mom looks from me then to Lauren.

"Okay. Is there a specific time for breakfast in the morning?" I ask.

"It's between eight and ten in the main dining room," Dad announces.

One of the servers comes around and gives each table a basket filled with s'more's kits. The staff lit a few more fire pits and has set chairs around each one.

"You girls pick out a firepit," Dad says, getting up from the table. "I'll get your mother another glass of wine then we'll join you."

Lauren and I get out our marshmallows and Hersey bars. I poke a marshmallow on my stick and work on making a perfectly toasted marshmallow. After eating two gooey s'mores, I'm feeling a little plump, like the Pillsbury Dough Boy.

"We're going to call it a night." Dad picks up his glass of wine and stands. He looks over at me and Lauren. "Please don't stay out too late."

Lauren and I stand and give Mom and Dad a hug.

"Happy birthday. I hope it's been great so far," I say, squeezing Mom.

"It's been wonderful," Mom says, kissing us each on the cheek. "Goodnight, girls."

146

After Mom and Dad are out of sight, Brian walks over from his family's fire pit and asks if he can join us.

Lauren looks up at Brian with a smile and says, "Yes, have a seat. My mom and Dad just went to bed." Lauren taps the chair next to her.

"I think I'll go to bed, too." I stretch my arms over my head then look over at Brian. "Nice to see you again. You guys have fun. I'll see you later, Lauren."

Walking into our room, I flip on the lights, and kick off my shoes. When I plop down on the bed and charge my phone, I notice the time. Changing clothes and brushing my teeth will kill some minutes. I don't want to call Lane too early. Flinging the curtains back, I peer out the window to see if I can see Lauren and Brian sitting by the fire. I barely see them, but I can tell they're out there.

I quickly text Lauren. *Stay out as long as u want, I'm about to call Lane.* A few minutes later she texts back. *It's all good. I'm enjoying the fire and talking w/ Brian. I'll text u b4 I come up.*

Snuggling down, I pull the covers up and lean against the headboard. I click Lane's number.

He answers with, "Hey babe."

"I'm so glad to hear your voice."

"Tell me about the island."

"It's breathtaking. There are wild horses, and deer everywhere you look. Lauren and I are having a blast. We watched a beautiful sunset on a deserted beach. We ended today with s'mores around a fire pit. My parents went to bed almost an hour ago, but Lauren's still out by the fire talking with a guy we met earlier today. So, I get to be totally alone with you while we talk."

"That's good. I'm glad you're having so much fun."

"Tell me about your day."

"It was filled with lots of extended family, lots of food, lots of small talk. It was a little boring. Now is the highlight. I've been thinking about you all day long."

"I miss you, too."

"What do you have planned for the next few days?"

"Lauren and I have plans to ride bikes to the opposite end of the island tomorrow with a picnic lunch."

"That sounds like another adventure."

"Yeah, I think it will be. Hey, I want to tell you about something I heard on Monday."

"Alright, I'm all yours."

"While working on my article, I went into the break room to fix myself some tea, and two editors for the *Crimson White* newspaper were in there talking. I overheard their conversation about *the Machine* controlling the SGA elections, and how they want them exposed and kept from allowing the Greeks to control campus politics." I hear Lane take a deep breath.

"One of them recognized me from Professor Brigg's class and asked what I was working on. I told her I was finishing an article for *Alice* and had just come in to find something to drink. When she found out about the article I was working on, she introduced herself and her friend to me. She said she remembered my name from what I'd written on homecoming. There on the spot she came up with the idea for me to write an article about the need for fair SGA elections by calling out *the Machine* for its unfair practices."

Lane jumps in with, "What did you say?" I sense concern in his voice.

"I told her I was just a sophomore, and a serious article like that is better coming from a junior or senior editor."

"What happened next?"

"I told her I left all my stuff lying out with my computer on the table and needed to get back to it. I wished her luck with the article. She said she agrees it should be written by an older more experienced writer. She also thinks it should come from someone who's a Greek."

"Mmmmmmm, that's interesting. You were in the right place at the right time."

"Yeah, you could definitely say that."

"Do you remember their names?"

"Olivia and Beth. Olivia is the one in our creative writing class."

"Do you have your computer?"

"Yes, I have it in case the article I submitted to the editor of *Alice* needs something corrected or changed."

"Okay, tweet something positive about the election and our candidate from the secret Twitter account. I'll work on having something printed in the *Crimson White* that would radiate so positively about our candidate that everyone will want to vote for him regardless of being Independent or Greek. But enough of that boring stuff. I want to talk about you. We should FaceTime each other tomorrow."

"Or I can call you back on FaceTime now?"

"That's okay. I don't want to hang up. Let's just plan on that for tomorrow night."

"So, what fun stuff do you have planned tomorrow?" I ask cheerfully.

"I have a lunch meeting with my father and my uncle in the city. Afterward I'm planning to do a little shopping with my sister."

"I've often wondered if your family owns a clothing store in New York, because I'm so impressed with the way you dress." Lane chuckles.

"No, my mother was elected Lieutenant Governor while we were living in Washington DC, and after she left office we moved to Manhattan. My dad is now a professor at Columbia. My mother finished writing her book a few years ago. The book is political, so I'd rather talk about how much I'm missing you. We've had too much talk about politics already tonight."

"Well, I think it's totally cool that your mom wrote a book. Speaking of changing the subject, I've been wearing and sleeping with your scarf every day. I wish I had thought about giving you something of mine."

"How about texting me a few pictures? I love the one you posted on Instagram, but it's you and your whole family."

"I have a bunch that Lauren and I took today. I'll text you the best ones later."

We talk for a few more minutes until I get a text from Lauren asking if I'm off the phone.

"Lane, I think my sister is ready to come in. She just sent me a text asking if I'm off the phone."

"Until next time gorgeous, girl."

"I'll send you some pictures in a few minutes. Goodnight."

I quickly text Lauren to come up. She marches in saying she smells like a campfire and heads to the shower. I continue scrolling through the photos we took today, do some quick edits, and text them to Lane. I'm definitely going to vlog during our adventures, tomorrow. After posting the pic of Lauren and me at the Dungeness ruins on my Instagram captioning it, "Seaside Sisters" and hashtag #cumberlandisland. I notice as soon as I post it, Lane's my first like. I look through his Instagram and do a little snooping, since I haven't taken the time to do that yet.

I see a picture from today of him with a couple of guys around his age. It is a great picture of Lane, and I double tap it. I continue to scroll down and see pictures of him and other DKE's at their house parties, and more pictures of him and some fraternity brothers in New Orleans. There's one of him and some guys smoking cigars, and one of him on a sailboat without a shirt on. I double tap that one, even though it's from several months ago. Continuing, I find one from the fourth of July where he's in a swimsuit and has the American Flag wrapped around his shoulders. It's an amazing picture. I screen shot it, and also double tap it, then I see a picture of Amanda, Lane and Ashley. It looks like they're at a party. I try not to think about him and Ashley together. I keep scrolling and see a photo of him with his parents, his sisters and with, of all people, President Barack Obama!

I gasp aloud. "Oh My God!"

Lauren walks out of the bathroom and asks what's wrong.

"Come look at this." I hold out my phone and show her the photo.

"Oh, wow, Bex, that's amazing. Lane must be really something special."

Lane sends a text that says, *Hey, cutie, r u stalking my Instagram?*

"Yes." I send him the screen shot I took of him wearing a swimsuit with the American flag around his shoulders. I add, *This... is so hot!*

He texts back, *You're hot!*

But u met President Obama!

Yes, and he's not hot like u.

I burst out laughing. He's apparently been scrolling through my Instagram looking at all my old posts from a few years ago, because he texts a photo of me when I was a senior in high school at the lake, wearing a bikini on a boat.

He texts, *This... is HOT*

That's from a few years ago.

Send me a recent bikini pic.

I look through the photos on my phone and go back a few months. I find one of me on the beach in Gulf Shores from last spring break and send it to Lane.

He responds with, *U r perfect, I'll be dreaming of u all night.*

I reach for his scarf lying next to me and wrap my face in it and inhale. Lauren looks perplexed. "Bex, what are you doing? I noticed you had that scarf on your pillow last night, and you've also been wearing it a lot. What's the deal?"

"Lane took it off on Monday and gave it to me to keep for him until I see him again. I've been sleeping with it and wearing it. It has his cologne on it."

Lauren rolls her eyes. "Wow, I've never seen you this crazy for a guy before. I must admit, if you're going to be over the moon about someone, Lane Townsend is a choice pick."

"Yes, indeed!" I say with fervor. "Your turn. Tell me all about Brian. How was talking with him at the fire pit?"

"He's really nice and fun, easy to talk to. He goes to a private school, but we know some of the same friends. He knows my friend Aspyn who started going to Greater Atlanta Christian School a few years ago."

"That's cool. Small world."

"It is. We exchanged numbers, SnapChats, and Instagram. He told me if you and I get back from riding bikes early enough he wants to walk with me on the beach tomorrow night."

"Oooooo, fun," I say cheerfully.

"We'll see how that goes. But yeah, it should be fun. I think he's pretty cute," Lauren says with a shy smile, almost blushing.

"Can I set the alarm for after nine? That's not too late, is it?"

"No," she says. "I just got out of the shower, so I'm just going to put on a hat, a sweatshirt, and leggings, and I'll be ready."

"Great, I'll take a shower in the morning. I promise to be quick. I'm looking forward to exploring the other side of the island tomorrow, especially that old church. And we need to make sure to time everything right so you're back in time for your *beach date* with Brian tomorrow night," I add with a twist of sass in my voice.

"Goodnight, Bex," Lauren says, rolling her eyes at me.

24

#Bea

I walk into the foyer and find the house alive with my sisters back from Thanksgiving. Our trip to Cumberland Island was magical, and Mom had a special birthday. Things are changing, so I'm going to cherish our family moments and vacation time. I wave to everyone and make my way up to my room. Opening the door, I see Bella sitting in bed, still in her pajamas.

She jumps up and hugs me. "I want to hear all about your trip. You posted some cool pictures."

Moving to sit next to her, I say, "I want to hear all about your trip, too."

"It was mostly just ordinary family stuff. I saw my cousins, aunts, uncles, and grandparents. The highlight was playing card games with everyone and just visiting."

I go on to explain the beauty of the island, the Dungeness ruins, the wild horses and the long bike rides.

"The island is so beautiful. It's peaceful and calm and has hundreds of wild horses and wild animals living freely. One of the oldest churches in the country is located there. It felt like pure peace walking into the historic sanctuary. Lauren met a guy the first day we were there. He goes to a private school and lives in Atlanta. They hung out while there and plan to continue seeing each other. Lane and I talked on the phone, texted and Snap-Chatted each other the whole time I was gone. We even Face-Timed each other one night."

Since it's only noon, I ask Bella if she wants to go to the kitchen to get something to eat. We see Lexi walk in and squeal as if it's the first of the semester again. While we share our Thanksgiving stories, Lexi and Bella are hanging on my every word about the rich history of Cumberland Island and our bicycle adventures.

After a leisurely lunch, we wander back to our rooms and chill for the rest of the afternoon.

"Amanda and I are leaving around six. The game starts at seven thirty." I say as I unpack my bags.

"I'm going to text Cat and Reese to see if they want to go," Bella comments.

"I have a date with Lane after the game. I'm excited about getting to see him after being apart for a week. He's taking me out to dinner."

"That sounds romantic," she says, batting her eyelashes.

After getting into my uniform, I choose a dress and heels for my date after the game and throw those into my duffle. Amanda and I meet downstairs and ride to Coleman Coliseum together. Along the way, I ask her about her Thanksgiving and ask if she and Ashley are from the same hometown.

"We're both from Dallas but went to different high schools. I didn't meet her until we were roommates freshman year."

"I was wondering about that since I saw you guys at the airport together and saw your Instagram post at a restaurant somewhere in Dallas."

"We travel together during holidays. We were roommates for two years before we decided to move into our sorority houses for our junior and senior years and we're still good friends. Seems like everything is still going well between you and Lane." She looks at me with caution. I smile and nod as I open the door and hold it for her to walk through.

During our meet-and-greet, Lane and some guys walk in, with Ashley in their crowd. There are a few other girls with them,

154

so I tell myself it's probably nothing. Lane waves to me as they walk past.

Our sequence is short tonight so the cheerleaders can do a full routine during halftime. I'm glad we don't do two full dances just coming back from the break. Looking into the crowd as I'm coming off the court, I wave to Bella and Lexi and Cat. Lane smiles at me from the stands. I run into the locker room and quickly text Lane. *I'll meet u at the front entrance as soon as I change.*

"Wow, you must have a hot date tonight," Amanda says, with an enthusiastic smile. She sees me changing into a dress and heels.

"My date is very hot. And yes, Lane is taking me to dinner somewhere. We haven't seen each other in a week, so I can't wait."

"Have fun. I'll see you tomorrow." She waves as she walks out of the locker room.

Lane is waiting near the entrance. He's alone and wearing a navy blazer, a button-down shirt, Khaki jeans, and really nice leather loafers. When he sees me, a huge smile comes across his face as he walks up to me and puts his hands on my arms and pulls me in for a kiss. As we continue to kiss, I realize we're still standing inside Coleman and people are walking around us. He takes my hand and my bag from me and leads me to his car. He smells amazing. I'm giddy, nervous, and happy, all at the same time.

Lane opens the door and tosses my bag into the backseat. He turns toward me. Pulling my face toward his, he kisses me again. I pull him closer and continue kissing him. Instantly, I lose track of anything like the day or time. Kissing me slowly, he traces his tongue across my bottom lip and looks into my eyes.

"I'm so glad to see you."

"Me, too. I missed you a lot," I say, catching my breath from his sexy kiss.

The drive to Evangeline's is quick. I mention to Lane how excited I am to finally get to eat here since I've heard a lot of my sorority sisters talk about how awesome and fancy it is. The hostess seats us at a private table featuring candles and a beautiful bouquet of red roses as the centerpiece. The restaurant is elegant, dimly lit, and romantic. Lane takes my hand and caresses it while we're talking.

"Is your family going to travel again over Christmas break?" he asks, looking at me with smiling eyes.

"No, I shake my head. We'll be home in Atlanta the entire three weeks, just having family time. What about your family? Any special plans for Christmas?"

"We'll be in Aspen, Colorado for two weeks, but I plan to leave before New Year's Eve." He grins, especially if Alabama makes it into the National Championship game and the team plays in the Super Dome on New Year's Day."

"My roommate Bella is from New Orleans. Her family said we could stay with them if Alabama ends up in the championship game."

"What could be better than watching Alabama win the natty and having you by my side on New Year's Eve at midnight?"

"Sounds priceless, let's toast to that."

"Cheers!" Lane says, winking at me.

We're just drinking water, but we laugh and clank our glasses together.

"I love this restaurant. It's beautiful." I say, glancing at the decor.

"This restaurant can't hold a candle to your beauty. No pun intended."

Blushing, I snicker and quickly change the subject. "Tell me about going to Aspen over Christmas. Will it be just your family?"

"It'll be some of my uncles, cousins, aunts, my three sisters, and my parents. They have a big house they rent every year around Christmas. It's a family tradition. We get together for skiing and snowboarding. Sometimes I wish I could do my own thing at Christmas since my birthday is right after."

156

"When's your birthday?"

"December 29th."

"So, you'll turn twenty-two?"

"Yes, I turn twenty-two right before the end of the year. When do you turn twenty-one?"

"I turned nineteen the first week of August. I won't turn twenty-one until right before I start my senior year."

"I need to find a way to stick around and not graduate in May. I've thought about getting a minor in journalism. I've also thought about law school here, too. Now I'm going to consider those two options a lot more seriously," he says with a smile that makes my heart melt. *Is his decision to stick around really based on his feelings for me?*

After dinner Lane and I walk hand-in-hand back to the car. He parks in front of the Phi Mu house, gets out, opens my door and gets my bag from the backseat. At the door, I ask him to step inside. It's really late on Sunday night, so I know no one will be up. Inside the foyer he drops my bag and grabs me by the waist, pulls me to him, and kisses me. Lost in the passion, he picks me up in his arms and carries me over to the sofa. He sets me down and takes off his jacket. He kisses me gently. Then he looks into my eyes as he caresses my face.

I whisper, "I think I'm falling in love with you."

He whispers my name, tilts my head back and kisses me with an intensity that makes me woozie. When I notice my phone buzzing, I sit up, take it out, Bella has texted me. *R u back?*

Yes, I'm saying good night to Lane downstairs now.

Looking at Lane, I say, "My roommate just texted me. Its midnight, and I'm about to turn into a pumpkin."

He smiles and presses his lips to my forehead. We stand, and he takes his jacket. We move toward the door. He reaches for my hand, kisses it lightly before walking out. I pick up my bag and float to my room.

"Hey," I say, quietly to Bella.

"Did you and Lane have a good time?"

157

"Yes, we went to Evangeline's for dinner. It was perfect," I say, slipping out of my shoes. "After he dropped me off, he kissed me. I get lost in him when he kisses me, and I whispered that I think I'm falling in love with him." I sit on the bed and cover my face with my hands, embarrassed that I actually admitted it to Bella.

She rushes over to me. "Oh my God, Bex! What did he say?" She sits next to me on my bed.

"He just whispered my name and started kissing me again, but way more passionately, almost out of control passionately, but then you called me and interrupted us."

"Oops, sorry." Bella looks embarrassed and walks back over to her bed. She pulls back the covers and turns off the lamp. "I set the alarm for seven thirty. I was waiting until you were home safe before I fell asleep. You're home now, and I'm tired, so I'll talk to you tomorrow. And you have another surprise on your pillow."

"Thanks, Mom," I muse in a sarcastic tone.

I turn around and see an envelope and red rose on my pillow. I flip on the flashlight on my phone, tear open the seal and use the flashlight to read the card. It's an invitation to the "Undertaker's Ball" at the DKE house for next Sunday. It says dress is formal and my escort will be Lane Kennedy Townsend. The writing is very elegant. I place the rose in the vase with the other two, which are now dried and wilted. I lay the invitation next to the vase and quickly change into something comfy and drift off to sleep, dreaming of fancy parties and Lane in a tuxedo.

25

#Noregrets

The alarm goes off, but I ignore it. The second time it goes off, Bella mumbles something about turning it off. She gets out of bed and turns on the Keurig then turns on her speaker which quietly plays "Never Enough" by The Hunna.

"Hey, Bella, turn that up." The song gives me enough motivation to pull myself out of bed and start the day. It's going to be a baseball cap day, for sure. Bella has the same idea; she's throwing on leggings and a sweatshirt. I mosey to the desk and grab a mug to make myself some tea, there I notice Bella's invitation.

"Hey, Bella, did you get an invitation to the Undertaker's Ball?"

"Yes, both Lexi and I got one yesterday. We were invited by Patrick and Jack. It's invitation only. Someone came last night and delivered them to four girls in the house. We're two of the lucky four." She looks at me with a hint of smugness, trying to impress upon me the fact that we're going to something exclusive at her favorite fraternity house.

"That's great. It will be a fun event, I'm sure."

"We've got to go dress shopping this week," she says, with a baseball cap in hand as she walks out the door for class. "Have a great day, Bex."

Since it's the first week of December, we have about a week before exams and dead week. All of the professors will be giving out pre-exam sheets. It tells us the date and time of the

159

exam or if we even need to take an exam for that particular class. The prep paper also tells us our standing grade and any upcoming assignments or study links to help us prepare. Exams and dead week are the worst, even nightmarish. Studying up to five or more hours in a day can leave you feeling like you've lost all contact with the outside world. It might be good to vlog about... *How to survive dead week*, ugh, the thought of it sucks, but since it's a college necessity, survival tips are useful.

My visual journalism class is first this morning. I get my exam prep paper and see that I have an A in the class but still have to take the exam. I know when we get our prep papers tomorrow in creative writing, it will show that our writing assignment will be our exam. About my intro to media production and my documentary storytelling class, I don't know yet. I already know I'll have Spanish and math exams.

Later in the day, I get the best news I could possibly ask for. The article I wrote for *Alice* magazine will be used for my final grade for my documentary class, and since my story for creative writing will be used as a final grade for the semester in that class, I only have four exams to study for. After class I wander back to the house for lunch. Lexi's in the kitchen, so I scoot in next to her.

"I'm excited that we'll be going to the Undertaker's Ball together on Sunday night," I say, sipping my Diet Coke.

"I know, right," Lexi says with excitement. "I've heard that party is pretty exclusive. Bella wants us to go dress shopping this Thursday. What does your schedule look like on Thursday or Friday?"

"I'm free. I only have a home game on Wednesday night this week, and the next one will be in January."

"That's good. You get a little break."

"A small one. I'll still have practice. We're working on a new dance that we'll need to have ready for the January and February games. I need to leave for practice in a few minutes."

My phone on the table buzzes with a text from Mom. *How was your first day back from Thanksgiving break?*

Good. I have my exam schedule. And I got invited to the Undertaker's Ball on Sunday night.

Ok. I'll Venmo you some money for a dress, but be thrifty in your choice pls.

Sweet. Thx Mom, Love u.

Then a text from Lane pops up. *Hey cutie. Hope ur having a good day so far. I have something for u.* He sends a photo of an advertisement featuring our SGA candidate that we're promoting. It's very impressive, a full-page color ad. It lists all his achievements and philanthropy. *Facilitated the V Foundation Event for Delta Chi Fraternity, helped raise 3,000.00 for the V- Foundation's Cancer Research, created the Gallettes Supports Vets event, Holds a 3.9 GPA, Phi Beta Kappa, Gamma Beta Phi, Young Life Leader and Mentor for Tuscaloosa High School, UA Honors, Business and Finance major.* The caption at the top is his name and, "Your SGA Candidate."

I know what Lane wants me to do with the photo. I say a quick goodbye to Lexi and run up to my room. I get out my computer and log in to the untraceable site. I post the photo then go back and delete Laine's text from my phone. I change the passwords for both secret accounts. Done. Not sure what I've gotten myself into, but I did want something exciting to happen, and this is definitely on the thrill level.

After dinner we have our regular Monday night chapter meeting. Tonight's meeting is all about finalizing our plans for our snow themed Christmas event. It'll be at Gallette's on the 15th at eight, which is the last day of finals before everyone leaves for Christmas Break. This is one of many parties that night. Ours is a *date night* event. I smile to myself with happy thoughts of Lane. The SEC Championship game is the next day in Atlanta. I'm not sure if he'll be able to go to that before he leaves for Aspen.

After the meeting ends, Bella and I head back to the room. I go about organizing my pre-exam papers and make a few notes and set an alarm for the morning. Bella asks again about going dress shopping on Thursday.

161

"We need to go somewhere where there isn't men's cologne," Bella says, laughing at her own joke.

"Too funny." I give her a sideways glance.

Of course, I think Lane smells awesome, and I think he *is* awesome, but more than that, there's something mysterious about Lane that intrigues me beyond my control.

26

#Hotoffhepress

The next morning, I spritz on a little perfume, grab my bag, stick my phone into my back pocket and gleefully walk out the door and head to my creative writing class. In the grand foyer there are stacks and stacks of the *Crimson White* newspapers on tables everywhere. The front-page is a full color ad. It's exactly what Lane sent me yesterday. Grabbing one, I walk into the lecture hall.

Lane is already in his seat. He leans over and kisses me on the cheek.

"Good morning, beautiful."

"It is a good morning now that I'm with you," I whisper, leaning closer.

"I like your scarf," he says, with a sheepish grin.

"I've worn it, I've slept with it, and I guess you may want it back?"

"You can keep wearing it. I like it better on you." His bright smile is radiant.

"I'm impressed with this front-page, full-sized ad on our SGA candidate. Also, the fact that the *Crimson White* seems to be front and center downstairs in the foyer today."

He just smiles his beautiful smile and doesn't reply.

Professor Brigg walks in and begins talking about an online quiz that's due at the end of the week. He explains that we'll do great on this quiz as long as we've been good note takers in class. The quiz will test our note taking skills as journalists.

163

We end up getting out of class fifteen minutes early, and Lane suggests we walk together across the quad before we go our separate ways.

He laughs. "I won't make you ride my bike this time."

I snort and smack him on the arm, but the comment *is* funny. Lane and I are standing together while he unlocks his bike. I notice Olivia walking down the stairs, she gives me a funny expression. I smile at her, but she only half-smiles back. She has a copy of the *Crimson White* newspaper tucked under her arm. Lane and I stroll together across the street and through the quad as he pushes his bike along.

"I have a date for the meet-the-candidate party," Lane says. "It'll be at Heat Pizza on January twelfth starting at seven——free drinks and appetizers. Info should read "open to everyone and invite your friends." Wait to post it on January fifth, then post another one a week later and a reminder the day of the event." He leans in for a kiss. "Bye, beautiful."

"See you," I say, as he gets on his bike and peddles away.

When I get to math, I write a few notes about Heat Pizza and the dates Lane gave me in a notebook. I'm glad he trusts me with all this information. But is this trust, or is it something else? There is a lot of secrecy. I guess that's the point of a secret society. I'm really starting to dig this whole *cloak-and-dagger* vibe. I stick the paper into my bag and push dreamy thoughts of Lane out of my mind so I can concentrate on math until class is over.

When I get back to the room from class, Bella's already back.

"What time do you want to go shopping today?" Bella asks, pulling a sweater over her head.

"I thought we could go later if Lexi has time. I'll text her and see when she's free," I say, setting my bag down.

"Yeah, sounds good. Let's plan to meet her downstairs. I have three shops mapped out I want to go to. Maybe we could go to Heat Pizza after we're done shopping," Bella suggests.

"Great, I love that you have a strategic shopping plan."

"If we don't find anything today, we may need to drive to Birmingham on Friday or Saturday."

"Let's hope we all find what we want today. I don't want to drive all over the state looking for a dress. By the way, I'm going to my tutor session, and then I'm checking out a camera to film my documentary story project." My phone dings. "Lexi says she'll be home in about an hour. I'll meet you guys back here as soon as I'm done."

Shopping goes quickly. By the third store we've decided on which dress we each want. I've chosen a black satin fitted dress with a split up the front left thigh. The top of the bodice is beaded with black sequined beads over a lace overlay. The sleeves are long but completely sheer and made of very delicate lace. It's extremely elegant and form fitting across the bodice. Bella chooses a grey sequined dress that comes up across one shoulder, leaving the other shoulder bare. It's full length with a sequined sheer overlay. Lexi picked a steel blue satin dress that's fitted with a sequined collar around the neck and is sleeveless. On the way to dinner, we chat about our hair styles and the shoes we want to wear with our dresses.

While at Heat Pizza, I decide to do a little creative filming with the camera I checked out. As everyone else is chatting away, I get the idea to interview the SGA candidate with a short two-minute interview, since my project needs to be under three minutes in length. It should work as a documentary, and Lane may even be interested in using some of the footage.

Back on campus, Lexi, Bella and I trek up the stairs carrying our long plastic bags with our ball gowns. Bella and I hang our dress bags on our decorative hooks then go down to the living room to hang out and wait for Bible study to start. This Bible study is geared toward exam week. The main verse featured is from Isaiah 41:9-10. I know this verse well, since I have it on a plaque in my room back home.

165

"Do not fear, for I am with you declares the Lord. Do not be dismayed, for I am your God. I will strengthen and help you. I will uphold you with my righteous hand."

Bible study wraps up with a reminder that exams are temporary but seeking and serving God has value for eternity. In other words, we should prepare for our exams and study, but we shouldn't worry. *Easy to say, a lot harder to do.*

I text Lane about my film project and ask if he thinks it'll be okay to do a short interview with our SGA candidate, Adam. I offer that it could be useful for publicity.

He texts back, *That's a great idea.*

He sends me his contact information and tells me he'll give Adam a heads up for me.

Perfect. TY. Have u completed the online quiz yet?

Yes, it's fairly easy. Have u finished it?

I'm planning to do it tomorrow or Saturday. I have to finish my editing project by midnight on Monday, and I want to get that and the online quiz out of the way so I can study for my other exams next week.

I set my phone down and look over at Bella. "I don't need an alarm for the morning, do you?"

"Nope, me, neither," she says, glancing up at me from the book she has her nose in.

"I have a few assignments to finish up before exams that I'll need to work on during the day. I'll probably go to the main library tomorrow," I say, turning off the lamp.

We say goodnight, then I fall asleep dreaming about showing up for one of my exams wearing my new formal dress.

I wake up to a text from Lane. *Good morning babe. Adam knows to expect a call from u.*

Cool. I'm glad my idea worked out. I'll call him in a few minutes.

I walk downstairs to make some toast and bring some back to the room for Bella. She's got coffee brewing in the Keurig. I pour myself a cup while dialing Adam's number. When he answers, I tell him I'd love to set up a time to interview him. We decide to meet for lunch at Heat Pizza, which was my suggestion, since I started filming there yesterday.

I have several hours to kill before my lunch meeting, so I decide to walk to the library to work on my online quiz. I look around for my notebooks and things to take with me. Bella sets her coffee down and pops her closet door open.

"Hey, Bella, what are your plans today?"

"Mostly studying," she says, throwing on a hoodie.

"Would you want to go to the library now then drive me over to Heat Pizza around one? I'm meeting someone there. I have to interview him for an assignment."

"Sure, sounds fun and better than studying in the room all day."

I pack up my books, grab the camera bag, and put everything into my backpack.

Bella and I find a quiet, out of the way, place in the library. We spread out and study for the next two hours. After I finish the online quiz, I text Lane.

I took the quiz.

How do you think you did?

I think really well. I feel good about it.

Awesome.

I'm meeting Adam for the interview at 1. I'll call u later.

I glace toward the other end of the table to check on Bella. As I stand, a guy and a girl walk past me talking in an animated whisper.

"They found all the *Crimson White* newspapers stacked in the basement of a building on the edge of campus."

I freeze in place, listening. They slowly walk past me, and I perk my ears up.

"I wonder why they stacked them in a basement on campus if they were trying to get rid of them? Whoever did that printed out new front-page covers, so why leave the old front-pages where someone might find them?"

"They wanted them found. The Machine wants everyone to know they control politics on campus. They've got to be the one's behind the new front-page ad for the SGA candidate"

"Bex, Bex, Rebecca!" Bella snaps her fingers, pulling me out of my daze.

"Are you okay, Bex? You were just standing there staring into space."

"Yeah, I'm okay, I stood up and got dizzy. Probably from sitting so long."

"Or too much studying. Let's go, girl, it's almost one." Bella waves her hand in the direction of the door."

Quickly, I brush away the thoughts about what in the world went on with the *Crimson White* front-page swap. Part of me wants to snoop and find out the scoop but it appears that someone or some group, I should say, took care to make sure they got what they wanted in the news.

A few minutes later, we arrive at Heat Pizza and pick out a table. I write down a few questions that I'd like to ask our SGA candidate. When I see Adam walk in, I notice he's a very good looking, at least 6'2" African American stud. I wave him over. I recognize him from the ad in the *Crimson White* and from the last time I was at a Young Life event. He was talking with a group of high school boys before I had my serious talk with Grant. Bella and I introduce ourselves. Bella says she'll place our lunch order and get some drinks delivered to our table while I conduct the interview.

I set up the camera for filming and make sure I have the right angle and height.

"Adam, I'm going to turn on the camera and begin the interview. Are you ready?"

"Yes." He smiles and nods.

"Let's begin," I say, pushing the button to start filming.

"I'm impressed with your credentials that were listed in the *Crimson White* this week. You're a very impressive candidate. Can you tell me about your work with Young Life?

168

Adam clears his throat and begins. "I was involved with Young Life in High School, and I feel that as a Christian program it has a lot to offer high school students. For one thing, it allows any high school student to be involved with a great group of friends. It may be a social thing they're looking for, but since it's meant to lead people to God it becomes more than social. I was invited by a friend. I'll be honest, I went because I knew there would be girls there."

He grins. "After several weeks I started to really listen to the leaders, the messages, and the Bible verses they were sharing with us. They started to mean something to me personally. I came to understand it was more than social. It was real, and it changed me, and changed my life."

He looks into the camera. "I wanted to be a positive influence on other high school students. I now volunteer once a week with Young Life for a breakfast devotional time with the 9th-12th grade boys from Tuscaloosa High School. We started out with just five guys showing up. Now we have seventeen each Thursday morning at seven at the Burger King."

He appears proud. "We have club night on Wednesdays for all the schools in the county to get together. This, of course, is a big social time for all the kids, but we leave them with a verse and a message that hopefully touches their hearts. We pray for these young students. Some of them have struggles and tough things they're going through, and they need real guidance and support. They need to know and believe that we care about them."

"I'm so touched," I say. "That's very moving." Tears well up in my eyes, I clear my throat, take a breath and begin again. "It sounds like you're a positive influence on young men in the community. My next question is why you want to be Student Government President."

Adam responds, "I was SGA President during my senior year in high school. I wanted to be a leader and a role model in school. I want to continue to lead. I love Alabama, the school, the classes, our sports teams, and our faculty. We have something very special here. Our traditions run deep. I want to be SGA President to continue the traditions but also bring positivity and great ideas to the program. I want to be able to work with a great staff of SGA representatives and work together to create the best school year we can for the student body on campus."

I turn the camera off, and notice Bella has been standing next to us, listening. I tell Adam we have some good stuff and thank him for meeting with us. Bella places our pizza on the table, offers Adam a slice, and sits next to me.

When Adam leaves, I turn to Bella and explain my filming plan.

"I'm want to shoot some footage of some icons like Denny Chimes, and the Bear Bryant statue in front of the stadium before we go back to the house, if you don't mind. I'll need to go to the lab tomorrow to work on editing this. I'll probably spend most of the day on it." I glance at Bella.

"You'll probably get a good grade. And Adam seems like a really good guy." She looks impressed. "Also, Lexi and I will have band practice most of the day tomorrow so you can work in the room undisturbed. But Sunday-Funday, can't wait for the ball!" Bella says earnestly.

27
#Thowshade

"Is it time to get ready for the Undertaker's Ball yet? I've been reading this page for an hour," Bella says, shutting her book.

"I'm starving," I groan out loud. "Let's go get something to eat. I think my butt is molded to this chair. We've been sitting here studying way too long." I lean back in my desk chair.

"Yeah, let's go downstairs and get something to eat. It's almost time for the Undertaker's Parade." Bella stands and stretches.

"I know. I've still got to take a shower, and I want to spend a lot of time on my hair and makeup," I add, closing my computer.

"I'm going down to Lexi's room. I'll meet you in the kitchen," Bella calls over her shoulder.

The three of us wander out of the kitchen with bowls and spoons still in hand when we hear commotion near the front of the house. The front door is standing open and girls are mingling around in the front yard. Lexi, Bella and I follow the other girls out to the front sidewalk. Ten minutes later our entire house is outside, and a huge crowd has gathered up and down sorority row.

In the distance we can see something coming our way, and the music is getting louder. A horse drawn carriage passes us, and behind it, a coffin carried on the shoulders of six DKE's comes into view. A New Orleans style jazz band follows with umbrellas and festive attire. Someone mentions it's called a second line.

Behind the Jazz band, I spot a large flag with the words "It's Never Over" printed across it. Lane has one end of the flag with Jack holding up the other side. Bella and I wave when they walk by. Lane winks at me. The end of the parade approaches with a truck full of DKE's on a trailer pulling the giant grim reaper statue, the one I saw at their party on Halloween. The smoke machine on the back of the trailer leaves us in a fog. After the parade has passed, we go upstairs to shower and change for the ball.

"Wow! that was interesting!" Bella says when we walk back into the house. "A real horse-drawn carriage, smoke machines, and a jazz band. I can't wait to see what the ball will be like."

"Yes, I'm a little nervous, excited but nervous."

Bella texts Lexi to bring her stuff to our room to finish getting ready with us. After primping, curling and powdering, we help each other into our dresses and slip on our shoes. I add rhinestone drop earrings then step into black kitten heel pumps. Bella puts on pearl earrings and a pearl necklace. Lexi's wearing her hair up. She adds small rhinestone earrings to match the rhinestone collar on her dress.

We admire ourselves and each other in the mirror. We take a few selfies and in unison say, "Okay we're ready." I pick up my small purse and put a pack of Kleenex, a lipstick, my ID and my phone inside.

The three of us glide out of the room and stop to look over the balcony railing. Down below our dates stand in the foyer talking. Slowly we descend the staircase. I truly feel like a princess about to meet my prince. When we get near the bottom Lane walks to the railing, smiling at me. He's wearing a black tuxedo with a red rose boutonniere. He greets me at the bottom of the stairs, and hands me a red rose. He kisses me on the cheek and whispers in my ear, "You're breathtaking."

I whisper back, "Thank, you, you look amazing."

172

Jack and Patrick walk up and greet Bella and Lexi with long stem roses, too. Lane offers his arm in a romantic, old-fashioned gesture. I slip my hand over his arm, and we walk out the door. Bella and Lexi follow.

I stop at the sidewalk in awe. Parked in front of the house is the horse-drawn carriage from the parade, and two DKE pledges in Tuxedos wait to open the door for us. Lexi and Bella giggle with excitement behind me, and when I turn around and smile, they are grinning from ear to ear. I ask Lane if one of the carriage drivers can take some pictures. We hand our phones over, and Lane and I pose in front of the carriage. Bella, Lexi and their dates get pictures, then we get a group shot before we take off.

Lexi and Patrick enter the carriage first, then Bella and Jack. Lane escorts me to the carriage door and I step inside with him following me. The door closes and the driver motions for the horses to walk on.

When the carriage starts to move, I look up at Lane and whisper, "Thank you. This is so special." He grins and kisses the tip of my nose.

The carriage pulls up to the DKE house, and our driver hops down to open the doors. A red carpet lines the sidewalk, and there's a fog machine creating a mist at the front entrance. The giant Grim Reaper statue lurks at the front door as we reach the top step. The doors are standing open, and we walk beneath the giant Undertaker's Ball flag hanging from the entrance. Inside, the only light is from candles, and there are hundreds on every surface. The atmosphere is magical. There are huge vases of red roses everywhere. To the left of the entrance, where the couches used to be, I see a coffin and a guy lying in it. We walk into a larger room where a band is playing jazz. The room to the right with the large blazing fireplace hosts buffet tables and an open bar.

Bella says she and Jack are going to get a drink. Patrick and Lexi follow. Lane and I drift to the back room. I notice the smaller room with the fireplace where he and I sat the last time I was here. Lane asks if I would like a glass of champagne. He leads me to a table featuring slender flutes filled with golden bubbly topped with strawberries. He hands me a glass then we wander over near the band. We clink our glasses in a toast. While sipping my champagne, my eyes scan the room, taking in the majesty of the party. I notice Ashley walking down the hall with a date. She walks toward Amanda, who has just arrived, and they embrace. I feel a little awkward, but I know at some point I'll run into Ashley when I'm with Lane.

Lane sets his glass down. "Would you like to dance?" He offers his hand with a bow.

He leads me onto the dance floor. He takes me by the waist, and I reach for his other hand. He's a good dancer. I can tell he's had some formal training. His movements are very smooth as we glide across the dance floor.

"Dancing to jazz with you is so romantic. This night is romantic," I say, flushed.

He leans in and kisses me softly then twirls me around. I'm laughing and enjoying every moment. He dips me playfully, and when I come back up, I see Ashley staring daggers at me. I try not to pay any attention. We move to a table for a dance break and casually sip our champagne.

Lexi wanders over and asks me to walk to the bathroom with her. We walk to the end of the hall into the small room with the fireplace. I show her the door to the bathroom. When Lexi finishes, we find Patrick waiting for her in the hallway. I scan the crowd, searching for Lane. I see him standing near the table where we left our drinks. Ashley has her hands on his arm and is standing way too close. Her face is almost touching his. I can't tell what she's saying. I stride toward them. Lane looks up, sees me, and pulls away from Ashley. When she notices me, she slowly reaches a hand up to Lane's face and whispers something in his ear. She slides her hand down his face to his chest, looks at me with a smirk, and walks away. That's enough for me, I can't help but feel anger bubbling up. I turn and go back down the hall

174

toward the bathroom. Before I can get to the door Lane grabs me by the arm.

"Rebecca."

I turn around with tears running down my face. Lane reaches out for me, and I pull away. I should probably give him a chance to explain, but Ashley's little show back there was like WTF.

"Rebecca, it's not what you think. Ashley's just jealous of you, that's all."

I wipe the tears from my cheeks but don't say anything.

"I care about you. You're my girlfriend. I only want to be with you. You need to believe that." He reaches out for me again, and this time he pulls me close. He looks so sincere.

I finally say, "I know you dated her. Amanda told me that Ashley still likes you and wants you back."

"That may be true, but I don't want her. I only want you. I've never felt the way I feel about you about anyone before. I promise you, Bex, it's you and only you I want." Lane pulls me closer and holds me tight. He looks down at me and wipes the tears from my cheeks.

Looking into my eyes, he says, "I care about you more than you know. I would never do anything to hurt you."

He lifts my chin, kisses me gently on the lips then my nose, and hugs me tight. "I don't want to let you go."

"I don't want you to let me go." I look up, searching his beautiful hazel eyes.

He kisses me tenderly. I smile. "I better go freshen up a bit," I say, taking a step back.

His hand brushes my cheek lightly. "Please come to me if something is bothering you. I want you to know you mean everything to me, forget about Ashley."

I walk into the bathroom and fix my makeup the best I can and re apply my lipstick. I can't help but think, *Is it really over between them.? Does Ashley have some sort of hold over him, or a secret? Should I have mentioned that Amanda told me about Ashley? And she warned me to stay away from Lane. But,*

175

honestly, I tried to stay away and couldn't. I brush off my worrisome thoughts and walk out of the bathroom over to Lane and take his hand.

"I'm sorry. Maybe I should have voiced my concerns about Ashley earlier."

He looks at me intently, searching my face. "You don't need to be sorry. Everything is okay."

"I hope Ashley gets the message soon," I say, hoping he'll divulge more information.

"Come on. Let's go dance." He holds out his hand for me.

After dancing, we check out the buffet. It's impressive. There seems to be a little bit of everything, shrimp, cheese, fruit, desserts, tiny quiches, all beautifully arranged. I ignore Ashley and concentrate all my energy on having fun the rest of the evening.

When it gets close to midnight the music changes and becomes a little spooky. The fog machine must have been brought inside because an airy mist is starting to creep through the house. Suddenly, a line of guys marches in with the coffin wheeled in behind them. They stop, turn, and face the band.

Three guys walk up behind them and begin announcing each guy one at a time. As they, do they turn and face us. Last, but not least, the guy in the coffin is announced, and he pops up. An explosion of fireworks breaks the deathly silence and eerie music. The band starts to play lively music corresponding with the fireworks.

Lane takes my hand. "Let's go outside and watch the fireworks."

We walk out to the back patio and watch the short but impressive fireworks show. After the final explosion, Lane explains the creepy announcement.

"Out of our pledge class we try to recognize the ones who've shown outstanding achievement through various tasks presented to them as well as the ones chosen to be in the coffin. We try to recognize them during the Undertaker's Ball in some small way. Each year we do it a little differently."

176

"This was spectacular. Everything tonight has been so beautiful. The carriage ride was special, and you make me feel special," I say, leaning into his chest.

"I always want to make you feel special."

He kisses me gently on the lips and on my neck, sending goosebumps down my arms to flutters into my stomach.

When we walk back inside, the fog is mostly gone, and all the lights are on. There are tables set up by the front door covered with black gift bags. Girls are taking gift bags as they leave with their dates. The jazz band is still playing, and a few people are still dancing. We walk to the dance floor, and Lane offers me his hand. We dance to another song. Lexi and Patrick are also dancing. Bella and Jack head toward the entrance. I glance up at Lane while we slow dance. "I think Bella and Jack are leaving. I wonder what time it is?"

"My guess is it's about one a.m. Are you ready to go?"

"I think Bella and Jack might have left."

"Wait here for just a minute. I'll be right back."

When he returns, he asks, "Ready?" and offers me his arm.

I wave to Lexi and Patrick. Lexi waves back, and I think she tells Patrick it's time to go. Lane picks up a gift bag for me. Walking down the stairs I notice the horse drawn carriage is parked out front. Lane helps me in and sits next to me. He takes my hand and kisses it. The carriage rolls on down the road, taking us back to the Phi Mu house.

"Did you have them get the horses and carriage just for me?"

"Of course, I wanted to make sure you got home from the ball safe and sound," he says smiling at me.

I put my hands up to my face embarrassed. "I feel bad for getting upset about Ashley."

"Let's not talk about her. You should know how I really feel about you by now. But if you need convincing …"

He leans in and traces his thumb across my lower lip. My breath hitches, I reach up and take his hand, keeping it at my

177

mouth, kissing it. Lane whispers, "Rebecca, as he kisses me, tugging on my lower lip with his teeth. I'm lost in the moment, this incredible, perfect moment. When the carriage stops, Lane helps me out. We pause near the front door. He kisses my hand and takes a bow.

I laugh and say, "You make everything perfect."

"Goodnight, gorgeous," he says, handing me my gift bag.

He turns to walk back to the carriage. Instead of getting inside, he jumps up and sits next to the driver, and they take off. I drift to my room in a dream state. I take off my shoes and slip out of my dress. I look inside my gift bag to find a long stem red rose and an Undertaker's Ball T-shirt. I slip the shirt then crawl into bed.

Bella comes in from the bathroom, holding a towel. "That was so much fun. Everything was beautiful, and the fireworks were impressive. Not to mention the carriage ride."

"Yes, I'm in love, totally in love."

I turn over and fall asleep, dreaming of horses and meadows full of roses.

28
#Sweaterweather

Morning arrives like a lion. Waking up, I realize I never washed my makeup off from the ball last night. After a long hot shower, I get dressed then wake Bella up to ask if she has an early exam. She says she has an alarm set and rolls back over. I pack my bags and the camera I need to return and walk over to Phifer to spend an hour studying for my camera, lighting, and sound test.

After that's done, I feel pretty fabulous about how I did, but with another exam to study for I head toward the house. As I'm walking down the hall, I get a text from Lane.

Good morning, I hope ur exams go well this week.

So far so good.

I'm immediately reminded of the awesome time I had last night and add another text.

TY again for the beautiful party last night, u made me feel so special.

U r very special to me. He adds a heart emoji.

Surely, I can trust Lane. Would I have chosen him over Grant just to have my heart broken? When I get back to the room, Bella's not there. Before I get into studying for my next exam, I email Lane the video interview I submitted for my class and share the unedited version. Scrolling through my pictures from last night, I post the group picture of me, Bella, Lexi and our dates standing in front of the carriage on Instagram and caption it "On our way to the ball." #undertakersball #uaDKE #rolltide

#phimu. Switching my phone to silent, I plan to study for several hours undistracted.

Finishing my second exam of the day makes me feel even better. Two down and two more to go between Tuesday and Friday. I get a reminder text from Amanda that we don't have practice again until Friday afternoon, but we do have a chapter meeting tonight about the party we're hosting at Gallette's. I walk back to the house after my second exam to find Bella studying.

"Hey," I say as I walk in.

"Hey, how were your exams today?" she asks.

"Good. How many did you have?"

"I had one today. I have two tomorrow and one on Thursday. I was exempt from one."

"Oh, wow, you'll be done by Thursday afternoon."

"Yes, I'm sleeping late on Friday."

"I'll try not to wake you up. I have a Spanish test at ten thirty Friday."

"Don't forget we have a chapter meeting tonight about the party at Gallette's Friday night," she says.

"Right, I need to do an inventory of the winter clothes in my closet. We may need to go shopping at KSO for some boots or something later this week."

"You know I'm always up for a shopping trip. Lexi invited Patrick, and I, of course, invited Jack. Let me guess you invited Lane?" Bella says, grinning at me. She knows the answer.

*****

The end of the week, end of finals, party night, *and* the beginning of Christmas break are all rolled into one day, and the celebrating starts tonight. While I'm walking back to the house after my Spanish final, I get a text from Lane.

I just finished my last final of the semester, how about u?
Yes, just finished, lunch? Walking thru the quad rn.

180

Lunch sounds good. I'm on my bike. I'll meet u on the strip.

I walk down to the strip and see Lane on his bike coming toward me. We pop into a taco bar, order food, and grab a table.

"So how did your finals go?" I ask between bites.

"Really well. I only had to take four. How about you?"

"I had to take four, too."

"Nice, I'm looking forward the snow party with you tonight," he says, with that sexy look he wears so well.

"Me, too." I smile back. "It'll be nice to start getting into the season of Christmas."

"Are you leaving early tomorrow morning to go home?" He asks.

"No, not really. I still need to pack. Bella and Lexi leave with the band on the buses around eleven thirty. She said they stop at their hotel first. The game starts at seven thirty. They have to be at the stadium by six. I'm going to find a ride with another Phi Mu to the game."

"How about you ride over with me?"

"Really? I'd love that. I'm glad you're going. When do you leave for Aspen?"

"I'll fly out Sunday afternoon from Atlanta. I'm planning on leaving my car at a fraternity brother's house, and I'll fly back into Atlanta at some point to drive my car back to campus after the break. By-the-way, I wanted to tell you that the clip of the interview you sent me is really good. You could edit it several ways and Tweet out different versions for promotions on the secret account."

"Yeah, sure. I'll do that this weekend." Glancing at my phone, I realize I need to get going. "I'm glad we got together for lunch, but I've got to scoot. I've got practice today because of exam week and Christmas break." I make a sad face and stand up.

Lane stands and gives me a hug.

"I'll stop by the house to pick you up at eight. We can walk to Gallette's together."

181

"That'll be awesome. I'll see you later." I wave as I walk out of the restaurant.

Back in the room, I quickly change and text Amanda to see if she's ready to go. We meet at her car and ride to practice. She's chatty on the way over and asks, "So, are you going to the game tomorrow?"

"Yes, are you?"

"No. I'm planning on flying home to Dallas tomorrow. I figured you'd probably be going since it's in Atlanta, and you live there. If we end up in the National Championship game on New Year's, I'm definitely going to New Orleans."

"I'm planning on doing that, too. Bella's from there, so we plan to stay at her house for a few days."

After rehearsal we're given a DVD of our new dance and told to practice it over Christmas break. *No rest for the weary.*

Back in the room, Bella is packing her big suitcase. I get my suitcase out and start putting things in, including my bag of laundry. I pull out the leggings, coat, and Lane's scarf I'm going to wear to the party and open the box of cute winter, waterproof boots I bought yesterday when we went shopping.

Bella stops packing and asks, "Are you riding to Atlanta with someone?"

"I was going to ride with Alexis, but I found out a little while ago that Lane is going to the game. I'm going to ride with him tomorrow afternoon, instead."

"Riding to Atlanta with Lane will be fun."

"I know. I'm thrilled to be able to spend time with him before we go our separate ways for two weeks. I wasn't sure if he'd be able to go to the game or not since I wasn't totally sure when he was planning on arriving in Aspen. I'm going to walk down to Alexis' room and tell her I'm riding with Lane tomorrow. I'll be back in a few minutes.

A few hours later, we're changed and ready to go to our snow themed date party.

Bella leaves with Lexi and a few other Phi Mu's early to help set a few things up before the party. I work on packing a

182

little more before I walk downstairs to wait for Lane. I see him stroll up and open the door. He's wearing a Ralph Lauren black and white ski jacket, ski pants, a black hat with ski goggles and a red plaid scarf.

"Wow, you look amazing," I say taking in every inch of his gorgeous looks. "You look like you just stepped off the ski slopes in Aspen."

He laughs and says, "Yep, but right now I'd rather get snowed-in with you."

I laugh as he pulls me into a hug. He takes my hand, and we head down the sidewalk and over to the strip to Gallette's for the party.

We smoosh our way inside. It's packed like a can of sardines. People are spilling over and out onto the patio. The music is loud, and the base is thumping. It feels amazing, especially with the crowds this tight. The videos on the screens have spliced in snow and skiing pictures of our sorority sisters from past parties and ski trips they've taken, which is really cool. There's even a fake snow machine blowing a dusting of tiny white flakes in the air. After Lane returns with drinks, we start dancing. The energy in here is explosive. A mixture of body heat, good music, and lots of drinking gives the feeling of complete freedom from tests and school. A feeling of *I'm on vacation for three weeks, and I'm going to party nonstop until January.* That strong vibe of total undeniable freedom is alive and tangible.

We find Bella and Lexi with Jack and Patrick and join them in the crowds. After several rounds of pictures and selfies, we ditch our coats and continue dancing. A few hours later, the crowds mixed with dancing and layers of ski themed clothing has made the air inside Gallette's too hot to breathe, we so decide to walk outside. Lane and I grab our coats and walk out to the patio. There's a light snow falling. I put my coat back on, and Lane and I walk hand-in-hand toward the quad. It's dark, and quiet and feels enchanting walking through campus in the snow. I get an inkling of what it might be like inside a snow globe.

The trees lining the campus have gone from sharp colored yellow and red leafed trees to solemn, looking dead sticks. Without all the green and color, the red brick paths and red brick buildings stand out. As we walk along the crimson path to the quad, the snow falls onto the bricks and melts away. The snow falling on the frozen ground forms a light dusting. We continue walking through campus, engulfed in the magic of the night, and end up in front of Woods Hall, the art department building. Woods Hall has a beautiful courtyard setting, and the red brick is offset by black rod iron balconies along the outside of the buildings. We find a bench and sit down.

"Over the past three years I've spent a lot of time in Woods Hall and across the street at Morgan," Lane says, as we lean back into the bench. "Do you know the ghost story behind Woods Hall?"

"No, but tonight would be the perfect time to hear a ghost story."

The campus is quiet and still, and the snow fall gives it a serene look. Lane puts his arm around my shoulder and begins the story.

"So, after Woods hall was completed in 1868, it was first used as a barracks for university cadets. There was a gunfight between two male students over the honor of a female. The two men decided to settle the score the traditional way with a duel. After the gunfight, one man fell over the balcony, and he either died from the fall or the gun shot. Today, they say that on some nights you can see this student's ghost walking along the top balcony of Woods Hall."

I look up at the balcony as he says that. I don't notice anything, but I feel a chill go through me. "Wow, that's an interesting piece of history."

I snuggle up to Lane and tuck my hands inside his coat.

"I have another ghost story for you. There's a story about the Little Round House, the one we sat in during the night of the bonfire. According to this story, during the Civil War, three Union soldiers were lured there by the promise of whiskey, only

184

to be shot by a Confederate cadet hiding inside. You can sometimes hear the soldiers digging around for the whiskey that was promised them."

"Oh my gosh, I'm so glad you didn't tell me these ghost stories the night we were in there, it would have totally spoiled the romance."

We both laugh, and Lane pulls me close and kisses me gently. We hear laughter behind us and notice a group of students has come out to play in the snow, and they've started a snowball fight. We decide to walk back to Gallette's to see how the party's wrapping up.

The walk back is not as peaceful or as quiet. The campus, now white with snow, is alive with co-eds running, laughing and playing in the light dusting. At Gallette's, most of the girls and their dates are outside taking pictures and running around in the snow. Bella and Lexi have built tiny snowmen on top of a table. It's cute, kinda like a snowman forest. Bella waves us over when she sees us walk up.

"Hey, what do you guys think of our tiny snowmen?"

"Adorable. Lane and I just got back from a long walk across campus. It was quiet at first, very peaceful and beautiful. Now most of the campus is out playing in the snow."

Lexi comments, "I wonder how long it will last."

"I don't know. I don't remember anyone mentioning snow in the forecast for this weekend. It will probably melt by the time you guys leave on the bus tomorrow. It didn't look like it was sticking to the roads."

Lexi announces, "I'm going to walk back to the house with Patrick. I may see you guys at the game tomorrow, but if not, Merry Christmas."

We say goodnight to Lexi and Patrick then Lane and I wander back inside with Bella and Jack as the end-of-term party continues into the night. After a while we decide to call it a night.

Lane walks with us back to Phi Mu. Inside the foyer, he leans down and kisses me on the nose. "What time do you want

185

me to come by to pick you up tomorrow? I don't want to rush you, if you still need to pack."

"I'll get up to see Bella off. I think I can be packed up and ready to leave by noon."

"That sounds perfect. We'll get to the stadium in plenty of time before the game. We'll even be able to enjoy eating dinner after we arrive. I'll text you in the morning."

Lane kisses me goodnight while running his hands up the back of my sweater. A wave of butterflies washes over me. I say goodnight and smile dreamily as I walk to my room. I open the door and see that Bella's already in her Pj's. I quickly get ready for bed and drift off to sleep dreaming of snow, ghosts, and Christmas.

29
#Epic

I wake up to the sound of Bella zipping her suitcase. "Good morning," I say, sitting up yawning and stretching.

"Hey, I didn't mean to wake you."

"No, that's okay. I should be up now anyway. I need to finish packing and get dressed."

"I'm going to head down for breakfast," she says.

"I'll come, too, and help you carry your bags."

Over breakfast we chat about the travel plans everyone has over the break. Lexi's roommate Jessica tells us she'll be in France for Christmas. That totally beats Atlanta for sure, but honestly, I love being home for Christmas.

After breakfast, I help Bella and Lexi to the door with their stuff before going back to the room to finish packing my bags.

I look around the room to make sure everything is neat and tidy. Just as I place the room key into my backpack, I get a text from Lane telling me he's on his way. I grab my bags, throw my backpack on, and bolt down the stairs. I hug a few of my Phi sisters, good-bye and wish them a Merry Christmas on my way out the door.

Outside the snow is mostly melted, but there are still remnants of snow on the roof of the Alpha Delta Pi house next door. Lane parks along the curb and takes my bags from me and puts them into his trunk. The radio is playing softly. He leans in and kisses me at the first traffic light we stop at. As we're driving, I send Mom a text, so she knows I'm on the way to the game with a friend. I still haven't told anyone except Lauren that Lane and I are dating. I probably need to mention him to my parents over the Christmas holidays. Mom only knows that I had a date to the Undertaker's Ball with a guy named Lane.

"Do you want to drive through Starbucks?" Lane asks.

"Sure, I'll have a mint hot chocolate." I dig my Starbucks gift card out of my bag and try to hand it to him, but he just kisses my hand instead.

We stop for gas next then make our way onto the interstate toward Birmingham and Atlanta.

I'm elated to spend this time with Lane. We talk about snow skiing and what he thinks he may get for Christmas. He asks about my sister and my parents.

"I need to tell my parents about you over the holidays."

"I'd love to be able to meet them soon."

"If we end up in New Orleans for the National Championship game, you'll be able to meet them there."

He laughs and says, "Good. You won't hide me forever."

"No, I'd never do that." I take his hand in mine, giving it a squeeze.

"There's a private party after the game tonight. Have you said anything to your parents about what time you'd be coming home?"

"Not really. They know I'm on the way to the game. They'll be watching it at home with friends. I think Lauren has friends coming over to hang out tonight. She may even have some friends sleep over. They know that it'll be late when I get home."

"But do you think you can tell them you're sleeping over with the friend that you're riding to the game with?"

I look over at him with a big question mark written all over my face but don't answer.

"Since the game will end around eleven thirty and there's a private party I want to take you to afterward, it might be best if you tell them you're sleeping over at a friend's house."

"Uhm, where will I actually be sleeping?"

"We won't be sleeping. The party will go until the wee hours of the morning. I can have you home before sunrise, but it just might be best to have your parents think you're sleeping over at a friend's house."

"Oh, right, okay, I can do that. I should text Lauren and let her know the plan. She can leave the basement door unlocked for me. I can text Mom and tell her Alexis will drive me home early on Sunday. I'll be asleep in my room by the time anyone wakes up."

An hour or so later, we pull into the security lot at the Mercedes Benz stadium, and Lane pulls out a pass. We park and have direct access into the new sleek stadium. The stadium is massive and impressive. We go through the tunnel gates and pop out into a restaurant decorated with mirrors, TV's, chrome lights, and shiny marble. Lane takes my hand as we walk to find a table. Once we're seated a waiter arrives and places menus in front of us. Lane is texting with someone while I sit and enjoy the moment. I text Mom and Lauren to let them know we're at the stadium.

When our food arrives so do a couple of Lane's fraternity brothers. He introduces me to James, Brock, and their dates Christina and Erin. They tell us they'll see us later and wander off. A few minutes later a few more guys that know Lane show up. He introduces me to them and their dates. I notice that they're Sigma Nu's, and I recognize the girls from the Tri Delta house. They sit with us, order food and hang out. After we finish eating, we walk to the railing that overlooks the field. It is so cool being able to walk out at field level. When I hear the band playing, I look up to see Bella, Lexi, the Crimsonettes and Big Al. The cheerleaders are down on the field stunting and tumbling. The stadium is starting to fill up.

We make our way to our section, and I wave to a few Phi Mu sisters. The Cheerleaders are lined up in front of the player's entrance, and the excitement is riveting. Smoke explodes from the entrance, and the cheerleaders take off down the field with

189

Bama flags waving, and Big Al is jumping up and down to the band playing the fight song. We stand waving and cheering as the team runs out onto the field behind Coach. We're playing Florida for the SEC Championship, and they look like they have almost as many fans as we do.

At halftime our Million Dollar Band performs first. We watch them exhibit an impressive half time show. Afterward, Lane and I decide to walk down and hang out along the field. It's also easy access to the restaurants and the bathrooms. We take a few selfies and I text them to Lauren. She responds. *Wow, ur right down on the field, how cool.*

Our seats are on the lower level, and we can walk right up to the field.

Lauren texts back. *I've got friends sleeping over tonight. I'll unlock the basement. We'll be staying down there. What time do u think u will get home?*

5 a.m.

Stay out of trouble. I send her a thumbs up emoji.

The game is tied at the start of the fourth quarter. Everyone in the stands, the players and coaches hold up four fingers announcing that we'll own the fourth quarter. Our QB throws to a receiver a clean catch. He runs all the way to end zone before he's tackled, but he manages to get the ball over the line. The extra point is good, and we're now up by seven. The gators don't have good field position. With only a few minutes left on the clock, Florida's QB throws the ball high and long, but Bama intercepts it.

With seventeen-seconds left on the clock we line up and take a knee. The clock runs out and the ceiling in the stadium opens. Fireworks go off, with confetti falling from the sky. Lane and I are jumping up and down, and the chant all across the stadium by thousands of Bama fans becomes louder and louder, "Hey, Gators, we just beat the hell outta you! Ramma Jamma Yella Hammer Giv'em Hell, Alabama." The crowds continue the chant, while the students and band rush out on the field to congratulate the players. I find Bella and Lexi, and we run up and hug each other. Alabama has just won another SEC championship game. Press, newspapers, television stations and reporters are on the field in droves. Lane and I are covered in confetti and filled with joy.

We watch with anticipation as Coach, dripping with Gatorade, takes the stage for his speech, flanked by players in the starting lineup. I film the speech live on my Instagram as confetti continues to fall from the ceiling. The fireworks end, and the ceiling closes. Bama fans remain in the stadium for the SEC trophy presentation and speeches from the coaches. Bella, Lane, Lexi and I move off the field and over to the side and watch the presentations.

When the players finally head to the locker room, Bella and Lexi say they're going to walk back to their hotel to change. I tell them I'm going to hang out with Lane tonight. I hug them both and we say our goodbyes.

Lane takes my hand and asks, "Ready for the party of a lifetime?"

I smile and say, "I hope so."

He laughs and says, "Let's go."

We get on the elevator and Lane presses a special button. He pulls out a key card to insert into the elevator that takes us to a private entrance. We get off the elevator and walk into a beautiful room with marble floors and dim lighting. I hear music playing, a song by Migos called "Culture" is turned up loud. We continue walking, and I see it really is Migos in person. My knees buckle. I almost hit the floor. I grab Lane by the arm and scream "Oh My God! Migos are actually here!"

Lane smiles at me and places his hand at the small of my back as we move into the party. I see more people that I recognize from earlier tonight who spoke to Lane and me during dinner. It looks like only twenty-five people are here. But there's a full bar, a full buffet, and a few of Migos' entourage hanging out with us, too.

The bar and buffet are set up overlooking the field, so we can see cleanup crews cleaning up the confetti. From the reflections in the glass that overlook the field I can tell that Lane and I still have confetti in our hair. Lane asks if I want a tour. We grab a few drinks and walk up a marble staircase onto a balcony that overlooks the main floor. From above I can see people dancing and taking selfies with Migos in the background. We turn around to find a huge room with glass sky lights. There are plush sofas, chairs, a gas fireplace and a large animal rug over a beautiful tile floor. Off to the right is a bedroom with a king-sized bed and a door open to a large bathroom. I walk into the bathroom and marvel at the size. "This bathroom is as big as my bedroom," I say in awe.

The floor and the walls are marble. There is a huge crystal chandelier hanging from the center of the ceiling. The ornamental piece of the bathroom is a huge jacuzzi tub. Directly behind the tub is a wall of floor to ceiling windows. Lane follows me into the bathroom.

"Is this where Coach is staying?"

He laughs and says, "No, it's the owner's suite."

"Does he know that we're in here? I mean I guess someone does, since we had private access to the private entrance."

"Yes, he knows that there's a private party in here tonight."

"How in the world are we able to be in here for a private party with famous Atlanta rappers?"

"My fraternity brother James' grandfather founded the Zaxby's restaurant chain. Migos are big fans of Zaxby's. They get free food, other perks and were paid well to do a private show. James' grandfather is also friends with the Falcons owner. He and his grandfather helped set up this special celebratory event tonight. They probably knew Alabama would win."

We walk over to the window. Lane pulls me close, and we gaze out at the beautiful view. Looking out the window, we can see for miles the impressive nighttime skyline of Atlanta.

"This is the most breathtaking view."

192

Lane whispers, "This is what I've wanted to do all night, have you all to myself, somewhere romantic and elegant."

He leans down, we kiss, and I'm lost forgetting about everything. Our kisses become more passionate, but we're interrupted by a girl named Haley.

"Hey, y'all, someone's in the bathroom downstairs so I came up here."

Lane and I walk out onto the balcony that overlooks the main room.

"Let's dance and see if we can get pictures with all three of the guys when they take a break."

We dance to "Pipe it up" before they take a break. One of their entourage puts on a soundtrack. Lane and I introduce ourselves, and we get several pictures with Quavo, Offset and Takeoff. Someone hands them drinks, and they walk out to the seats overlooking the field just beyond the wall of windows.

"Wow, we just met Migos. This is the best night ever. I feel like I'm in a dream," I say, giddy and silly.

Lane and I walk over to the couch in front of the fireplace and sit for a while. I snuggle up to him and put my head on his shoulder.

"This is the perfect private party and the perfect way to end a perfect game day."

He leans down, kisses my cheek, and whispers, "I am going to miss the hell out of you these next few weeks."

"What time does your plane leave tomorrow?"

"Around two. After I drop you off, I'm staying with James, he doesn't live too far away. I'll get a little sleep and leave my car at his house. He'll drop me off at the airport at one."

I pull out my phone to check the time then I scroll through pictures from tonight. I want to post the one of Lane and me with Migos. Lane tells me not to tag the location. He tells me to use a different location for the photo and reminds me this is a secret private event and not to mention where the party took place. I nod and say, "Okay" then add my caption for our photo with Migos. "BAMA made the plays, and MIGOS made our night."

#bama #rolltide #SECchamps I let Lane look at it. Since he approves, I post it.

Migos comes back from their break and start up a new song. All the lights go out and it's just candlelight, the lights on the Christmas tree and the glow of the fireplace. We stand and slow dance to the next song before they break into "Out Yo Way." Their last song picks up speed, and they end the night with "Bad and Boujee." A couple of police officers show up and escort them and their entourage through the private elevator entrance. When they let the cleaning crew in, we decide it's time to leave. We say good night to the others and walk down to the parking garage. I give Lane my address, and he puts it into his GPS.

We pull up to my house at four thirty in the morning, and all is quiet. Lane kills the engine and the lights. Trying to be stealthy, we parked along the street instead of the driveway. He pops the trunk and helps me carry my luggage through the gate into the backyard. The basement door under the deck is unlocked, just like Lauren promised. We step inside the living room and see two girls asleep on the couch. One is Lauren and three more are asleep atop air mattresses on the floor. We tiptoe upstairs to the main floor.

I whisper to Lane, "I can manage the bags the rest of the way."

"No way, I'm this far into your house, I'm going all the way into your room."

We try to be as quiet as we can, but I'm on the verge of busting out laughing. We get to the top of the stairs with only a few minor creaking sounds. I hear the dog come running out of Mom and Dad's room. I quickly grab him up in my arms to keep him quiet. I tiptoe into my room and Lane follows me. He sets the bags down, and I put the dog on my bed. Lane and I both try to suppress our giggles as he pulls me in, one hand around my waist, the other grips the back of my head. I tilt my head back, and close my eyes as our lips meet, soft and gentle, before becoming hungry and passionate. All I want to do is continue to

194

kiss him for a million, trillion years, but I know he has to drive to his fraternity brother's house then later get on a plane to Aspen.

I whisper, "I'm going to miss you so much. I'm glad I got to spend all day and night with you."

"I wish I could stay in your room all night," he whispers while lightly kissing my neck.

He leans in and kisses me again, his tongue softly meeting mine. Not wanting him to leave, I finally pull away and walk him back down the stairs, back to the basement and out to the patio under the deck. We kiss again and whisper goodnight. I watch as he walks out the gate. I lock the door and quickly run back to my room and watch from the window as his car drives away.

I pull out my favorite Pj pants, slip them on and crawl under the covers. My dog Micky crawls under the covers with me and snuggles down. I plug my phone into my charger then pat Micky on the head and whisper, "Wow, I've just had the best day of my life."

30
#Jomonotfomo

Rolling over feeling groggy and totally incoherent I think I hear people up moving about making breakfast and talking. Micky starts to bark at the door, so I open it to let him out. I look at my phone. It's only seven thirty. Seeing a text from Lane from an hour ago makes me smile. *I'm at James' house about to go to sleep. I miss u already.* Sighing with contentment, I fall back to sleep. I'm awakened again, this time it's Lauren standing over me. I ask her what time it is.

"Nine," she says.

"I'm staying in bed," I say, pulling the covers higher.

"Okay, I told Mom you were asleep. She still wants me to ask if you're going to church with us."

"Tell her no, please."

"I will. But I saw you posted a picture with Migos."

I've got my eyes closed, trying to go back to sleep, so I'm not looking at Lauren. I know she's hovering over me. I can feel it. She's probably standing over my bed, wringing her hands, looking like the Grinch about to steal Christmas.

"I'll tell you about it later," I say, angry and annoyed.

When she realizes I'm peeved she leaves. Later that afternoon, Mom wakes me.

"Bex, everyone is back from lunch," she says, peering into my room. "We brought you something to eat, if you want to come downstairs."

I mumble, "Thank you, I'll be down in a few minutes," from deep under the covers.

After lunch I wander back to my room to shower. Lauren walks in and asks if I want to go Christmas shopping with her.

"Sure, give me fifteen minutes."

We have three cars, and the one Lauren drives now is the car our parents bought me when I got my driver's license. After I went off to college Lauren started driving it to school, and my parents didn't really think I needed a car at college. I think they thought at eighteen I was too young to be driving myself back and forth to Tuscaloosa, but I'm hoping for a car for Christmas. I let Lauren drive, since I feel like it's her car anyway.

As soon as we get in Lauren looks at me with a wicked gleam and says, "Spill, you and Lane were partying with Migos last night?"

"Yes, but you have to swear to me that you won't tell anyone where the party was. It was a private party in a secret location."

"Like how private?"

"There were only about twenty-five people there, including Migos and their entourage."

"Start the car or I'm going to drive," I say, motioning with my hands to get going.

She starts the car, but her mouth is still hanging open.

"Look, Lauren, I'm serious. I'm not supposed to tell anyone where the party was."

"But I'm your sister. You can trust me not to say anything."

"You can't tell Mom and Dad, you can't tell your friends, you can't tell Brian, no one and nobody. And that goes for as long as you live. I feel like you need to swear on a Bible or something."

"Well, if you look in the console, you'll see my Bible and my notebook."

I open the console, and sure enough, it's there. I take it out and hold it in my lap. When we get to the parking deck, I hold up the Bible and Lauren puts her left hand on top and holds her right hand in the air.

"Swear you'll never tell anyone what I'm about to say, and if someone asks about it, tell them that I was at someone's home in Buckhead."

Lauren nods and says, "I swear to keep your secret forever."

"We were in the owner's suite inside Mercedes Benz stadium, and it was just a few of Lane's fraternity brothers and their dates from the secret society."

Lauren looks like she's about to combust. "Secret society, private party with Migos, inside a suite at the Mercedes Benz stadium. OMG, this is just like in *Gilmore Girls* when Rory was dating Logan at Yale, and they were in that secret society and had crazy secret parties."

"Yeah, kind of, but this is real life."

"Your sophomore year is turning out to be more than a little interesting."

I roll my eyes at her as I step out of the car.

Christmas cheer is in the air as we walk around marveling over the enchanting decorations and the skaters on the ice rink. We go inside all our favorite stores. Lauren finds something for one of her best friends and something for Mom. We go into Vineyard Vines, and even though I know everything in the store looks like Lane, I feel like there's nothing here that would seem special enough for a gift.

"I just don't know what to get Lane," I say, a little flustered.

Lauren is combing through men's shirts but turns to look at me. "What does he like?"

"Well, he would like everything in here, I think, but none of its unique enough. What do you get someone who seems to have everything?" I ask, not really expecting her to answer.

"I know that's a hard one. I'm sure you'll think of something." Lauren gives me a knowing look, with a hint of drama in her voice. "I can think of something he hasn't had that he would *love* as a gift."

She's still giving me that look with a smirk on her face. I figure out what her meaning is, and I slap her butt.

"Lauren, I can't believe you," I say, a bit embarrassed. "Your mind is in the gutter, and it needs to stay out of there. You know I'm not like that, and you shouldn't even be thinking that way."

"It was supposed to be a joke. I was just trying to make light of the situation."

I exhale with a loud huff. "You better be joking."

We continue shopping, and I find a golf shirt for Dad. Lauren picks out a flannel for Brian. We wait on our packages to be wrapped then leave Vineyard Vines to walk to the KSO store. I find a gift for Mom and a little something for Lexi and Bella. On the way home, I get a text from Lane, saying he's arrived at his house in Aspen. I text back a heart emoji, and *I miss u.*

He texts back a kissy face emoji, and *I miss u more.* I almost start to cry. I tear up a little, and Lauren asks if I'm okay.

"Yes, just missing Lane. He just texted me that he's at his house in Aspen."

We stuff our shopping bags into the car and head home. Walking inside, the aroma of fresh popcorn and pizza is welcoming. Mom saved one of our three Christmas trees for us to decorate as a family. We have one tree in the living room, one in the foyer, and a tree in the basement. Lauren and I each have trees in our rooms. The tree Mom left us to decorate together is the tree in the foyer that she calls *the travel tree.* This is the one with ornaments from a lot of the places we've stayed, vacationed, or visited over the years. Lauren and I grab a slice of pizza and wander over to the tree to work on decorating it.

Mom hands me the latest ornament, a mermaid with the words Cumberland Island printed across the mermaid's tail. Dad turns on Christmas music, and we're all in a festive mood as we decorate the tree. I love remembering each place we've visited as we reminisce, talking about each ornament. We each share something fun about a trip as we pick up an ornament from the box. We have lots of ornaments from Disney World. Lauren says she wants to go back one more time before she leaves for college.

By ten o'clock everyone but the dog and I have gone to bed. Since I slept so late, I'm not feeling sleepy, so I turn on the TV to see what's on. I flip through the channels and something catches my eye. It's a documentary about JFK, Jr., and it shows him and Carolyn Bessette on their wedding day. They're walking out of the little church on Cumberland Island. That snags my attention. I hit pause and replay it. I watch the entire documentary. I'm intrigued with the magazine he started, his life, his fun-loving carefree personality, like kayaking in the Hudson with his best friend at midnight. The fact that he got married on Cumberland Island in the little church, the very same place I was at just last month, all of this is fascinating. An idea for a story hits me like a ton of bricks. I run up to my room, turn on my computer and I start writing my story for Professor Brigg's class.

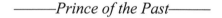

———*Prince of the Past*———

It's been almost twelve years since we left the monastery in Cadaques and arrived in the coastal city of Valencia, Spain. The monks helped me track down my great aunt's family and connected us with her daughter, a doctor at Santa Maria De Ripoll. I can't believe Jackson (Joaquim, as he's known here in Spain) will be eighteen in a few weeks. Watching him now as he maneuvers his sailboat toward the dock, he looks so handsome like his father. I'm starting to feel melancholy with his graduation approaching. It's time that I tell him his story, the story of his parents, and the story of his miraculous birth. I know he vaguely remembers the lessons at the monastery before we arrived here when he was six, but he knows nothing of his birth. The monks kept us safe and stored our papers and detailed documents provided by the hospital in Stockholm until we were ready to move. The monks provided us with new papers, so we could blend in once we arrived in Valencia. Having found the daughter of a distant relative, who is also a doctor, has been a blessing for us, and I owe her my life.

Joaquim walks off the dock toward me, and we decide to walk to the plaza and find a cafe for dinner. It's late March, and the burned statues from Las Fallas (St. Joseph's Day) are still smoldering. As we pass several burned Ninots from the festival, I notice one in the image of Donald Trump. It's been nice these eighteen years being in a place that's calm, relaxing and safe. Spring is a beautiful time here in Valencia. The delicate smells from the orange blossoms fill the air, and the ocean is more enjoyable. We sit at a table outside at Taverna La Mora. I look at Joaquim and say, "Estoy muy orgullosa de ti." I love you and I'm so proud of you."

"Gracias, Mama."

"Es hora de decirte algo muy importante sobre tu vida y tu futuro." "It's time to tell you something very important about your life and your future."

"Si, Mama."

"Todo lo que he hecho en mi vida ha sido protegerte. Everything I've ever done has been to protect you. Ahora que cumples 18 anos, te confieso algo que podra determina tu futuro. Haz con ello lo creas oportuno. Now that you will turn eighteen in a few weeks, you will take this information and use it wisely to decide your future. Te voy a contar mi historia verdadera, en ingles. I'm going to tell you my story in English."

The phones were always ringing, I was always busy, but the best kind of busy. New York City never sleeps and a lot of the time neither did I. I worked for Jack Kent, Jr, as his personal assistant right before and during the time he started his political and pop culture magazine, The American Spirit. I did everything from plan his private wedding on a secluded island off the coast of Georgia, to telling him when to write a Thank you note. I was best friends with his wife Kaitlyn, as well as Mark, who was his right-hand man and co-founder of the magazine. The press, fans, and crazies were always following him and tracking his every move. I had to answer phone calls from people trying to find him

201

and open letters from crazy stalkers. I protected him as much as I could. Kaitlyn hated the press and the lack of privacy more than anything in the world. But Jack had grown up in the spotlight, he was used to it, it was part of who he was and a staple in his life.

When I met him, I was a secretary, but after I had worked for him for two and a half years, I became much more important. I loved being able to get into the hottest restaurants in New York, wear the best clothes, and work for one of the most famous and adored men in the world. He was American royalty and adored by most. But some say his family had a curse. His father had been murdered as well as one of his uncles.

Six months after he and Kaitlyn were married, she hired extra security whenever they were together. It was her way of trying her best to deal with the press, publicity and cameras. One evening Jack stayed late to work at the office with some of the staff, and Kaitlyn had the entire security follow her home. Alone in the apartment, she began making dinner and asked one of the guards to help her open something. A sniper bullet came through the large window in the kitchen, hitting the guard in the ear, but the bullet ended up lodged in Kaitlyn's head. She collapsed, and the guards went into action, calling in the police, closing the blinds and turning off all the lights.

Jack was on his way home when he got the call, and I met him at the hospital. Kaitlyn was in a coma, and one of the doctors realized she was six weeks pregnant. No one knew about the pregnancy. Jack told me that they had not planned to tell anyone, including family for another two months. The doctor suggested they fly Kaitlyn to Sweden to a special hospital, where he knew they could save the baby. The grave news about not being able to save Kaitlyn but at least save the baby had us all on the verge of hysterics. Jack said he didn't want anyone to know about the baby, and he didn't want anyone to know we were going to Sweden. The press had already gathered outside the hospital, and the news reports on TV were saying Kaitlyn had been shot by a sniper bullet meant for Jack. There had been no other news, and no one was going to leak anything to the press. The floor we were on was locked down and heavily guarded, so no one knew what was happening but us.

At three in the morning, a helicopter landed on the roof of the hospital, and Jack, I, two doctors and a nurse helped wheel Kaitlyn into the helicopter. We flew to Washington DC and boarded a special Air Force plane to Sweden. We flew directly to the hospital, where a staff of doctors and nurses rushed Kaitlyn into a secure room. The doctor in charge met us in the hallway and took us to a private room to talk. He explained that he had done womb transplants that were successful, and in order to save the baby a surrogate would be needed. A healthy woman who had never had children would be pumped with hormones to shock her body into thinking it was pregnant. After seventy-two hours of IV drugs, a surgical procedure would take place to implant the fetus into the donor. The surrogate would have to remain in the hospital until the child was born. Jack told me I needed to be the surrogate.

"We know Kaitlyn won't recover." Tears ran down his cheeks. "We will have to make a tough decision at some point. The baby needs to be saved by any means possible."

Jack broke down sobbing uncontrollably. When he hit the floor, a nurse helped him up and sat him in a chair next to me. I leaned down in front of him. I knew what I needed to do and what I needed to say to Jack.

"Of course. I will do it. I will be the surrogate. I will help save your baby."

Joaquim has tears running down his cheeks, and I move my chair over and put my arms around him and hold him tight. I continue my story.

I'm immediately hooked up to IV's, and drugs are pumped into my system. After seventy-two hours, I'm prepped for surgery. As soon as the baby is transplanted into my womb, Kaitlyn, the two doctors, the nurse and Jack board a private plane back to Washington D.C. where they will get on a helicopter back to the hospital in New York. No one knows they left, and the American press has gotten little word except that Kaitlyn has been in a *coma for several days. Jack tells me he will be back as soon as he can. I tell him not to worry about anything. He leaves and I never see him again. Their plane crashes into the Atlantic Ocean off the coast of Virginia. The bodies of Jack, Kaitlyn, the doctor and nurse are found. I am never found. My body reportedly is lost at sea or eaten by sharks.*

I give birth to a beautiful healthy boy. I name him Jackson, close to the name of his father. The doctors take care of the birth certificate and document all the procedures that were done to save this precious baby. The information is stored in a secure locked waterproof box. The baby, the secure box with important papers and I are whisked away to a monastery in the north part of Spain. After six years, I am reunited with a second cousin named Carmen Tous, and you know the rest of the story. Joaquim has stopped crying and asks, "Why did you wait so long to tell me?"

"I wanted you to be old enough to make your own decisions. I couldn't go back to New York. The press and the lifestyle I would have led there would have been too much for me to handle. I had no way of knowing if the sniper had been caught. I didn't want to live in fear for my life or for yours. I wanted only to keep you safe and protected. I wanted to be able to tell you when you were old enough to decide for yourself what you want to do with the information. I have all the proper documentation from the doctors in Stockholm. You can now choose to go to America, find your aunts, uncles, and cousins. Share with them what you know and who you really are, or you can keep it a secret forever. You look so much like your father."

"Mama vamos a la Iglesia, y hablemos con Don Jose, para que nos ayude decidir sobre el futuro. Come with me to church now, Mama. Let's find Don Jose, he will know how to guide me about deciding the future. Quiero hablarle sobre el camino despues de la graduacion. I want to know what path to take after my graduation."

We leave the cafe and walk to Catedral de Valencia. We light candles, and we begin to pray.

204

It takes me two hours to write the story. I re-read and double check for any misspelled words. I check the word count and it is over 1,000 so it falls into the range for the assignment. I save my document and turn off my computer. I fall asleep dreaming about working at a famous publishing house in New York.

The next morning my phone rings me awake. I pop up, grab my phone off the nightstand and notice it's Lane calling me. I answer with a sleepy sounding . . . "Hey you."

"Good morning, beautiful."

"I just woke up when the phone rang."

"Good for you, sleeping in today."

"I stayed up really late writing my paper. Have you finished yours?"

"No, I need to get started on that. I'm sorry I was so short with you on the phone yesterday. I had just gotten to the house here in Aspen after the plane ride and an almost four-hour car ride. I was totally beat."

"I understand. I was so tired yesterday that I slept almost all day. Then I wasn't tired last night so I ended up flipping through channels on TV and saw something that gave me an idea for a story. I wrote it in about two hours."

"That's awesome, Bex."

"I want you to read it first before I submit it, just to get your opinion, especially since you're an English major."

I hear Lane laugh. "Email it to me today. I'll read it tonight. I'm about to hit the ski slopes, but I wanted to talk to you first. It's still fairly early here, a few hours behind Atlanta time."

After we hang up, I open my computer and email him my story file just as Lauren barges into my room.

"Good, you're awake." She hands me the sports section of the newspaper. She points to a photo. I begin reading.

"Alabama to play Oklahoma in the College Football National Championship Game in New Orleans on January first."

"Yay." I squeal. "I need to call Bella."

"Mom just got off the phone with Bella's mom about the plans to go down there. She said we'll leave here on the 27th and stay at their house until the 30th. Bella checks into the hotel at two that day. The game is set for seven the evening of the first, and we're staying at a hotel near where the band and the team will stay called Hotel Monteleone. Mom said that Bella's parents are staying there too. Two nights at their house and three nights at the hotel."

"That sounds perfect. Thanks for the update, but I'm still calling Bella."

Bella doesn't answer, so I leave her a voice mail. I go down to the basement and pop my DVD into the Xbox and practice my routine for an hour. When my phone rings, I notice it's Bella. The first thing she says to me is, "You and Lane met Migos?"

"We got to meet them at a party with one of his fraternity brothers. It was really cool."

Before hanging up, we talk about what she's been doing the past few days of Christmas vacation and how excited we are about the National Championship game.

Lauren comes down to the basement and asks if I want to see a movie at Phipps Plaza with her and Brian.

"Sure." I ask, "Which one?"

"We want to see the new Star Wars movie at six thirty, but we want to do a little more Christmas shopping first, if that's okay. We'll go to Brian's house and ride to Phipps with him. He told me to come by around three."

A few hours later we pull up to Brian's beautiful house in Buckhead. Brian's Mom answers the door and ushers us into the kitchen for some drinks and snacks. Brian pops in and gives Lauren a hug. I'm thrilled that they're still into each other after meeting randomly on Cumberland Island last month. We leave in Brian's car, and it's a short drive to Phipps Plaza from his house. Brian says something to me about meeting Migos, and I act cool.

"Yeah, Lane has fraternity brothers here in Atlanta and one of them has family with connections to Migos." I'm super nonchalant about it, and he drops the topic.

I love going to Phipps. It's such a treat to see all the fancy stores. Something catches my eye when we walk past the Gucci store.

"Hey, guys, do you mind if we pop in here?"

I see a scarf that might be nice for Lane. I also notice some loafers that look similar to the one's I've seen him wear. I look at the price tag $530.00.

"Wow," I utter a little too loudly, and Lauren and Brian turn and look at me.

"Are you looking for something for Lane?"

"I think he would like this scarf," I say, picking it up off the shelf.

"It's over $200.00. That's a lot to spend, but it's your money."

"I know, but I have a pet sitting job for the next four days, and I'll make it back. I'm going to get it and see if they'll wrap it."

After our shopping spree, we go to the movie then back to Brian's house. We follow him to his basement. It's really cool, with exposed brick walls and floors. He and Lauren plop down onto a large leather sofa and get snuggly. Brian turns on the stereo speakers and asks us what music we want to listen to. He chooses John Mayer. I decide to sit at the bar and scroll through my Instagram. After about an hour, I am bored. "Hey guys, it's late and probably time for us to go."

Brian and Lauren look over at me. Lauren eventually says, "Yeah, I guess you're right."

Brian stands. "I'll walk you guys upstairs."

He pulls Lauren up with him and walks us upstairs to the front door.

I tell Brian bye, walk out and sit in the car while Lauren spends the next ten minutes saying goodbye.

31
#Christmas

On Christmas Eve, we go to church for a special candlelight service and enjoy dinner at one of our favorite restaurants with our grandparents. When we get home, Mom asks Lauren and me about plans for the morning.

"Do you girls want to sleep late?"

I look at Lauren. She looks back at me and says, "Bex, do you want to sleep in the basement and watch Hallmark Christmas movies?"

"Christmas movies, hot chocolate, popcorn, and let's plan on sleeping in tomorrow. It's Christmas Pj time," I say, running up the stairs to change.

Lauren and I make popcorn and hot chocolate then look at Netflix for the first Christmas movie we want to watch. Just before the movie starts my phone rings. I answer and tell Lauren to pause the movie. She makes an annoyed sound and starts texting with someone.

"Hey, babe," Lane says when I answer.

"Hey, sweetie," I reply back.

"What are you doing?"

"Lauren and I are just about to watch some Christmas movies. We made popcorn and hot chocolate."

"That sounds like a lot of fun. We've got a full house with some munchkins waiting on Santa to arrive. We're hoping they're settled in for the night. I'll have to go up and help set gifts under the tree in a little while, but first I wanted to call you."

"I'm so glad you did. Merry Christmas Eve."

"Merry Christmas Eve to you, too. I read your paper last night, and its good. It's got one heck of a cliff hanger."

"Yeah, I wanted to leave a little mystery."

"It sounds like you wrote about JFK, Jr., his wife and his magazine, but changed all the names."

"Wow, how did you figure that out? You are super smart." He laughs.

"Do you remember the day we met? I mentioned that I read a lot of history."

"I remember. How could I forget meeting you? I tripped over you. Do you think it's good enough to submit for the assignment?"

"Yes, definitely. I have to finish mine soon. I've started but need to finish up."

"What's your story about?"

"It's about a boy who goes sailing without permission, gets caught in a storm and is rescued by the coast guard."

"Oh, wow, is it a true story?"

"Yes, actually it is."

"Sounds scary."

"It was at the time."

"Uh, oh, were you the boy who went sailing without permission and had to be rescued?"

"Guilty," Lane says. I laugh.

"I hear my aunt and my mom coming down here to find me," he says "They're probably ready to start putting all the gifts under the tree. I should go."

"Wait just a sec. I guess you saw that Alabama is playing in the National Championship game?"

"Yes, two of my cousins are going to fly down with me. Where did you book your hotel?"

"Hotel Monteleone, it's close to where the team and band will stay. We'll be at Bella's house for two nights, then three nights at the hotel."

"I'll see if I can get a reservation there, too. Merry Christmas, baby," he says before hanging up.

Christmas is my favorite. Not that we're kids anymore, but just being home with family and all that entails feels magical. Lauren and I fall asleep after watching two Christmas movies.

When Lauren and I finally wake the next morning, we run upstairs to find Mom and Dad in the kitchen making pancakes and bacon.

"Merry Christmas, girls," Dad says, putting pancakes onto a plate. "How many pancakes do you want?" he asks.

"Three, please."

"Look," Lauren says, using chocolate chips and strawberries to make a face on her pancake. We giggle then I squirt whipped cream along the top of my pancakes making it look like a Santa hat. After breakfast we move to the living room to open gifts. Dad hands us our stockings to open first. I take out a small box with a bow and open it. Inside is a key to a car. I scream and jump up off the couch. Mom and Dad are beaming.

"It's in the driveway." Mom and Dad start walking toward the door.

Lauren and I run out to see a red Mazda 3 hatchback. I get inside, and it smells wonderful. I love the new car smell.

"It's used but in great condition and only has 50,000 miles," Dad says, pointing to the dash.

I squeal, "I love it."

"Well, you'll get to drive yourself back to Tuscaloosa after the break."

"We're both so proud of the young lady you've become and the success you've had so far in college. We thought you deserved your own car at school," Mom says smiling at me.

I'm gushing, beaming, and squeezing Mom and Dad with joy.

Later that evening Brian and our grandparents come over for a family Christmas meal. After dinner I tell Mom and Dad that I have another pet sitting job in the neighborhood.

"I'm taking my new car. I'll be back in about an hour," I yell, walking out the door.

When I get back, Lauren and Brian are in the basement exchanging gifts and watching a movie. I go upstairs to hang in my room while texting Bella and Lane. I tell them both about my car and how excited I am about it. Lane texts me back that he got a new car for Christmas, too. He says he will call me in a few days, since tonight is a little crazy with all the family, kids and stuff.

The next day Lauren and I head to the mall in my new Mazda for all the after Christmas sales. We want to hit our favorite stores and spend some of the Christmas money from our grandparents. When we get home four hours later, Mom has taken down lots of the Christmas decorations and is working on taking ornaments off the main tree. I go upstairs and work on packing for our trip to New Orleans and sort out my new outfits. I turn on my speaker and play "Unbelievers" by Vampire Weekend. As I go through clothes and continue to pack, my phone rings. I look at the screen and see that it's Lane.

"Hey, whatcha doing?" he asks when I answer.

"Hey, just working on some laundry and packing. How about you?"

"Actually the same."

"What time is your flight?"

"We leave here on the 30th around nine and our flight is at two. We should be at the hotel by six thirty."

"That's great. We should be there by then, too. Were you able to get a room at Hotel Monteleone?"

"Yes. It's a small room but it should work for the three of us guys."

"I think Mom and Dad booked a suite for us. We're leaving tomorrow to drive to Bella's home in Covington."

"How long is the drive?"

"Just over six hours from here, and they're a little less than an hour away from downtown New Orleans. I'm super excited to go but not looking forward to the long drive. That reminds me, you have a birthday in a couple of days."

"Yes, I think my cousins, my parents and my aunts have some type of surprise planned for that day or night, not really sure what yet, but they're up to something. My best birthday gift will be the next night when I see you again."

That makes me smile. I sit on my bed and lean my head back on the pillows. "I got you something. It's kinda a birthday/Christmas gift."

"You didn't have to do that."

"I saw it, and it made me think of you. I wanted to get you something."

"I know I'll love it."

Mom pops her head into my room. "Make sure you're ready to leave by ten in the morning, goodnight."

I nod in Mom's direction and hold up my hand for her to wait until I'm off the phone.

"Lane, my mom just walked in. I'll text you tomorrow while I'm in the car for the long drive. I'll talk to you later. Have a great birthday. I can't wait to see you."

I set the phone down, focusing on Mom. "I need to stop at a house down the street so I can finish up my pet sitting job in the morning. The family returns tomorrow afternoon."

"Do you want to take Micky to Camp Bow Wow before you do that?"

"Not really, can you ask Lauren?"

She closes the door, and I hear her go into Lauren's room. I get ready for bed, and Micky jumps up and snuggles up next to me.

32

#Rideordie

After five hours in the car, I am about to scream. I've texted with Lexi, Bella, and Lane for hours. Lauren is watching Netflix on her phone. Bella and I plan to watch the last three episodes of season one of *Stranger Things* when we get to her house tonight, so I'm not really interested in watching Netflix in the car. When we stop for a late lunch in Hattiesburg, Mississippi, I ask Dad how much longer.

"About an hour," he says.

"Praise the Lord," I proclaim. Lauren laughs at me.

Mom says, "I second that emotion." I roll my eyes thinking maybe I can last one more hour. If not, I'm toast.

Finally, at Bella's house, we pull into the drive and see her younger brother playing basketball with some friends. When he sees us, he stops dribbling and tells us to go in through the open garage. Dad knocks on the door. I hear someone yell, "They're here." Bella and her family greet us and take our luggage. I'm staying in Bella's room, Mom and Dad have the guest room, and Lauren's staying in the game room on the upper level. The weather is nice, sunny and 62 degrees. Bella's mom leads my parents on a tour, and Bella and I go back up to her room. Lauren wanders outside to play basketball with the guys.

Bella and I get comfortable in her room, turn on the TV and start up episode six of *Stranger Things*. We get almost half-way through when her dad comes to the door and announces dinner. I follow Bella downstairs and out to the backyard. She has a massive backyard that is super flat. There's a fire pit area, a covered patio with a large table that seats eight, and an outdoor grill with a refrigerator built into a large stone counter. They have a swimming pool and a hot tub with a fountain spilling over the edge. The ambiance with the lights and the fountain from the pool is tranquil and relaxing. There's a large stone fireplace at the far end of the pool next to the hot tub. Bella's dad has cooked a meal of barbecue chicken and corn on the grill, with a side of red beans and rice. We enjoy the evening sitting around talking and being near the fire. A lull in conversation allows Bella to stand and motion for me to come with her.

"Bex and I are going to watch a movie. We'll see you guys in the morning."

We watch the rest of episode six and episode seven before we fall asleep with the TV on.

When I wake up, I notice Bella is still asleep. I remember Atlanta is an hour ahead and I'm on a different time zone. I wander downstairs and find my parents up, having coffee in the kitchen. Bella's mom has a spread of eggs, bacon and King Cake laid out.

"You need to try some King Cake," Bella's mom points to the colorful sugar topped cake. "Mardi Gras is next month, and we have King Cake almost every day up until Mardi Gras Day," Bella's Mom says, handing me a plate.

The cake is delicious and sweet with a sugary topping that's a little like coffee cake but better.

"This King Cake is perfectly savory with this Diet Coke," I say with a bite in my mouth, licking my fingers.

Mom laughs and says, "The breakfast of champions."

A few minutes later Bella comes down and joins us. "What would you like to do today?" she asks.

"I don't know. Whatever you want to do is fine with me."

"How about I take you and Lauren down to the lakefront?"

About that time Lauren pops in fully dressed and ready for breakfast.

214

"Perfect timing. We were just talking about you." Lauren gives us a sarcastic expression.

"As soon as you finish eating, Bella says she's taking us on a tour of the town." I hand Lauren a slice of King Cake.

"We'll start off at Lake Ponchartrain," Bella says, picking up her phone and keys.

After a short drive we arrive at the lakefront. It's beautiful, and full of old moss-covered oak trees and great views of Lake Pontchartrain. The lakefront goes on for miles. As we drive along the waterfront, Bella tells us about Hurricane Katrina.

"A lot of the old houses along the lake front were ruined. We were without power for several weeks. Most of the houses have been rebuilt and are just as breathtaking as the originals." Bella points out the window as we drive past.

We park the car, get out and walk around. I snap a few pictures of the fancy Mardi Gras decorations on the front of the gorgeous houses along the lakefront. We walk along the sea wall, balancing like gymnasts on a balance beam with the waves splashing onto our pants and shoes. Lauren climbs into the lower branch of a huge oak tree. Bella and I follow her and climb onto one of the overhanging branches above her. After a while tree hanging gets dull, so we walk to a seafood restaurant close by.

"New Orleans is the best place in the world to eat seafood," Bella muses.

"Agreed, but also the beach. I've been to some great places in Destin," I add.

"What else is unique to the area?" Lauren asks.

"How about I take you guys to try any flavor snowball you can think up."

"Any flavor?" I say questioning.

When we get to the snowball stand, Lauren and I marvel at all the flavor choices. I choose the Cajun red-hot, Lauren chooses a blackberry and Bella gets creamy tootsie roll that has condensed milk drizzled on top. We sit at a picnic table and swap samples. I take a photo of my snowball and text Lane *Happy Birthday* with the photo added to the text. I tell Bella and Lauren that today is Lane's birthday. They want to wish him a happy birthday, so I take a quick video of us singing to him and send it.

We pull back into Beau Chene subdivision and decide to walk down to Bella's neighborhood park and hang out. Before we leave on our walk, Mrs. Campbell reminds us we're going to dinner in Madisonville and wants us to be ready to leave by five thirty.

"Got it, Mom," Bella says as we head toward the river along the golf course path just behind her house.

"It's so pretty here," I say, admiring the swamp like river.

"Keep an eye out for alligators," Bella directs.

"The water is brown like coffee. How can you see anything?" Lauren scoffs.

"We grew up swimming and boating in this water, so we're used to not being able to see anything once we're in it."

Lauren mutters, "Gross."

"I think there's something mystical and magical about the moss dripping from the giant oak trees. I loved the moss-covered trees on Cumberland Island, too. There's something spooky, yet romantic about them."

"Yeah, I guess." Lauren says

"I'm with you on that girl. I love spooky, mystical and romantic trees too," Bella adds jokingly.

Back at the house Bella and I take our time getting dressed for dinner to the annoyance of our family members waiting for us to leave. We arrive at the waterfront restaurant and have a private table for eight in front of the windows overlooking the Tchefuncte River.

Bella's dad explains, "This is the same river that flows through Beau Chene and then out into Lake Pontchartrain."

My dad asks how to spell it, and we are all amazed, since it sounds like chew- funk-ta and nothing like it's spelled.

Bella's mom says, "There's a Mardi Gras boat parade along the river tonight. We'll want to walk outside and get a good spot close to the riverbank."

216

After dinner, we walk outside where hundreds of people are lined up waiting for the parade. Lauren, Bella and I squeeze into a spot up front. Bella's dad begins telling us about the traditions of Mardi Gras.

"Mardi Gras is the celebration of being able to party and do any and everything up to the day lent begins. Mardi Gras is a forty-day celebration and lent is forty days of giving up something to prepare your heart for Easter and the sacrifice of what Christ did for us. Mardi Gras means, Fat Tuesday. All day on Mardi Gras day parades go from sun-up to sun-down. The day after Mardi Gras is Ash Wednesday. All partying ends and the sacrifice of choosing to give up something important to you begins."

My dad asks, "So it's a religious holiday?"

"Yes, it's considered a Catholic holiday here, and all the schools throughout the state are closed on Fat Tuesday. Here in Louisiana, we love a party and a festival. Anytime there is reason to party, we're ready."

The boats coming down the river are decorated with Mardi Gras flags, and gold, green and purple tensile, wreaths, and decorations. Some of the boats are large and filled with people hanging over the sides waving and throwing beads to us.

Bella explains, "Make sure to wave your hands in the air to get their attention, and they'll throw beads to you." Bella demonstrates, waving her hands above her head.

Lauren and I are getting the hang of catching beads. Mom gets in the spirit and in no time is right along beside us waving her hands at each passing boat. When it ends, Bella, Lauren and I have a massive collection of beads around our necks. I even have some dangling from my arm. I set my phone on Boomerang and have Mom film Bella, Lauren and me waving beads in the air. I notice a Mardi Gras filter on Snapchat and send it to Lane. Then I quickly send him a text. *Can't wait to see u.*

Counting down the hours, babe.

217

33

#NOLA

Hotel Monteleone in downtown New Orleans is beautiful, historical, and only one block from where Bella and the rest of the band are staying. The historical aspect is more exceptional when I find out that many famous authors have stayed here. There's an impressive display in the foyer of all the authors who have frequented the hotel. I stop to admire the display and read the list aloud. "Ernest Hemingway, Tennessee Williams, Ann Rice, William Faulkner, John Grisham, Eudora Welty and Truman Capote. "Lauren look at this list of authors who've stayed here," I say, pointing at the glass cabinet. "They've all written books set in and around New Orleans." Lauren vaguely glances in my direction and moves on.

The lobby is striking, with massive vases of fresh flowers, marble floors, mirrored walls, paintings on the ceiling and large crystal chandeliers grace the high ceilings.

Mr. Campbell points across the lobby. "The Carousel Bar is very famous. You have to wait in line in order to get a seat on the carousel, and the bar moves slowly in a circle."

I ask if Lauren and I can go over there while they're checking in. We walk into the Carousel Bar, and, sure enough, an exact replica of a carousel slowly rotating in a circle is smack dab in the middle of the bar. The people seated are in chairs painted to look like animals on a real carousel. The entire bar is very large with lots of tables and seating, but I can understand why people would want to wait in line to get a spot on the moving carousel. I stand and observe for a few minutes——totally picturing Gatsby and Daisy sitting on the carousel, laughing, smoking, and drinking. With all the authors who've stayed here, I can feel the energy from the bar and sense the liveliness from days gone by.

When we get the room keys to our suite, we're told it's located next to the rooftop pool. Bella's mom tells us their room is on the fourth floor. Standing outside our room, I notice the sign on the door says, William Faulkner Suite. I feel a thrill as I slide my fingers across the brass name plate.

Lauren brushes past me. "You're such a book nerd. Wanna hang out by the pool?" she asks, dropping her bags.

Lauren and I snag two chairs in the sun by the pool. I pull out my Kindle to read. Lauren scrolls through her Instagram, posts a selfie, and starts texting Brian. After a few minutes, Mom and Dad walk over to us and say they're going to the Carousel Bar with Bella's parents for an hour. I get comfy and continue reading a book. When a crick in my neck wakes me from dozing, I look around but don't see Lauren anywhere. I walk back into our room to find her lying on the sofa watching TV.

"Hey, Lauren, I'm going to change for dinner. How long was I asleep?"

"I think thirty minutes or so. Mom texted me a few minutes ago and said Bella will be finished with practice by six thirty. We're supposed to meet everyone in the lobby a hour later to walk to Pat O' Brien's."

I change into jeans and a sweater with fringe, and Lauren changes, too. I get a text from Lane saying he's here and staying on the seventh floor. I text him back that we're in the William Faulkner Suite right by the rooftop pool. He texts back *I can meet you at the pool in five minutes.* I tell Lauren that Lane and his cousins are staying at our hotel, too, and I'm going to hang out with him until it's time to meet everyone in the lobby.

I open my suitcase and pull out the gift box that's nicely wrapped in Gucci paper. I take the box with me and sit at a table next to the pool. When I see Lane walk up, I jump out of my chair, and he hugs me tight. He pulls my face to his and kisses me sweetly on the lips.

"I'm so happy to be here with you," he says.

"Me, too, happy birthday." I hand him the gift box, beaming.

"I have something for you too, but I'll give it to you later," he says taking the box from me.

Lane opens it and takes out the scarf. He puts it on and pulls me into his lap.

"I love this," he says, playing with the scarf around his neck.

"I'm so glad. I had no idea what to get you. When I spotted the Gucci store, I went in and thought this would be something you would wear."

"It's perfect. Knowing you picked it out for me makes it even more special. What are your plans tonight?"

"My family and Bella's are going to dinner at Pat O'Brien's. We're walking over there in a few minutes. Do you and the guys have plans?"

"We'll probably meet up with a few of my fraternity brothers and hit a few bars on Bourbon Street."

"Do you know about the big Bama party tomorrow night?"

"I know there's one at the hotel where the team's staying."

"Right, so tomorrow night there's a Bama pre-game fan-fare dinner and New Year's Eve party at the team's hotel. Bella was telling me about it on the drive down here today."

"What time is that?" he asks.

"I think the buffet is from six to eight. Then the band and the cheerleaders will do a performance. Afterward there will be a New Orleans band and some type of Mardi Gras show that goes until midnight. I know our families are planning to go to that. I'd like you to come, too."

"I'd definitely like to join you."

220

"How about you come downstairs and meet everyone, now? I'm meeting them in the lobby."

"Sure, I'm ready to meet your parents," he says, leaning in for a kiss.

"First, let's walk to my room and see if Lauren's ready."

I knock on the door. Lauren peeks out at me through the crack then opens the door to let us in.

I can tell when Lane and I walk in that Lauren wasn't expecting to see him.

"Lauren, this is Lane." I gesture with a wave of my hand.

"It's nice to finally meet you, Lauren. I've heard a lot about you." Lane reaches out to shake her hand.

"Same, I've also heard a lot about you, and it's nice to finally meet you, too."

I can tell by the expression on Lauren's face she's impressed with Lane. She looks like she's trying to hold in a giggle fit.

Together, we get on the elevator. My palms are sweaty, so I wipe them on my jeans and fan my face. I'm nervous about introducing Lane to Mom and Dad. Lane puts his hand on the small of my back as a calming gesture as we step into the lobby.

I can see Bella's family and my parents standing around talking. Lauren, Lane and I walk up to them. Mom notices us and looks startled.

"Hey, Mom and Dad, this is my boyfriend, Lane." I say with a cat that ate the canary smile, and the Band-aide is ripped off.

Dad says, "Boyfriend? This is news."

"I was waiting until we were all together to introduce you," I say, while glancing at Mom with a look that says 'help, reel Dad in if things go south'.

Lane reaches out and shakes Dad's hand. Bella is looking amused and whispers something to her mom.

Mom, still looking surprised, says, "It's nice to meet you, Lane. Is your family here for the game?"

221

"I flew in today from Aspen with two of my cousins, but the rest of my family is staying at our house in Aspen for another week. My family usually vacations for two to three weeks in Aspen during Christmas."

I move the introductions toward Bella's family and introduce Lane to them.

"So how did you and Rebecca meet?" Dad asks.

"She tripped over me the first day of class."

Everyone laughs, I turn bright red, and Lane squeezes my hand.

"We're both taking Richard Brigg's creative writing/journalism class." Lane's manner is just the right amount of respect and friendly.

I butt in, "I know we have plans for dinner, and Lane has plans with some fraternity brothers tonight, but he's planning on joining us for the Bama tailgate, New Year's party tomorrow, if that is okay with you guys?"

Mom nods. "Absolutely, we'd love to have you join us."

My parents say goodnight to Lane, and he turns to me. "Bex, let me introduce you to my cousins really quick." He takes my hand, and we turn around.

Two handsome guys walk up. He introduces me to Conor and John. After the quick introduction, Lane kisses me on the cheek, then he and his cousins walk into the Carousel Bar, and I walk out to the sidewalk where everyone is waiting.

First thing Mom says is, "He's the guy you went to the Undertaker's Ball with."

"Yes, we've been dating for about a month."

"What happened with Grant?" Mom asks.

I'm glad Bella's family is wrapped up in their own conversations and are walking ahead of us, so they don't hear all the embarrassing interrogations I'm getting.

"I had a talk with Grant and told him I liked him a lot, but I had feelings for a guy in my class who asked me out, and felt I wanted to date him to see how things go."

"How did Grant take it?" Mom's tone is serious.

"He was nice, understanding, and appreciated my honesty. I know I hurt his feelings, and I felt bad about it, but I had stronger feelings for Lane."

"What can you tell us about this Lane?" Dad prods.

"He is in the Delta Kappa Epsilon fraternity. He's from New York. His Mom is in politics and has written a book. His dad is a professor at Columbia University, and he has three older sisters. You can ask him all the questions you want tomorrow night."

Lauren jumps out with, "And he's really rich."

I poke Lauren in the ribs and give her a nasty look. She rolls her eyes.

We have to wait for a table at Pat O'Brien's, so our parents go to the bar and order Hurricanes. Bella and I hand Cade our phones and ask him to take pictures of the three of us girls in front of the Pat O'Brien's sign.

Once seated, we order alligator bites for an appetizer. I am totally in love with New Orleans' food and lively atmosphere. The streets are crowded with partygoers and Bama fans yelling *Roll Tide* across the streets and back again. Walking back to our hotel is quite the experience. Jazz bands play at every corner. People dancing, people in costumes, and Bama fans all mix into one big party scene.

When we get back to the lobby, we make plans to meet everyone at Café Beignet around the corner for breakfast.

I blurt out, "I'll walk Bella back to her hotel."

"Take Cade with you, so you're not walking back by yourself," Mrs. Campbell says, motioning toward Cade.

"I'll come, too," Lauren adds.

When we get to the lobby of her hotel there are even more Bama fans mingling around.

Bella points down a hallway and says, "The ball-rooms where the party will be are that way. You guys will probably want to meet here tomorrow night before for the party."

"I'll make sure to tell everyone. We'll see you tomorrow at Café Beignet."

223

34
#Natty

In the morning, our group wanders out of the hotel, down the street and into the small cafe to indulge in beignets.

"I'm in love with beignets, I can't get enough. It's like heaven in my mouth" I say, picking up a third one from the plate in front of me.

Lauren and I are covered in powdered sugar and look a mess. Bella and Cade are used to eating them but joined us in pigging out.

After we stuff ourselves with beignets, we walk down to Jackson Square and the Riverfront to decide on a carriage tour. We choose an hour-long horse-drawn carriage tour through the city and learn all about the history and battles of New Orleans and a little about Napoleon Bonaparte. After our carriage drops us back at Jackson Square, we walk inside Jackson Cathedral. There's organ music playing. The inside is designed with huge arched ceilings and paintings. We sit and listen to the beautiful music for several minutes while deciding on our lunch destination.

We choose The Court of Two Sisters. The walk over allows us to experience jazz bands, magicians, and other street performers. At the restaurant, the waiter escorts us to the patio, where we delight in the sounds from the water fountain and the live jazz trio. The patio where we're sitting is covered in the largest wisteria vine I've ever seen. After lunch Mom wants us to take a family picture in front of the fountain, and Bella's mom decides to do the same with her family. After the family photo sessions, we walk back toward the hotel but stop inside several shops along the way. By the time we arrive at the hotel, it's five. I call "shower first" when we walk into the room.

I get dressed in a short black dress and kitten heels. My silver, satin cropped jacket pulls the outfit together. Lauren is wearing a shimmery dress with boots. Dad is very dapper in a suit and tie, and Mom looks sophisticated in sequins.

Lauren says, "I hope this New Year's Eve party is lit."

"I'm sure it will be," I say, posing with a hand on my hip showing off my dress. "Lane is meeting us in the lobby," I mention as we step inside the elevator.

When we get out, I see Lane. He's wearing a black jacket, button down shirt in light purple, black pants with expensive looking loafers, and black socks with purple polka dots. He's also wearing the scarf I gave him. He looks breathtaking. Seeing him gets me all tingly. He winks at me, shakes Dad's hand and greets Mom with a dashing smile. He's always so smooth talking with people. Lane and I walk together down the block to join Bella's family for the party.

The ballroom where the buffet is set up has hundreds of red and white balloons on the ceiling. I see Big Al and a few cheerleaders posing for pictures with families at one end of the room. There are at least a hundred round tables set up with black tablecloths, candles and Alabama themed table runners down the center of each. We stop at the entrance and present our tickets. The parents get coupons for free cocktails. We find an empty table and put our stuff down to mark our places before we get in the buffet line.

During dinner Lane seems to be charming everyone with his smooth approach to conversation, and I get the feeling that Mom and Dad are quite impressed.

Lane explains his plans. "I'll major in art history and English, and I'm thinking about a minor in journalism. My parents want me to go to Law School after I get my first degree. I

226

haven't completely decided against that, but for now I'm leaning toward a journalism minor which means I go another semester over the summer and might start grad school next year, depending on my decision."

I look at Lane and grin at him. He smiles back.

"Rebecca tells us you're from New York and your father is a professor at Columbia, how did you decide on Alabama?" Dad asks.

"Most of my family went to Yale or Brown, but I wasn't interested in going to a school in the Northeast. I did a lot of research on colleges in the South and a few out in California. After touring the Alabama campus, I liked it so much I told my parents that I was thinking about going to school there. They reached out to some family friends and were able to connect me with some families and legacies in the DKE fraternity, and we went from there."

After dinner, we move to the next ballroom which seems even larger. There's a stage set up on one end and round tables set up with black tablecloths, candles and Mardi Gras decor. Each seat has an Alabama shaker lying in it. We hear the band coming, so we move to the side to make a path for them to walk through. Lauren goes to the nearest table and retrieves the shakers and hands them out. There are several hundred people lined up cheering for the band as they march in.

When Bella and Lexi walk by, we yell, hoot and holler really loudly, and her dad whistles more loudly. The tubas and the drum line go up onto the stage. Marching in next are the Crimsonettes with a short baton routine. They line up on either side of the stage along the stairs.

Next comes Big Al, running, waving and jumping, followed by the cheerleaders. They run around with Alabama flags and get the crowd pumped. They do a few cheers and some stunting then sit in front of the band at the front of the stage. There's now a narrow pathway leading to a podium. The band begins the fight song, and we shake our pom shakers to the beat. Coach, flanked by two State Troopers, jogs toward the podium.

When the rowdy cheering dies, he greets the crowd and talks about the National Championship game and the team. The band plays another song, and the Crimsonettes and Cheerleaders get the crowds going again with cheers and back flips. The band leads them out with the drum line playing a rockin' beat.

Once it's quiet in the room, Bella's mom says, "Bella and some of her band friends will be joining us after they change out of their uniforms."

The lights get dim, and a jazz band starts setting up on stage, tuning their instruments. Several minutes later, another band with costumed performers enters the room where the Bama band exited. They're marching very close to each table, and the people marching with them are in full Mardi Gras costumes, some on stilts. They throw Mardi Gras beads into the crowd as they continue playing lively Mardi Gras music. Lauren and Cade jump up and catch several beads. A small Mardi Gras float makes its way inside. The jazz band continues circling the crowd, playing "Mardi Gras Mambo." Lane and I stand in front of our table next to Lauren and Cade to catch beads being thrown from the float. Another float enters the room. This one has a king and queen riding on it. It makes its way around the room with the king and queen waving to the crowds as they slowly ride toward the stage.

The king and queen are escorted off the float then graciously walk up the stairs, their costumes dragging in a long train behind them. Their headpieces, tall and stately, glitter in the spotlight as they walk toward the large royal chairs set for them. When the music stops a man in a tuxedo announces, "Ladies and Gentlemen, may I introduce to you the King and Queen of Krewe of Endymion."

While the king and queen are pronouncing their blessings upon the party, Bella, Lexi, Jack, and Patrick show up. The band on stage begins to play and the king and queen rise and make their announcement.

"It's time for dancing and *Laisser Le Bon Temps Rouler*. (Let the good times roll.) They extend their hands to the crowd, then return to their chairs. The king and queen sit majestic in their royal chairs, signaling the beginning of the party. Mom, Dad, and the Campbells get up and make their way to the dance floor. The rest of us stand around talking, wandering over to say hello to Lexi's family.

When the jazz band takes a break, a DJ shows up and plays music for us to dance to. The younger crowd hits the dance floor for the next forty minutes. I notice the parents heading to the bar for cocktails. When the band comes back to the stage, the lead singer announces, "It's fifteen minutes until midnight." He points to a large clock being projected onto a screen to count us down.

Lane reaches out his hand for me to take. "Would you like to dance with me until midnight?"

"Of course. I wouldn't do midnight without you," I say glowing.

We move to the dance floor and slow dance to a spicy jazz tune. A minute before midnight, the countdown begins. "10, 9, 8, 7, 6, 5, 4, 3, 2, 1." The band breaks into "Auld Lang Syne." Confetti and balloons fall from the ceiling.

Lane kisses me and whispers, "Happy New Year, baby."

I whisper, "Happy New Year."

I put my head on his shoulder and soak in the magic of the moment. Confetti still falls like glitter in the air, and the soft sounds of the familiar New Year's tune plays as we gently sway to the music. My dream state is shaken by Bella and Lexi yelling in my ear.

"Bex! Happy New Year! Let's get a group selfie."

All eight of us squeeze in for a selfie. Horns are blowing in the background, and I see everyone's parents out on the dance floor enjoying a slow dance. I hear Jack say to Bella and Lexi that a lot of the guys from the Bama band are heading out to Bourbon Street. They look over at Lane.

"Lane, do you want to go with us?" Jack asks.

He responds, "No thanks, I want to stay right here." He looks into my eyes.

I put my head back on his shoulder, absorbing the moment, and close my eyes.

Bella and Lexi say goodbye to Jack and Patrick. Lauren and Cade are sitting back at our table, looking at their phones. Mom walks over to talk to Lane and me.

"Dad and I are going to call it a night and head back to our hotel. I'm going to tell Lauren to come back with us. Please don't stay out too long."

Lane and I say goodnight to Mom and Dad as they leave the dance floor.

Lane asks, "What would you like to do now?"

"I want this moment to last forever. It's been a dreamy evening. I just want to stay with you as long as I can."

"How about we go back to our hotel and hang out there for a while?"

"Sure, we can go up to the rooftop pool since my hotel room is right next to the pool, Mom won't be able to say I stayed out too late, if I'm really just outside our door."

Lane smiles at me and shakes his head. He's probably thinking—*Girl logic.*

We walk a block over to our hotel, in the cool breezy air. There's a lot going on in the streets with people living it up, as if New Orleans could get any crazier. The night seems magical and feels alive. When we get to the rooftop, there's no one around. The pool is lit up and makes for a quiet and romantic setting. We walk over to the railing and view the New Orleans skyline. Lane reaches inside his coat pocket and pulls out a slender blue box tied with a silver satin ribbon.

Holding the box, he says, "This is a late Christmas gift."

I take the box and tug on the ribbon and remove the lid. Inside is a beautiful gold and silver charm bracelet.

"It's beautiful," I purr.

I pick it up and examine it carefully. The charms dangle and glisten in the moonlight. I touch each one and mention each aloud.

"My Phi Mu symbol. A heart with the date August 23rd?"

"The day we met. The day you tripped over me." He grins.

"This is so romantic. What a perfect gift."

I continue looking at each charm and notice one that looks like a DKE pin.

"Is this your DKE pin? Have you had it made into a charm?"

"Yes, I had the entire bracelet made just for you. It's made of platinum and 18 karat gold. I wanted you to be able to wear it with either gold or silver jewelry."

I bite my lip while feelings of happiness overflow and I burst out, "Oh Lane, this is the most thoughtful and beautiful gift I could possibly imagine."

There's one final charm, a round University of Alabama emblem with rhinestones.

"You can add to it, of course, with other charms if you'd like."

"This is so special, its perfect. I love it."

I'm teary eyed now, so Lane takes the bracelet from me and places it on my wrist and fastens the clasp.

He takes my hand and kisses it gently.

"I'm glad you like it."

"I want to wear it every day. I'm thrilled you came up with something so thoughtful and creative."

"I want you to know how much I care about you, Rebecca."

He leans in and kisses my forehead, then our lips touch gently, and we continue to kiss more passionately. I take Lane's hand in mine and lead him to my door. We step inside the living room area of my suite. I look up at him and whisper, "We're planning an early dinner at Commander's Palace tomorrow at five thirty. I've already asked my parents if you can join us. You are welcome to, if you don't have anything else going on."

"I don't have any plans except going to the game with you tomorrow night. So an early dinner with you and your family would be enjoyable. I think Conor and Jack will be sleeping most of the day, anyway."

I suppress a giggle into his chest and say, "I think everyone will be sleeping until game time tomorrow night."

He kisses me lightly on my ear and whispers, "Good night, beautiful. I'll see you tomorrow."

I close the door behind him and slowly and quietly tiptoe into my room to show Lauren the bracelet.

"My gosh, Bex, that's really pretty," she gushes.

"I know. It's also custom made just for me. Look at each charm, my Phi Mu symbol, his DKE pin made into a charm, a heart with the date we met, the UofA symbol, it's so special."

"Is that the box it came in?" Lauren asks, pointing to the box. "It's from Tiffany's. That makes it even more special."

"You're right. I opened the box but didn't notice it was from Tiffany's. I was so stunned by the bracelet."

"He's definitely a keeper, Bex."

"I have to agree with you, sis."

"I guess you'll show it to Mom and Dad tomorrow?

"Yeah, but I hope they know we're sleeping 'til noon. I'll poke my head into their room and let them know I'm back and to let us sleep late."

When I walk back in our room, I ask Lauren if she's heard from Brian.

"What did Brian do for New Year's Eve?"

Lauren gets under the covers and says, "He had a party at his house with some of his guy friends, and they're all sleeping over."

"So, no girls?"

"No, I'm not worried about that. He didn't mention any girls. He would tell me if he wanted to date someone else. Brian is great, and we're pretty serious right now, too."

"That's good news. I'm happy for you, Lauren."

The next morning, I wake up to the sound of the TV in the next room. Lauren is watching the Rose Parade. Mom and Dad look up from the newspaper.

Dad says, "Look who's awake. We ordered room service, and there are some left- overs."

I walk over, pour some juice, and take some toast and strawberries over to the couch. I plop down next to Lauren and watch the rest of the Rose Parade. When the parade ends Lauren jumps up.

"Can I walk over to Cafe Beignet and pick up some takeout?" she asks.

When Lauren leaves, I think about getting in the shower. Then I remember my bracelet. I show my wrist to Mom and Dad, who've been busy reading the paper.

"Look what Lane gave me for Christmas."

Dad moves his newspaper to one side, and Mom perks up and looks at my wrist that I'm holding up. She comes over for a closer look and I show her each charm, one at a time.

"Bex, this is gorgeous and so thoughtful."

Dad asks, "How serious is this? I thought you've only been dating a month?"

"Yes, I know, and I think he's a keeper."

Dad scowls. "You need to take things slowly."

Mom jumps in with, "It's a beautiful bracelet and a thoughtful gift. But I'm with your dad, take it slowly. You said you've only been dating a month, and it looks like he's given you his fraternity pin forever."

She's right. His fraternity pin is permanently fixed onto my bracelet. I feel a wave of emotion rush over me. This is getting serious, but I'm okay with it, I think.

"You guys remember he's coming to dinner with us today before the game, right?"

Mom says, "Yes, I remember, and we're looking forward to getting to know him better."

Lauren comes back with a large bag of beignets. I devour one, muttering, "It's like mana from heaven."

A little later, Lauren and I hang out by the pool while Mom and Bella's mom go shopping, and our dads hang out at the Carousel Bar.

I finish the book I'm reading and look at the time. I tell Lauren I'm going to go in to decide what to wear. Lauren's on the phone talking to Brian and gives me a wave as I walk away. I decide on the solid red knit dress and tall black suede boots I wore to the homecoming Game. I spend extra time on my makeup and hair. A few minutes later, Lauren walks out of the shower, drying her hair with a towel.

"Can I borrow something of yours to wear?" she asks.

"Sure, anything you want."

Then Mom knocks on the door.

"You girls have fifteen more minutes, before it's time to leave."

I text Lane to meet us in the lobby.

Lane is waiting when we get off the elevator, looking divine. He's wearing a red button down with a navy blazer and khaki pants. He smells amazing. He greets me first with a kiss on the cheek, shakes hands with Dad, then greets Mom and Lauren with polished politeness.

Dad signals for us to walk out the front entrance.

"I've called for an Uber to Commander's Palace because I don't want to bother with getting the car out of the parking garage," he says, walking toward the curb.

Commander's Palace is huge. We're escorted up a staircase and down a hallway into an all-glass room with beautiful views and incredible chandeliers. The wait staff is very formal. When Lauren and I go to the restroom they escort us by offering an arm and walk us all the way there. I'm also impressed by the food and the presentation. I can tell Lane's impressed, too. He says this is his first time to eat here but says he's been to New Orleans on several trips with his fraternity brothers over the years.

Dad laughs. "I'm sure this is not the normal hang out for fraternity guys when they come to New Orleans. But it is one of the most famous restaurants here." After a four-course meal we're feeling a little fat and happy. When our Uber arrives, we hop in and make our way to the Superdome.

234

At the stadium entrance, we wave goodbye to my family as we walk through the gate. Mom turns around as she's walking away, "Remember to meet back at this gate when the game is over."

Lane and I find our way to the student section near the band. We wave at his cousins, Conor and John as they head toward us. They both say hi as they settle into their seats.

"How has your New Year's been so far?" I ask.

John answers with, "I love New Orleans."

Conor nods his head, hands Lane a beer, and says, "It's becoming one of my favorite destinations."

Lane tells them about our dinner at Commander's Palace.

"That sounds like a great place. We just ordered room service this afternoon," John says, looking from us to Conor.

The game begins, and we're up on our feet cheering. The game goes into overtime, and we win with a field goal. Another National Championship is in the books, and history is made. After the celebration and trophy presentation, Conor and John tell us they're going back to the hotel and give me a hug as they leave.

While we're waiting for my family to meet us at the curb, I ask Lane about his plans.

"When does your plane leave tomorrow?"

"My flight's at five thirty."

"Are you flying back to Aspen?"

"No, we're flying to Atlanta, and I'll hang out with Conor and John one more day. Their flight from Atlanta to Aspen will leave Thursday, then on Saturday I'll drive back to Tuscaloosa. Now that you have a new car, what day do you think you'll drive back to campus?"

Lane is smiling at me and takes both my hands in his.

"I think I'll be back on Sunday. But I'm not looking forward to class Monday. It'll be hard to get back into a routine. We have a home game later that week, and a new dance to perform. We have three home games in January and four in February with the last one on February twenty seventh. Then

235

we'll get a bit of a break, unless the team goes past the SEC playoffs and into March Madness."

Lane reaches out and brushes the hair out of my eyes. "Hopefully you'll get spring break off, too."

"Yes, I doubt our team will be in the final four. But since you'll be in Atlanta for a few days, maybe you can come to dinner at our house on Friday night?"

Mom, dad, and Lauren walk up waving excitedly.

"That was some game," Dad says.

"We were on the edge of our seats, holding our breath those last seconds. How were your seats?" I ask.

Dad says, "They were pretty good. 45-yard line, a little high up, but we were able to see well."

Lauren moans, "I'm so over football, with the overtime it seemed like it would never end."

The Uber arrives. When we get out at the hotel Mom asks, "Are you guys staying out? It's pretty late."

I look over at Lane. "Would it be okay if Rebecca and I just hang out for a few more minutes?" he asks.

"Sure. Rebecca, just let me know you're in for the night when you get back to the room." Mom smiles as she turns to walk away with Dad and Lauren.

Lane takes my hand and we pop into the Carousel Bar and find a corner couch seat. Lane orders a scotch, and I order a pomegranate spritzer. Even though my drink is nonalcoholic, it comes with a sprig of rosemary. Lane and I toast, touching our glasses together, and I snuggle up to him on the sofa. The bar is crowded, and I see Bama fans wandering in from the game. Everyone is in a great mood. I hear *Roll Tide* being shouted back and forth in the distance.

Lane says, "Happy New Year's Day."

"Cheers to that." We touch our drinks together with a clink.

After about forty-five minutes of hanging out, Lane looks at his phone. "I don't want to keep you too long and make a bad impression. I'll walk you up to your room."

We walk hand-in-hand to the elevator and get in. Once the doors close, we're alone. He pulls me close and looks into my eyes. "I'm falling in love with you, Rebecca," he says, then kisses me.

We kiss until the elevator doors open, and a couple walks in and smiles at us. We back up and sneak glances at each other until we get to my floor. Lane walks me to the door, and we step inside. It's quiet, and I know everyone's asleep. Lane takes my hand, and I feel butterflies on trampolines. I lean into him.

"I'm falling in love with you, too," I whisper, staring into his eyes.

He pulls me close, and we kiss. He puts his hand on my cheek and whispers, "I'll see you in a few days."

I close the door and walk to Mom's room to let her know I'm back. Tiptoeing back to my room, I snuggle down under the covers absolutely glowing. *He's in love with me.*

35
#Itsadate

On the long drive home, I text Lane to make sure he still wants to have dinner at my house on Friday. He does, so I decide to see if Mom and Dad are cool with it. If not, heavy pleading will be involved. When Lauren finds out I invited Lane for dinner, she asks to have Brian, too. I thought she should have asked me first just to get my feel, but I really like Brian, and it's not going to rain on my parade to have both our boyfriends over for dinner at the same time.

Friday morning, I spend the day cleaning, putting away decorations, and helping Mom plan the meal. I'm excited, giddy, and nervous, because it feels so official. *My boyfriend is coming to dinner!*

"Just be casual and normal," I tell everyone.

Dad raises an eyebrow at me. "Who are you telling to be normal?"

Lauren pipes up, "OMG, Bex, it's not like we haven't had dinner with him before."

"I know, but he's coming *here* to our house."

Then I remember he and I snuck in at five a.m. the morning after the SEC Championship game, and it makes me smile. When seven thirty rolls around, I'm nervous when the doorbell rings. I feel like it's our first date or something. I practically attack him when he walks in the front door. I show him off to Mom and Dad like he's a new toy. When they met him at the hotel in New Orleans, I kinda sprung it on everyone that he was my boyfriend, but tonight it seems real and planned.

Mom pours herself a glass of wine, and Dad offers Lane a beer, and they settle into comfortable, casual conversation. The doorbell rings again, and Lauren goes to let Brian in. After all the introductions, we sit out on the screened porch, where Dad has the fireplace lit. Everything feels nice and cozy, warm and welcoming.

After Mom's spectacular chicken piccata dinner she says she's set up dessert for us at the bar in the basement. The four of us go downstairs and leave Mom and Dad to the cleanup. Our basement is kinda bland in comparison to Brian's, and I have no clue how cool and awesome Lane's house must be. We do have another fireplace lit downstairs, and Mom has an impressive display of candy, snacks, and desserts set out for us on the bar counter. Brian asks if we want to play Xbox. Lauren and I end up watching as Brian and Lane battle it out in *Lego Star Wars*. I suggest *Rock Band,* and Brian calls drums, Lane and Lauren get the guitars, and I grab the microphone. We rock out to "Livin' on a Prayer" by Bon Jovi then "Anyway You Want It" by Journey.

"Great Voice, Bex," Brian says.

Lauren adds, "Bex had the role of Belle in *Beauty and the Beast* her senior year in high school."

"That's cool," Brian says, nodding in a cool guy way.

Lane smiles a sexy smile at me and looks charmed by this info.

Lauren and Brian walk over to the bar and start throwing gummy bears into each other's mouths. The dog comes bounding downstairs and jumps up on the couch with Lane and me.

"Micky really likes you and thinks you're a keeper."

"Well, he's definitely a dog with good taste." Lane rubs Micky behind the ears.

When Brian gets ready to leave, Lauren follows him upstairs. Finally, alone, I cuddle next to Lane on the couch.

"Will you be driving your new Christmas gift around campus?"

Lane shakes his head and sets his drink down.

"My new car will stay in New York, and I'll keep the one I have now for driving around Tuscaloosa. I'd love for you to come up and see it, maybe over Spring Break?"

I smile at him but don't answer.

At midnight I walk with him out to the driveway. I show off my new car parked next to where we're standing. I lean up against the side of the car and pull Lane close.

"It's very sporty," he says smiling down at me. "I like it. The color red suits you. You'd better be careful driving to Tuscaloosa Sunday. I want to see you when you get back," he says, rubbing his nose against mine.

"I want you to be safe driving tomorrow, too." I slip my arms through his.

Kissing me tenderly, he whispers, "I want *you* to come back to me safely." Our lips touch gently.

"I promise I will." I close my eyes and drink in his kiss.

On Sunday morning, Mom, Dad, and Lauren stand in the driveway waving bye as I pull away. It's about four hours to Tuscaloosa, but it goes quickly. There's not much traffic through Atlanta, since its Sunday, and I gain an hour when I cross the state line, which I love.

I pull into a spot near the Phi Mu house, grab my bags out of the back, and walk inside in search of our House Mother. I have a gift for her, but I also need a temp parking slip for my new car. I drop my bags off in my room, run out, and place my parking sticker in the dash.

Bella's not back yet, but she should be here soon. I walk down the other hall to see if Lexi's back. I knock, and Lexi's roommate, Jessica, opens the door to let me in. Lexi is unpacking. I find an empty spot on her bed and sit down. She shows me the new clothes she got for Christmas. Jessica mentions there's a house Bible study later tonight if we want to join. A text pops up on my phone, and my cheeks burst with an enormous smile.

"I know what that means." Lexi says in a sing song voice.

240

I say, "Yep, Lane is outside. He's just pulled up. I'll see you guys later."

I run out the door and jump into Lane's arms.

"That's what I call a greeting. Have you had lunch yet?"

"No, I've been back less than an hour. I'm not all that hungry, but I'll go anywhere you want."

We end up in the quaint area of downtown Northport with lots of cute shops and trendy places to eat. I ask him to drop me off at Coleman after lunch so I can be at dance practice on time. I tell Amanda all about my new car on the ride back from practice.

"Why didn't you drive it here? she asks. "It's your turn to give me a ride," she says with a laugh.

"I rode over with Lane, and he dropped me off."

"I saw you guys at the game sitting with his cousins."

"I didn't see you. How did you know we were sitting with his cousins?" Amanda gives me a weird smile and says, "I just know who his cousins are. I was sitting about seven rows behind you guys. It was a great game. I got in town on New Year's Eve, but we didn't stay out late. We were back in our room by midnight."

"I was at the Bama New Year's Eve party with my family and Lane. We had a blast. Oh, by the way, this is what he got me for Christmas." I hold out my arm.

She holds my arm up and carefully inspects at the bracelet.

"Wow, it's a custom charm bracelet. It's gorgeous, Bex. I have to say I had no idea Lane had it in him. I may have misled you when I told you he was a total playboy. Or maybe you've changed him."

I smile back at Amanda, thinking maybe I have.

When I walk into the room to change for dinner, Bella is unpacking her stuff. I'm so glad to see her even though I saw her less than a week ago. I feel good about being back at Phi Mu house with all my sisters. It's fun listening to their stories about the things they did during Christmas break. Jessica has us in stitches telling us how she and her mom got lost driving through a little town in France where they stayed at a Chateau in the Le Voir Valley and waking up each morning to screeching peacocks. Mealtime is always a great way for us to get caught up.

Afterward we gather in the living room for the back-to-school Bible study. Lexi's roommate Jessica opens with a prayer and reads a verse from Psalm 20:4.

"May God give you the desires of your heart, and make your plans succeed."

I love this verse. We talk for a few minutes about God knowing our needs before we ask. Jessica suggests we "popcorn pray" where anyone in the circle can pray if they feel led. When we get back to the room, I pull out my markers and draw a design around the verse and outline it to make the lettering bolder. I tear it out of my notebook and pin it on our memo board. I gather my things for class tomorrow and set the alarm. I tell Bella goodnight and roll over and ponder what my heart may want, wishing for warm sunny days, longing for spring, and sitting in the sun.

36
#Savagenotaverage

The alarm goes off excessively early, making me want to stay in bed longer. I'm just not quite ready to get back into the swing of things. I turn on "Midnight Memories" by One Direction for motivation as I shuffle around the room. Bella and I walk out together, and I wave bye to her as I cross the street to Phifer. Classes go well, practice goes well, and I'm feeling good about performing the new dance at the basketball game tomorrow night. Lane and I text back and forth throughout the day. He reminds me of the SGA party, so I log into the anonymous Twitter account and post it.

By Tuesday morning I'm more chipper when I get up, but it's raining, so I put on my Hunter rain boots, grab my raincoat, and make my way to the lecture hall. My journalism class and my Spanish class are the only classes that stayed the same since those are one day a week classes and cover different material each semester. All my other classes are new. By continuing Spanish, I now have a minor in it. By the end of this semester, I'll be close to a minor in journalism, too.

I slip my raincoat off before walking into the lecture hall. When someone grabs my hand, I turn to see Lane, who's wearing a pullover rain jacket with a hood and he's dripping wet.

"Good morning on such a lovely day," he says.

"It's a good morning now." I smile.

He leans close and whispers, "Good job on the video interview post. It's gotten almost 2,000 views. I've heard lots of good buzz about the upcoming party, too." He smiles and squeezes my hand as we walk down the stairs to take our seats.

When Professor Brigg walks to the front of the room to begin class, he greets us with "Happy New Year" which causes cheering and whistles and a few "Happy New Year's" yelled back. After everyone settles, he continues with normal announcements then tells us something very interesting.

"I've selected three stories from the assignment. I've made copies of the stories, removed the names of the authors and added discussion questions to each. You will each take a folder with the stories and questions with you when you leave today. Your assignment will be to read each, and answer the discussion questions, which will be our lecture for next week. Please be prepared to answer and discuss in class, each question per story. You will also select which story you feel is the best. There will be a voting link on the class website where you'll cast your vote for the story of your choice. I will collect your notes and discussion questions in class next week. I do have final say on the chosen story but will certainly take into consideration the votes. Remember that the one selected will be published in *The New Yorker*. Good luck to the three authors."

When Lane and I receive a folder, we open them and find my story and his to be two of the three. We give each other a side-glance and a smile. This should be fun. I get to critique and discuss Lane's story in class next week, and he gets to do the same with mine. This should be interesting. I am so excited that I'm in the running for *The New Yorker*.

After class ends Lane says, "I've added another writing class to my schedule this semester, so I'm in Phifer for my next class. I don't have to ride my bike across campus today."

I perk up, "What other class do you have?"

"News writing and reporting."

"Oh, yeah, I'm taking that next year," I say, nodding. "I'll see you tonight after the game."

244

I give him a quick hug and a kiss on the cheek, getting a good whiff of his cologne, which causes my eyes to close in dreamy contentment.

Our rainy Tuesday lets up a little by game time, and I'm thrilled our new half-time dance goes over well. We lose the game to Auburn by 3 points, so that sucked, but Lane is waiting for me after. He takes my hand, and we walk together out to my car.

"You did great tonight."

"Thank you. I'm glad you're here."

We stop next to my car. He leans on the side of it and pulls me to him, his hands around my waist.

"What are your plans for tomorrow?"

"Mm, I can't think of anything special."

"How about we get together at the library and work on the story assignment?"

"Sounds like a plan."

"Let's meet at the Gorgas library at two."

"Great, I'll meet you then."

"Goodnight, Rebecca." He kisses me before he turns to leave.

In a lustful state, I watch him walk to his car before I throw my bag into the back. Amanda walks up, smiles a knowing smile as if she now approves of Lane. She gets in, and we drive back to the house.

After a shower, I sit on my bed and pull out the folder for my creative writing class to read through the stories and discussion questions. It looks like we have to answer six discussion questions for each story. The third story is called "Freedom of Speech—Freedom of Choice. As I read it, it occurs to me that this may have been written by Olivia, one of the editors for *The Crimson White*. It reminds me of the discussion she and I had a month ago when I accidentally overheard her and another girl discussing their feelings of injustice toward the SGA elections and the Machine's interference. I read a portion of the story.

245

...There seems to be a sense of entitlement when it comes to the involvement of the Greek's and the secret society known as the Machine. They have controlled the votes on campus for years and even some state elections. It's a new age, a time for us to take a step forward in voting our conscience. Let's put forth an effort to stand together, united but unique and unsolicited in our thoughts, decisions and our votes. We are each individuals with thoughts, abilities, and judgements. We have no need for only the mere illusion of democracy. We don't care for dictatorship or controlled elections. Let freedom ring, and the machine hear our cry . . .

I finish the story and read a few of the questions that Professor Brigg has added.

1.) Is this simply an opinion from an Independent or is this story true for all students Greek or other?

2.) Does the story appear too biased?

3.) Does the story engage the reader until the end? Yep, this will be an interesting discussion with Lane tomorrow.

I switch to the next story titled "Storm before the Sun." I know this one is Lane's. It's a true story, that much I know. It's engaging until the end, and it reads almost like fiction. One portion strikes me, and I read it again.

The fog rolls in and the glassy surface of the sea shines light like a mirror. I anchor out just far enough from shore that it's a distant horizon. I lie on my back flat on the deck and feel the silence of the sky staring down at me. Just before the break of dawn, the only sounds are the lapping waves against the side of the boat.

I feel the pressure of family, school, friends, and demands ease from every pore of my body. I can feel the knots untying from my mind. I'm lulled to sleep, wrapped in a sense of security, my blanket is the sea. Suddenly, I am awakened by pelting rain hitting my face that feels like needle pricks on my skin. The wind is blowing hard, and the swells of the waves are crashing over the sides of the boat.

246

I've sailed in Regattas many times with my father and uncles, so my decision to venture out alone was not irresponsible of me, but the fact I never told anyone I left to take the sailboat out was certainly a mistake. I make it to the emergency radio and signal for help. I use my phone to dial 911, then I call my dad. He doesn't answer, so I leave a quick message. "I'm in the harbor, four miles south west, and a storm has come up; need help." I work quickly to adjust the sails, but the strong winds break the mast, and I have to use the jib sail.

There's an order and a sense of discipline to sailing as well as a calmness to it. Rough storms can prove how strong a sailor you are and prove how tough you are. I wasn't expecting a storm or a rescue before dawn that day. I was only after the comfort and peacefulness of being on the sea, but I got more than that. I gained knowledge that confronting a storm on the ocean can be like fighting God and having the universe against you. It gave me the courage to see truth, the security of calmness to feel safe, and the ability to understand twenty years from now I know I won't be disappointed by something I didn't try. Instead, I'll face things head on, try new things, and live without regrets . . .

His story is so good. I'm almost in tears reading it. I feel like I've climbed into his soul, his person and his spirit, that causes me to feel something tangible and honest. I read the discussion questions for Lane's story, so I'm prepared for our study date in the library tomorrow. *Study date . . . this is going to be the most fun studying I've ever had!*

37
#OTP

I'm totally looking forward to my study date on this wonderful hump day. After my last class ends, I head back to my room to freshen up and gather my things to take to the library. Bella wanders in while I'm packing my stuff.

"Hey, where are you off to?" she asks, getting a Coke out of the fridge, before landing on her bed.

"Lane and I are meeting at the library to work on an assignment that's due on Tuesday. By the way, are you planning to go to the party at Heat Pizza tomorrow night?"

"I don't think I'm going. I'm definitely voting for him. He seemed like a great guy from what I could tell when you were interviewing him but I'm not sure I want to go to a campaign party."

I step closer to her. "I get that, but I think it'll be a lot of fun, and you get tickets for free drinks. I think everyone gets at least two. If you change your mind let me know. I'm going with Lane."

"Yeah, okay, sounds good—I'll think about it and let you know tomorrow. Have fun on your study date," Bella says, with a Cheshire cat grin.

As I near the library, I see Lane walking up the sidewalk, and I run to catch up. He sees me, smiles, and takes my hand.

"How was your day?" he asks.

"Much better now that I get to spend it with you." I lean my head into his shoulder.

We get on the elevator, get off on the third floor, and find a quiet table in the back corner. We pull our chairs next to each other. I get out my folder, notebook, and a pen. I silence my phone and set it on the edge of the table and throw my backpack underneath.

Lane asks, "So, did you read the stories and answer all the questions?"

"I did read the stories, and I read all of the discussion questions, but I didn't answer anything yet. I figured we would go over it together."

"Do you want to start with "Freedom of Speech," my least favorite?" he asks.

"Sure, I figured that one would be the hardest for us maybe. Well, maybe not hard, but you know what I mean." *Since it's a blow to the secret society.* I laugh and giggle. I'm feeling a little bit silly right now and find it hard to be serious and study next to Lane. He looks *so* good and smells divine.

He pulls out the "Freedom of Speech-Freedom of Choice" story questions and reads the first question aloud.

"To answer this question, I'd say it's absolutely the opinion of an Independent and non-Greek student."

"So, you think the story is totally biased?"

"Yes, our elections are democratic. We allow everyone to vote their own choice. The elections are not rigged. We are not padding votes. If they're complaining that the Greek campaigns are more impressive or we spend more money to promote our candidates, then they should do the same. They have the same campaign options we have. This is America, and though it may be true that one team has the upper hand with spending more money or has more influence, it doesn't mean that the election is unfair. Everyone has the opportunity to vote their choice. I also don't think they can complain that the campaigning is unfair. This is a political office, and this is simply politics."

I remember Lane's mother was the Lieutenant Governor and ran for Governor when they lived in Washington D. C. before they moved to New York. I feel like he probably knows a

249

lot about politics. Even with all the rumors about the Machine controlling politics on campus, so far, I haven't seen control, only campaigning. I decide to agree with him on his answer. I jot down some notes for the first two questions, and we move on and finish the last two.

"For the third question I thought it was well written, and it held my attention to the end."

"I agree with that, too," he says.

"Does it get your vote?" I look at him with a big smile.

"Nope. I have another story in mind that will be getting my vote."

I start laughing again and put my hand over my mouth to keep from being too loud, since we're in a library.

"You really have the giggles today, but it's super cute."

"I know, I'm sorry, I can't help it. You smell amazing. Have I ever told you that before?" I lean in close to him and nuzzle his neck with my nose.

He kisses the top of my head. "It's going to be really hard for me to keep my hands off of you if we keep this up," he says, taking a deep breath.

I pull away and straighten my posture. "Let's get back to business," I say, sitting up straight and tall.

"Shall we move on to the story titled "Storm before the Sun," I ask, getting serious again. "I loved this story. It brought me to tears, and I felt like I could feel your soul. It's so well written. It's dramatic and scary but has so much feeling and emotion. I know it was scary for you having gone through the experience of being close to death."

Lane looks at me and says, "Yes, it was scary, and I was afraid at the time, but I had gone out there to clear my mind of stress. When I was rescued and back on shore, I felt a sense of accomplishment and a drive that made me feel I could do anything. It was a bad thing that lead to a good thing. It helped me get through my sophomore year of high school and allowed me to pursue things I felt unsure of doing before the boating accident. You could say it was a major turning point in my life.

250

I'll never forget it. It gave me confidence, and it made me who I am today."

I'm stare at him, speechless and in awe. A feeling of pride fills me. I reach over and hug him.

Lane gets very serious, "Okay, this is a study session not a make out session."

I start laughing again and snorting. I put my head down and cover my mouth to keep the laughter stifled. I jerk my head up and flip my hair out of my face. When I do, I hit my phone, and it slides off the table and onto the floor and continues sliding across the slick floor under the table next to us landing with a thud against the wall.

"Oops," I say, meekly.

I crawl under the table on all fours to get to my phone. When I get to it, I notice Lane has crawled under the table with me. My giggle fit starts up again. He presses a hand over my mouth to keep me quiet. I can tell he wants to laugh, too. He pulls me close, pulls his jacket off, puts it over our heads like at tent, and we start making out. *Our library date has turned into a hot make out session after all.*

While under the table, we hear voices and hurried walking. It sounds like two men talking to each other about finding someone. I start to crawl out from under the table, but Lane pulls me back and puts his finger to his lips and makes the "Shhhhh" sound. We're huddled close together facing each other, and I'm trying so hard to keep all my giggling quiet. Lane takes the jacket off of our heads and crawls out from under the table. I follow behind him. When we sit in our seats, I notice two guys with long lens cameras get on the elevator and some guy standing next to our table. He has reddish blonde hair shaved at his neck and above his ears, but the front is long and hangs down over one eye. He whispers something to Lane then leaves.

I ask, "Who was that? His hair reminds me of the lead singer for COIN. Your hair might look cute like that, too." I reach up and play with his hair and move it to hang down in front of one eye. We both start laughing again and he pulls me close and shushes me.

"That's my fraternity brother, Ben. "Read the first question. You can play with my hair later. I want to finish this assignment before ten tonight." He gives me a sideways glance when he says that.

"Okay, so the knots being untied in the author's mind could be like the knots that you tie a boat to the dock with or even the knots that calculate the speed that the boat is going. Those could both be symbolism." Lane nods his head in agreement.

"And the glassy surface of the sea shines light like a mirror could be the writer baring his soul to the sky just before the storm approaches." Lane nods again.

"Question two you've answered for me."

For question three I say, "The story has a dramatic feel but also emotional elements, and the storm reflects the emotions that the writer was facing before he lay down on the deck and fell asleep. The storm could also be symbolic for the troubles the author was trying to get away from by sailing out onto the sea, in the first place. I don't think anything needs to be changed or improved. In my humble opinion this story is perfect, and it's getting my vote, for sure," I say, lightly rubbing my nose against his.

"Babe, you're making me want to crawl back under this table with you again, but we need to finish these last questions, and we saved the best for last." He gives me a sexy smile.

I make a face and pretend I'm sliding down my chair back under the table.

Lane grabs my arm and says, "Uh, uh, uh." He remains serious and gives his answer for the first question. "I liked the switch from Spanish to English. I thought it was clever, and you are minoring in Spanish, so I thought it was a good use of that."

I say, "Mucho Gracias." and try not to laugh. I hold it in, but it's hard. Lane moves on to the next discussion question.

"The story reminded me of JFK, Jr., his wife Carolyn Bessette, and his former assistant Rose Marie. I find it hard to answer question three. I like the cliffhanger, which gives readers an option of guessing what happens in their own mind. I also agree it does have the makings of a novel. I could see where the cliffhanger ends, and the story picks up with the main character arriving in New York. And the final question, yes, this story gets my vote. I think you should vote for your own story, too, instead of mine."

"Why?" I ask, looking a little sad.

"Because yours is good, and its fiction. Mine may be good but it's a story about something that happened to me when I was fourteen. Since you used creative writing skills as well as your imagination to write it, I think you should get as many votes as possible and win the spot in *The New Yorker*."

I give him a puppy dog sad face and say, "But I really want to vote for you."

He tries to give me the same puppy dog sad face and says, "But, I really want you to be the winner."

I roll my eyes up to the ceiling and say, "I'll think about it."

"That's my girl. I'll walk you back to the house," he says, closing his notebook.

Lane and I walk hand-in-hand across campus laughing and talking. My heart is so happy and full right now it wants to burst. We get to the sidewalk near the front door and he stops, leans down, and kisses me. I reach up and pull him close, kissing him back with soft gentle kisses. We're interrupted by a loud whistle from some guys walking down the other side of the street. We glance their way then turn back toward each other.

Lane says, "I'll pick you up an hour before the campaign party starts. If you don't mind coming early and helping with some of the set up?"

"Perfect, I'll be glad to help."

He takes my hand and kisses it before he turns to walk away. I'm all smiles as I walk inside for dinner with my Phi sisters, bursting with feelings of being in love.

*****

When we arrive at Heat Pizza the next day, some of Lane's fraternity brothers are outside setting up the check-in-table. Inside, most of the tables have been pushed to the back or to the side, leaving a large open area. There's a small stage set up on the far end where a DJ is hooking up speakers and a microphone.

Lane says, "I need to check on a couple of things. Would you help with blowing up some balloons?"

We walk behind the bar to find a helium tank and a box of balloons. I start cutting ribbon, and Lane wanders off. A few minutes later a few freshmen KD's show up and come over to help me with the balloons.

One of the girls says her name is Mary Margaret and asks, "Who are you here with?"

"I'm Lane's girlfriend, Rebecca."

Her eyes get big and she says, "Oh wow, Lane is so cute."

She glances at her friend, and they smile at each other. *I wonder, has Ashley started some sort of Lane Townsend fan club at the KD house?*

Mary Margaret and her friend Sophia help me tie balloons to each of the ten balloon weights. We set them around the restaurant to create a festive party look. I see more KD's hanging campaign posters on the walls and windows. When the DJ turns up the tunes, Lane appears by my side.

"Thank you for helping out tonight. The place is looking great," he says.

Adam walks up, shakes Lane's hand and says, "Hi Rebecca, how are you? Thank you for helping put this event together tonight. I know it will be a huge success."

254

"We're glad to do it, Adam. Anything to put the right candidate in office," Lane says, cheerfully. I smile and nod in agreement.

Adam turns to meet, greet, and chat with others around the room. People are coming in by the droves, and Adam is going to have a busy night talking and shaking hands with everyone. I text Lexi and Bella, telling them there's free pizza here as well as drinks and a DJ.

Bella texts back, *U had me at free pizza. We're on the way.*

By the time Lexi and Bella walk in there are at least five hundred people inside, and it's a tight squeeze trying to walk around. There are even people hanging out on the patio. Bella and Lexi make their way over to where Lane and I are.

"Thanks for coming," I say happily.

"This is quite the party," Bella says. Her eyes roam around the room.

"Yeah, it's like frat party times two in here," Lexi says, with a short laugh.

Lane excuses himself and hops onto the stage. He taps on the microphone to get everyone's attention. He greets the crowd and introduces Adam. He's so polished and self-confidant I'm beaming at him. Before he hops off the stage, he gives me a wink and a smile.

Adam makes an awesome speech, and the hundreds that have gathered are now in a very good mood, and the cheering is contagious. When the noise dies down, Lane is interrupted by someone wanting to talk to him. Lexi and I walk over to get more drinks. On the way through the mass of people, I see Ashley with Amanda and some other senior KD girls. Ashley has the attention of the eight or so people gathered in her circle. I don't want to think about her right now or have any type of contact with her after her display at the Undertaker's Ball.

I point her out to Lexi and Bella and whisper, "That's the girl I called you about the day you left for Thanksgiving break.

255

The one that Lane used to date. She's so animated right now like she's performing. What could she possibly be talking about?"

Bella yelps, "Stop looking at her. I remember seeing her at the Undertaker's Ball. You know Lane's not into her. She's just a diva chick. She's very pretty, but she has nothing on you. You're genuine. It's obvious Lane prefers you to *that*." She motions with her hands toward Ashley when she says that. Somehow Ashley happens to look our way just as Bella flings her hand in her direction. She gives a deadly look. I turn back to Bella and roll my eyes.

A few people are starting to leave, I'm feeling less claustrophobic and can breathe more easily. Lane comes back with a drink, looking more confident than ever.

"What do you think about the party? A success?" he asks.

"Absolutely," I say. "There had to be over six hundred people here tonight."

"Yes," he responds. "And there were even more outside. I had someone film a little tonight. I'd like you to edit some clips to post. We'll have another party like this at Innisfree the day of the election. I can take you back to the house now, if you're ready to go. I'll need to come back and help take some things down and pack up. I don't want you to have to hang around for that."

"That's okay, I can get a ride back with Bella and Lexi."

The three of us walk to the parking lot toward Bella's car. Before we get to the car someone pushes into me. I almost fall into a puddle of water, but Bella and Lexi grab both my arms before I tumble. Stumbling to stand upright, I look up and see a group of girls laughing and running away from us, one of the girls is Ashley. Lurching toward them, I yell, "he doesn't want you! I'm his girlfriend now. Get that through your thick head, you scud."

Ashley starts to make her way back toward me, looking every bit the evil witch, I think she is. She moves to hit me, but Bella moves in front of me blocking Ashley blow.

256

Ashley's friends pull her away. I hear them say, "Come on she's not worth it."

38
#W/L

Walking into the lecture hall on Tuesday morning, I'm nervous. I feel really weird about people discussing my story in class. I know no one will know who wrote any of them, but it's still going to be a little strange. I sit down next to Lane, who leans over and kisses me hello.

"Are you nervous about the discussions today?" I ask.

His glorious smile is radiating. "No, and you shouldn't be either."

"Well, I don't know about that, but I'll try to stay calm," I say, half laughing.

When Professor Brigg walks in, he asks each row to gather all the discussion questions so he can walk by to collect them. He asks us to write our name on each sheet before we send it down. He turns on the projector and the discussion questions for Freedom of Speech pop up. A heated discussion breaks out between Olivia and Lane during the discussion of *Freedom of Speech—Freedom of Choice*. Professor Brigg has to intercede so we can move on. Lane's story gets lots of praise.

My story provokes some very interesting discussion about my story line, and I can tell that most of the class would love to read the rest of the story. It appears that Lane is the only one who figured out that the story was a spoof on JFK, Jr., his wife and assistant. I couldn't tell if Professor Brigg was impressed that Lane knew this or annoyed that only one student was able to figure it out. Class ends five minutes later than usual, and

Professor Brigg tells us to be on the lookout for an email that will let us know which story wins.

The rest of January is cold and damp. I spend most days walking to classes wearing rain boots and a raincoat. Tonight, will be our last home game performance for the month. I've come back to the room to work on assignments and get out of the freezing rain before heading over to Coleman for the pre-game festivities. While I'm finishing up an assignment submission, I receive a new email from Professor Brigg. A shiver of nervous energy shoots through my body when I open it and start reading, *Congratulations to our story winner, Rebecca Brant. Rebecca's fictional cliffhanger Prince of the Past" has won the opportunity to be published in The New Yorker. I've worked out the details with the editors, and I've listed the information that goes along with this honor below. I know all of you will want to congratulate Rebecca in class on Tuesday.*

I continue reading the rest of the email. My article will be published in the April issue of our campus magazine *Alice*. Wow, my Netflix piece was just in this month's issue, and I'll have another published piece in there a few months later. I continue reading the rest of the email.

It says, I will be flown to New York in April to meet with the staff and editors for a tour, and the final proofs of my story. The story will be published in the July issue. It says I have the opportunity to intern for eight weeks during the spring semester next year under the supervision of two of their editors. I jump off the bed and start bouncing around the room. Grabbing my phone, I immediately call Lane. When he answers I'm out of breath and can hardly speak.

I finally get out in-between puffs of breath, "They chose my story. Lane, I can't believe it. My story is going to be published in *The New Yorker.*"

"I knew you could do it. I had every confidence in you, babe. I am so happy for you. Let's go out after the game tonight to celebrate."

"Yes, I'd like that. I need to call my parents and tell them. I'll see you later tonight."

I hang up and dial Mom's cell. She answers on the first ring. I'm still jittery and running around in circles. I burst out, "Hey, Mom, you're not going to believe this."

She answers, "What is it, Bex?" with concern in her voice.

"The assignment I wrote over Christmas break was chosen to not only be published in *Alice* the campus magazine, but also in *The New Yorker* in July. They'll also fly me up in April for two days to meet with the editors."

Mom's voice sounds out of breath, too. "Bex, that's incredible. We're so proud of you. You never cease to impress us. Can you send us the story? We would love to read it."

"Yes, it's on my computer. I can email it now."

"Do you think we can all fly out to New York with you and make it a family trip? Maybe we could all be on the same flight and stay a few days longer and make it a mini vacation?"

"That might work. They didn't give me a specific date. It says for me to choose the best two days in April to come out. I have the address, phone numbers and the name of the person to contact at *The New Yorker*. It also gives a few hotel options. They aren't paying for my hotel room, only my plane ticket."

"That's good they let you choose the dates that work best for your schedule. If you choose a Thursday/Friday date, we could leave on the same flight on Wednesday night from Atlanta and return together on Sunday."

"Yeah, that sounds like a plan. It's a few months away, but I think by the first of March I'll have a better idea which days in April will work. Make sure to tell Lauren when she gets home, please."

"She'll be thrilled for you. Have a great performance tonight. We love you and are proud of you, Bex."

After hanging up with Mom, Bella walks in. "Guess what! You're never going to guess." I grab her in a bear hug.

Bella looks at me like I've gone crazy, "Mmmm, let me see, Ashley has been stricken with a fatal disease."

"I wish, but no. My story was chosen to be published in *Alice* in April and in *The New Yorker* in July. I get to go to New York to meet with them for two days in April."

Bella's eyes are huge. "Bex, that's amazing."

She hugs me, and we both jump up and down.

"I know. I still can't believe it. I just got off the phone with Mom. I called Lane first, and he said we'll go out and celebrate after the game tonight." My voice comes out a little high pitched from holding in my breath too long.

"Bex, this is so exciting."

Bella sits on her bed, and I fall back on mine, my head still spinning. A text from Amanda pops up on my phone about riding to the game with me tonight. I send a quick text back and take a deep breath, trying to relax enough to gather composure to get into my uniform and get ready to dance at the basketball game.

*****

Lane greets me after the game with a bouquet of red roses. We end up at Innisfree for a casual celebration dinner.

Lane says in a soothing tone, "So, I know you're excited about *The New Yorker* and your trip to meet and work with the editors. Have you been to New York before?"

"No, but I'm really looking forward to it. In fact, my mom asked if I might be able to choose a Thursday/Friday trip and turn it into a long weekend for the whole family. I know my parents went there years ago, and they talked about taking us on vacation to New York, but it just never happened. Since you live there, are you going to recommend all the best places to visit?" I ask, batting my eyelashes at him.

"I could give you a list of all the best tourist places and some local favorites. Your family is probably wanting to see all the sights. I would recommend a Broadway show. I can help you get tickets for some of the best. If your parents have any specific

261

questions, make sure to let me know and I'll help answer as best I can."

I change the subject. "Tomorrow's Groundhog Day, we get to see how many more days of winter are left."

"Like if he sees his shadow there's five more weeks of winter, and if he doesn't there'll be an early spring?"

"Yes, exactly, and speaking of five more weeks, I only have four more games to dance at in February. The last basketball game before the SEC championship is on the 27th of February. No basketball on the 14th, by-the-way."

Lane with a coy smile says, "Oh, do you think you might have special plans for February 14th?"

"I sure hope I do." I give a shy smile.

After dinner Lane drives me back to the house and helps me carry in my bag and roses. We step into the foyer and say goodnight. He kisses me on the forehead, and I wave bye as he walks out the door.

Back in the room, Bella's in bed but still awake and immediately perks up when she sees my roses.

"Wow, those are divine."

"Lane was waiting for me after the game with these in his hand. He looked like a modern-day Prince Charming standing there. I'm going downstairs to look for a vase big enough to hold them."

I find an array of vases in a cabinet and select one. It looks beautiful sitting on my desk. After positioning it just so, I plop down onto my bed to study.

"Do you have plans for Saturday night yet?" Bella asks

"I haven't made any plans for Saturday yet, what's up?"

"Lexi, Cat and I are signed up to volunteer at the Young Life banquet Saturday night. It involves a free meal and an opportunity to meet some of the directors and learn about job opportunities for summer camps and other leadership roles."

"Sure, count me in."

*****

Only three more months left in my sophomore year. It's hard to believe. I wish this year could last forever, since it feels like the best year of my life, so far. This week has flown by since I found out about winning the assignment in *The New Yorker*. Lane's been a huge motivation these past few months, but my besties, Bella and Lexi, have been in my corner for two years now I don't know what I'd do without those two. I'm glad to be volunteering with them at the Young Life banquet tonight. It'll be a blast. Only problem is I'm still not sure what to wear.

"Bella, what are you wearing to the Young Life Banquet tonight?" I ask, staring into my closet.

"A dress but nothing really dressy. It's nice but not fancy."

I poke through my closet and take out a floral romper dress and pair it with leather booties. After Bella, Lexi and I are ready to leave we text Cat to meet us. Cat walks over, and we meet her in the parking lot next to my car. I set my phone in the charger just as a text from Lane pops up. *Have fun with the girls tonight. I miss u.*

I'm glad he's cool with me hanging with my friends tonight. He knows it's a fundraiser and a volunteer opportunity for me, so he doesn't mind.

When we arrive one of the directors offers us several options, check-in-table, greeter, or food service. Lexi and Cat choose greeter, and Bella and I choose check-in-table. Cat and Lexi greet everyone as they arrive with a program and send them to us to check-in and get their name tags and table numbers. Most of the guests are parents of middle or high school students who have children involved in Wyldlife or Young Life. Bella tells me this event is their biggest fund raiser of the year. While we're working the check-in, Grant, Adam and a few other guys walk in.

263

Grant is talking as he walks by and doesn't notice me. After they walk past, I nudge Bella.

"I just saw Grant walk in. I haven't spoken to him in months. It feels weird to see him."

Bella shrugs. "He's probably one of the guest speakers tonight."

At the start of the event, Bella and I take seats in the back of the room. When it's time for us to make our way to the buffet line, I know there's no way for me to avoid running into Grant. I take a deep breath and push on trying to be calm and collected. When we get closer to the buffet, I see his group walk toward us. He sees me, and I smile.

"Hi, Grant, it's good to see you. How have you been?"

He looks a little surprised to see me but smiles and says, "Hey, Bex. I've been great. It's good to see you, too. Glad you could come tonight."

"Thank you. Are you one of the guest speakers?"

"Yes, I'm talking about working for the middle school Wyldlife camp and the Young Life camp in North Carolina I worked at last summer."

"Nice," I say, picking up a plate and moving into the line with Bella and Cat.

After we get our food, Lexi, Bella, Cat and I walk back to our table in the back of the room. A worship band comes on and plays a few songs. One of the directors opens with a prayer and a welcome speech. A slideshow presentation about Young Life events and summer camps is shown on a big screen, and I see lots of fun pictures of Lexi, Bella, and Grant working but looking like they're having the best time of their lives.

The slideshow ends, the music is turned down and Grant is introduced. He takes the stage and talks about why he's been a camp counselor for the past two years and what the experience means to him. He's so cute, earnest, and endearing. His speech is heartfelt, giving me inspiration to want to serve whole heartedly this summer while working at camp, too. My heart twinges a little thinking about Grant and me at camp all summer together.

He has that sweet South Carolina accent and a volunteer giving heart. *Not to mention he's still hot.* A few old feelings emerge. After Grant speaks, Adam is introduced. His speech is similar to the one he gave during our interview.

Adam leaves the stage, and one of the directors introduces more of the volunteer leaders to talk about the programs for middle and high school students during the school year. They also give information on becoming a leader, serving as a camp counselor, and the opportunity to donate financially, since they're nonprofit. When the event is over, I notice a cute girl talking with Grant, and they look like they're leaving together. As they walk past, he gives me a slight wave. I feel a little dissed, which I know I shouldn't. I look over and get Bella's attention.

"Do you think Grant is dating the girl he left with?"

Bella huffs. "I'm not sure, Bex. Why does it matter? You have a boyfriend that you think you're in love with anyway."

"Um, yeah, I know, I was just asking."

She gives me a look like "Can't fool me."

In the car on the way home, Cat and Lexi are talking about volunteering to lead a group of high school girls again next year, and about working at summer camp again. Lexi leans over the seat and taps me on the shoulder.

"Bex, do you want to work with us at summer camp this year?"

"Well, it would definitely be a lot of fun, that's for sure. I'll think about it."

Cat warns, "Make sure to decide before the end of April. The application has to be turned in around the 20th."

Later, as I'm getting ready for bed, I decide to vlog about volunteering today and caption it *Fun ways to volunteer while in college* When I finish, I can't help but remember seeing Grant leaving with a girl. *But I'm not still into him, right?*

39
#Highkey

I'm up early putting on one of my uniforms for the *Crimson Cabaret* volunteer day at the children's hospital. It's been a crazy, busy week. Honestly, I didn't know if I was coming or going. Both the *Crimson White* and *Alice* had me do a quick photo shoot and interview session about my story being chosen for *The New Yorker*. It felt surreal, for sure. On top of that we decorated the house top to bottom for Valentine's Day and during our chapter meeting we drew names for "secret Valentines." It's like playing secret Santa. That spurred on a shopping trip to Target. Lexi asked me what I was getting Lane. Guys are hard to buy for on Valentine's Day, in my opinion. Bella suggested buying him cologne. She's never going to let me live down my stalker moment in the men's department. When Lexi suggested getting tickets for the Tucfest music festival at the riverfront amphitheater, I knew that would be a great idea, especially with the cool bands coming, Haim, COIN, Mumford and Son's and Kid Rock. I have no idea what Lane has planned for me for Valentine's Day, but I'm sure he'll make it special. My phone rings, pulling me out of my thoughts, and I grab it, answering quickly to keep from waking Bella.

"Hello," I whisper into the phone, walking into the hallway still trying to be quiet.

"Hey, babe, I just wanted to see about doing something fun with you after the game tonight?"

"Sure, I'm up for doing something later. Why are you up so early?"

"I wanted to get some studying in before the day got away. Do you want to see a movie?"

"Yeah, that would be a lot of fun," I whisper.

"How about the new Stephen King movie?" Lane suggests.

"Okay, hopefully it's not too scary."

"Have fun today with your service event. I'll see you after the game. Bye, babe."

I sneak back into the room, quietly finish getting ready and text Amanda to see if she is ready to go. We stop to pick up two more girls along the way. It's a short drive to the hospital because it's so close to campus. We take the elevator to the children's floor and meet up with the rest of our team in the hall. Local TV camera crews are set up to film us in the large common room. The children's faces light up when our team walks in. The basketball team came out today, too. Making these children smile and feel better for a while is a great feeling. We do a short routine then pass out the goodie bags and take pictures with the kids and their families. The hospital asks us to stop by the rooms of the children who were unable to come to the common room, and the TV crew follows us, filming the whole event.

When I get back to the house around noon, I head to my room to change. Bella's not there, but I see a small stuffed animal with a note attached to it sitting on my bed. I read the card from my secret Valentine. I get out one of the cards I got for my secret Valentine, and I add a gift card to it then I walk down the hall and slide it under her door. After changing clothes, I go down to the kitchen for something to eat and see Bella and Lexi eating lunch.

"Hey, Bex, how was your children's hospital thing today?" Bella asks, cheerfully.

"It was so fun, and the kids were so sweet. Some of them were really sick, which was sad, but the day was fun. It's all probably going to be on the local news tonight."

"Oh wow! We should try to catch that," Lexi trills.

267

"Yeah, that's cool," Bella adds.

Between bites of my sandwich I say, "It is, and tonight TV crews are filming us prior to the start of the game, actually before the last four games. We've switched off with the cheerleaders. They're doing the meet-and-greets and photo ops, and we're being filmed while we do a pregame performance."

Bella laughs. "You're going to be famous, one way or another, from being published in *The New Yorker* or from dancing on TV."

I shake my head at Bella, pick up my drink and scurry up to my room to decide what to wear on my date. I send a text to Mom and Dad to make sure they remember to watch the game on TV and record it. These last four games feature us more than the cheerleaders, and it'll be nice to have some good routines on film to save for posterity, my kids, or something along those lines.

The game ends in overtime, and we win with a three-point buzzer beater. I follow my teammates into the locker room to change. Lane meets me out front, and we walk hand-in-hand to his car.

"How was your service project?" he asks. I love that he's always so interested in what I do.

"It was fun and sweet seeing all the kids and their families. It's funny, I'll be on TV a lot today. The local news crews were filming us this morning, and tonight the ESPN crews were filming us. Mom texted me that they saw me and recorded everything. Mom and Dad thought it was cool watching me on TV tonight instead of being at the game."

"I like being at the game. I'd rather see you in person." Lane chuckles and gives my hand a squeeze. "So, do you feel like popcorn, candy or both?"

"Ooooo both, for sure. If this movie is too scary, I'll be sitting in your lap."

"That's why I picked the movie," Lane says, with a wink and sheepish grin.

40
#Beminevalentine

My eyes open to a dozen pink and red balloons floating above me on the ceiling. One of the strings has a note attached. I pull the note off the string and read it. *I want to wine, dine and have you, be mine. You mean more to me each new day, in every way, my sweet Valentine.* It's signed LKT. I flip the card over, and it says, *Look for the scarf.* I notice one of the balloons has a red scarf tied around the bottom and untie it. Another note falls down. I unfold that. *Put me on and we'll be gone; walk out to the lawn and you'll see John. I promise to have you home before dawn.* In tiny print it says, *over.* I flip the note to the other side and read, *5 p.m. outside with scarf in hand,* and it's signed with Lane's fancy signature. Bella wakes up and screams.

"What the heck, man? Has your secret Valentine gone overboard?"

"They're from Lane and had a few notes attached to them. Apparently, I'm supposed to be outside ready to go at five o'clock with this red scarf in my hand and something about seeing someone named John."

"Wow, Bex, I wonder who got these balloons in here?"

"I don't know, but Lane had to have one of our Phi Mu sisters do it. He's known Amanda for a while, so I could ask her about it, or I can wait and see what my surprise is and ask her about the balloons later."

"Yeah, ask her about the balloons after you've gone out and had a fabulous Valentine's date. If this is the prequel, then the actual date must be mind-blowing. I'm going to take a quick shower," Bella says, as she opens the door. "Oh, look, Bex, our secret Valentines are outside our door. You have a box of chocolates and a card, and I have a cute stuffed animal and a card. Have you done your secret Valentines for today?"

"I'm having something delivered to her this afternoon. How about you?"

"I left a card and flowers on the kitchen table for mine to find at breakfast this morning."

"Cool, Happy Valentine's Day, Bestie." I walk over, hug Bella, then pick up my box off the floor.

I lie back on my bed and take a picture of the balloons covering the ceiling, then post it to Snapchat with the caption *"From the greatest BF eva!"*

The day drags on. I'm too excited about my mysterious date tonight that it's hard to pay attention to what's going on in class, so I text Lane instead.

Happy Valentine's Day. Loved the balloons in my room this morning.

He texts back, *Happy Valentine's Day to my favorite girl.*

"What should I wear 2night, something really dressy and formal or just a nice dress?

A nice dress with a jacket, the red scarf, of course, and some shoes that are easy to slip off.

Mm, sounds specific, can't wait.

Me, too. He adds a heart emoji.

After class, I go back to the house, kick off my shoes and sit on my bed between the dangling strings from the balloons floating on my ceiling. Before I start on homework, I send my sister a text.

HVD. Do u have big plans with Brian?

We r going downtown 2night, but I don't know where yet, it's a secret. He sent me roses 2day with balloons.

Same. Lane secretly had a dozen balloons put in my room sometime after midnight. I woke up to pink and red balloons

270

*floating on my ceiling. And I have no idea where he's taking me
tonight, but it involves a red scarf. So, I'll have to let u know ltr.*
Cool, call me tomorrow. I want to hear all about it.

I look through my closet and find a short black knit skirt
and a long sleeve white blouse to go with it, red pumps that I can
easily slip off and my satin jacket in silver. I add a red rhinestone
necklace with matching earrings and curl my hair. Bella walks in
as I'm putting on lipstick.

"Hey, Bella, which purse do you think I should take?"

"I have a cute, beaded clutch that has red in it." Bella
reaches the top shelf of her closet and hands me a sequined clutch
with tiny red flowers on it.

"I think I'm all set." I twirl around to Bella's applause.

"You still don't know where you're going?" she asks.

"No clue, but I'll text you a pic when I get there."

"Lexi and I are going to dinner with Jack, Patrick, Cat and
Ryan. I'll text you a pic, and we can compare them and decide
who wins Valentine's Queen for a year."

I laugh and say, "Okay. Deal."

I stuff a few things into the purse and give Bella a hug as I
leave the room. I walk down the stairs to the front door. Opening
it, I see a black limo parked out front with a driver leaning
against the hood.

"Are you John?" I ask, walking toward him.

"Yes, ma'am. Let me help you with the scarf."

He opens the door to the limo, and there's no one inside.
He ties the scarf around my eyes and helps me in. "We're going
on a short fifteen- minute drive."

The car starts and soft piano music begins to play. When
the car stops and the door opens, someone takes my hand and
helps me out. The same person reaches for the scarf and unties it.
I open my eyes to see Lane standing in front of me holding a
dozen red roses tied with a huge bow. Starring at him stunned,
excitement leaks out from me as a smile plasters my lips and my
heart pounds ferociously in my chest.

271

"Ready?" He moves to the side and takes my hand. When he steps out of my way, I see that he was standing in front of a small private airplane.

I gasp and say, "Oh my God. Lane, are you serious? We're getting on a private plane right now?"

"Yes, it's just a short flight."

We climb the stairs up to the plane and sit side-by-side in the back. There is only one pilot and the two of us, and it's so romantic.

Looking into Lane's beautiful eyes, I say, "This is the most romantic thing in the entire world. There is no possible way my Valentine's Day could get any better. I feel like I'm dreaming."

Lane leans over, kisses me gently, and whispers in my ear, "You don't have to ever wake up."

"I dream of a lot of wonderful things, but I don't think I could have ever dreamed this up."

The flight is just under an hour. When we get off the plane, another limo waits for us.

Lane asks, "May I?" and pulls out the red scarf. "Just a short drive for the second part of the surprise."

I turn around so he can tie the scarf, and he leads me to the limo. Once we're seated soft piano music begins playing. Lane leans over and gently kisses my neck. Shivers go down my spine, and I gasp for breath.

He whispers as he kisses me softly, "You're so beautiful."

The limo stops, and Lane helps me out, takes my hand, and we walk for a while.

"It's not too much farther," he says.

When we stop, he unties my scarf, and we're standing in front of a table covered with a canopy set under palm trees next to a large swimming pool that overlooks the ocean. It's beyond breathtaking. There are lit candles everywhere. There's a table set for two and even a candle lit path that leads from our canopy covered table down to the beach. I stand in stunned silence.

272

"Lane, it's breathtaking. I don't have words. I don't know what to say."

He turns to face me. "You don't need to say anything. I want you to know you are very special to me." He pauses, staring into my eyes. "I love you, Rebecca."

I gasp for breath. "I love you, too," I say, as we stand staring into each other's eyes, frozen in time.

He leans in planting a gentle kiss on my lips then says, "How about dinner? May I?" He offers me his arm.

Lane pulls the chair out for me. He sits across the table and pours sparkling water into my glass. He holds his glass in the air.

"A toast to my beautiful Valentine."

"And to the best night of our lives," I add.

"The best night, so far," he says with a wink.

"Yes. The best night, so far." I hold my glass up again in a mock toast.

After studying the menu, I choose a salad and baked grouper. A few minutes later a waiter comes out and takes our orders.

"I'm curious as to how you're able to pull off a private plane and private dinner for two beach side, four driving hours from campus," I say, rubbing his leg with my toe under the table.

Lane smiles. "There's no need to know the details. Those are boring, anyway. Just know I want to make you feel special. I fell for you the first day I saw you. My heart has never felt like this before, and you mean everything to me." Lane takes my hand in his.

"I fell head over heels for you that first day, too."

We laugh and joke with each other over our romantic dinner. Lane and I take a selfie, and I text it to Bella, but I know it is impossible for her to guess where we are. She texts a picture of her, Jack, Lexi, Patrick, Cat and Ryan at what looks like a fancy restaurant.

After dinner, our waiter arrives with a plate of chocolate covered strawberries and two glasses of champagne. Lane and I feed each other strawberries, while sipping champagne.

"Do you want to go for a walk on the beach?" I ask.

I pick up one of the roses from the centerpiece and grab my phone. We both slip off our shoes and leave them on the sidewalk near the table before we walk down the boardwalk into the sand. At the water's edge I bend down and draw a heart with my finger and lay the rose in the center.

"Lane, stand next to me so that our feet are at the edge of the heart." I turn my flash on and take a photo of our feet together on the edge of the heart just as a wave comes up and almost washes it away. Then I text it to Bella. I post it to my Instagram with the caption *Best Valentine's Date Ever*. I search the location and find we're in Orange Beach, Alabama. I show my phone to Lane.

"I finally know where I am now."

We laugh, and he grabs my hand and pulls me toward the water. He rolls his pants up to his knees, and we splash around like kids.

We walk hand-in-hand back to our table and sit next to each other sipping our champagne.

I get a text from Bella with words in all caps *U R AT THE BEACH RIGHT NOW?*

Yep, quite the surprise, I may win best romantic date. And the photo I just texted you is going on my VSCO ltr. I might also become Valentine date VSCO famous, too. LOL.

Bella texts back, "*Holy Crap, will u be home 2night?*"

Yes, in about two hours or so. There might be a private plane ride involved.

U r telling every single detail when you get back 2nite. Don't even think about leaving anything out, and BTW, you've won Valentine Queen for the rest of your freaking life. VSCO fame or not.

I burst out laughing.

Lane says, "Should I even ask?"

274

"Just girl stuff." I shrug and tuck my phone back inside my purse. "I'm going to walk inside and use the restroom before we get back on the plane. I don't really want to go home," I say, giving Lane a pleading look.

The limo is waiting when we walk out of the main restaurant. We slip into the back and snuggle up close as Lane pushes the button on the privacy window, and we watch it go up. His fingers gently move up and down my arm, lingering near my neckline, I lean in, and we kiss nonstop until the limo parks in front of the plane. Lane helps me up the steep airplane steps and buckles me in.

"I want you to come with me over spring break next month," he says staring into my eyes. "My family is getting together on Cape Cod, and I'd like for you to meet my them," he says, after we take off.

Totally surprised by the invitation, and not sure of what to say. I say the first thing that pops into my head. "I don't know if I would be able to do that. My parents are spending money to fly with me to New York a week after spring break. I don't think they'll pay for me to fly to Cape Cod or even allow me to fly that far to spend a week with a boy."

"We would fly this plane from Tuscaloosa to New York. My new car would be waiting at the airport, and we'd drive that to Cape Cod. You would have your own room and bathroom in the house. My entire family, including my niece and nephew and my sisters would all be staying there. Your parents wouldn't be spending any money on the trip. I can ask them for you if you'd like."

I smile at Lane. He's being so sincere and serious. "You are so sweet to offer to do that, but I know that won't help. My parents are very old fashioned about me dating. Each time I had a date, I would have to bring him inside to meet my family first before we were allowed to go out together. Going on vacation with a boy would be out of the question."

Lane looks gloomy. "I really want you to come with me and meet my parents."

275

"I'd really, really like to."

"What would you normally be doing over spring break?"

"Last spring break I was with Lexi, Bella, and Cat. We stayed in one hotel room on the beach in Gulf Shores. It was all very tame. Seriously, the only wild things I've done have been with you, and those haven't really been wild, just crazy fun. I would probably be with Bella, Lexi, and Cat again at the beach this year."

Lane tries to give me a puppy dog sad face. "The house we would be staying at is right on the beach and has a heated pool. I love you, Bex. I want you to be with *me* over spring break somehow."

We stare into each other's eyes for a minute, then I say, "I'll think it over and see."

I lay my head on his shoulder and fall asleep. Lane kisses the top of my head to gently wake me up.

"We're back home, baby," he says quietly.

I blink as my eyes adjust to the light. We get into the first limo and arrive in front of Phi Mu within a few minutes. Lane walks me to the door, kisses me, then places soft gentle kisses down to my collar bone.

"Goodnight, I love you."

I whisper, "I love you, too."

I suddenly realize that I left his gift sitting on my desk. I quickly say, "I got you something, come inside for a second while I run up and get it."

I run into the room. Bella is asleep. I grab the box and run back down the stairs, trying to be as quiet as possible. I hand Lane the box. He opens it, and a happy smile appears on his face.

"The music festival. I love this. This will be fun."

"I'm so glad. I had no idea what to get you."

"It's perfect, babe."

He hands me my bouquet, then kisses my cheek before opening the door.

I slip off my heels and carry them and my roses to my room, then lay the roses across the desk. Quietly, I slip out of my clothes, crawl into bed, and think about skipping my first class in the morning. I fall asleep easily dreaming about private plane rides, the beach and being in love.

41

#YOLO

Surrounded by papers covering the floor, I'm studying when Bella walks in and leaps to her bed to avoid stepping on my mess.

"Shhheeesh," Bella huffs.

"Hey, girl. Sorry about the mess. Hard day I presume?"

Bella rolls over, looks at me, and says, "Just long. I'm tired."

"I know that feeling. I've been studying for almost two hours."

Bella slides off the bed onto the floor next to me.

"I bet you're kinda glad last night was the last game you had to dance at this season?"

I look over at Bella and give her a side nod. "Yeah, sort of. It's a long season with practices starting in September and going through the end of February and sometimes into March. So, it's good to get a break for the rest of the year."

Bella rolls onto her stomach and props up on one elbow. "I wish someone would crack my back."

I put down my pen. "Do you want me to stand on your back?" I ask.

"Yes, as long as you're barefoot."

I carefully stand on Bella's back with my bare feet, and we hear a crack.

"That felt great. I'm feeling better already. Oh, look what I found under the bed." Bella pulls out a balloon from Valentine's Day. "Look, it's still blown up but super tiny."

"Awwwwww, maybe it was meant for me to save," I say, with nostalgia in my voice. "I would never have guessed I'd meet someone like Lane."

Bella looks at me questioningly. "Like how? You've got that dreamy look again. Do you mean someone really good looking or really rich?"

"I don't know. I guess both."

"You don't give yourself enough credit, Bex. You're very smart, very talented, in your case a true triple threat, and if this writing gig you've got going doesn't work out, you can always be on Broadway. You're drop dead gorgeous."

I reach over, grab Bella's arm and pull her over for a hug. "Thanks, bestie, I love you too. You're a fantastic friend. I don't know what I'd do without you. Seriously, you keep it real."

"Any time," she says, smiling at me.

Bella gets up, grabs a drink out of the fridge, and sits on her bed. "We should start planning spring break. It's a little less than four weeks away."

I lean back against my bed with my knees up and look at Bella, "You know what Lane asked me on Valentine's night? That was several weeks ago, and I haven't really thought about it again until you said we need to plan spring break."

Bella shakes her head at me. "No, what did he ask you?"

"He wants me to go to Cape Cod and stay the week with him and his family. He said we would use that same private plane. It flies him into New York whenever he needs to go home. His car will be waiting for him there, and we would drive to his vacation house. He said he really wants me to meet his family." I start cleaning up all the papers I have scattered around me.

"Wow, what did you say?"

"I said I'd love to go, but my parents would never allow me to go on spring break with a guy, especially that far away. We

279

haven't talked about it since. I mean, I guess if my parents think I'm at the beach with you guys they'd never know."

Bella sets her drink down, looks me in the eye, and says, "Wait, what? You want to sneak off with him, fly to New York or Cape Cod, and tell your parents you're at the beach with me, Lexi, and Cat?"

I exhale loudly. "I don't know, Bella. I want to be with Lane, and he really wants me to go. I guess I figure everything will be fine, and what they don't know won't hurt."

Bella shakes her head and says, "Yeah, I don't know. I see your point, but it's a bit risky, I think."

"I know it is. I won't decide today. But if he asks me again, I may just tell him I'm going. Sometimes I lose all contact with reality when I look at him. It could happen that I magically say I'm going, and the next thing you know I'm on another private plane ride." I stand with my hands on my hips and give Bella a smarty pants face, as if to say, *you know what I mean.*

She rolls her eyes at me. "Oh, my gosh, Bex. Well, I know Lexi is in for the beach for sure. I need to text Cat and book our hotel room in Gulf Shores. Oh, by the way, now that the weather is warming up, some people were talking about going up to "the cliffs" this weekend."

"I'll be at Tucfest with Lane."

"Oh, that's right. You got him those concert tickets for Valentine's Day."

I turn on my phone to look at the weather for Saturday.

"Saturday will be sunny and 78 degrees, gotta love it," I say, smiling at Bella.

*****

I'm digging through my dresser drawer trying to find my favorite cut off shorts when I get a text. I look at my phone. *Hey, babe, what time should I pick u up for the concert?*

I'll be ready in 30.

280

I find my shorts and a white knit top that's open in the back, put them on, then French braid a long strand of hair down one side. I wander down the hall to ask if anyone has any glitter. I could only get red, silver and pink, so I mix all three colors together with some hair gel and add glitter to my braid. Then I apply some around my eyes, using a little Chapstick for the adhesive. I open the closet and find a cute pair of strappy sandals that tie around my ankles. Bella and Lexi walk in, both wearing swimsuits and cut off shorts.

Lexi says, "Hey Bex, you look awesome, love the glitter!"

"Thanks. You guys headed up to the lake to hang at the cliffs today?"

"Yes, we're looking for Bella's beach towel."

I bend over to tie up my sandals. "Y'all have fun. I'll be back late tonight. The concert probably won't be over until around eleven."

"Okay, see ya, Bex," Bella says, as she picks up her towel and flip flops. I wave bye and walk downstairs to wait for Lane.

By the time we arrive at the amphitheater, there's already a line—at least a hundred people or more. As we walk through security, we're handed a seat saver which allows us to leave our seats to get lunch, meet the band members at their meet-and-greets or shop the vendors at the festival.

We end up with center row seats about half-way back from the stage. Lane and I put our seat savers across our seats and tear off the claim tickets. We each take one then we head over to check out the food truck vendors.

I brought a small blanket with me to sit on and spread it out under the shade of a tree. We sit on the blanket eating our lunch, listening to the warm-up band playing, totally chillin' and enjoying the music and food.

"I'm curious, what's on your playlist?" I ask.

"I don't think I have any music from any of the bands playing today on my playlist. What's on yours?" he asks.

I open Spotify on my phone. "I have a few COIN songs and Kid Rock."

Lane laughs and says, "I don't think I know many Kid Rock songs."

I smile and put my hand on his knee. "I think you'd like them. Can I look through your playlist?"

Lane opens Spotify and hands me his phone.

I scroll through. "Wow, a lot of old school stuff. Boston, The Police, Steve Miller, a lot of rap music, oh and John Mayer. I like John Mayer, too."

Lane holds out his hand, "Show me your playlist."

I had him my phone. "Mm, no old school stuff at all." He reads my playlist aloud as he scrolls through. "A lot of country music, AJR, 21 Pilots, Rainbow Kitten Surprise, Post Malone, John Mayer, The Killers, Ed Sheeran, Jonas Brothers." He laughs.

"Our playlists are a lot different."

"Well, not too different. We both like Ed Sheeran, Post Malone, and John Mayer. I think the main difference is I have a lot of country music on mine. I think you could get into some of it." I give him a coy smile.

The opening act ends, and Lane and I pack up our picnic and head back to our seats. COIN comes on, and I'm up dancing. Lane seems to be enjoying himself, too. When their hit song "Talk too Much" comes on, I sing along and get Lane to dance with me.

"I could totally get used to this. I didn't think I could love watching you dance more than during the halftime show at the basketball game, but this is great."

When COIN's session ends, we decide to walk around and check out some of the vendor merchandise. I see some friends from dance team, and Lane and I walk over so I can introduce him. They invite us to stand in line with them to meet the members of COIN for photo ops. I look at Lane.

"Go ahead, babe. I'll grab us some drinks and meet you back at our seats."

I give Lane a quick kiss and happily join the girls in line, laughing and giggling about taking selfies with the band members.

By the time the third band is done, Lane and I have had several beers. We decide to get some snacks and more drinks. I drink a little water, but I'm definitely feeling buzzed. The last band is about to come on, and Lane walks up with more beer. Kid Rock opens with "Tennessee Mountain Top" and I dance and sing along. I notice Lane watching me with a smile out of the corner of my eye. I'm feeling really good. I know all the words. I stand in my seat and continue dancing. I hear whistles coming from behind me. I look down and smile at Lane. He has a permanent grin on his face. I throw all my inhibitions to the wind and let loose a little more as I enjoy Kid Rock's performance.

After the concert I take off for a potty break, and Lane tells me to meet him at the docks just below the amphitheater. It's late at night and a little cooler as I walk down to the river. He puts the blanket around my shoulders, and we sit on the dock with our feet dangling just above the water. The moon is full, the stars are out, and things are quieting down after a rowdy day. We lie back on the dock and stare up at the stars. I'm still feeling lightheaded like I've had way more to drink than I should have. Lane pulls me onto his lap, my legs straddle him. He kisses me passionately and slowly, then pauses, looking into my eyes.

"I really want you to come with me on spring break, Rebecca."

"I will," I say, and continue kissing him.

When he drops me off back at the house, we kiss goodnight, and I run up the stairs to the bathroom. I splash a little water on my face to wake up a bit. I walk into my room and find Bella and Lexi watching Netflix.

"Hey, how was the music festival?" Lexi asks, pausing the movie.

I walk over to the fridge and get out a bottle of water. "It was so much fun, but I think I drank a little too much. I was

283

dancing a little wild during Kid Rock. Like standing in my seat and getting whistled at and all."

Bella says, "Wow, Bex, that's not like you."

"I know. I was having a great time, though." I sit down on my bed, untie my shoes, and kick them off.

"Did Lane like the concert?" Lexi asks.

"Yes, I think so. Mostly he was enjoying watching me dance. So, I'm pretty sure he had a great time, too," I say with a grin.

"We saw your Instagram post with COIN. That was cool," Bella says.

"Did you meet any other bands?" Lexi asks.

"No, I stood in line with some friends to meet COIN but didn't want to stand in the long lines for the rest of the bands. I would have stood in line to meet Kid Rock, but it was getting late, and Lane and I walked down to the dock after the concert."

I start changing into an old T-shirt then stop and look at Bella and Lexi.

"I told Lane I would go with him on spring break."

I hear them gasp. "What do you mean?" Lexi asks.

"He asked me on Valentine's Day, and I told him I would think about it. I told him my parents wouldn't allow me to go that far away with a guy they've only met a few times. I had a little too much to drink today and got caught up kissing him on the dock tonight after the concert. I really want to go, like really bad. I'm not going to change my mind."

Bella and Lexi get up and sit on my bed on either side of me. Lexi puts her hand on my shoulder. "What are you planning to do? Will your parents think you're with us at the beach?"

I look at Lexi then over to Bella and nod. I lean my head down on Bella's shoulder.

Bella looks at me, "You're my best friend, Bex. You know I'll support you."

I grab Bella and Lexi by the hand. "Operation spring break is a go!" I say, lifting our hands in the air.

284

42

#Nobrainer

I stay in bed most of the day Sunday trying to recoup from my slight hangover. By two o'clock I take a shower and work on homework. I send Mom a text letting her know that I'll be at the beach for spring break again this year with Bella, Lexi and Cat. I've never lied to my parents like this before, and it feels odd. I add another quick text before she can answer me, *I think the following week after spring break I'll go to New York to meet with the editors.* I suggest the Thursday/Friday meeting dates just like Mom wanted so it will be a long weekend with the family. Maybe this will consume her thoughts more than my spring break plans and she won't get suspicious.

Bella and I came up with the plan of how many Instagram posts we'll do while we're gone and plan to make some of the pictures look like I took them by the way they're tagged. I'm planning to take some at the beach in Cape Cod and change the location to say Gulf Shores. Spring break is only a week away, and I get goose bumps thinking how fun it will be to go away with Lane for a whole week. I'm hoping the excitement will overcome the guilt I have about lying to my parents. I mean keeping this from them stops them from worrying about me being on vacay with some boy far from home anyway, right?

I get a text from Lane about meeting him at Innisfree tomorrow for the SGA election party. I shoot off a text back.

I'm there.

Ur the best. The party starts at 4:30. The polls close at 6. I think we will have way more people at this event than the last one. The election results won't post until 11, so hang on for a long night. Pls do another IG post and Tweet so everyone knows the time and that they'll receive one free drink ticket on arrival.

I'll do that right now, babe.

One last campaign plug for Adam. Boom it's posted.

*****

Arriving at campaign party headquarters, I notice some of the members of the secret society setting up a large inflatable screen and sound system. I help with balloons and drink tickets for a while then I turn the ticket table over to the guys manning the door. Lane's in a great mood as he walks around talking with everyone. I decide to do the same, since I know a lot of people here. It's going to be a long night waiting on the results, and I should make the best of it. Ashley walks in with some friends. I make a mental note to keep a close eye on her in case she decides to encroach on Lane. If so, I'll need to make a bee line over to him and let her know to back off. No more Ms. Nice-guy where she's concerned. As the night goes on, the crowds get thicker. Lane is right about the numbers tonight, way more than the first campaign party a few months ago.

At ten forty-five the DJ stops playing music and the screens switch from music videos to our campus broadcast of the election. I scan the room for Lane and see Ashley nearby. I move through the crowds quickly and soon I'm by his side, taking his hand in mine. He leans down and kisses my cheek. I'm nervous about the election, but Lane is cool, calm, and relaxed. We're about to hear who's won. I squeeze Lane's hand, and I look over at Adam, who's smiling and talking with someone next to him. All eyes turn toward the screen. They pronounce Adam the winner by a 75% margin. The crowd cheers, and he takes the mic for his speech. Lane lifts me up in the air and slowly brings me down into a kiss that lasts several minutes.

I whisper, "Congratulations, I love you."

43

#Beachorbust

Bella and I carry our bags downstairs and meet up with Lexi and Cat and Cat's friend Reese outside. Reese is taking my place at the beach with the girls. They're driving Cat's car, and I notice the back windshield is painted with *Beach or Bust.* We ask Reese to snap a photo of the four of us standing next to the painted car window so I can text it to Mom, letting her know I'm on the way to the beach. Well at least *a beach,* anyway. Reaching out, I take Bella's hand and wrap my pinkie around hers. We pinkie swear that we'll check in with each other every day in order to keep our stories the same. The girls pile into Cat's car, and I wave as they drive off.

*****

The plane ride only takes two hours. Soon Lane and I land at JFK and walk down the stairs onto the tarmac where a fancy sports car is waiting. Someone helps load our luggage into the trunk. Lane pushes a button on his keychain, and the doors of the car rise like wings.

"Are you okay with the top down?" he asks.

I pull out a hair tie. "I'm up for the time of my life," I say, smiling at him.

We get in and take off. The wind in my hair feels like freedom.

"What type of car is this? It's like the coolest car I've ever seen."

He turns the radio down. "It's a McLaren limited edition spider. This was my Christmas present."

"Wow," I say, making an OMG-I-can't-believe-it face.

As we drive on, we take turns listening to each other's playlists.

After an hour or so Lane asks, "How about a lunch break?

I nod, smile and give his arm a gentle squeeze.

We pull up to a cool waterfront restaurant in New Haven, Connecticut, where we're seated outside since the weather is nice and sunny with a gorgeous view of the boats in the harbor.

After placing our order, I glance at my phone to see a text from Bella. *We r at the hotel about to head to the beach. It's time for u to text ur mom that you've arrived safely.*

Quickly, I send mom a text, letting her know we're at the hotel. I feel weird about doing that but also kinda exhilarated at the same time. I've never in my life done anything this crazy or this bad before.

Just texted my mom we made it to the hotel.

R u at Lane's vacation house yet?

"Lane, how much farther until we get there?" I ask.

He reaches over and squeezes my knee. "About two hours."

I text Bella the time I think we'll arrive. She sends a thumbs up.

The hours fly by. Soon we're pulling into a large circular drive that has a massive house attached to it.

Stepping out of the car, I can't help but stare at the house. "Lane, this looks like a resort."

He laughs. "It's been in my family for a long time. My parents, my oldest sister, her husband, and their kids should be inside. My other sisters arrive tomorrow with their boyfriends. Some of my other family members own the house next door, so my cousins you met over New Year's will be here."

288

We walk into the foyer and set our luggage down. Lane takes my hand, and we walk toward the back of the house where we hear people talking. Lane's mom sees us and jumps up, followed by his sister. They greet us with hugs and kisses on the cheek. Both are holding glasses of wine.

Lane's niece and nephew run over and pounce into Lane's arms. He picks them both up in a giant bear hug. It's the most adorable thing I've ever seen, and I'm standing there grinning like a silly schoolgirl.

Lane's mom jolts me out of my daze. "Would you like a glass of wine, Rebecca?"

Not thinking about it, I answer. "Sure." Then I follow her to the kitchen. There's a centerpiece of snacks, plates, bottles of wine and sodas on ice. Lane's mom hands me a glass and pours Chardonnay into it. More introductions follow as I'm led into the living room. I meet Lane's father, Don, and his brother-in-law, Matt. Lane's sister ushers the twins away from Lane toward the kitchen and busies herself with their snacks at the table. I hear one of them say, "I don't like that kind of cheese."

Lane takes my hand, and we sit together on the sofa and fall into casual conversation with his family. They ask me about school, my family, my interests, hobbies, and my major. After several minutes of chit chat Lane's mom says, "I know you'd both like to freshen up before dinner. Let me show you to your room, Rebecca."

Lane and I stand and follow her up the stairs. We walk down a narrow hallway to a room at the far end. His mom opens the door to a beautiful story book room with yellow floral curtains, white wicker furniture and a white antique iron bed. The window overlooks the ocean.

"Mrs. Townsend, this is stunning."

"Please, call me Colleen. We'll leave you two to get ready. Dinner will be in an hour. Please take your time."

I notice my suitcase has been placed in the room. She walks out leaving Lane and me standing there.

I glance at Lane. "What should I wear to dinner? Are we dining out?"

He walks over and puts his arms around my waist. "No. We'll be in the dining room downstairs tonight. I think we may eat out tomorrow night."

With a slight laugh, I say, "I'm still confused on what to wear."

Lane twirls me around. "I love the blue jean cut offs a lot." He slides a hand down to my butt and gives it a squeeze. "I think Mom expects a sundress or something along those lines. Just not shorts and a sweatshirt."

I breathe in deeply and nod. "Got it."

Lane shows me the bathroom. I poke my head in and look around. It's well-appointed with fancy soaps and shampoos. I notice a beautiful clawfoot tub.

"I feel like I'm staying in a bed and breakfast," I say, quietly enough that Lane probably didn't hear me. "Will you show me your room?"

He takes my hand and places it over his arm very proper like. "This way, my darling," he says in a theatrical tone.

Along the hall Lane points out that his sister and her family have a Jack and Jill style suite and down at the end of the hall is his room. It's painted blue. His bed has a plaid bedspread with large boating oars on the wall above it, very nautical.

There's a photo on the dresser of Lane with his sisters from several years ago. He has his own bathroom, too. His suitcase is opened on his bed, as if someone has already unpacked most of his things.

"Did someone unpack for you?" I ask, pointing to his suitcase.

"Yes. Our housekeeper's name is Greta. She probably hung my shirts in the closet." Lane walks over and opens an antique armoire. I follow him over and, sure enough, six shirts are hanging inside.

"Wow, it's like you have your own butler. Or is it called a valet? Like in Downton Abbey?" I say with a hint of sarcasm.

Lane rolls his eyes at me and shakes his head. I look through his shirts. There are a few Robert Grahams, I've loved seeing him wear in class, to the point I even looked them up online. I realize I can't afford to buy him one, so I just have to admire him in the ones he already owns.

I pull out a light-blue-checkered print with a white paisley overlay, "Would you wear this one tonight?"

Lane smiles at me. "Whatever you'd like." He pulls me in for a kiss.

I hear kids running in the hall, and I quickly pull away and feel nervous about someone seeing us making out.

Lane kisses me reassuringly.

"I guess I should get back to my room and get ready for dinner," I say, walking to the doorway.

Lane taps my butt, giving it a light spank, making me giggle as I step into the hall.

Walking past Lane's sister's room, I can hear her through the closed door reminding the kids to be on their best behavior. I start unpacking but remember I need to text Bella. Pulling my phone from my back pocket, I send her a text.

Sry it took so long to text u. I've been here about 2 hours and just got caught up meeting Lane's family and it slipped my mind.

It's ok, I'm glad everything is going well.

The house is beautiful. I feel like I'm staying at a B&B. My room overlooks the ocean, and my bathroom has a clawfoot tub.

For real? I'm glad to hear u r not having to rough it in a small hotel room with three other girls. She sends a goofy faced emoji. I send back a smiley face and continue unpacking.

Dinner is in a large dining room near the front of the house. There's a fireplace in the center of the far wall. The fire creates an intimate ambiance in the elegant room. The table looks large enough to seat twenty or more people comfortably. Tonight, it's set for eight. During dinner Greta is our server. All the adults, including me, are served wine. I get the feeling they think I'm

291

twenty-one, but I don't want to explain that I won't even turn twenty for four more months. Instead, I take only a few tiny sips of wine and drink my water instead.

Conversation is light and fun. The twins, Ross, and Reagan, announce they have a birthday party coming up in a few days. Their mother, Lane's sister Renee, tells them to explain what they want to have at their party.

Ross begins, "It's a Star Wars theme. Han Solo and R2D2 will be there."

Reagan adds, "And Princess Leia and Luke Skywalker will be there, too."

They start talking about light sabers and cake.

Renee says, "On Monday we have to finalize the cake design and other party details. Their party will be on Tuesday evening in the backyard. More of the family will be here for that."

I smile and nod and look at Ross and Reagan. "It sounds like it'll be the best birthday party ever."

They seem to agree with me and announce they turn seven. After dessert Renee tells the kids it's time to get ready for bed. They ask for stories and she looks over at Lane and me.

"Rebecca and I would love to do story time," Lane announces.

Ross and Reagan cheer loudly. I laugh and glance at Lane, who squeezes my hand under the table.

Renee ushers the twins up the stairs, saying, "Let's quickly get baths and Pjs on."

Lane's dad gets up and offers everyone an after-dinner drink and a game of cards. Renee's husband, Matt, joins him, and Lane and I follow. We walk into a sunroom where several gaming tables are set up. Three of the walls are all windows and overlook the swimming pool. Beyond that is the ocean. One wall is floor to ceiling shelves and full of board games, puzzles and books. Don asks me if I know how to play Euchre or Crazy Train dominos. I tell him I've played both games at least once but would need a refresher.

Colleen joins us at the table, and we play one round of Euchre before Renee walks in.

"The munchkins are in bed waiting for stories," she says sitting down.

Lane and I get up and walk upstairs. Reagan is sitting up in bed with a Princess nightgown on.

"What's the name of the Princess on your nightgown?" I ask, sitting on the edge of her bed.

Animatedly she says, "It's Moana. She's a Princess that lives on an island and fights the bad guys in the ocean." She has a slight lisp, which makes her more adorable. "I wanted a Moana birthday party, but Ross wanted a Star Wars party, but it's okay because Princess Leia will be there."

I ask her about the books she has sitting on her bed.

Ross interrupts. "I picked out three books," he says, holding them up.

Lane says, "How about we read one of yours and one of Reagan's choices, then you can choose the third book together." The twins nod in agreement.

Lane begins reading Ross's first book choice. I think how adorable this scene is. Cute twins snuggled up in twin beds with Lane reading a fairy tale while we listen, hanging onto each word. He finishes the story, and I begin with the one Reagan chose. After the third book Lane kisses them goodnight and turns out their lamp. We tiptoe out the door back down to the card game.

Renee looks up and says, "How did it go?"

"They're perfect angels," I say in response.

"Well, thank you, but I can assure you they are not." Everyone laughs.

Colleen says, "I sure think they are." She beams as only a grandmother can.

Lane announces we're going for a walk on the beach. Colleen reminds us everyone is expected to go to church in the morning and breakfast will be served at nine thirty.

Walking outside in the cool, windy air, Lane takes my hand as we pass through the gate onto the sand toward the ocean.

"Your family is lovely, and you have the most adorable niece and nephew. Twins are so cute."

"I'm glad you like everyone." He turns to face me, and it seems as though he wants to say something else.

Instead, he looks down at the sand, picks up a shell, and hands it to me.

"I'm really glad you're here with me. It means a lot that you came."

"I'm glad to be here. My parents think I'm at the beach with Bella and the girls, though."

He looks a little surprised at that but doesn't say anything. Loud laughter is coming from the house, and we both turn in that direction. We can vaguely see figures through the window.

"The card game must have gotten a lot more interesting after we left," I say smiling up at Lane.

Lane steps closer to me. "They love competition. Tomorrow my other two sisters will arrive, and things will get more rambunctious."

We move to sit in the sand, facing the water, and I stretch out my feet and lean my back against Lane's chest. He wraps his arms around me, and we gaze up at the moon and stars.

"It's so pretty here," I say softly.

"Yes, it's probably my favorite place on earth," Lane adds. He's very quiet, solemn, and peaceful.

"I guess your favorite place on earth makes you feel peaceful and tranquil?"

"It does. One of the many reasons I love it. It reminds me of family, quiet times, fun, no pressures, no ..." He stops mid-sentence, gently kisses my neck and says, "Are you getting cold? Do you want to go back inside?"

I nod, and he lifts me to my feet. We walk hand-in-hand back to the house in silence. The only sound is the quiet stillness of the night and rolling waves.

Inside, the card game is still going. When we walk in, they ask us to join in. Lane leans down and gives his mom a kiss on the cheek.

"I think Bex and I are going to go to bed. It's been a long day."

I smile. "Thank you so much," I say. "Dinner was lovely. I appreciate you having me this week."

Colleen and Don smile back. "We're glad to have you," Don replies.

We wish everyone a goodnight then head to the back staircase.

In the hallway Lane says, "I hope it was okay that we didn't start up a new card game."

"It's totally fine. I could use the sleep, and you're right, it was a longer day for us with the travel time."

He walks me to my room and sweetly kisses me goodnight. I soak in the tub with bubbles and candlelight before going to bed. Warm, relaxed, and still a bit tired from traveling today, I fall asleep content.

44

#Vacay

As soon as a wake up, I walk to the window and view the sunrise over the ocean. Pulling out my phone, I take a picture then post it to my Instagram and change the location to Gulf Shores, AL, just as I do, a text from Lane pops up.

Hey, babe, u up?

Yes, I'll be out in about fifteen. HBU?

I'll come down to ur room in a few minutes.

When Lane knocks on my door it makes all thoughts of anything else flee. I hurry to the door and open it. He looks and smells so amazing. I drink in his scent. He grins at me. "Good morning, gorgeous. You look beautiful," he says with a wink.

"I'm glad. I packed three dresses," I say, twirling around.

We walk together down the stairs and into the formal dining room. Breakfast is set up buffet style. Lane's parents and the twins are already sitting at the table eating.

"Good morning, kids," Lane's dad greets us as we walk in. "There's juice and coffee over on the far buffet and eggs, bacon, and toast on this one." He points to both, and Lane and I head for the food.

The centerpiece on the table is a large display of fresh fruit sliced and paired with tiny jars of yogurt. I still feel like I'm in a fancy bed and breakfast. Renee and her husband Matt walk in carrying shoes and sweaters for the kids.

Lane's mom looks over at me. "Tell us about your church in Atlanta, Rebecca."

"It's a large non-denominational church," I say, then add some details about the campus locations and the style.

"The church we'll attend today is an Episcopal church. We normally attend a Catholic church in the city. But for many years our family has attended this church whenever we're on the island."

I nod and smile. She says she's heard of my pastor and remembers hearing him speak at Barack Obama's pre-inauguration service.

*****

The church service is beautiful and formal. It's totally different from the "rock band" mega church I attend in Atlanta. Lane and I sit next to the twins and try to keep them busy with crayons and paper. I can tell he adores his niece and nephew.

After church, our group descends on a European restaurant in town called Bistro de Soleil and is escorted to a private area where Lane's sisters, Macy and Meg are sitting. Both have their boyfriends with them. Lane introduces me to Macy and her fiancé and says their wedding is in early June. Meg introduces her boyfriend from law school. I learn Meg is in her second year of law at Yale, and Macy works in New York for a publishing company.

"Rebecca has won the writing contest in our journalism class and will have her story published in *The New Yorker* this summer," Lane announces during lunch. Everyone at the table ooh's" and "ahh's and wants to know all about it. I give them a very brief description of the story, telling them it's about a mother and son and that she reveals an incredible secret to him that will change his life forever.

"I'll actually be meeting with the editors in New York in about a week," I add.

Lunch is a very casual but long. By the time we're back at the house it's three thirty. Lane tells me he's going to talk with his dad for a while, and they go into an office or library in the front of the house. Renee takes the kids upstairs to change

297

clothes. I decide to hang out and talk with Lane's sisters and the guys outside by the pool. Renee and Matt come out with the kids clad in swimsuits carrying pool floats and a sand bucket full of toys. The kids get in at the shallow end and Renee and Matt relax on lounge chairs near the pool steps.

Meg looks at me and says, "I don't know about you guys, but I think I'll change into my swimsuit and come back out."

Macy agrees, and the three of us stand, leaving the guys to continue enjoying their beers. Meg and Macy wander down a long hall on the first floor, and I notice at least four doorways along the hallway. This house must have eight or nine bedrooms.

Before I get to the staircase Lane pops out of the office and closes the door behind him.

"Hey," I say, startled.

"Hey. Sorry about leaving you," he says.

"It's okay, I've enjoyed getting to know your sisters. Everyone is changing into their swimsuits." Lane seems a little distracted.

"Is everything okay?" I ask. We get to the top of the stairs and he stops.

"My dad always wants to know about my plans for school, career, future and all that. I think since I'm the only boy he looks to me as the family leader, even though I'm the youngest. My oldest sister, Renee, used to work as a campaign manager for a politician in Washington before she married Matt and decided to stay home with the twins. Matt's a lawyer and is running for Mayor, since they moved to Connecticut five years ago. Meg is in law school but of course has a boyfriend, and dad thinks she'll end up giving up her career to have a family. He and Mom have always wanted me to go to law school after I graduate. It's time for me to apply, and I've given him some other ideas I've had and some options I've been thinking about."

We walk into my room and sit on the bed.

"So, how'd that go?" I ask.

"He took it better than I thought he would. He wants me to make sure I have a plan and a job lined up by fall."

I look into his eyes and see a tiny bit of stress creeping in. I pat his hand, not knowing what to say.

"That's why I wanted you here. You make everything feel right."

I smile and put my arms around him. He gently strokes my hair and kisses me on the forehead. "I'll go change and meet you at the pool." He stands and walks down to his room.

I walk over to my bag, pull out one of the swimsuits I brought, pull my hair into a messy bun and walk back out to join Lane and the rest of the family poolside. A pool volleyball game has just started, so Lane and I jump into the pool to join the game. Lane, Meg, her boyfriend Luke, and I are on one team. Macy, her fiancé Stephen, Renee and Matt are on the other team. If anyone were keeping score, I'd definitely say our team won. Lane puts me on his shoulders, and we celebrate. Meg and Luke do the same, and the next thing you know all the girls are on their guy's shoulders, and we start tossing the ball around again.

Greta comes outside with a tray of lemonade and cookies. Ross and Reagan put down the sidewalk chalk they were playing with and rush over to the table and take a cookie. Lane and I get out of the pool. The guys get beers in hand before they park themselves in pool chairs. I wrap a towel around myself and sit on Lane's knee. Colleen walks out and announces that there's a food truck event in town tonight and asks if we all want to go. Everyone's in agreement that the food truck festival is a good idea.

"The event is at the park and close enough that we can drive the golf carts," Colleen informs us.

I whisper in Lane's ear, "What should I wear?"

Lane laughs and starts tickling me, and I squeal and squirm, and almost fall off his lap before he catches me.

He whispers back, "This is the perfect opportunity for you to show off your cutoff shorts."

Macy stands. "I better go change."

Stephen gets up to follow her. Renee tells Ross and Reagan to clean up. I hear one twin say, "Can we get some ice cream?" Meg and Luke go inside, which leaves Lane and me by ourselves. I drink the last drop of lemonade from my glass and scoop out a piece of ice. I start to pop it into my mouth, but instead I rub it across the back of Lane's neck. He jumps, and I quickly hop off his lap, dropping my towel. He chases me around the pool until he catches me and picks me up, acting as if he is going to throw me in.

"No, no, no, please no, don't throw me in. My hair is almost dry." I'm half-laughing, half-pleading with him.

He sets me down and pulls me in and kisses my neck and continues all the way up to my mouth. I look at him shyly and feel weird kissing him when I'm not sure if anyone can see us from the windows. He notices I'm being really shy. I think he can tell it makes me nervous to show affection around his family. He picks me up, tosses me over his shoulder, and carries me upside down giggling into the kitchen before he sets me down. His mom and dad are watching The Master's golf game on the large TV.

His mom smiles at us and says, "You better be careful with her, Lane." She gives him one of those *Mom looks.*

45

#Justbeachy

The next morning, I put on my new bikini since Lane and I plan to spend the day on the beach. After tossing my portable speaker and sunscreen into a tote I bop down the stairs. It's super quiet in the house, no sounds of munchkins running around. I walk into the kitchen to find a breakfast spread of fruit, bagels and juice on the counter with a note from Lane's mom lying next to it. *The guys have gone to play golf for most of the day. Renee and the kids are at their horseback riding lessons, and the girls and I are finishing birthday shopping for the twins. We're meeting Renee and kids for lunch in town to wrap up all the details and plans for the birthday party tomorrow evening. Greta left breakfast for you guys, but lunch is on your own. Love, Mom.*

I fix myself a plate and turn on the speaker I brought down with me and set it to a Luke Bryan song. I'm dancing and singing as I spread cream cheese on my bagel when Lane comes up behind me. Surprised, I scream and turn around. He puts his hand around my waist and pulls me to him. "I love to hear you sing," he says with a huge grin on his face.

"You scared me to death," I say, out of breath.

"Just keep doing what you're doing."

"Okay, so you want to dance with me?" I give him a questioning *come hither* look.

I turn the volume up, take his hand, and pull him out to the center of the kitchen, swaying and dancing as I go. Lane follows along and we're dancing and laughing hysterically. He picks me up and sets me on the counter. I wrap my legs around his waist. Both of us only in our swimsuits start making out. I'm much more into it than I was yesterday, since I know no one is home. Suddenly Greta walks into the kitchen carrying a stack of beach towels. She looks at us but keeps walking out to the pool and sets them on a table. I laugh and press my face into Lane's chest embarrassed to be caught by the housekeeper.

Lane lifts my chin up and says, "Bex, it's just Greta. We were just kissing. It's okay, really."

I roll my eyes, hop off the counter, and turn the volume down on my portable speaker. To change the subject, I say, "How about we pack a picnic?"

"Great idea, I'll find a cooler."

Lane and I busy ourselves making sandwiches and packing fruit and cheese into our container. He throws in a few beers and some bottled water.

"I think we're set," he says, closing the lid.

I grab my speaker and phone and pick up two towels from the table as we pass the pool toward the path leading to the beach. We set our stuff in the sand. When I take off running into the water, Lane chases me in. We play and splash around a while then head back to the beach. I spread out my towel and lie on my back. Lane does the same. He reaches out for my hand, and we lie there, holding hands with our eyes closed while the warm spring sun dries our skin and warms us up.

We fell asleep. I open my eyes and look at Lane. He's definitely asleep. I flip over onto my stomach and turn on some music just quiet enough to hear but not loud enough to wake him. I scroll through some posts on Instagram for a few minutes until Lane rolls onto his side and props up on his elbow.

With a sweet grin he asks, "Why didn't you wake me up?"

"You were too cute sleeping. In fact, we both fell asleep. I just woke up a few minutes ago."

"What time is it?"

"It's one thirty. We slept for a while. Are you hungry?"

I open the cooler and take out a bag of grapes. Lying on my side, facing him, I pop a grape into my mouth and grab another. I try to throw it into his mouth when he starts to yawn. I miss and try again.

"Hand me some grapes," Lane says, trying to catch the ones I keep throwing at his mouth.

"Finally got one." I say, as one flies back at me and hits me in the nose. We continue trying to throw grapes into each other's mouths until they're all eaten. Lane opens the cooler and pulls out a beer.

"Do you want your sandwich?" he asks.

"That'd be great." I say, sitting up cross-legged as he hands me a sandwich and a bottle of water.

"Cheers, to the best boyfriend in the world." I touch my water to his beer.

Lane shakes his head. "No, to the best girlfriend in the world."

I smile to myself, thinking this is way too perfect. Suddenly a football lands next to us. Lane picks it up and jumps up to throw it back to the guys it belongs to. I watch as he runs and throws the ball to them. He's muscular and athletic, with a hint of a six pack but nothing like a swimmer's body. Just the really nice, toned body of a model. Lane starts throwing the ball back and forth with the other two guys. Realizing it's his cousins, Conor and John, I get up and start walking toward them. They notice me and shout, "Hey, Bex!" Conor throws the ball to me, and I actually catch it, but I'm not so good at throwing it back. After tossing the ball around for a while, John asks if we want to meet up with them later at a place called The Beachcomber.

"We can meet at seven for dinner. There's a band playing at nine. We might need to buy tickets online," he says.

Lane looks over at me. "What do you say, Bex? The Beachcomber's a beach bar on the North end of Cape Cod directly on the water."

"Sounds cool. I'm in."

"I'll go in and see about tickets for the concert," Lane says to the guys. "We'll meet you there." Lane tosses the football to Conor, then we walk back toward our stuff we left on the beach.

Moments later, I set the towels down in a pool chair as we walk by. Lane takes the cooler inside and says, "I'm going to purchase tickets for the band at The Beachcomber. I'll be right back."

I nod and spread out my towel on a lounge chair. Pulling my phone out of the tote, I flip open my Spotify playlist, set it on shuffle, then turn on my speaker. Lane walks out and sits down next to me.

"We have tickets for the band tonight. We should probably leave before six thirty."

"What should I wear? I know, I know, it's the question of the day. I'm just not used to dressing up as much."

"This place is a total dive bar. It's really casual. They're only open this week and next week for spring break. Their official season opens late May."

"It sounds fun," I say, spraying Coppertone on my shoulders and chest.

"Here let me spray some sunscreen on you, we've been out here for a while." I say holding the can of Coppertone toward Lane.

Half an hour later our tranquil pool time is interrupted by squeals of laughter and splashing. Lane's mom and sisters have returned with the kids.

"Watch me, Uncle Lane," Ross says in midair landing a cannon ball with a splash.

Reagan copies her brother. Lane jumps in with them, and the twins converge on top of him. He takes turns lifting them up and throwing them as high as he can into the deep end. I watch in total amusement from the lounge chair. Macy, Meg, and Renee have changed into their suits and joined us.

When the kids move on to playing with pool floats, Lane gets out and dries off. Colleen walks up with a glass of tea in her hand.

"The tent and table rental people will be here to set up for the party at ten a.m. tomorrow," she says. "The giant Star Wars spaceship bounce house should arrive by four, and the caterers just after that. The party starts at five, so, we'll need some help blowing up balloons and setting up Star Wars decorations around three." She turns and looks in Lane's direction.

Lane says, "Sure, Bex and I can help with anything. We can even take the kids out for the day and keep them busy until you need us to work on setting up. By the way, Bex and I made plans for dinner with Conor and John. We're meeting them at The Beachcomber at seven and staying for a concert. We'll be home late."

The guys arrive back from their day of golf and join us by the pool. Greta follows behind them with a tray of drinks and snacks. Colleen tells Don that Lane and I are going out with Conor and John tonight. Lane's dad gives him a stern look. "Stay out of trouble and no bar fights," he says to Lane.

I arch my eyebrows at that statement. I'm glad I'm wearing sunglasses. *Wonder what that's about?*

Lane gets out of his pool chair and offers me his hand. "We're going to get ready to leave. Don't wait up for us."

I follow behind him, waving to everyone as we walk into the house.

In my room I pull out my favorite pair of ripped jeans and a sleeveless lace top, pair it with sparkly sandals and curl my hair. I add a touch more makeup than usual, hoping to look a little older since I'm not sure what this New England beach bar scene will be like.

A knock on my door startles me, I crack it open and see Lane leaning against the doorframe.

"Wow." You look amazing." He whistles, nodding his head in approval.

Lane looks like he stepped out of GQ with his shirt unbuttoned half-way down. A look of style and money exudes from his every pore. He reaches for my hand, and we walk down the staircase.

When we get into the McLaren, he leaves the top on, since it's only 56 degrees tonight.

"Do you mind if I pick the first song?" I ask. I choose Keith Urban's "John Cougar, John Deere, John 3:16" and start jamming. I can tell by Lane's grin he approves of either the dancing or the song. I turn the volume down and look at him.

"So, you didn't want to play golf with your dad and the guys today?"

"No, I would've had to leave you. I knew Mom and Renee were going to be busy with shopping for the kids and last-minute party arrangements, giving us a day to ourselves. I'm glad we got to spend the whole day together."

"Me, too." I lean over and kiss him on the cheek. "What did your dad mean when he said don't get into any bar fights?"

Lane chuckles. "That was referring to Conor. He got into a fight in Aspen over Christmas break when we went out for my birthday. Don't worry, everything will be fun tonight. I'll probably have to play golf with Dad and the guys later in the week. After the birthday party is over you and Mom and my sisters can spend some time together shopping on Wednesday."

"Yes, I think I would enjoy that a lot."

We pull up to The Beachcomber and can actually park on the beach right at the front door. Lane gives a valet some cash to keep an eye on his car and we head to the entrance.
Inside, the appearance doesn't disappoint with wood floors and wood beams on the ceiling accented in colored lights and beer signs. This is the perfect beach bar. We meander through the tables of people out to the patio area with amazing views of the ocean and the sunset. Conor yells for us to come over where he, John and a couple of girls have a table.

Lane orders a fruity drink for me with a Rum floater on top, and I only drink half, switching over to water, trying to be conscious of not drinking too much. Lane and I share a delicious lobster roll. It's a lot of fun hanging with his cousins and their friends. When I leave to go to the bathroom, I come back to find more girls camped out at our table. One of them is absolutely drop dead gorgeous with long dark hair and beautiful features. Come to find out, it's John's sister and some of her friends. I panicked for a minute. The fear of losing Lane to someone more dynamic, more intelligent, or more beautiful always looms in the back of my brain.

The band is great, and we dance and sing until we are hoarse and shut the bar down. Sneaking into the house, we try to be as quiet as possible. Lane kisses me goodnight and whispers, "It's okay to sleep in a little tomorrow." I shut the door behind me, take a quick shower, and crawl under the warm downy blanket, drifting off to sleep dreaming about sunsets and birthday parties.

46
#WOKE

The next evening everyone is happy when the rental truck drives off with its final load of tents and chairs from the party last night. We're all feeling a bit lazy and chill after Star Wars bounce houses, costumed characters and too much cake. Ross and Reagan haven't skipped a beat and are busy painting their birdhouse gift sets on the patio. Lane and I are snuggled in a pool chair watching Don and the guys grill shrimp and steaks for dinner. Matt pops open a beer and sits next to us.

"How about a bonfire on the beach after dinner?" he asks, to whoever is listening.

Ross hears him and asks, "Can we do smores?"

His dad answers, "Sounds, like a plan. If you guys put away the paint you can help dig the pit for the fire on the beach."

Renee walks over and helps the twins pack away the paints. They scurry off to find their shovels.

Lane stands and pulls on a shirt and heads to the beach to help Matt set up the wood for the fire.

Macy shows me where they keep the stones that go around the firepit, so Meg and I follow her over and bring back several stones to go around it. Matt and Luke get a load of wood from the side of the house and build a tall triangle of logs which they'll light after the sun goes down.

After a leisurely dinner poolside, Lane and the guys light the fire. It's dark and a little chilly, so I go upstairs and put on a sweatshirt and come back down. The twins are now wearing coats and have marshmallows on the ends of their sticks. Conor, Jack, Kayla, and two of her friends have walked down to join us around the fire.

Lane takes my hand, and we sit on a blanket he's spread out for us. He gathers a plate of s'more's supplies and sits facing me.

"I have the perfect s'more process," he explains. "First, I lay out two graham crackers, add one piece of chocolate to each side, and then I toast my marshmallow, continuously turning it while holding it over the fire. When it's toasted on all sides, I lay the marshmallow on one Graham cracker, pick up the other one and press and pull the marshmallow to get it off the stick. Voila, the perfect s'more."

I watch his process in total amazement. I try to do the same but end up with a lopsided, half-on-half-off marshmallow, and we crack up laughing. I can't stop laughing, and neither can Lane. Tears are running down my face. I look at him and feel so much love in this moment. He seems to feel the same. I stop laughing long enough to take a bite, and I get marshmallow goo on the side of my face.

"You got something right here." He starts to lick it off, which sends us both into a laughing fit again.

Luke has his guitar and starts strumming a John Mayer tune. We sing along. Soon everyone notices I can really sing, and they start asking for requests. We decide on the "Hallelujah" song. I start off softly, "Now I heard there was a secret chord ..." I get louder with each Hallelujah, and I close my eyes and feel the song pouring out and belt out the last Hallelujah to a round of applause, whistles and cheers. I feel a little embarrassed.

"Bex, that was amazing," Macy and Meg say in unison.

"Have you thought about trying out for American Idol?" one of Kayla's friends asks.

I lean my head on Lane's shoulder, and he wraps his arm around me. "No. I've never really thought about it much. I've always been a dancer and have concentrated on that."

"Your voice is beautiful, Rebecca," Colleen says.

309

"Any more requests?" Luke asks.

Reagan raises her hand. "The Moana song." She looks over at me, "Bex, do you know that one?"

"Yes, but you have to help me sing it." I motion for her to come sit with me. Reagan comes over, sits in my lap, and we begin. Luke joins in on the guitar, and everyone joins in singing the chorus.

Reagan stands and takes a bow. Renee and Matt get up and tell the kids it's time for bed. Ross and Reagan walk around, giving everyone a hug and kiss goodnight before they walk back to the house. The rest of the adults decide to follow and say their goodnights, leaving just us college kids curled up around the fire. Apparently one of John's sister's friends is with Conor, so they're coupled up. Kayla and her other friend are on their phones. John gets up to poke the fire, gets a beer out of the cooler and sits back down. Lane starts kissing my neck, sending shivers and butterflies through me like an electrical charge. My feelings for him are stronger than ever. After a few minutes of quiet kissing and snuggling, we decide to call it a night. The guys pour water and ice from the cooler over the fire until it's out. Lane grabs the blanket, and we wave goodnight to his cousins as we head toward the house.

He walks me to my room and kisses me in the doorway.

I whisper, "I love you."

He kisses my nose, then lips and says, "I love you, too. I really love you, Rebecca."

We stare into each other's eyes. I feel as if I can see into his soul.

"I want to take you out on the sailboat tomorrow."

"That sounds awesome."

He reaches for my hand, lifts it, kisses it softly and whispers, "Goodnight."

I close the door slowly, watching him through a tiny crack as he walks down the hallway. He knows I'm still watching him, and he looks back over his shoulder and winks at me. I float over to the bed, feeling as if I have wings, lifting me up and gently setting me down into a dreamy slumber.

The next morning Lane sends me a text. *Good morning, Angel. Sleep well?*

I did, and u?

Dreaming of u all night. This text makes me swoon. I send him another text. *Well, u can c me in a few minutes I'm about to walk downstairs.*

Everyone is having a big breakfast in the dining room this morning. We fix our plates and join them.

"What are your plans today?" Lane's dad asks looking from me back to Lane.

"I'm taking Bex out on the sailboat."

Macy says, "That will be a lot of fun. Have you been sailing before?"

"No, this will be my first time," I reply.

Colleen says, "I'll have Greta fix a basket of snacks for you guys to take."

"Remember, Grandma, we're going to make mosaic stones," Reagan says with a flip of her fork, spilling egg on the table.

After breakfast I run upstairs and put on a swimsuit under my T-shirt and shorts, slip on my sandals and pull my hair into a messy bun. Walking through the kitchen on our way to the beach, Lane picks up the snack basket. We stroll down the beach toward the pier. It's a sunny day with only a few clouds.

"The weather is perfect," I say as Lane helps me up onto the sailboat.

"It is. I'm glad it's been unseasonably warm this week. I checked the weather before we left. No rain, no storms, and just enough wind to be a perfect day for sailing."

Lane tells me what to do, and I help him with the ropes. He gets the sails up and slowly eases the boat away from the dock. I stand with him at the helm. It's an amazing feeling, the breeze, blue skies, the sun, and the gentle waves lapping the sides of the boat as we move across the water.

311

"I love this, Lane."

"I knew you would." He smiles back at me.

"Is this the boat you took out when you were fourteen, the one from your story?"

"Yes, this is the very boat. I grew up sailing with my uncles, my cousins and my dad. We would spend a month or two up here in the summers. I can remember as far back as two or three year's old being on the boat, playing in the sand, and inside the house. That was when my grandmother was still alive. I have the happiest memories of my life here on this boat and in the house where we're staying. Everything happy, joyful, and fun I associate with this place. Good memories and good times with family. We'll go out around this bend and anchor out next to that island over there." Lane points to an island in the distance.

I nod my head and wrap my arms around his waist.

We get to the spot where Lane wants to stop, and he starts working on getting the anchor out. I walk down into the galley to look for the basket of snacks we brought from the house. The snack basket is sitting on a table. I stroll over to get it when I notice the bedroom and the bathroom in front of me, so I wander on in. It's a tiny bathroom, but I'm glad there's one on the boat. Before I use the bathroom, I set the basket on the bed. I can hear Lane walking around at the front of the boat. When I come out of the bathroom, I take off my shorts. My hair tie gets caught as I'm pulling my shirt over my head. I reach up, yank the hair tie out, flip my hair over, and shake my hair around. When I flip my head up, I see Lane standing in the doorway.

"There you are. The anchor is set," he says, walking toward me.

"I found the bathroom and the snacks," I say, picking up the box of crackers.

Lane pulls me into a tight embrace, and we kiss. He picks me up and sets me on the edge of the bed. I wrap my legs around his waist. We are kissing so passionately I'm breathless and breathing heavy. I'm totally lost in him. He kisses my neck, down to my collarbone then between my breasts and back to my neck.

312

He whispers in my ear, "I love you so much, Rebecca."

I am grasping for him, pulling him closer to me kissing his neck, his chest.

He softly says in between kisses, "I want to make love to you." He lowers my head onto the pillow behind me, and we continue kissing. He moves onto the bed on top of me and slowly moves his hand down my stomach to the top of my bikini bottoms.

I suddenly stop kissing him and open my eyes. Lane is smiling at me and starts kissing me again, but I push him off and sit up.

"Lane, I, I, I." I stumble for the words to say as tears start streaming down my cheeks.

"It's okay, baby." He pulls me close and holds me tight.

"It's just that I've never ..." I'm still struggling with what to stay.

Lane says, "I know, and I'm sorry if I scared you. I had not planned on this. It's just I saw you in here, and I got carried away. I would never do anything to hurt you." He strokes my cheek gently.

"I know. It's just I've never had the feelings that I feel for you. And I've never gotten physical in any way with a guy other than kissing. I made a promise to myself when I was in eighth grade, during one of our church retreats, that I would wait until I was married. I want to give myself in that way only to my husband. It was a decision I made a long time ago. It's stuck with me all these years. But the feelings I have for you are so strong it scared me just now."

Lane is looking at me with so much love in his eyes. He pulls my face close to his.

"Sweet Rebecca. I fell in love with you because you're different from the other girls I've dated in the past. With what you just said, it makes me wish I could turn back time and re-do things. You're a precious gift, and you have my heart and soul. I love you and want to protect your heart and your feelings. I love and respect you too much to want you to do something that would be against how you feel. It makes me care for you even more because you're choosing to wait and give yourself only to your husband on your wedding night. I know how special that is, and you should keep that promise you made years ago. It's a good promise to keep."

He wipes the tears from my cheeks, pulls me close, and holds me.

I look into his eyes. "I love you, Lane. I love you so much."

"I love you too, Rebecca, more than you know." He presses his lips to my forehead, then stands and picks up the basket of snacks.

"Do you want to go sit up top in the sun?" he asks, reaching for my hand.

I wipe my cheeks, take his hand, and follow him up to the deck. We lie on the deck of the sailboat for hours, just talking about school, my New York trip and the fact that we leave in a few days.

When we arrive back at the house, everything is quiet. We walk inside and notice the kids in the front yard. We walk outside and see Colleen, Renee and the twins planting red, white, and blue flowers in the flowerbed around the flagpole. Colleen sees us walk up and waves us over.

"How was your first sailing trip?" she asks.

"It was perfect," I say with a big smile.

Reagan takes Lane's hand and pulls him over to the flowers and starts telling him what kind they are. Colleen asks if we can go to the store and pick up some things on her list for tonight.

"Sure, I'll be glad to. Rebecca may want to go up and change and relax for a while, though."

Lane and I follow Colleen into the kitchen to get her list. Lane sticks the list into the pocket of his shorts and says he'll be back in a few minutes. When he leaves, I pop into my room and turn on the shower. After washing my hair, I wrap it up in a towel. Picking up a bag off the floor, I pull out the new dress I

314

bought on my shopping trip with Lane's sisters. I slip it on, blow out my hair and add a touch of makeup.

My phone dings a text from Lauren asking if I'm at the beach. I text back *Yes* and send a picture that I took with my legs stretched out in the sand with the ocean waves in the background. She texts me a blurry black and white photo that looks like it's from a newspaper of two people that look like me and Lane getting into a car that looks like his. Her text reads, *Is this u*? I have no clue what she's sent me or why she's asking. I decide to ignore it, because I don't have time for Lauren or any explaining right now, and I can hear Lane downstairs.

I walk down the stairs and help him unload the bags in the kitchen before he wanders upstairs to change. I notice Macy and Meg sitting out by the pool. Colleen and Renee come inside with the twins, and Renee takes them upstairs to change. Colleen and Greta begin working on a salad and an appetizer to take to the dinner party we're having next door with the extended family. I offer my help to Colleen and Greta who are busy washing vegetables.

The dinner party is more relaxed than I thought it would be, and conversations are easy with Kayla, her two friends, and John and Conor, whom I already know well. Lane's aunts and uncles are nice, and after dinner we enjoy a rousing game of Trivial Pursuit.

When there's a break in the game, Lane and I wander into the kitchen to get a drink. I pull him aside around the corner so we're out of sight and take both his hands in mine.

"Thank you for this trip. I know I lied to my parents, but I plan on telling them the truth later. Maybe when I get back home in May. But I want them to know why I came with you and how much you mean to me. I'm going to tell them I'm in love with you."

Lane smiles down at me, and he pulls me in tight and holds me. Then he puts his hands on each side of my face and we stare into each other's eyes. He searches my face, as if he's looking for something, as if he wants to tell me a secret. Finally, he speaks, "I want you to know how much I'm in love with you. It means a lot that you came. I feel like I can trust you with anything."

Suddenly, Colleen yells for us from the other room, "Lane and Bex, come back, it's your turn."

Lane kisses me gently and says, "Ready for more Trivia?"

47
#SWERVE

I'm thinking about how this feels like paradise as I roll out of bed and look out the window at the sunrise over the ocean. It's the last full day of spring break, and I wish I could stay here forever. Ready to get this wonderful day started, I jump into the shower and quickly put on a swimsuit and shorts, then I walk downstairs to say my goodbyes to Lane's sisters and their boyfriends, since they're leaving this morning. We stand waving to them as their car drives away. Back inside, Renee is getting cereal out for the twins and asks Lane and me to keep an eye on them while she and Matt go upstairs to pack.

A few minutes later they bring down three suitcases. Lane and I walk outside and help them load their SUV. We kiss and hug everyone goodbye. As they pull out of the driveway, we can see Ross and Reagan waving to us from their car seats.

Colleen asks if Lane and I have plans for the day. Lane tells her he's taking me to lunch later.

"Your dad and I have dinner plans tonight with friends and we plan to leave around four. We'll be home late."

Joking, Lane says, "Don't do anything I wouldn't do." Don and Colleen laugh and shake their heads, leaving Lane and me standing in the foyer.

"Come on, let's go out to the beach," Lane says, taking my hand.

Lane and I walk out to the pool, grab some towels, and continue to the beach. I throw my towel down, pick up a stick, and begin drawing in the sand, a heart, the date and our initials. I take Lane's hand in mine, and we hold hands over the large heart and date I've drawn and take a photo. I take another one with my toes in the surf. Lane picks me up on his back piggy-back style and twirls me around. I take a video and a few selfies of us being silly and goofing off.

As I'm putting my phone inside my towel, Lane runs over and tosses a crab near my feet. I scream and start running. He chases me around the beach. When he catches me, I fall breathless into his arms. Finally, we stretch out on our towels and lie on our sides facing each other, talking about almost nothing, but it feels like everything.

"So, the restaurant we're going to later today, can I wear the dress I had on last night?"

"I love the dress you had on last night. It would be perfect."

"I'm glad you like it," I say, leaning in for a kiss. "I had fun shopping with your sisters the other day."

"I know they like you a lot. You've made the cut with the sisters, for sure."

"I like them a lot, too." I say, staring into his beautiful face.

I don't want to move from this position, but eventually we go in and change out of swimsuits and into something dressier for our lunch date.

Lane has the top off the car when I walk out the front door.

"It's a perfect day for a drive. I want to show you around The Chatham Resort."

"Sounds wonderful," I say, as I pull my hair into a bun and put on my Ray-Bans, ready for a beautiful drive up the coast.

The restaurant is set on the beach, and we have a perfect table for two with incredible views of the ocean. Lane points to a location in the distance and shows me the seals sitting out on the rocks.

He's still looking in the direction of the ocean and says, "We can walk around later and maybe spot a whale."

"How exciting. I hope we see one."

We hold hands across the table, and he rubs his thumb across the bracelet he gave me.

"Macy and Meg noticed the bracelet the other day when we were out shopping." I say cheerfully. "Macy told me she was the one who helped you when you went to Tiffany's to design it."

"Yes, Macy was glad I called her to ask her advice with it."

"Your family is great," I say, setting my water glass down.

Lane looks slightly distracted, like he did the first night we were here, as if he wants to tell me something. The waiter interrupts our moment when he walks up to talk about the menu.

After lunch we walk out to the beach and watch the seals. We walk through the Inn's farm and gardens. I point to a rustic looking barn.

"Let's go check out the barn."

We walk hand-in-hand over to the barn. Lane leans against the wood frame and pulls me in for a kiss. "This has been one of the best weeks of my life," he says.

"Mine too. I wish it could last forever."

"You do?" he asks. "Forever with me?"

I laugh and say, "I wish this could last forever." I twirl around with my hands up in a gesture of lightheartedness. I'm not sure how serious Lane was trying to be, but I gave the moment a lighter mood.

On the ride back to the house Lane reaches for my hand. "How about we sit on the beach for the next few hours and watch the sun go down?" he asks.

"That sounds like the perfect ending to a perfect day and a perfect end to a perfect trip."

Pulling up to the front of the house, he says, "I'll get some drinks and snacks and put them in a basket and grab a blanket."

"I'll meet you outside. I'm going in to use the restroom," I say, walking through the front door.

I get to the powder room in the foyer next to the office where Lane had a meeting with his father on Sunday afternoon. The door is open, and the room is large and filled with books from floor to ceiling. It's a beautiful library. I know no one is home, so I walk on in and look around.

There's a baby grand piano near the bay window. Another door leads to a smaller office located at the far end of the room that boasts a massive oak desk. The library has a long couch and coffee table in the center of the room. There's a table behind the couch with lots of framed photographs.

I walk over for a closer look. I pick up a frame that has a photo of Lane's mom with an older woman. I'm guessing its Lane's grandmother. The photo next to it is Lane's mom with ... *What the . . . ?* I stare at the photo in my hand. It's of Lane's parents with Jacqueline Kennedy Onassis. I continue looking at all the photos on the table, and there's more on the bookshelves and on the piano. I walk over to the piano, and there's a photo of John Kennedy, Jr. and his wife Carolyn Bessette on their wedding day. Another one of a young girl with JFK and another man who looks familiar, maybe Robert Kennedy. There are photos of Lane's mom with the entire Kennedy family. The entire room is filled with photos of Lane's family. Photos from years ago and photos from last year fill the room. This is a family library filled with books and memorabilia of the Kennedy legacy. I hear Lane calling my name, but I'm frozen and can't move. I feel like I've been punched in the stomach. I think I'm in shock by what I've just discovered. Lane *is* a Kennedy. I feel betrayed, angry, hurt, and let down by the one person I felt I could trust.

I step out of the library into the foyer. Lane is standing there, and he knows I know his secret.

"Bex, I was trying to tell you."

I push past him and run up the stairs to my room, close the door and put my hands over my face and cry.

"Rebecca, Rebecca," he calls after me.

320

I can hear Lane knocking on the door. "I wanted to tell you the first night we got here. I was afraid to tell you. I've had to live with the pressures of being a Kennedy all my life. That's why I knew who your story was about. That's why I knew about The Greyfield Inn and Cumberland Island."

Of course, I should have put two and two together, I feel so stupid. He continues talking, and his voice is more soothing. "I know I should have told you sooner. I was just so happy to have found a girl far removed from the life I've had to live. There's more pressure on us because of who we are, on me in particular than on my sisters. There's a legacy, it's political, and there's also supposed to be a curse on the male members of the family. It felt so good to be away from all that. It feels right when I'm with you."

He pauses a beat, and I feel bad for him, but I'm so hurt that he didn't tell me—— we've gotten so close on this trip. "Please believe me when I say I was planning to tell you, and I've tried to find the right time a few times this week. I have, really, I have. I was just about to tell you on the beach tonight. I know you don't believe me, but it's true, and it's true that I love you. Please open the door, Bex."

I open the door a little. I'm still crying but manage to say a few words. "I feel hurt right now, Lane. I feel lied to. I trusted you, and you kept a secret from me. I feel stupid. I feel used. I don't even know what I feel. I'm going to pack so I'll be ready to leave at seven a.m., and I'm going to bed." His face is sad, and he has tears in his eyes. "Goodnight, Bex," he says, and I close the door.

I finish packing and set my alarm. I wish I could talk to my mom right now, *but I freakin' lied to her about where I am.* I don't know what to do. I don't know if I'll get any sleep. My emotions are tied up, but I don't think I can talk to anyone about this yet because it's too raw. I pace the room and glance at the clawfoot tub in the bathroom and decide to draw a hot bath. Sliding in, the bubbles cling to me. Leaning my head back, I try to relax. Maybe lying to my parents caused bad mojo. Geez, have

321

I fallen in love with someone I don't know? Maybe Lane did try to tell me——and I'm just gullible. The clues where there. He's from money, from the east coast and part of the secret society. Ugh! I'm driving myself nuts thinking about this. My mind is a mess. I get out of the bath, dry off and turn out the lights. I fall into bed and can't help but cry myself to sleep.

When the alarm goes off, I feel like I've been hit with a truck. It's still dark outside. I turn on the hot water and splash my face. I'm all red and puffy. I apply enough makeup to cover any signs of crying. I walk down the stairs, carrying my suitcase, and set it near the door. Lane's mom walks by.

"Good morning, Rebecca," she says cheerfully. "There's breakfast on the counter in the kitchen for you."

"Thank you so much, I'll fix myself something."

I pick up a bagel, some fruit and juice and sit down at the table. Colleen gets herself another cup of coffee and joins me.

"I've had an amazing time this week. Thank you again for having me."

"It was our pleasure." She pats my arm, and I notice I'm still wearing the bracelet Lane gave me.

Lane walks in, glances in my direction, and picks up a plate.

"Good morning," he says.

I can tell he is trying to be friendly but definitely putting on a show of sorts. I don't think anyone else has noticed our solemn mood. Since it's so early in the morning, being less enthusiastic would come with the territory.

"Good morning," I say, trying to smile.

He sits down with coffee cake and a cup of very strong-smelling coffee. Colleen starts talking about something, and Lane and I try to follow along and act like we're paying attention. Don walks in with the newspaper in one hand. "What time are you two heading out this morning?" he asks.

Lane looks at his watch and says, "Right about now. Ready, Bex?"

I get up, hug his mom, and say thank you again to his dad. His dad picks up my bag and puts it into the trunk of Lane's car. They hug and kiss Lane and make plans to see him in a few weeks. We get into the car and begin the four-hour drive to his private plane in New York.

We drive in silence for what seems like forever, but it's probably just an hour. It gives me time to post a photo of my toes in the ocean and add some random caption about having the best spring break ever. I change the location to Gulf Shores. I also texted Bella letting her know I'll be back at Phi Mu house this afternoon. Out of the staunch silence Lane speaks. "Please talk to me. I want us to be able to work through this." He looks over at me with a pleading concern.

"I don't know what to say right now, Lane. I'm hurt. I have a lot of things that I'm feeling, and I need to sort them out somehow. I think you should give me some time to do that. I'm guessing your family just assumed I knew whom I was dating. It feels really awkward knowing they'll probably read my story in *The New Yorker*. I wonder if they'll think I wrote a crazy fictional story about JFK, Jr. having a long-lost child because I was dating you? I don't want to seem like some crazy stalker fan girl. I don't want anyone thinking that about me."

"I'm going to explain to my parents that you just found out right before we left. I'm going to let them know that it's my fault for waiting too long to tell you, and it's caused a bit of an argument between us. They are not going to think bad of you. They love you. They can tell you are much different from girls I've dated in the past. And I want to give you as much time as you need to sort out your feelings. But I also want you to believe me when I say I would never hurt you on purpose for any reason. I love you more than words can say. I want you to understand that. I want us to work this out. I want to be able to talk to you more about it when you're ready."

When we get on the plane, there are snacks waiting for us, but I have no appetite. I fall asleep during the flight, and it's not until we've landed in Tuscaloosa that I wake up. Lane and I walk

323

slowly down the stairs to the tarmac. The BMW he drives around campus is waiting for us.

He pulls up to the curb in front of Phi Mu, gets out and helps me with my bag. Our hands touch, and I feel the electricity go through me that I've always felt when I've been near him. He notices it, too, because we glance up at each other.

"I'm here when you want to talk," he says, looking at me like there's been a death. He gets into the driver's seat and starts the car. I take my bag and quickly walk into the house, up the stairs, and into my room, barely speaking to anyone as I pass them along the way.

I shut the door behind me, fall face down on my bed, and cry my eyes out, an ugly gut-wrenching cry that tears through my soul and feels like I'm dying inside. My insides feel like they're being ripped apart piece by piece and will never be put back together. I feel angry, lonely and hurt. I feel like I'll never be happy again for the rest of my life. What if I've lost the love of my life?

My phone dings with a text. I look at it. It's Lauren asking if I'm back from the beach. *Yes*, I text back. Then my phone starts ringing for a FaceTime call. Again, it's Lauren. I accept.

"Hey, why didn't you text me back the other day?" I see a look of concern dance across her face. "Bex, are you crying? What's wrong?" she asks.

"Nothing. I just got home, and I'm really tired."

"Okay, well I sent you that photo, and you didn't respond."

"I guess I didn't understand what you were sending me."

"It was a photo from *The New York Times*. I was working on homework in Dad's office, and I knocked the paper on the floor and that page fell out. When I put it back in, I noticed the photo, and it happened to look just like you and Lane, but I knew it couldn't be you because you were with your friends at the beach, right? When I read the caption, "New York Bachelor, Lane Townsend of The Kennedy Legacy leaves for Cape Cod with mystery girl in his exclusive limited addition McLaren

Spider," it freaked me out. I wanted to find out what the heck it was? Seriously, Bex, you look like you've been crying, and Lane is apparently a celebrity or something? Did you guys get into a fight? Did he break up with you for some girl that looks similar?"

Frustrated, I scream. "Oh my gosh, Lauren, it was me in the photo! I didn't go with my friends. I went with Lane to his family's house in Cape Cod!"

"No way. Are you kidding me right now? That was you getting off that plane and into that cool car? And he's like the son of some famous politician or something?"

I sit up, flip over and lean my head against the pillows and stare at Lauren on my phone screen.

"Bex, are you just going to leave me hanging here or what? Tell me what's going on with you. I'm your sister, remember?"

"Mom and Dad didn't see the photo, or did they?"

"Well, it's Dad's paper, but he doesn't read the gossip page anyway, so I don't think he saw it. Then later I saw it in the recycling bin."

"Good, they still don't know. I'm planning on telling them about it later, so don't say anything. Give me a chance to talk to them. I'd rather wait until I'm home for a few days this summer. I just can't handle anymore drama right now. I've got my trip to New York in a few days, and finals two weeks after that.

"Yeah, thanks for planning that trip over *my* spring break, by the way. Now I can't go to the beach with my friends, which I would actually be doing, instead of going to New York with you."

"Here's the short version of the story Lauren, I'm in love with Lane. I fell in love with him maybe the first time I saw him in class. I have a hard time thinking straight when I'm with him, and when he asked and pleaded with me to go with him over spring break, I caved and said yes. Everyone thought I was at the beach, and I made it look that way on Instagram. Bella and Lexi knew all about it. I had no idea that Lane was from a famous

325

family. I can look back on things now and see that I glazed over a lot. I'm a gullible person, I guess. I found out on my own by walking into their family library which had photos of all the Kennedy family members. Lane claims he was trying to tell me about it. But the last night we were there I find out on my own, and now I feel like I've been lied to."

Lauren's mouth is hanging open, and she's staring back at me dumfounded.

"Lauren," I say, trying to get her to say something.

"So, you're fighting with him over the fact that he's from a famous family?"

"No. I'm upset and angry with him because he never mentioned it. Now I feel like a complete dumb ass. I was so smitten that it never occurred to me. I feel used and lied to and confused about my feelings for him."

"You said he was trying to tell you about it but didn't get around to it?

"He claims he was trying to tell me about it the first night we were at his house. He claims he tried to tell me again, then he was planning on telling me the last night we were there, but I wandered into the library. The door was open, it's a beautiful library—I couldn't resist."

"Book nerd backfire," Lauren says, moving her head side to side with each word. "So how did you leave things with him?"

"I told him I needed some time to sort out my feelings. I told him I was hurt and that I had trusted him. I mean, my gosh, we talked about everything, I felt like he was my best friend. I loved him, still love him."

"Does he love you?"

"He says he loves me and wants us to work this out. I told him to give me time, but I'll see him in class on Tuesday, and it will be so hard. I just don't want to talk to him or see him right now."

"I've gotta go, Bex. Mom's calling me. I hope you can forgive him and work things out."

326

"Thanks, Lauren, I feel a lot better after talking to you about this. I'll see you on Wednesday night."

I work on unpacking, taking all my clothes out of my suitcase and moving them to my laundry basket. As I go to close my empty suitcase, there is the shell that Lane picked up the first night we were at his vacation house. I reach for it, close my hand around it, and start to cry again. Bella bursts into the room. "Bex, Bex, I'm so glad to see you."

I turn around to face her and she sees that I'm crying. She drops her bags and hugs me tight.

"Bex, what happened?"

We sit on my bed, and I tell her the whole story from beginning to end and leave nothing out. I even tell her about my experience with him on the sailboat. When I'm finished, I say, "I'm just so hurt."

"I understand why you would feel that way, but I think you should find a way to talk to him about it, Bex. From everything you've just told me, I can tell that Lane really loves you. Especially with what happened on the sailboat and how you told him you plan to wait until you're married to sleep with someone. He was glad you felt that way, right? That's what he told you. What guy says that? Unless he really cares about you and loves you. I mean that's the kind of guy I want to find, too. If you think about it, he probably came to Alabama to get away from the Ivy League schools in New England. All the schools that his family members have gone to for generations. He was searching for himself and his own identity. He met you and found you different from other girls. You're innocent, sweet, thoughtful, smart, talented, and gorgeous. Most importantly, you're real, you're genuine, and he could see that right off the bat. I think that drew him to you."

"Yeah, I guess so, but I just can't help how I feel right now."

48

#Stressdoesntgowithmyoutfit

The next morning, I reluctantly go to church with Bella and Lexi. They try everything to cheer me up. Later in the afternoon while I'm trying to get stuff ready for class, I start scrolling through all the pictures Lane and I took together, including the video of us goofing off on the beach when he's carrying me around on his back. It makes me sadder. Bella tells me to stop looking at pictures and videos of Lane and pick up the phone and call him, but I can't. I know I'm being stubborn, but my pride is hurt especially since Amanda warned me about him in the first place.

I drag around campus on Monday from class to class in a listless existence. I pour myself into my homework and send Mom and Dad an email with ideas and plans of what I'd like to do while in New York. I add my itinerary from the editor at *The New Yorker,* which includes the times I'll be working with them, so my parents can plan to do things they'd like while I'm in meetings.

I plan out what I'm going to wear each day and hang outfits on my wall hooks, adding jewelry and shoes then stand back and stare at each one. Bella gives me her opinion on which necklaces to take. I notice the bracelet Lane gave me on New Year's Eve, and it throws me into a saddened state again.

There's a knock on our door and Bella answers. "Come in." It's Amanda. "Hey, guys what's up? She says looking at me. "Looks like you're packing for your trip to New York?"

"Yes. I'm working on it." I glance at what I have hanging up.

"Well, I came to see if I could talk to you privately for a few minutes downstairs if you don't mind?"

"Sure." I say, setting down the jewelry in my hand, and follow Amanda down to the library.

We sit across from each other.

"What's up?" I ask, getting comfortable in the chair.

"Lane called me yesterday and told me what happened. You know I've known him for four years. I know that he's changed this year. It's been a good change for him, and I think it's all because of you being in his life."

"So, you've known all along that he's a Kennedy? You warned me about him, but never told me *that*?" I pull a face.

Amanda wiggles around in her chair and looks me in the eye. "I warned you about him, because I knew how he was with Ashley. She and I were close our first two years on campus when we were roommates, and we're still good friends. I knew those two were toxic together, but she desperately wants him for herself. She wants him because of who he is. Ashley is the niece of George Bush. Ashley, in her warped mind, thinks because she's a Bush and he's a Kennedy that it's a match made in heaven. Lane saw through her."

I roll my eyes at Amanda. "But Bush is a Republican, and the Kennedy's are Democrats."

"I know, but it's still a political publicity thing. She doesn't care who's with what party. She wants the attention it would give her. American Royalty marries American Royalty, etc. It's about power and prestige for Ashley." Amanda clears her throat.

"This year Lane is different. He's not a powerful snotty jerk like he's been in the past. He's matured, and I think he really wants to find himself and separate who he is personally from his family's legacy. He wants to create his own legacy and be known for himself. That's what I've noticed this year. Amanda scoots forward and looks into my eyes.

329

"He's so worried about you, Rebecca. He wanted to tell you, but he worried it would change how you saw him or even how you felt about him. A lot of people just want to be around him or friends with him just because of who he's related to. He keeps his family legacy to himself, just so that people don't try to use him for his family's name. Early on, when you first met, it scared him to think if he were to tell you, something might change with your relationship. He was going to tell you the night that you guys planned to watch the sunset on the beach. His feelings for you are very real. He talked to me about it for over an hour. He wants me to persuade you to talk to him and give him another chance."

I stand, walk to the window and look out for a few seconds then turn back to Amanda. "I don't know. Finding all of this out kinda does change the way I feel. When I think about the press chasing him with cameras and the pressure he says he's under to be in politics and live up to what his family expects of him, it's a lot to think about. I mean, who wants to be chased by cameras and the press for the rest of their lives? Who wants to be under a microscope all the time and have all of America in your business? I'm surprised cameras aren't following him down here, too."

"He has a service that alerts him and keeps him one step ahead of the press. They work with the campus police to protect his privacy. They've given him the ability to get into any building on campus to hide, if needed."

When Amanda says that it dawns on me that day we were in the library when I crawled under the table to get my phone. He got under the table with me. I remember two guys with cameras getting on the elevator who seemed like they were looking for someone.

Amanda stands and walks over to the window next to me. "Just think about it, Bex. See if you can talk to him and maybe work things out. I was so happy for you guys, especially seeing the change in Lane this year."

330

"I'll think about it, but I have a lot on my mind right now, and I'm leaving the day after tomorrow for New York."

"I'm going to tell him I've talked to you and that you're going to consider talking to him."

Back in my room, I drop onto my bed and throw the covers over my head, trying to drown out the stress and thoughts of everything I've learned about Lane. I'm starting to wish I could just forget him altogether and move on to the simple life I used to have which may actually be the best thing for both of us at this point. But I don't know what I want.

*****

Waking up, I realize its Tuesday morning and I have to go to my journalism class, and I guess see Lane——totally dreading this more than anything. Before heading out, Bella hugs me. "I'll be thinking about you this morning and hoping everything goes well."

"Thank you, Bella. You're the best."

My favorite class has turned into my most dreaded. Begrudgingly, I grab my backpack and head out the door.

I walk into the familiar lecture hall and take my usual seat. Lane's not here, yet, and I breathe a sigh of relief then cross my fingers and hope he won't show up. But low and behold, just as I think that he walks up next to me, waiting for me to move my feet so he can pass.

"Hi Bex," he says hopeful.

I look up at him. Geez, why does he look so good *and* smell so good? I thought I could just forget about him and move on. Oh yeah, I tried that earlier in the year and failed. I quietly say, "Hi," and move my feet out of the way. I pretend I'm busy getting stuff out of my bag and flip through pages in my notebook.

"How have you been?" he asks, staring at me.

Why does he have to talk to me? I glimpse at him. He looks so good. I can't stand it. I'm about to freaking cry right here, right now in class. I take a deep cleansing breath and turn to face him.

"I've been okay. How about you?" I try to give a smile or at least a pleasant look.

"I've been thinking about you nonstop since we got back Saturday. I've been worried about you and hoping that you're doing okay."

"Yeah, I'm okay. Just trying to get ready for New York. I leave tomorrow afternoon."

"I remember," he says, still looking at me.

Oh. My. God. I want to crawl under this desk right now. I turn and look away.

Thank goodness Professor Brigg walks in and starts the lesson. Our assignment is to research articles from eight newspapers around the country. Three must be from outside the U.S. He tells us we can look up all the details of the assignment and when each portion is due online. I'll have to look this up later, because I'm having a hard time focusing on the assignment. I had no idea how hard it would be sitting next to Lane. Trying not to look at him is not that hard but sitting this close to him when he smells amazing is torture.

When class is over, I start packing up and stand to leave. Lane reaches out for my hand. I turn and look at him. The electricity I feel with him holding my hand right now is insane. It makes me want to drop my book bag, jump into his arms and kiss him nonstop for about five years. Instead, I start to cry, turn and run up the stairs into the hall then back down the steps out of Phifer and all the way back to Phi Mu. I run inside, almost bumping into Lexi. I close the door to my room and drop my bag and sit on my bed, trying to get a grip. I hear a knock on the door.

"Bex, it's Lexi, can I come in?"

"Yeah, sure, Lexi, come in," I say, trying to wipe the tears away and sit up cheery faced as she walks through the door.

"I just wanted to see if you were okay. You looked upset coming up the stairs just now."

"Yeah, I was upset, am upset, uhm, yeah," I stammer over my words. "I just had my class with Lane, and it was hard to be around him."

"I'm so sorry, Bex." Lexi sits on the bed next to me and puts a hand on my back. "You still feel angry toward him and can't stand being around him?"

"Nope, that's not it." I spring up off the bed and stand in front of Lexi. "I wanted to pretty much jump his bones just now. He looked so freaking good and smelled amazing, and he reached out and touched my hand."

Lexi is looking at me strangely. I start pacing back and forth in front of her. "He looks too good, he smells too good, he is irresistible. I'm so glad I'm leaving tomorrow afternoon. I need to get him off my mind, out of my head, and out of my heart for good," I say with animated movements, still pacing back and forth.

"Are you sure you want to do that? It sounds like you still care about him."

I stop pacing and look at Lexi. "That's the problem, I do care about him. I'm crazy head over heels in love with him. But I shouldn't be."

"Why not?" She looks earnest.

"He lied to me, and I trusted him, and it made me feel really stupid, hurt and just not good. I want to forget about him and push him out of my mind. I want to stop hurting and let these feelings go. I got in way over my head, and maybe it has more to do with the secrets I've kept and the lies I told my parents. It's hard to explain, Lexi."

49
#NYNY

Bella and Lexi walk me to my car Wednesday afternoon. We hug each other goodbye as I get in to drive to the Atlanta airport to meet my family. The funk I've been in is really getting old. I need to ditch the negative feelings somehow. I click open Spotify and choose *Watermelon Sugar* by Harry Styles. I turn it up and hit the interstate to Atlanta.

I get a text from Mom telling me which park and fly lot to go to, so I can leave the car and hop on the bus to the Delta terminal. On the bus I text Mom I'll meet them at Delta baggage check. Jogging inside, I see Mom, Dad, and Lauren standing in line and I run up to them. I hug them tight like I've haven't seen them in years. It's comforting being with my family while I'm feeling so crappy. After our plane arrives at LaGuardia airport we take an Uber to our hotel on 32nd street and Madison Avenue. Mom opens an envelope while in the Uber. "Look what came in the mail on Monday. They're from Lane."

I do a double take. She has tickets for *Hamilton*. I can't believe it. No one is able to get tickets for that show. It's the hottest thing on Broadway right now. But of course, Lane can get whatever he wants whenever he wants it. He's Lane KENNEDY Townsend. As I'm thinking this, I'm glad no one can read my mind.

"Wow, that's awesome, Mom. I thought you bought us tickets to *Cats*, I say staring at the tickets.

"I did, that's tomorrow night. This show is for Saturday night."

"Oh," I mouth the word without making a sound and stare out the car window.

Lauren is smiling at me, clearly enjoying this conversation. I can see her reflection in the window. "That was really nice of Lane to think of us and get us tickets for a show that's hard to get into," Lauren says, her eyes on me.

I stick my tongue out at her when Mom isn't looking.

After checking in, Mom suggests I take an Uber in the morning to the World Trade Center, the new structure built after 9/11, since I need to be there by nine. I set the alarm on my phone and set out the skirt and blouse I plan to wear. I'll take a purse big enough to put a change of shoes inside.

I get out my kindle and snuggle up in bed reading. I hear Lauren saying good night to Mom and Dad. Then she comes back into our room. "Did you tell Lane thank you for sending us the Hamilton tickets yet?"

"No, I just found out about it a few hours ago."

"Yeah, but you should call him."

"I don't want to talk to him. I'm trying to get over him, Lauren," I say in a clipped tone.

"You're being ridiculous and unbelievably stubborn, you know."

"I'll text him." I say, closing my kindle and reaching for my phone. I give her a get-out-of-my-business-look while sending Lane a text.

TY so much for the Hamilton tickets. Mom showed them to us earlier. That was very thoughtful of u. I'm looking forward to going.

I go back to reading my book. A few minutes later my phone dings with a text from Lane.

I'm glad to do it, and I hope u have a wonderful time. Good luck with your meetings at The New Yorker tomorrow.

TY, I'm have an early meeting in the morning. Goodnight.

335

I set my phone down and go back to my book, but now all I can think about is Lane. I try to go to sleep. I turn off the light and close my eyes, hoping for sleep to come soon.

In the morning, I'm full of excitement when I get up. My appointment today makes me feel so grown up and New Yorkerish, like I'm actually going to work at *The New Yorker* for real. The offices are located on the 38th floor of One World Trade Center. I get a full tour with introductions to the staff and even the editor-in-chief. I hope I didn't come across too star struck, since writers are like rock stars to me.

After the tours, I work with one of the fiction editors and cartoonists who create sketches for the publication. We have lunch on the 101st floor with astounding views of the city. I get to come back tomorrow morning to finalize the sketches and the proofs.

After lunch I meet up with Mom, Dad and Lauren, and we tour the 911 memorial. The tour is so emotional——we find ourselves crying through most of it. We take the subway back to the hotel to get ready to see *Cats* on Broadway. Staying busy with no down time is doing me a lot of good right now.

The next morning, I knock on Mom and Dad's door to let them know I'm leaving.

Mom opens the door quietly for me to come into their room. "Rebecca, we're going to sleep in this morning, so just take an Uber back here when your meeting is over. You can change, then we can all go to lunch together."

"Okay, Mom." I say, leaning in to give her a kiss on the cheek. My phone alerts me my Uber is downstairs and I beeline it for the elevators. I get out in front of One World Trade Center, and today I don't have to wait in the lobby. I was told to go on up to the conference rooms. I'm excited to see the final sketch and to hear about the internship opportunity for next spring.

When I get back to the hotel at noon, I find Lauren in the bathroom putting on lip gloss.

"You're back, thank God. I'm starving and ready to eat. I'll go next door and get Mom and Dad while you change into something more comfortable for a long day of walking."

She spins out of the bathroom and out the door, her shoulder length hair flipping. I hear Dad answer when she knocks.

The four of us troop out of the hotel, bounding down the sidewalk toward Central Park. We rent bikes and ride through the park to a restaurant on the water and sit at a table outside where we can watch people rowing, it's all so tranquil.

While we're waiting on our food to arrive Mom eagerly asks about my meeting.

"I got to meet so many editors, and I was taken around and shown the radio station pod cast area and the sketch rooms. The internship package they presented to me is in a binder back at the hotel room. I'll need my advisor or my dean to sign off on it if I decide to take it next spring. They gave me phone numbers of the current interns and said I can call them and maybe tour the apartment where I'll live for those eight weeks if we have time today, I'd like to do that."

"I think we can squeeze that in," Dad says, approvingly. "Tell us more about the internship opportunity, hon."

"It would start at the end of February and go through the end of April. I'd be assigned to work with two editors as an assistant, so I'd have a variety of tasks. Some of it may be busy work. But the entire experience of working at *The New Yorker* even for eight weeks would give me so much knowledge. I'd live with three other girls in a small apartment. I'd have to pay a portion for the rent. But they do allow us to eat for free at the restaurant on the 101st floor, and they pay for my plane ticket.

"What do you guys think? Is it possible? Would you and Mom let me do it?"

"We want to read over the packet of information they gave you first, and we'll talk about it further with you in a few weeks. Are you still planning to bring Bella home with you for Easter?" Mom asks.

"Yes, we'll leave next Friday after class ends and stay until Sunday afternoon before we drive back to Tuscaloosa."

"What are Lane's plans for Easter?" Mom smiles at me when she says this, and I feel almost like crying. I swallow hard before I answer her.

"He's flying to New York on Friday morning and he's supposed to fly back on Sunday night, so he'll be with family, Easter weekend too." I'm glad our food arrives. Now everyone is busy chatting about the food and stuffing their mouths. I'm hoping the Lane questions have ended.

Lauren knows I don't want to talk about Lane. She gives me a quick glance then says, "How about we return the bikes after lunch and walk over to the Metropolitan museum?"

"Oh, that sounds like a good idea." Mom smiles. "What do you guys want to do tomorrow before we see *Hamilton*?"

"How about "Top of The Rock?" Lauren and I say in unison.

*****

Our plane back to Atlanta leaves at three thirty today, and Lauren and I want to do some speed shopping at Barney's with Mom before we leave. We make it to the airport in the nick of time, back to Atlanta at six, and I drive home and sleep in my own room with my dog. I leave early on Monday for Tuscaloosa but miss my classes, anyway. I plan to look online later and see what I've missed. I unpack and leave a gift for Bella on her bed, so she'll see it when she gets back from class, then I lie down for a nap. When I wake up, Bella is working on homework.

"Look who's finally awake, New York Girl. I love the necklace you got me. Thank you for that," she says, smiling at me.

Sitting up in bed, I yawn and stretch my arms over my head. "I'm glad you like it. I didn't want to get you anything that was too touristy."

Bella laughs. "Like a foam Statue of Liberty crown?"

338

I nod and smile. "Yep, exactly."

"Tell me all about New York, and don't leave any details out."

I lean my head back against the wall remembering every detail.

"First, when we were on our way to our hotel, Mom pulls out tickets to *Hamilton*, the hottest show on Broadway, next to impossible to get tickets for."

"How did she get them?"

"Lane sent them in the mail."

Bella's eyes are like saucers.

"Yeah, I know, right? anyway, I texted him thank you a few times. So, we've technically talked a little, I guess you could say."

"I guess that's good?" Bella looks concerned.

"Well, it depends. I'm trying to get over him and move on, but I can't."

I finish telling Bella about the New York trip then go online and look up assignments for the week and notice that Professor Brigg posted an announcement stating we can work on the assignment on our own and don't have to come to class on Tuesday.

I let out a loud "Yipee!" startling Bella. "Good news, girl, some good news, I'll be sleeping in tomorrow." I say, closing my computer.

By Friday afternoon, I'm re-packing my bag. Bella and I are heading to Atlanta for Easter weekend. This will be her first time in Atlanta, so we plan to do all of my favorite things. We start on Saturday morning with the World of Coke, then go to the Aquarium, followed by the SEC Hall of Fame museum, all within walking distance of each other. We end the night at Krog Street Market, and we're back home by midnight.

"That was the most fun day I've had in a long time," Bella says, falling back on my bed.

"Me, too. I'm so glad you got to come with me this weekend. This is what I'm wearing tomorrow." I pull out a new sundress I bought recently and show it to Bella.

"Our church is really casual. I think you'll like it. But it will be major crowded tomorrow, so we're planning to leave thirty minutes earlier than we usually do."

I hear Lauren walk in from her date. I open my door, watching for her to walk past. "You're getting home a bit late, aren't you?"

"At least I *have* a boyfriend." Her tone reeks with sarcasm.

As she walks into her room, I notice the dog following behind her. "Wow, she's a grump tonight. But the dog is going with her, anyway. That makes me a little sad. Micky always used sleep on my bed."

"I wonder why Lauren is acting like that." Bella comments.

"I don't know. She may think I've given Lane a raw deal. She thought I had the perfect set up, the perfect life, and I think she wanted things to work out between Lane and me. I'll talk to her later.

The next morning we're up early for Easter. Mom cooks a fabulous breakfast, and we enjoy the church service then brunch at Mom's favorite restaurant in Milton. Bella keeps mentioning how shocked she was seeing so many thousands of people at one service. Now that we're back at home, I want to find Lauren and ask if there's anything bothering her. Although she seems totally fine now, it was obvious last night she was angry. I walk across the hall to her room and knock on her door.

"Come in," she says.

Walking in, I say, "Hey there, I just wanted to talk to you for a few minutes before I have to leave again. Are you okay? I'm worried you're mad at me. You seemed angry last night."

"Oh, that, I'm sorry, Bex. It wasn't really meant for you. I'm mad at Brian. He's talking about breaking up since we may be going to different colleges. He needs to decide if he's going to

Auburn or UGA, and I need to decide if I'm going to Alabama or UGA. I think he feels like our relationship is complicating his decision. And we had a fight."

"Have you decided which one?

"I'm leaning more toward UGA, simply because it's closer to home and I want my own identity. I thought I wanted to be at the same college as you, because your life there is so amazing. I realize I need to decide for myself what I'd prefer. I'm trying not to tell Brian my decision, because I want him to make his own choice. Since I wouldn't tell him last night, he got mad. But I didn't want my decision to change his mind and vice versa."

"Okay, well, I'm going to say with conviction, honesty is the best policy. I know I need to talk to Mom and Dad about a lot of things. You may think I'm the last person who should be talking to you about honesty after lying to Mom and Dad about spring break."

"I appreciate you talking to me about this. I'm going to call Brian today and tell him my college choice and let him know that it has nothing to do with where he wants to go. Either way, I'll still care about him." Lauren looks at me seriously, "What have you decided about Lane?"

"I haven't decided anything yet. I've tried to get over him, and I guess I think avoiding him all together will allow me to do that and move on. If I don't see him, don't talk to him, I'll eventually get through it. Again, you can see why it's so important to be honest with each other," I say with a frown.

"I don't know, Bex. I'm not convinced you should get over him," Lauren says with a knowing look.

"I don't really know what to do, and I want to talk to Mom about it, and if I do *that,* I'll have to confess that I lied about where I went for spring break."

"I know you think you can push this aside and get through the last few weeks of school without dealing with it, but I don't think you can. I think you need to talk to Mom and go ahead and get this all off your chest."

"You're right, everyone has been telling me to talk to Lane and give him a second chance, but all I've wanted to do is talk to Mom, but I'm so scared of what she and Dad will think. But I'm going to. I'm going to find her now and tell her before Bella and I leave. Thanks, Lauren. You, know you're a lot smarter than you think."

"Well, I've had the perfect big sister showing me the way for years."

I lean in and hug Lauren tight. When we pull apart, we both have tears in our eyes. I wipe the corners of my eyes with the sleeve of my shirt. I stand and give her another quick hug before popping my head into my room to see what Bella's up to.

"Hey, Bella, I'm going to talk to my Mom for a few minutes. After that we can head out, okay?"

"Sure, I'll be ready when you are. I'm about to call my mom and tell her happy Easter."

I walk downstairs in search of Mom and find her in the kitchen putting cookies into a to-go container for us to take with us when we leave.

"Hey, Mom, can I talk to you somewhere private for a few minutes?"

She sets the cookies down and says, "Of course, honey, let's go to my room. Dad's in the garage looking at your oil and checking your tires."

Mom shuts the door and sits on the bed and pats the spot next to her for me to sit. I sit down and face her and start to cry. She holds me for a while before I lift my head.

"Rebecca," she says, hugging me tighter. "Sweetie, talk to me."

I take a deep breath. "I've done something that I thought would be okay. I thought I needed to grow up and be on my own and do things my own way and live my life without being so cautious about everything. And when I met Lane, I couldn't help how I felt about him. I love him, Mom. I really do, but I lied to you guys and went with him on his private plane to his family's vacation home in Cape Cod over spring break." I bite my lip.

342

"His whole family was there even his niece and nephew. I had my own room and bath, so it wasn't like we shared a room or a bed or anything. But I felt I couldn't ask permission because I was afraid you guys would say no. He really wanted me to meet his family, and they're great. In fact, they may be too great." I pause, lowering my head and wring my hands.

"The last day there, I stepped into their library, finding family photos, of the Kennedy legacy. He's the grandson of a famous Kennedy and he had kept that secret from me. He told me he was trying to tell me while we were there but kept chickening out because he was afraid of how I would look at him and it might change our relationship and how I felt, and it scared him." Mom rubs my back gently and pushes a strand of loose hair behind my ear.

"But because he lied, I felt betrayed and hurt, and I wanted to forget him and go back to the way things were with Grant. He was safe and uncomplicated. Bella and Lexi introduced us because they thought he was perfect for me. But I wanted more and with Lane he was larger than life, I was drawn to him. He wants to work things out with me, and he's waiting for me to come to him when I'm ready to talk. He waited for me when I was deciding between him and Grant. And Mom, there's one more thing."

"It's okay, you can tell me. I'm not going to be upset with you. I'm glad you've come to talk to me about this."

"Ok, well, we went out on his sailboat, and we were alone down in the cabin room after he anchored the boat. Things got very physical, but I stopped. I told him that I wasn't ready, and that I'd planned to wait until marriage to have sex. He was gentle and sweet, and told me that that was one of the reasons he fell in love with me because I was so different from the other girls he'd dated. He told me he thought it was a good choice. He apologized and told me he hadn't planned on anything happening, and he just got carried away." I take a deep breath.

"Please don't tell Dad any of this. The lie has been a burden on me and when I found out that Lane lied to me and wasn't a hundred percent honest, I just wanted out. I wanted my life to go back to the way it was. I wanted to forget I'd ever met him. I felt really stupid." I roll my eyes and wipe them with my back of my hand. Mom gets up and goes to the dresser to get a box of Kleenex. She hands it to me. I blow my nose before continuing.

"I'm worried about what his parents will think about my story when they read it in *The New Yorker*. I don't want them to think I wrote it because of who Lane is, and I don't want them thinking the reason I dated him was because he's from a famous family. I've been running from a lot of feelings and assumptions. I'm glad I finally got the courage to talk to you."

I look into mom's eyes. She has a huge smile on her face.

"Whew, Rebecca that's a doozie. I'm so glad you came to talk to me before you left to go back to school with all of this weighing you down. I understand why you thought you had to lie to us, but you shouldn't have. If you had come to us first and explained why you were going to Cape Cod, what the plans were and the sleeping arrangements, your Dad and I would have been receptive to allowing you to go. You never know until you ask." She smiles then takes my hand in hers.

"You're nineteen and in a few months, you'll be twenty. You've been on your own away from us living your life, doing your thing at college for two years making us proud of you. We love who you've become. You've grown into a woman with a good head on her shoulders. I think you can make choices that you think are best for yourself then when you need to, come to me or to Dad whenever you have questions or doubts or need advice. We're here, and we'll always be here. I won't tell Dad any of this if you don't want me to, it can stay between us. But you need to talk to Lane and figure out what you really want."

She pauses and puts her hands on either side of my face, pulling me close to her, looking me straight in the eye.

"You choose what *you* want. You are so smart, Rebecca. Trust your heart."

344

Just then Dad walks into the room wiping his hands on a towel. He looks at us and asks, "Oh, was I interrupting something?"

"No, Dad. Mom and I were just chatting, girl stuff, nothing you'd be interested in."

He laughs. "Okay, hon, your oil looks good, and I checked your tire pressure, everything is A-ok, and I filled up the tank for you."

I walk over and give Dad a hug, and Mom joins in kissing me on the top of the head.

"I guess Bella and I will head back now." I say, pulling out from the group hug.

50
#GUCCI

On Monday, life seems better, and my head seems clearer. My talk yesterday with Mom gave me some clarity, so I feel a huge weight lifted, and I can breathe again. The late April sun is out, bright and shining. All over campus, spring is in the air. People are sitting out on the quad, and everyone is talking about going to the cliffs on Lake Tuscaloosa to hang out. I'm working on an assignment on my computer at my desk when Bella walks in.

"Hey, are you going to the cliffs with us?" she asks.

"I can't today, maybe later in the week. I've got to turn in my assignment for my journalism class before nine tomorrow. I'm also meeting with my advisor today to go over my internship package and all my classes for next year. She's pushing me to double major—— journalism and creative media with a minor in Spanish. The other thing I'm planning to do today is get my application turned in for working at the Young Life camp this summer with you guys."

Bella's face lights up. She hugs me and says, "I'm so glad we get to spend the summer together. It'll be so much fun. Which area are you going to say you'll work in?"

"I'm going to select journaling and lead one of the book study sessions."

"That sounds perfect."

"Yeah, one of the books they list is *I Choose the Sky* by Emily Wilson. I've been wanting to read that anyway."

"I'll see you later, Bex." Bella grabs her towel and a drink, leaving me to finish my work. Hopefully, I'll be able to enjoy lake time later this week.

I finish my assignment and submit it. As I'm gathering my things for my appointment with my advisor, there's a knock on my door. Opening it, I find someone standing on the other side, holding the largest bouquet of flowers I've ever seen. I set them on my desk where's there's barely enough room for them. My large bouquets of dead roses have been retired to the upper shelf of my closet. I haven't been able to bear parting with those, even though they're dead. It's nice to have a beautiful, fresh, fragrant arrangement. I open the card, already knowing who they're from.

Bex, I miss you greatly. I wish I could talk to you one last time.

Love, Lane

As I walk out the door to go to my meeting, I send Lane a text.

The flowers are beautiful. I love them. I agree we should talk, and I know I've been putting it off. Maybe later this week?

His text back is quick. *See u later.*

When I walk into the house after my meeting, Amanda greets me in the foyer.

"Pack a bag." she tells me.

"What? Why?" I look at her weirdly.

"Pack an overnight bag. You're coming with me."

"Coming with you where?" I ask, with an almost hostile tone.

"A special end-of-the year party."

"What special end-of-the-year party?"

"Bex, just be ready to leave in thirty minutes and don't ask so many questions."

I grab a small Vera Bradley duffle and throw a couple of changes of clothes and shoes inside.

Bella walks in, looking a little sunburnt and asks, "Where are you heading off to?"

347

"Amanda said something about a special end-of-the-year party."

"I thought your *Crimson Cabaret* party was on Sunday night?"

"It is. This is something else. I'm not even sure what it is," I say quietly. "I'll be back sometime tomorrow, I think, in time to go to Cat's softball game. I only have one class tomorrow, which is good. I won't miss much. And I finished my assignment and submitted it. Good thing I didn't go to the lake today," I say, feeling encouraged.

"Okay. Be safe and have fun with whatever it is."

I wave bye to Bella and walk downstairs to find Amanda waiting for me in the foyer. We walk outside and see a stretch limo waiting for us. Inside are six more girls, and now I realize this special end-of-the-year party has "secret society" written all over it. In the seats are small white gift boxes tied with crimson-colored ribbons for each of us.

The ride takes about three hours, and we have a total dance party in the limo on the way down. We've been playing our favorite songs and drinking champagne along the way. When we pull up to the house, it looks like it's as big as Lane's vacation home in Cape Cod. It's enormous.

"Where are we?" I ask.

"Mobile Bay in Fairhope. Nick's parents left for Europe today," Haley says, bouncing up the front stairs.

We grab our bags and walk inside. The home is beautiful but furnished very comfortably. Walking toward the back of the house, we hear loud music and what I think may be a gunshot. Following the girls out onto the screened porch, I notice the beautiful lagoon-style pool. I'm wishing I had brought a swimsuit. Hopefully someone brought an extra. I bet Amanda did. We walk past the pool to a beach path that leads to a wooden walkway out to the bay, which ends at a boathouse hosting a double decker porch on the dock.

About ten guys are on the deck atop the boathouse, shooting skeet, smoking cigars, and drinking expensive scotch

348

when we walk up. Two of them have shotguns in their hands and are wearing safety glasses. I notice one of the guys with the shotgun is Lane. I hear Lane yell, "Pull" and a skeet flies up and over the water. He shoots it and it smashes into a bazillion pieces.

I call out, "Good Shot."

He turns and looks at me. "Hi, Bex," he says, and I melt into a pile of goo right there on the dock.

Amanda leans on my shoulder and says, "Some of the girls are going in to put on their swimsuits."

"I wish I had packed one," I reply.

"I brought two with me."

"Thanks, Amanda." I follow her and the other girls back toward the house.

After changing into a bikini, I decide to open the small gift box. I slide the ribbon off and open the lid. Inside is a gold necklace with a small round charm. It's the Alabama crest symbol, the one with the Greek Goddess holding leaves in one hand, but below her other hand is a skull and cross keys symbol. There's also an envelope inside the box. I slide the card out and read——*Wear this and you will be allowed places you never thought you'd be. Your loyalty will be rewarded, and the position of editor will be granted.*

I'm not sure what this means. I've only applied for assistant editor for the *Crimson White* next semester. I won't even find out if I got it until sometime over the summer. I stuff the card back into the box and close the lid. I put the necklace on. I glance at myself in the mirror. It's pretty and dainty, but deep down I know there's something powerful behind wearing it and having power may not be such a bad thing after all.

I rush back outside to find the girls and notice the sun has set, and the guys have moved to the swimming pool and the hot tub. Colorful lights light up the pool and hot tub. Music is playing on the outdoor speakers, and there's lots of laughter and splashing going on around me. I sit on the edge of the pool and dip my feet in. The water is warm with steam rising from the surface. Lane joins me with a cigar in one hand and his glass of scotch in the other. He smiles at me, and I smile back.

"You want to go somewhere to talk?" he asks. He tilts his head to the side——there's a slight grin on his face.

I nod my head and stand. He sets his glass of scotch down, sticks his cigar in it, and takes my hand. The familiar feelings and butterflies come back as though they'd never left.

We walk to the end of the pier and sit on the porch swing. We stare into the darkness of the water for several minutes until Lane breaks the silence.

"I've decided I'm getting a double major in English and art history and a minor in journalism. I'll be finishing my minor in June. I'm also going to start grad school this summer."

I look at him in shock, thinking he may be talking about law school at Yale.

"I'm getting an MBA from Alabama," he continues. "I start this summer and will finish the following May. I'm staying another year for my master's. I want to do something in publishing and plan to have a job worked out by the time I finish my MBA next May."

"That's awesome, Lane." I look at him, beaming. "I'm so happy for you."

"I'll be around. I'm not going anywhere, and I just want you to know that," he says with a serious look. "I'll be gone for a week in June for my sister's wedding, but other than that I'll be in town and in classes all summer."

"I've worked out some things, too," I begin. "I'm taking the internship at *The New Yorker* next spring. I'm going to take five classes in the fall and two online classes in the spring that work with my internship. My advisor encouraged me to double major in journalism and creative media and I already have a minor in Spanish. This summer, I've decided to work as a camp counselor at a Young Life camp in North Carolina."

"Wow. It sounds like you know what you want to do. That's great, Bex."

"Yes, I feel good about everything. I think working at the summer camp will help clear my mind and get me down to basics again. And I'm looking forward to the internship this time next year. Look, Lane, I'm sorry I got angry with you." I turn my body and face him head on. His eyes grab mine in a magnetic gaze. "I understand your delay in telling me about your family history. I know you didn't mean to hurt my feelings. At the time, it felt very overwhelming. I told my mother everything last weekend on Easter Sunday. I couldn't hold it in any longer. I had lied to her, and I felt like you had lied to me. I was trying hard to shove everything under the rug and move on, but I knew I couldn't, and all I wanted to do was run to my mom and tell her. She was great, and she encouraged me to trust my feelings and to trust that she and Dad will always be there for me."

I hesitate to say the rest and look down at the ground gathering my courage. I know I'm changed, and there's no going back, I know what I want, and in truth, it's been there all along. I look up into his eyes and a warm feeling burns inside me.

"I also told her that——Lane, I'm very much head-over-heels in love with you."

He pulls me into his arms, runs his hand gently over my neck touching the necklace, pulling me in tight and holding me like there's no tomorrow.

Epilogue

Two weeks later, I'm with Lane the evening prior to his graduation, at the graduate honors reception inside the grand, historic President's mansion on campus. I feel privileged to be with him as we mingle through the crowd meeting the elites of the university.

While Lane introduces me to several distinguished alumni, there's one in particular, an Alabama Supreme Court Justice who is the keynote speaker tomorrow at graduation.

"Justice Melton, this is Rebecca Brant, my girlfriend."

He's an older man, maybe around my father's age. He's been a justice for a long time and is highly respected. As we shake hands, he comments on Lane's decision to complete his MBA at Alabama, then he turns to me, his eyes seem to land on my necklace.

"Ah, yes, the new *Crimson White* editor. It's lovely to meet you, Rebecca, I've heard so many good things about you and not just your GPA," he jokes.

I notice the gold pin on his lapel, its exactly the same as the charm on my necklace, the one I received during the secret society party. There's more to the secret society I know that now, and I've just skimmed the surface. I'm anxious to find out its secrets, and I think my junior year will be very telling. Between being an editor for the campus paper and working in New York next spring, my journalism career will go anywhere I want to take it. I'm ready for the challenge and whatever comes my way. And Lane——I'm happy he'll be here another year for his masters, his decision mainly being because he's in love with me.

352

Sophomore year didn't disappoint, but junior year, heck, it's gonna blow up and if there's one thing I've learned this year——is to follow my heart …

Because sometimes you have to let your heart lead and your dreams follow.

Acknowledgements:

Thank you to my friends who believed in me and this dream of mine to write and publish a book. Many, many thanks to those who took the time to read really rough drafts in order to give honest feedback in order to improve the story. Thank you to my editors who taught me a lot of things about the writing process. Sue Grimshaw, you were a cheerleader, pushing me to try my best. Thank you to my copy editor, Mary Marvella who spent a lot of time on my manuscript looking for mistakes. Thank you to everyone who gave me their support in the completion of this book...Mary Beth Bishop, Laura Sinabria, Lisa Lucas, Faith Kummetz, Catherine Abbate, Dana Ridenour, Eileen Tucker, Zann Kennedy, Jane Peay, and all of my book club ladies at Polo Women's Club. Last, but certainly not least, my husband Jeff Tucker.

Find out more…

Song: "Death Was Arrested" Northpoint Inside Out Ministries

Northpoint Community Church Alpharetta, GA (found on Spotify)

Northpoint Inside Out high school ministry… www.northpoint.org

Younglife Forsyth County Georgia, Instagram: @focoyl @focowyldlife @wfhs_younglife

To find a Younglife group in your area go to www.younglife.org

University of Alabama Younglife Instagram: @bamayounglife

For more of the "Walking the Crimson Road" experience….

The soundtrack for "Walking the Crimson Road" can be found on Spotify…

Perrie Tucker Walking the Crimson Road playlist

Discussion questions for groups:

1. Bex thinks she's been cautious, and strait-laced throughout high school and her freshman year at college and wants something exciting to happen sophomore year. Explain what you think she wants to happen and why you think she feels this way.
2. After meeting Lane in class, Bex can't get him off her mind. In your opinion do you think she acts like a stalker, or just a regular girl with a crush?
3. Amanda, Bex's Phi Mu big sis, and dance teammate encourages her to be in the secret society. Why do you think Bex is hesitant to join them? Do you think she

should join them? What would you have done in that situation?

4. Bex struggles with her feelings for Grant. If Lane had not been in the picture, where do you see Bex's relationship with Grant going? What would you do in the same situation?

5. For their creative writing/journalism class Bex and Lane have to submit stories they wrote. Bex comes up with a doozie and writes a fictional tale based on a former American heartthrob who was from a famous political family. What did you think about Bex's story? Did you like it? From Lane's story, what are some of the things you learned about him from reading it? How do you think what happened to him in the story changed him or made him who he is today?

6. How do you feel about Bex lying to her best friend about the secret society? Do you think it's right for her to keep that secret since it is a very secretive society and those are the rules? What are your thoughts on the whole secret society thing?

7. When Bex decides to lie to her parents about her whereabouts over spring break and take off with Lane, were you thrilled or scared for her? Would you have done the same thing?

8. When Bex discovers the secret that Lane has been keeping from her, she feels upset, hurt and lied to. Do you think she's being fair to Lane? Are her feelings justified? Can you see yourself feeling the same emotions as Bex? Would you have handled the situation in a different way?

9. Were you glad that Bex came clean and told her mom everything, and I mean everything… Did she do the right thing?

10. In the final chapter during the secret society party, Lane and Bex have a heart-to-heart talk. Are you glad

they made up and got back together? How did it make you feel?

11. During the pre-graduation reception at the President's mansion, Bex is introduced to some powerful people and seems to have accepted the secret society for who and what they are. Is accepting the potential opportunities that these powerful people can provide good or bad? Why or why not?

12. How do you think Bex has changed since the beginning of school in August? In what way is she better or worse?

13. Are you looking forward to the sequel?

Follow me on social media: IG: @always.n.style Twitter: @PerrieT Website: www.perriepatterson.com Facebook: Perrie Patterson

About the author...

Perrie is the mother of two who are both in college now. She is a 1989 graduate of the University of Alabama where she majored in fashion merchandising. Years later, she had no idea that she would be writing romance novels. With both kids in college Perrie has a lot more time for writing. She and her husband, Jeff live just north of Atlanta with their three fur babies, enjoying their empty nest. *Walking the Crimson Road* is her first novel.

Since this book was first published, in December of 2019, Perrie has written the sequel. *My Blood Runs Crimson.* She has also written a YA competition cheer romance titled *Hit Zero.* She plans to write a third in the "Crimson series" giving the "Crimson books" closure. The title of the third book in the "Crimson series" will be *All the Crimson Roses.* Perrie's books can be found online at Barnes and Noble, and the Kindle additions can be found on Amazon, as well as her website www.perriepatterson.com. Please feel free to reach out to me for speaking engagements. You can email me at perrietuck@mac.com.

Made in the USA
Columbia, SC
21 November 2021